PRAISE FOR
The Electric Michelangelo

"A vivid depiction of changing seaside culture on both sides of the Atlantic, and a smart study of a subtle but disreputable art."　　　　　　　*—The Independent*

"An auditory delight. Sentences are threaded with internal rhyme, textured by syntactic inversions, and one can hear at times a distinct metre—the author's own rhythmic tattoo—beating beneath her prose. *The Electric Michelangelo* is a pleasure to read."　　　　　　　*—Zembla*

"The torrential Lawrentian flow of her prose offers many heady pleasures."　　　　　　　*—The Times* (London)

"Her gorgeously embellished prose compels the narrative, along with the beguiling vignettes she conjures up . . . [and] the effect is intoxicating."　　　　　　　*—Financial Times*

"Sarah Hall's second novel is richly descriptive, an evocative exploration of misfits and exiles searching for a home."　　　　　　　*—The Lady*

"Hall is a writer to indulge, and her sensuous, poetic prose is every bit as evocative as sand poured from a pocket at the end of a holiday."　　　　　　　*—Daily Mail*

– THE ELECTRIC MICHELANGELO –

by the same author

HAWESWATER

The Electric Michelangelo

— SARAH HALL —

HARPER

PERENNIAL

HARPER ● PERENNIAL

A paperback edition of this book was published in 2004 by Faber and Faber Ltd., United Kingdom. It is reprinted here by arrangement with Faber and Faber Ltd., United Kingdom.

P.S.™ is a trademark of HarperCollins Publishers.

HarperCollins books may be purchased for educational, business, or sales promotional use. For information please write: Special Markets Department, HarperCollins Publishers, 10 East 53rd Street, New York, NY 10022.

FIRST HARPER PERENNIAL EDITION PUBISHED 2005.

Library of Congress Cataloging-in-Publication Data

Hall, Sarah.
    The electric Michelangelo / Sarah Hall--1st Harper Perennial ed.
        p. cm.
    ISBN-13: 978-0-06-081724-4 ISBN-10: 0-06-081724-0
    1. Tattoo artists—Fiction. 2. Coney Island (New York, N.Y.)—Fiction. 3. Morecambe and Heysham (England)—Fiction. 4. British—New York (State)—Fiction. 5. Mothers and sons—Ficiction. 6. Single mothers—Fiction. 7. Immigrants—Fiction. I. Title.

PR6108.A49E47 2005
813'.6—dc22   2005040610

05 06 07 08 09 ❖/RRD 10 9 8 7 6 5 4 3 2 1

For all our Reedas,
And all our Rileys

– THE ELECTRIC MICHELANGELO –

'Good and bad, two ways
of moving about your death
by the grinding sea . . .'
                    Dylan Thomas

– PART I –

– Bloodlights –

If the eyes could lie, his troubles might all be over. If the eyes were not such well-behaving creatures, that spent their time trying their best to convey the world and all its gore to him, good portions of life might not be so abysmal. This very moment, for instance, as he stood by the hotel window with a bucket in his hands listening to Mrs Baxter coughing her lungs up, was about to deteriorate into something nasty, he just knew it, thanks to the eyes and all their petty, nit-picking honesty. The trick of course was to not look down. The trick was to concentrate and pretend to be observing the view or counting seagulls on the sill outside. If he kept his eyes away from what he was carrying they would not go about their indiscriminating business, he would be spared the indelicacy of truth, and he would not get that nauseous feeling, his hands would not turn cold and clammy and the back of his tongue would not begin to pitch and roll.

He looked up and out to the horizon. The large, smeary bay window revealed a desolate summer scene. The tide was a long way out, further than he could see, so as far as anyone knew it was just gone for good and had left the town permanently inland. It took a lot of trust to believe the water would ever come back each day, all that distance, it seemed like an awful amount of labour for no good reason. The whole dirty, grey-shingled beach was now bare, except for one or two souls out for a stroll, and one or two hardy sunbathers, in their two-shilling-hire deck-chairs, determined to make the most of their annual holiday week away from the mills, the mines and the foundries of the north. A week to take in the bracing salty air and perhaps, if they were blessed, the sun would make a cheerful appearance and rid them of their pallor. A week to remove all the coal and metal dust and chaff and smoke from their lungs and to be a consolation for their perpetual poor health, the chest diseases they would eventually inherit and often die from, the shoddy eyesight, swollen arthritic fingers, allergies, calluses, deafness, all the squalid cousins of their trade. One way to tell you were in this town, should you ever forget where you were, should you ever go mad and begin not to recognize the obvious scenery, the hotels, the choppy water, the cheap tea rooms, pie and pea restaurants, fish and chip kiosks, the amusement arcades, and the dancehalls on the piers, one way to verify your location was to watch the way visitors breathed. There was method to it. Deliberation. They put effort into it. Their chests rose and fell like furnace bellows. So as to make the most of whatever they could snort down into them.

There was a wet cough to the left of him, prolonged, meaty, ploughing through phlegm, he felt the enamel basin being tugged from his hands and then there was the sound of spitting and throat clearing. And then another cough, not as busy as the last, but thorough. His eyes flickered, involuntarily. Do not look down, he thought. He sighed and stared outside. The trick was to concentrate and pretend he was looking out to sea for herring boats and trawlers returning from their 150-mile search, pretend his father might come in on one of them, seven years late and not dead after all, wouldn't that be a jolly thing, even though the sea was empty of boats and ebbing just now. The vessels were presently trapped outside the great bay until the tide came back in. Odd patches of dull shining water rested on the sand and shingle, barely enough to paddle through, let alone return an absent father.

Outside the sky was solidifying, he noticed, as if the windowpane had someone's breath on it. A white horse was heading west across the sands with three small figures next to her, the guide had taken the blanket off the mare, the better that she be seen. As if she was a beacon. Coniston Old Man was slipping behind low cloud across the bay as the first trails

8

of mist moved in off the Irish Sea, always the first of the Lake District fells to lose its summit to the weather. So the guide was right to uncover the horse, something was moving in fast and soon would blanket the beach and make it impossible to take direction, unless you knew the route, which few did in those thick conditions. Then you'd be stranded and at the mercy of the notorious tide.

– Grey old day, isn't it, luvvie? Not very pleasant for June.

– It is, Mrs Baxter. There's a haar coming in. Shall I be taking this now or will you need it again shortly do you think?

– No, I feel a bit better, now I'm cleared out, you shan't be depriving me. And if I need to go again I'll try to make it to the wash room. You're a very good boy, Cyril Parks, your mammy should be proud to have a pet like you helping her around here. Well spoken and the manners of a prince. Is it a little chilly to have the sash open today, luvvie?

The woman watched him from her chair. She resembled a piece of boiled pork, or blanched cloth, with all her colour removed. Just her mouth remained vivid, saturated by brightness, garish against her skin, and like the inside of a fruit when she spoke, red-ruined, glistening and damp.

– Yes, Mrs Baxter, I'm afraid it is. Would you like some potted shrimp? Mam made it fresh today.

– Oh yes. That would be lovely. I do so enjoy her potted shrimp, just a touch of nutmeg, not too heavy handed, salt and pepper, and never anything but fresh butter. Some of these places here leave their butter out of the pantry to spoil and use it all the same, I can tell. I've a delicate palate that way and can spot a cheap tray. Nothing worse than rancid butter, is there, luvvie? You tell your mammy I'm of the opinion that hers is the best potted shrimp in Morecambe. I won't mind telling her myself next time I see her. And is it her?

– Is what her, Mrs Baxter?

– You know. Is it her that King George gets his potted shrimp from? I know he has it sent specially to him from Morecambe Bay. I read it in the papers, that he's very partial

9

to it and has it sent to him from a mystery person, a secret source. Would she be that mystery person? Because now that wouldn't surprise me, wouldn't surprise me in the least, I do so enjoy her potted shrimp.

– No, it's not her, Mrs Baxter.

He shook his head and picked up the basin. The trick was not to look down, to think of anything else other than that which was in his hands, but he always did look. He was self-torturing that way. He had eyes for the grotesque things of life, though in all fairness, given the current situation, he was provided ample opportunity to indulge his morbid curiosity. His mother said that human eyes saw no more nor less than the human brain commanded them to, a glass half empty or a glass half full, the Lord's leftovers or Satan's finest dining. In which case, he feared, he tumbled headlong into the realm of pessimistic and suspicious divination. Which, furthermore, left him swinging in a rather grave and hazardous position, influenced not just by the fair and graceful winds of heaven, but by a forked-tongued, red-hoofed, south-to-north blown breeze.

≈

The consumptives in his mother's hotel coughed up blood into their basins and handkerchiefs hourly. They did it earnestly, guiltily, as if each time fulfilling a pact with the Devil himself that in the matter of their failing health there would be those intolerable moments when the undersigned must bring up their monstrous, viscous, bloody end of the bargain, involving immeasurable discomfort on their behalf, for the Devil had his humorous perversions after all, before they were allowed future reprieve and life. And merciful breath. They looked at Cy with apology as they hacked and gurgled but also with a measure of determination on their ashen, bulging faces, which was at heart impersonal and informed him his presence mattered not in the affair. Whatever the Devil did with the by-product of the deal after it washed down the sink he did not care to know. He hated the pink wash of fluid that broke on their temples before the coughing began, for there were little giveaways of the disease he'd learned to interpret, and if he saw them in time and his mother was not around to prevent him, he would put down the fresh linens, the bars of pungent soap he was distributing, and back out of the room. Tuberculosis gave him the wither-ing-willies. That and the other sick industrial legacies did not seem to bother his mother. She went about the hotel with no such trepidation. They needed the money to keep the hotel afloat and these guests were as welcome as any others, money was money after all. But Cy knew that Reeda Parks possessed a tolerance for these patients that went well beyond financial solvency and that many had lost their jobs due to poor health, so he suspected her rates must have been lower than those for ordinary folk. None of the other Morecambe boarding houses and hotels were as keen to take consumptives as Reeda. The Bayview Hotel had become known as a sanctuary, though it was not advertised outright in the papers as such. Even folk on their last legs often got room and board within, so that she acted as both bed-nurse and hostess. She was immune to the effluent, the slime, the smell and the sense of false hope that hung around their rooms like flies about finished with a corpse. She did not get that weak-kneed feeling when they coughed and spat. She didn't object to the proximity of mucus and fluid and damp spillage in her environment. She was toad-like in that fashion. Nor was Cy encouraged towards a better frame of mind by her resolve. It was distressing to him that she abdicated her common share of distaste, and it made her seem overly stern, even a touch Gothic. But if he took it up with her she simply lost her temper.

– What ails you boy! What a cold heart you have! Cyril, they did not ask to be struck with this disease. They received it for a lifetime's honest toil. I'm just looking after my own, as should you, my boy. We're not all born with our hands and feet above deck, port-out starboard-home, now are we? Manners to strangers, whether your equals or your betters, should be one and the same, young man. One and the same. That is to say equal to the courtesy you pay yourself.

Still, this did not change the fact that the consumptives coughed up blood and phlegm into basins like unholy spawn and he could not abide it.

– Now take this shrimp up to Mrs Baxter and inform her that the Territorial Band is marching at three o'clock if she cares to take a turn on the prom. I shall be available to take her arm if she's feeling wan.

The consumptives appreciated Reeda's immunity and mistook it for compassion or some kind of heightened sense of social duty, and for her kindness they would often take her hand in theirs and kiss it with their roe-red mouths.

– Reeda, Reeda. You're an absolute angel.

They sat next to the open bay windows of the hotel if they were too weak to stroll on the promenade with the rest of the summer masses in straw hats and with breeze-tugged umbrellas, letting the curtains blow in and eager for the wind on their faces. Their basins tucked like upturned helmets on their blanketed knees. They were desperate for air. More specifically, they were desperate for the air in Morecambe. They sucked it down in between their fits and held it inside their lungs like opium smokers in a den. They inhaled like they were performing exercises: loudly, with determination and regiment. They exhaled the way people sometimes did behind closed doors at night in the Bayview when all were abed and Cy was passing on the way to the kitchen for a glass of milk, letting out breathy noises as if their lungs were working a fraction beyond their control. Morecambe's air was renowned, if not nationwide then reliably in the north, for its restorative properties, its tonic qualities. It was soft. That was how everyone described it, including the *Morecambe Visitor and General Advertiser*. Soft, soft air. Healing. Medicinal almost, and if only someone had known how to bottle it, fortunes could have been made worldwide. Beautifully soft. This was, in large part, a tourism ruse, but of course the claim was a feature endorsed in every advertisement for every hotel or boarding house in the town. See Naples and Die, see Morecambe and Live! they read. When a white lie was told here, it was told in bold. So as far as the unwitting, desperate, industrially ravaged workers of the north were concerned the air possessed mystical, salving, qualities. It might even save them from Old Chokey if they were lucky. They wanted to believe it, and so they did believe it. And in the end, with the proliferation of the claim, year after year, season after season, even Morecambrians half-believed what they were issuing as truth, thus their maintenance of the fib took on extremely convincing proportions. Including Reeda Parks's.

– Cyril, if they ask for open windows, just open the windows, for pity's sake, and fetch more blankets if it's chilly. Best we let them have what they came for. Nothing like fresh air to improve the inflicted and we have plenty of it to spare, and it is very special.

Now Cyril Parks knew that this claim of miracle air was a fiction even at his age. The townsfolk of Morecambe were no more robust than anyone else he had met in England and they had access to it all the time. Locals still passed away in old age and were driven in carriages to the graveyard on Heysham Hill by men in tall black hats and horses with creaking black bridlery and sinister feather head-plumes. The consumptives sometimes died in the hotel while on holiday, if they had a sudden decline in condition and could not be transported to the sanatorium under Blencathra mountain, or home to loved ones in Glasgow, Bradford or the Yorkshire towns in time. Upon consideration the air was quite soft, he supposed; you didn't particularly notice it going in and out, though he had no idea what hard air was like in comparison. The air over in Yorkshire seemed about the same when Cy had visited his Aunt Doris there, two Christmases ago, though the wind on the Yorkshire moors had had something different about it, a spirit that was not coastal, a tone that was dry and dirge-like, and it had sent shivers down his spine as it fluted and lamented during his stay, haunting the rocks and trees and grass. Perhaps London had hard air. Perhaps it was what they called a city phenomenon. Or perhaps the lack of sea had something to do with it. No. Morecambe's air was not discomforting. It didn't make your lungs bleed, unless they were bleeding already. The consumptives liked it, trusted it, used it. They could obviously tell the difference between a soft and hard climate where he could not.

~

There were times his mother caught him backing out of the hotel rooms looking disgusted, and he'd find her hand on the back of his neck. A cool hand that might have been, of late, near the puckered mouth of a consumptive. A hand that told him not to move back another inch. A hand that felt as pale as the sick body it had been joined with. And he would shiver. He imagined if he ever touched one of the customers with tuberculosis they would feel cold like snow, even on their necks where they should be warm. Like a stone house already abandoned. Or a candle, since their appearance was deadened like the waxwork figures in Madame Tussaud's. But he was careful not to touch them, if at all possible. And he was careful to try not to look at the soupish mess in their basins, that substance with its disagreeable appearance which had led him to avoid eating stewed tomatoes and thick-shred marmalade for going on three years now purely because of the cursed similarities.

They were always so grateful. Grateful to have their basins emptied and disinfected so they could cough into them clean again as if to convince themselves that there wasn't so much blood and disease coming out of them, and grateful to be holidaying in Morecambe where there was soft air. All told, it was a sorry state of affairs. Especially as he knew that

Morecambe's air wouldn't save them, these strange, pale, red-mouthed ghouls who smelled slightly metallic or like vegetables fermenting, who preferred their windows to be open and liked to consume potted shrimp almost as much as the King of England himself did. A very sorry state.

Once, after catching him in the act of slipping his basin-emptying duties, having spotted a telltale sour-cherry glaze on the face of a customer as he had, Reeda sat him down at the kitchen table, and with the stern sympathy which was her calling card she instructed him to buck up.

– Look, love, I know it's not the cat's whiskers to have to care for these folk in this manner. But, honest to goodness, you're beginning to riddle my grate with your behaviour. I don't wish to judge you uncharitably, son, but I do consider it a rudeness. Now pull your socks up. I've not the time to tend to everything myself. Some might think us foolish for taking those we do. You might think us foolish. But these people deserve a little holiday as well as anyone. And some deserve it more. They've worked their lives away digging the coal that keeps you warm, and fixing the threads that bind your pant-seat, and I won't have you spoil their fun. You'll simply have to find a way to cope, please.

Her eyes, the colour of a smithy's anvil. She had, of course, a guilt-inducing and persuasive case. Also, if his mother had more than her fair share of consumptives in the hotel in the spring and summer seasons, compared with the other guest houses of the town, she also never complained about her gas bills, or worried that the present war would rob her of her best customers.

~

Reeda Parks had run the Bayview Hotel for seven years, since Cy's father had died in the Mothering Sunday storm of 1907, captaining the *Sylvia Rose* when it went down with three other local fishing vessels, never to be recovered. There was a photograph of him in the hall of the Morecambe Trawlers'

Cooperative Society building, moustached, wellingtoned and sou'westered, leaning an elbow on a stack of heave nets piled on the stern of the boat. So Cy had come to know his father as a man who had only one position, upright, at work, dead, and he could never really imagine him otherwise, not sitting in a chair smoking a pipe or snoozing full-bellied after Sunday lunch, nor lifting a pint of frothy ale, nor shaving at the mirror. There was a pocket watch and a pair of cufflinks which Cy had inherited, when it became apparent the *Sylvia Rose* was not going to find her way back to the great bay, though they seemed to have little to do with the man in the photograph, who would undoubtedly tell the time via the position of the sun in the sky and whose oilskin was fixed at the wrist by a rough string tie which his salt-cracked hand could manage better.

The day after the storm Cyril Parks was born. He gave his first scream while the last of the south-westerly gale blew out, having taken the sea walls, the new jetty, most of the west end promenade and eleven fishermen of the town with it. Reeda said afterwards that the troublesome weather front had brought only one thing worth having, her son, even if it had also taken a husband. She said she'd been made a mother on the back of Mothering Sunday and she could not complain about that. The storm had been one of the annually expected disturbances, folklore had some saying it would be a monster, wicked as it had been in 1853 when the town was all but swallowed by the Irish Sea, and that the men who went out that morning were madmen who didn't heed the caution. Reeda Parks disputed this, often without the slightest provocation, turning from what she was doing suddenly to confront her son, as if she had heard a phantom slur to her husband's name from some imaginary quarter.

– Your father was a good fisherman. He knew the sea as well as anybody can know it, there was salt in his blood. The sea will give when it faces you and take when it turns away. And your father was the first to say that. He did right by his crew, and he did right by his family. He was not a reckless sort. There was only one occasion he ever acted heedlessly, it was in my defence as he saw it, and that doesn't concern you. He was a good man, Stanley Parks. You remember that of him.

Cy knew to sit and listen to her and not interrupt when she spoke of his father. There was an unconditional sort of praise that she paid him, but he could see from the crease in her brow and the concentration in her eyes that it had been worked upon. Whatever information came from her about the man had passed through a mill of some kind, so that it was lighter, finer and more easily kneaded into the dough of his young life than it might have been if he had lived and she had made comment upon him. He sensed that his mother had prepared her statements, they were benign, considerate, sifted, and he wondered if all good wishes and positive out-looks did not require first crafting in some fashion. When he was old enough Cy went to the town library and looked in an old newspaper for an account of the storm. A full spring tide had met a bay full of rainwater from the estuary mouth of the river, and the run-off from the Lune marshes, for it had been raining solidly for a month. The land was a full sponge trying to squeeze itself out, and with the help of the wind the already strangely tempered body of bay water had become livid, sending waves inland taller than Alderman Birkett's Clocktower. Boats had broken their moorings and were strewn along the promenade, land-locked and splintered, silt and jetsam was everywhere and the wreckage to the front of the town looked like Morecambe had been visited by a drunken giant.

Reeda Parks had been solely responsible for the hotel's upkeep since then, though she was already well acquainted with its management. She did it with a minimum of grace, with wearyless effort and very much out of habit. Her hair grew thinner and her son grew taller. Summers were lucrative, winters were penny-pinching. Whatever financial weather the Bayview encountered Reeda Parks etched it down in her small notebooks, firmly in pencil, figures to spend and figures to save, allotments of income and expenditure, money for food, for upkeep, for bills and for advertising. She was not alone in her financial stringency. If there was one thing the guest house owners of Morecambe Bay took seriously it was the necessity for annual duration of the summer season's income. When Cyril was old enough to carry things she set him to work in the sixteen rooms, and she never took a second husband. Her reptilian ability to manage the sick provided the hotel with its minimum stability. The mines and mills and the poverty of the north continued to provide the working classes with wheezes and diseases. The *Morecambe Visitor* continued to promote the restorative seaside air that could cure them. And Reeda Parks continued to cater for them during their brief leisure time. She always managed a full house in the softer months, and the Bayview was clandestinely known as a sanctuary for the ill. So when Mr Baxter died of black lung, his sick wife naturally continued to vacation once a year there, loyal to the end, and eternally speculating about whose potted shrimp was worthy of the royal palate.

∼

There was something almost storybook about Cy's birth and his father's death, so closely were they allied. Reeda spoke of the matter in sweeping, tale-mongerish tones to him, using words like 'deceased' and 'destined' and nodding her head with a deep expression on her face – her face in those moments was an etched region where significance and yarn and solemnity combined and understood the fates, the gods, the loving, brackish, tossed-together and torn-asunder human heart. With that face alone she could give credence to the fairytale correlation of suffering and joy, of gain and loss, of life and death. As if all meaningful events and altered fortunes took place together and on celebration days to justify a star-crossed calendar. As if Cyril Parks from the very moment of his mortuary nativity was destined to find that out. Fires on Easter Sunday, funerals on April the first or anniversaries, the events would come and seem greater for their timing than they would have otherwise. Thus, it went beyond his mother's old-timey, rhymey tongue, throughout the winding streets and cheap hotel porches, past the Methodist churches, the seaside enterprises, the public houses, the novelty stages and the fishing factories; small troubles loomed large, were given generous lip-service, yarns were daily fare, luck was just another word for happiness, tragedy became a strand of time that wove itself into the ordinary folklore stitching of Morecambe Bay's history. And if you wanted, you could catch it all in allegories and pictures, memories and scriptures, in facial expressions and human productions. It was an anecdotal sort of town.

~

A solution to the problem of the bloody basins did present itself, the week of Mrs Baxter's potted shrimp that June. One day, while he looked down into the discharge bucket he was carrying, a small miracle occurred. He had of course looked down, being of an eternally curious and vitiating disposition. Blood and bleach swill had made patterns in the bowl as he carried it out to the washroom where he was to rinse the container in the big Burbridge sink. There, in distressed shades of red, was a man on a boat far out to sea, far out for the waves were tall, and he waving. At least a stream of blood masquerading as an arm was waving. Cy held very still, and for a brief moment his eyes saw a journey played out of a man to the sailors' famed Elysium. Cradled within its mucus, red shapes appeared like spilled ink on a blotter, to form an accidental painting, except the shapes were never-setting, they continued moving and in a moment the image changed and was reformed. The boat became a seagull with crooked wings, which then became a blooming flower, which then became the turret of a castle. He moved the basin in a circle, like Gypsy Alva the fortune teller in the Curiosity Arcade rotating upturned cups to charm the tea leaves from which she would divine a life. Blood down the side of the basin wall was all at once like the distant shallow mountains unflattening the bay's horizon. Then to the other side of the bowl the blood spun, there was another mass of red land, unrecognizable, until the ruddy wash came around once more to recreate the Westmorland mountains yonder.

Cy put the bowl down at the side of the sink and blinked. If he had been inclined towards such assumptions he would have sworn it was a prophecy of some kind. Or that his well-behaving, deck-swabbing eyes had engaged in some kind of mutiny. And for once his hands were not tacky with sweat, nor was his tongue furling in preparation for a retch. He had forgotten to feel disgusted. He was not thinking of the foul nature of the basin's contents, instead something magical had been granted him beyond the grotesque, a counter-curse to the original hex. Perhaps he had Mrs Baxter's consumption to thank for the vision, or the insistence of his mother that he continue with the task at hand, Cy did not know. Or perhaps, and he did not rule this particular option out, taking a moment from his contracted bargain, the Devil himself had painted Cy a little picture for amusement or aesthetic purposes, being not entirely wicked after all.

So. What if blood could tell you stories? What if blood could lure you into pictures? What if there was something worthwhile underneath the shudder and jitter of a body's mess and spill, some redeeming wonder beyond the grit and gristle and ghastly cavalcade of the flawed and festering human anatomy? He was not entirely sure why, but that thought was oddly pleasing.

∼

Where one confusion ended another was sure to arise. There were uncertain occurrences within his home, mostly out of season when the hotel was emptier of guests, that ravelled and knotted up the strait-laced brain. Arrivals and departures late at night, when muffled soothing voices and muffled cawing cries could be heard. Usually the sounds emanated from behind the fastened parlour door, so that Cy, having made his way up to it stealthily, barefooted and in his nightshirt, could never interpret their exact meaning, nor what might lead to their issuance. He had never yet found the courage to peer through the keyhole, for reasons similar to his theory that a foot kept safe within a blanket was less susceptible to being nibbled and gnawed on by boggarts and trolls beneath the bed. When the caw-caw cries and soothing voices intensified he would retreat timidly upstairs. There were serious notes to the music of the voices that suggested to him the hidden situation was a deeply adult matter, where the sudden presence of a sleepless child would result in a severe scolding or even a boxed ear. So he hid and he listened and he watched. After a while he would see his mother coming out of the door with a bloody basin of her own, covered by a cloth, then minutes later she would return to the room of strange noises. Later, tucked behind the banister, tired but bright with worry, he might spy his mother and another lady that he knew from town leaving the parlour, helping a third party – always a lady moving sore and slow – through the passageway to the front door. Their arrival was never heard, never apparent to him, as if the visitors stepped from a conjurer's chest within the hotel or came in via the building's creaky water pipes. Rarely, perhaps only once that he could recall, a man was present in the hallway also, a soldier, from the new army base at Bare hamlet. He stood pale against his uniform and said not one word. Mostly, however, it was a matter concerning only ladies. Before the discreet visitors left the Bayview, his mother would usually kneel down and lift the skirt of the unknown female, adjusting something beneath her while she sniffled and sobbed and winced.

– Is she clotting?

– Yes. Good. S'all right luvvie. All over now. Just keep off your feet if you can manage. Don't wash for a day or so, stand up when you do it, and no bath, not for a week. Oh, luvvie, you're all right, hush now.

Then as she closed the door to her visitors his mother would pause and smooth down her dress, or put a hand to the wall and lean for a time. She might pour herself a sherry from the cabinet, and drink it using her stiff head to take it back in one long finishing sip, or she would come upstairs to check on him in his room, and he would have to race silently back, remain very still below the covers and feign sleep, hoping the racket of his heart would not convey past his chest as it pounded and pounded and he felt he might go deaf himself from all the noise. Twice he had witnessed Reeda and her friend carrying a visitor in a sling made from their linked arms because she could not walk, and as he ran to the window of his room he observed them moving up the dark street, away from the dull yellow glow of hotel windows – for the lamps on the promenade were extinguished by eleven at night and it was long past that hour on both occasions – so that joined together they appeared to be a heavy, misshapen creature lumbering through the murk. And then, when she was gone, the hotel would seem ugly and massive about him and echoing full of unrest.

～

The Bayview was not a beautiful building, it was grey and fortress-like from the outside, with tall chimneys and brown, seaweed-coloured stains on the walls, molested as it had been over time by the salty sea air, the Anglo-Saxon damp, and it sat within a row of similar looking guest houses so it seemed like one of several poorly brushed ivories in a lower row of teeth. Jonty Preston and Morris Gibbs and Cyril Parks spent many a wet afternoon rampaging through the hotel's hallways, on the hunt for mischief and distraction. The three had been friends since they could remember and if there was trouble being produced about the town they were seldom far behind it. The clatter of thrown boots, the scuffle of furniture being moved and the tinkle of shattering glass were sounds that often accompanied the trio on their rounds.

Reeda Parks and Mrs Preston were also friends of sorts. It was a practical relationship, which never extended to a shared pot of tea and a piece of currant cake in the Tower tea room. Nor were they cordial over the punch stall at the annual fancy dress parade. It was not a friendship at all really by the usual standards. The two women did not ever seem to enjoy each other's company all that well if they met in the street, nor would they pass conversation idly at a grocery counter, not in the fashion that some ladies fell about laughing over gossip at the fishmongers, pointing to one of the young, lipsticked munitions workers from the White Lund factory as she strutted past the window, and sniping.

– All fur coat and no knickers, am I wrong, Muriel, or am I right? Talk about salvage, she won't salvage much of her own brass or her own pride dressed like that!

It was not a pleasanter friendship either, where they pinned each other's hair or shared a powder compact at the mirror in the public lavatories. No, theirs was a partnership on an altogether different level, a darker level. That is to say the two mothers had a relationship which meant Mrs Preston only visited the Bayview late at night, a hooded cloak about her, a small leather case in hand, and in the company of different ladies who might be very young and filled with tears, or older, weary-looking and gaunt, as if haggard from an insubstantial diet or excessive work. And always sore they were when they left, and sometimes needing to be carried and sometimes vomiting into a bowl. It was something of the shadowy world that bound Mrs Parks and Mrs Preston.

The latter was a large-small woman, rotund but petite, and she ran, with the assistance of her husband who was banished from the house from three in the afternoon until suppertime and her daughter who was sentenced to remain incarcerated at the house for those same hours, a small residential and apothecary venue on Lord Street, which catered to the rather eccentric pseudo-medical needs of Morecambe's public. In her front room, 'The Surgery', as a sign read on the door, she had bottles of hair-restoring lotion which smelled of old varnish, devices for scouring hard spots at the elbow or heel, poultice presses for headaches, acid for warts, salts for bellyaches, roots for excessive libido, roots for dwindling libido – the boys hadn't the foggiest what a libido was but it did sound painful and poorly behaved – talismans for love, crystals for luck, snuff powders for melancholia, jars with handwritten labels and with dubious inscriptions such as 'Marvin's Magical Cold Cream, Never Age a Day, Never See a Wrinkle'. Her potions and concoctions bordered on the tinker gypsy variety, though she had a clientele who showed surprising fealty and were willing to undergo the crudest, most suspect and experimental of treatments if they proved affordable, in the hope that they would become younger and prettier and stronger. Or at the very least not quite so ailed, so warty or so deviant.

Mrs Preston's true speciality was electro-therapy. It was all the rage in town, but Jonty's mother professed, and was widely held to be, the most skilled local administrator of the best medical panacea since leeches. The boys had no end of paralysing amusement with her equipment when she left it in an unlocked dresser. The headpiece was adjustable and looked rather like a fishing net had bred somewhat unsuccessfully with a hairdresser's perm dryer. The settings were easy to master, though the unleashed voltage did not necessarily correspond with the mark indicated, for it seemed electricity often had a mind of its own. Above all else the gear was far too tempting to resist, sitting in the dresser like a toy from Frankenstein's workshop. Since Cy was the tallest of the three boys he was frequently the test-subject for increased voltage, the theory being, according to the other two, that the longer the legs the further the electricity had to travel and the more diluted and harmless it became. Once treatment began there was always a moment when the entire world went rigid and buzzing and illuminated and Cy felt like he was part of a working machine, deprived of independent motion and yoked by magnificent force, or like a bulb in a lamp on the prom exuding luminescence. His arms and feet were lost to him, his muscles championed by a sudden ceasing rust, but they were not rendered useless, quite the opposite, there was passage through him, along his veins and arteries, along his skin and all the parts of him that usually felt of nothing. He could sense a rush of energy. He became a bridge to somewhere splendid. And afterwards, when the power crackled off, the world was crisp at the edges and tingled. Since the experiments did not kill him, Jonty and Morris then wanted their turn, and they fought over the hybrid headset. After a time all three of them upped the bets on who could endure the switch the longest. The medical miracle got into the brain and singed away reason.

– I'm a star! I'm a star in the sky!

Electricity. What a mystery and a marvel! Like wasp stings in your bones. Like lightning harnessing you, whipping your whole body and riding you around the room. Theirs was an intrepid, fearless leap through the zapping doorway of the dazzling new electrical age. Mrs Preston, of course, got wise to the illicit use of her therapy equipment, which always seemed to be set too high when she came to use it again on a patient. And once or twice she shocked the curled hair straight on an unsuspecting soul, and had to produce some rapid explanation. Ever after she kept it in a suitcase under the bed in her room, which the boys were forbidden to enter on pain of a sound hiding. There were other intriguing oddities at Jonty's parents' house. The beauty was you never quite knew what you might find rummaging through the drawers and cupboards of the Surgery.

– Look at this thing, Jont. Your mam's name is Widdershin Winny. So's your pissy sister's.

25

– So? Your mam's a tuppenny street walker with a pole up her crack. And she smells like a dog's backside.

– Yes, well, his mam lives in Garlands 'cause she's a lunatic.

It was all fun and gaming until Cy came across a small leather case tucked away at the back of one cabinet, which he recognized and which, when the catch was released, folded out to reveal several long, sharp metal instruments strapped against a velvet inlay, one curved at the very end with a tiny overlay designed for picking, plucking, tearing, like a seagull's bill. The chill hands of every dead sailor in Morecambe trailed the length of Cyril Parks's spine.

– Jonty. What's this for?

– Mam's crochet and knitting kit. She's useless at it, mind, as best I can see – never makes us anything. She doesn't send socks to the trenches either. Now then. Look at this fetching item.

Untroubled by the discovery, Jonty had a string of dried vole skins about his head. Cy didn't mention that the case was used by his mother in the Bayview some nights and he was fairly convinced that knitting was not quite such the brutal and exhausting hobby for the women that the sounds within the parlour suggested. Not knitting at all going on in fact, he suspected. Not where there was a locked-door brew of hocus-pocus and basins of blood and the mystery women called out clamorously as if they were night-ravens.

On these nights of careful company and whispers and bird-like screeches, Cy gradually began to tolerate what was sinister and wonder about the night-wound ministry on the other side of the wall. The keyhole seemed to expand a fraction each time he stood holding breath outside the door, as if bidding him use it. Like his eye had once upon a time been summoned to the consumptives' waste before Satan had shown him a gallery the other side of his squeamishness. And so one night Cy bent forward and peeked. And inside was a terrible story that couldn't ever be told in friendly childish pictures made from red paint. It was the Devil's joyless laboratory and in it his dabblings were mirthless, invasive, and they produced wet slop like pulled fish-gut when the gulls have flocked and pecked and ruined a catch. And Cy would never, never look again.

There was no name for what he saw, and no possible explanation for him at that age had Reeda wanted to present him with a tricky revelation. If one lesson was to be learned by her son that night, it was that there were practices which went beyond a doctor's formal world of medicine, and which ordinary folk might be better versed in. Because his mother undertook them and she was not a bookishly educated woman. There were rituals in blood, aspects of the human body which lived beyond official stewardship and out towards an altogether stranger keeping. So when the town authorities announced stiffer gaol sentences for local abortionists caught and prosecuted successfully, without having any connection to the term for such a thing he did not know to be afeared for the safety of his mother. Having not the vocabulary to discern relevance, there was no crime that she conformed to, she was no official malefactress. And if she was indeed a witch in all her raised-leg, sharp-hooked female rites with Mrs Preston, she was still his mother who also clothed and fed and loved him.

～

If it was not entirely forgotten, the parlour incident was shoved sufficiently far back in Cy's mind so as to trouble him less and less with the passing of time. Life could be cruel and it could be strange and it was certainly messy, that much he knew. But there were the pressing amusements of childhood to enjoy also. So it was that later that same year the boys came to be standing in a line on the concrete wall of the bathing pool, engaged in one of their favourite occupations. The piddling competition. Above the bay the sky was fast with cloud, drifting fat shadows over the town, stuck between coy sunshine and a squalling rain that had kept mostly out to sea all day so far. The boys had their backs to the town and had hold of their dickies in preparation. It was low tide and once again the flat plains of the beach were exposed, fishing boats were tipped on their sides and resting on the sand. Cy was about to burst. He had been saving himself all afternoon while drinking a good quantity of lemonade, the better to get some force with. The strategy proved to be not such a terribly good idea, however, as Morris Gibbs was late in arriving and by the time he made it to the pool Cy felt as if he had a hard football in his stomach. He wasn't sure he could go even if he wanted, so tight the blockage felt, though in fine tradition he bluffed and told them all he was going to hit the fells on the other side of the bay, if not manage Scotland that day. Jonty Preston, who was not one for long-distance urination and preferred to referee, shouted the mark.

– Ready? Aim. Fire!

All five let go a welcome stream in five golden arcs across the sand and shingle. Ten feet away the beach spluttered and gurgled like a drain. It could have been his height that helped him out, he was tall for his age, or his urgent need to go, but after getting a delayed start Cy knew he was winning the competition by a good few inches.

– And halt.

Jonty had five sticks in his hand, ready to plant next to the wet patches. This had to be done quickly before the piddle was lost into the dry sand or evaporated. The rules of the game meant you were supposed to stop the flow for a few seconds so that the referee could score. Then if you still needed you could finish up at your convenience. Jonty was bending down with his twig-flags when Cy hit him warmly on the ankle. With all the lemonade and the unkindness to his bladder things had gotten away from him. He couldn't have stopped that day for all the toffee in Ashworth's sweet shop. The boys jumped off the wall holding their stomachs with laughter while Jonty raced after Cy, yelling that he'd bash his head in and make him eat his shit. A woman cycling by on the promenade called out and shook her finger at them.

– You filthy little buggers! I know what you're up to. Clear off. People have to swim there!

– There's worse than piddle down there. Show us your knickers then, missus.

– Filthy little gutter-snipes!

The Bare Pool, as the structure had unfortunately and controversially been christened, was a large square enclosure that had been the scene of seasonal bathing since its construction in the late nineteenth century. Tidal dangers meant that it could within minutes become the scene of perilous gnashing waves, the sea churning up pebbles and muck against the wall as if cranking the handle of an enormous meat grinder. Several bathers had been knocked unconscious against its sides during the facility's operation and been hauled out of the pool by passers-by. Cuts and bruises were all too common; the pool was not a masterpiece of engineering. At high tide it filled with muddy water, jellyfish, seaweed and equally unwelcome human detritus and pollution – Morecambe, as a thriving though modest resort, had, in truth, neither the capacity nor the economy to deal with the excessive summer waste and the masses were frequently reacquainted with their bodily expulsions as they swam or strolled along the beach. There were of course moral implications to swimming in the Bare Pool. Mixed bathing was a heavily disputed occurrence, rigorously condemned by the conservative council since men and women were first seen to be splashing and barking with laughter like rowdy sea lions in the pool's arena, swallowing great gobfuls of salty water and groping at each other. It was simply not English to have men and women in states of undress carousing in the water and examining each other's parts, they maintained; this was not the colonies, after all. Young gentlemen could clearly be seen to be aroused by the proceedings. Clubs were formed to regulate decency, with bathing huts and vans where old ladies in high collared dresses inspected the attire of lady swimmers to ensure that it was properly lined and old men tested the strength of hemming around the suits of gentlemen with the perfunctory tug of a finger. Fines could be levied for wandering inside the stipulated ten-foot distance to be kept between the partially clothed sexes. The names of offenders were, of course, to be published in the *Visitor*.

Reeda Parks snorted loudly when she read about this development in the paper.

– What will those tiresome old masons ban next, I wonder? Holding hands in the Alhambra picture house? The human body is god-given and sacred, Cyril, nothing of it is vulgar, don't ever be ashamed of it.

She lived by this mandate and was not ashamed to have him see her as she dressed, see her well-worn, menially utilized, hard-handled body as she bathed, with its broken stomach, the gathered flesh, the discolouration at its crevices. Nor did she make unkind comment about her fellow citizens, the weighty, the narrow, the bent or twisted, as some people did. He never asked her if that philosophy meant you could give up your body to those nocturnal procedures, including hers, which seemed withdrawn and mysterious and by nature turbid, like the rips and towing undercurrents of the water in the bay you always knew were there, writhing, even under a calm green-grey surface. Instinct told him it was likely wiser that he not expose his knowledge of his mother's pointy midnight craft and so he never did.

Regardless of new codes of conduct, the Bare Pool was seldom empty of suited bathers and there was no finer platform anywhere on the beach from which to hold the weekly piddling competitions.

≈

In the days of Cyril Parks's childhood, the town was the scene of summer straw hats, Sunday-best attire and flagpoles clanking in the breeze, of bowling and boating competitions at Happy Mount Park and shows in the pavilions. There was punting, affordable dining and false recuperation for the blighted. Cy's first memories were of laughter and crowds, the wind blowing through the fabric of the place so that everything moveable flapped, or rippled, or sashayed. Morecambe Bay in season housed the Yorkshire and Scottish masses, and the Bayview took its fair share, the former coming from May to August, the latter crossing the border in spring and September, and so many visited from Bolton and Bradford that Reeda jokingly referred to their home as Bradford-by-the-Sea. The town roomed its visitors in cheap hotels, provided them with entertainment and reasonably priced food and drink. Reeda would tell her small son that he was lucky, where he lived there was a never-ending holiday, rich with rewards for those who most deserved them. It seemed everywhere Cy went in summer there were seaside treats, seafood served along the pier, sugar rock, dripping ice-cream cones, quarter-sliced ham sandwiches, tea on the beach and a variety of sticky buns. The main attractions were the sea, the magnificent view over the bay to Grange and the air itself, which was infused with something vital, and Cyril Parks loved all three. Steamboats and paddlers jostled in the bay's current alongside fishing boats, the skippers of the vessels arguing loudly about foreshore rights and landing stages, so the noise of the place went right out to sea and then came back, drifting in through the Bayview's open windows. It was a place alive to his senses. Come July the smell along the promenade was sweet and salty with the warm sugges-tion of sewage at the back of it, and sometimes, in protest to unfair rental brackets which left the fishermen the worse off, catches were sorted in public shelters and gazebos, most often the ones located near to councillors' residences, leaving piles of stinking fish heads and guts and shells for the pleasure of the public, and the town was swamped by an odour of rotting ocean fare. The Bayview's residents, unwilling to do without their therapeutic air, rank or otherwise, would on these days take nosegays to their faces and handkerchiefs liberally sprinkled with lavender water provided by the pragmatic Reeda Parks, as they shuffled slowly along the sea-walk. That forty to fifty tons of cockles alone, plus baskets full of whiting, cod and mussels came down gangplanks and up in carts every single day made for a serious argument with mighty leverage, Cy thought. And sure enough it was a trump card for the fishermen to play and rents always adjusted themselves accordingly.

The music halls were always full. If Morecambe was the poor man's Blackpool then poor men danced as well as rich. What little money there was in the hands of northerners come summer often ended up in Morecambe's seafront pavilions, the Taj Mahal, the Crystal Palace, the Alhambra, each gave as many as three concerts a day in season. Often the Bayview's guests would insist that Reeda and Cyril accompany them, purchasing tickets as thanks for another lovely week's stay. Inside the pavilions there were orchestras with foreign, exotic sounding names, magicians and minstrels, dandies or local comedians, singing competitions. Nothing was too silly or cheerful or unpopular for the people of the north at leisure who otherwise spent nigh on fourteen hours a day at work for most weeks of the year. Cy watched the shows with interest, and he watched the watching crowds – some people laughed before a joke was even finished being told and he knew they had been to the show before, maybe several times, but their laughter never seemed forced and the gags never got old. It was as if the punch-line was really the joyful state of not-for-blessed-once having to lift a shovel or swipe a loom or smelt or saw or sew.

When the tide went out the crowds came in. Sandy, stony mud was eclipsed by a covering of bright bathing towels, fluttering tents and swaying sunshades. From his window in the hotel it seemed to Cy a delightful, wonderful thing. A jester's costume draped all across the beach. Hundreds of pale and lumpy legs appeared from under clothing. Skin pinked and peeled, lotions were applied too late to sore knees and rosy shoulders. Flowery-capped heads bobbed up and down in the water and feet splashed in the waves. Boys a little older than Cy in shorts and paper hats moved in and out of the heliolatrous northern masses and the striped red tents selling winkles and jellied eels and warm orange-syrup, swapping information as to where the breasts were biggest, where the legs were shapeliest, and where the bathing suits were lowest. Even the rain, reliable and persistent when it decided to appear, could not dampen the celebratory spirit of the promenade, people ran laughing and shrieking either into the sea where wetness would not matter, or into the cafés and public houses of the town, leaving sand prints on the seats and tablecloths when they departed, and the evening's merry entertainment simply got started early. There was no silver service, no operatic gowns, there were no foreign spoils, silks brought back for daughters, fine wine for sons, nor artistic decorated objects purchased for a collection. A postcard home, a box of sugar-rock or slab of toffee, a fond memory or two of the easy banter that arose from the collective solidarity of the poor but jovial masses and from the unity of those around you who were in the same boat, so you were all in it together, was souvenir enough for Morecambe's crowds. It was a place where England's working weary came to laugh and sing and cast away their cares, if only for a brief and temporary spell.

∾

When he was very young, almost too young to remember, Cy would be taken up and down the promenade mid-season with his mother and a group of younger women, who came to stay at the Bayview for a day or two from the city. The Ladies of Leeds, his mam called them. They came for three years in succession, each year for a day or so longer. Reeda looked forward to their visit enormously, she would make extra potted shrimp and even buy a better sherry for the occasion. Before the ladies arrived she got a funny look in her eye like a dog about to snatch a bone from the butcher's counter. They were kind, well-dressed women who would not let Reeda wait on them before first insisting that she did not, they would squabble over who would wash the dishes after supper and would compliment each other on what perfume was being worn or which stockings best flattered an ankle or the choice of book presently being read. There was a great sense that these ladies liked each other very well, they seemed close, perhaps related to his mother, though he knew of only one living blood-relation, his Aunt Doris in Yorkshire. The ladies never scolded him, but they did watch him closely, while he helped his mother to cupboard the crockery, as if they expected him to fumble at any moment and drop her china dishes. They gave him questioning looks, often without issuing any actual questions.

In the mornings, breakfast would be hurried and shoelaces tied quickly. The ladies were flushed in their cheeks and gave each other good-luck kisses.

– Best of luck, duckie.

– Yes, and best of luck to you.

– Best of luck to all of us, I say!

Then they marched out of the hotel with Reeda and Cyril in tow, their skirts snapping like sails in the wind as they strode, heading for the busy promenade. It was unclear to Cy what occurred during these outings, or their purpose, but the ladies all seemed very determined, taking turns to address the crowd and passing round a brass plate which seldom came back bearing much other than a piece of chewed-up fudge which would stick to the plate lip like glue, or shirt buttons or extinguished cigarettes. Though uncertain what the plate was supposed to collect he supposed it was not beachgoers' rubbish as the ladies would click their tongues in annoyance at their meagre alms. Votes seemed to be what his mother's friends wanted, and as he'd never seen a vote he did not know how to recognize one on the brass plate if it happened to be forthcoming. Cy spent these mornings holding his mother's hand and kicking the back of one foot with the other in boredom, looking up at her frowning face.

Frequently one or two of the women came back to the hotel in the afternoon for sandwiches after the pier walk, though most stayed out while his mother returned to her hotel chores. Once settled round the kitchen table with a pot of tea they would continue their talking about votes in louder, more irritated tones. Other times Cy and his mother would return alone, and Reeda would ferociously pound chicken liver into pâté for dinner that night. On the way back to the Bayview there would be trouble if his mother ran into one of the other hotel owners. The arguments were without exception begun by other women. Mrs Thelma Kirkstall from the Grand Hotel once caught hold of his mother's wrist as she passed by and hissed at her.

– My Ronnie saw you out on the promenade again. Reeda, you silly cow, why don't you get another husband instead of all this nonsense. Whatever's in you?

Cy's mother stood looking at Mrs Kirkstall, just looking at her and not moving until the woman took her hand off Reeda's wrist, then she turned and walked away. The woman went to pat Cy's head but Cy made as if to buckle his shoe, though it was already firmly buckled, half unwilling to be touched by the woman who had grabbed his mother, half suspecting that Mrs Kirkstall may also have touched consumptives in her time. He looked up at her squinting face, crumpled like a discarded fish and chip wrapper. She had a badly done permanent wave and cracked dry lips.

– Poor lad, she'll raise you to wring out her skirts if you're not careful. You'll end up selling ladies' bloomers and shoes in Anderson's. Come by ours if you want sometime. Mr Kirkstall will show you all you need to know, eh? Come round and he'll give you a wee drop of man's talk. There's a good lad.

And she boxed the air like a March rabbit, upright and punching on its hind legs. Cy unhinged and re-buckled his shoe, then ran down the street after his striding mother.

– Skirt-wringer!

He heard the woman shouting after him and when he caught up with Reeda he found she was cussing under her breath as bitterly as he had ever heard her cuss.

~

There were better ways to make money in Morecambe than passing round brass plates, Cy would find out. There were in fact more schemes for making money in the town than there were grains of imported Blackpool sand on the shores of the bay. Most of the lesser enterprises were unsurprisingly thought up by children, and Cyril Parks's gang was not innocent in this regard. The adult spiritualists, fortune tellers, novelty kiosk vendors, hoteliers, whores, the town planners and the contractors may have made more money and lost it out of season but the desperate entrepreneurial efforts of the young peddlers, hustlers and downright petty rogues were remarkable, breathtaking and prolific. Cy liked to think of his peers as the best inventors of the day, unfettered by trivial, traditional constraints, like guarantees or liability. If the town's tourist industry operated on the premise of vague flight-of-fancy fibbery with regard to its assets, beauty surrounding and health abounding, Morecambrians living to be 120 years of age on average because of the miraculous air, and so on and so forth, the individual juvenile protagonist was far more venturesome and frequently exposed in his swindlery. 'Buyer Beware' was the motto of the trio. Children annually sold tickets for tours to see the local boggarts, monsters, spirits and wee folk of the area, who supposedly lived in the dunes, the bushes surrounding the town and out in the Lune marshes. The boggarts themselves ranged from convenient stray dogs, vagrant tramps and drunks, to friends and younger siblings dressed in raggedy clothing with twigs entwined in their hair and mud on their faces. When, one summer, they ran out of suitable candidates for the role, Cy and Morris and Jonty drew lots to see who would have to dress up and cover himself with muck for the occasion. Cy lost the draw, though Jonty later confessed to having fixed it earlier on with Morris as revenge for Cy peeing on his leg.

– Why does the boggart have to have dog shit on him? Can I not just sit in the mud for a bit? It's all the same.

– No it's not, stupid. All boggarts roll around in it 'cause it keeps people away who want to kill them. Can't have a boggart without shit as anyone knows! Do you want your sherbet dip or not, Parksie?

Jonty winked at Morris and Cy eventually consented to the indignity.

They dressed him up in a pair of old waders belonging to Morris's dad, which stank to high heaven of flukes, and they stuffed grass into the holes of his shirt, around the collar and up the sleeves. Cy had brought a pocketful of potato peelings from the kitchen of the Bayview and he stuffed them into his mouth and practised his groaning while his pals went on the search for fresh shit. They came back over the marshes with two sticks on the ends of which was a nasty mess and proceeded to poke Cy with them while giggling and putting their noses against their sleeves. He protested through a mouth of peel.

– That's foul. Get off, it's enough.

– Wait here while we find our customers. And don't wash the dirt off, Cyril Parks.

Half an hour later, he was still sitting miserably in the swampy grass of the Lune marshes feeling thoroughly sick at the smell of himself and the rooty, soily taste of uncooked potato. He'd got bored watching the sea in the distance rolling in, shallow and foamy, watching the fishermen moving their hazelwood baulks, and collecting their shrimp. Try as he might he could not imagine being a fisherman like his father had been, not because the industry was not a good one, it provided food for the town, but because there was a quality of uncertainty, you could never be sure what the sea would bestow and what it would reserve for itself – he had seen many a fleet come back to the bay without so much as a mackerel scale or a halibut tail in the hold, the expressions of the men long and webbed, as if casting nets within themselves. Similarly, the clouds in the sky had ceased to form interesting patterns. He looked at the horizon where the sun would be disappearing in a few hours, and he remembered what his mother had told him about that as a very young child – that the sun's light never went out at night, it just went over to Ireland and then it went to America, then right around the world until it came back up again the other side in the morning. And it was like a lamp that all lost souls could follow. After the watching and the ruminating there was nothing left to do but putrefy in his own revolting stench. Then he heard a whistle, the signal for him to hide and ready himself for his performance. He ducked down in a puddle of water and parted the reeds to watch for the approach of the unsuspecting tourist. He could hear Jonty's voice warbling away, matter of fact, and informative, as if he were giving a tour of the Winter Gardens.

– Right around these parts he was last spotted, madam. He was eating the skull of an animal – crunch, crunch – they have very powerful jaws you see. Now they are quite smelly, so be warned. You may want to prepare yourself just in case he comes in close.

– Goodness gracious. Is it safe? I mean, won't it be quite cross with us if we tread near its home?

– Oh, they don't have homes, madam. They range around and wail at night. Sometimes they approach farms to eat the chickens and they make necklaces out of the feathers, but there's never been a complaint of one attacking a human being. At least not in Morecambe, in Blackpool possibly. Just a little further, madam. Right around here. Super day, isn't it?

– Quite lovely.

The lady did not sound convinced, suddenly preoccupied by the thought of powerful jaws and headless chickens, no doubt. But it mattered not; that question was the code-sign

38

for the boggart to reveal itself. Cy leaped up out of the marsh, wailed, and disappeared behind a clump of grass.

– Over there, madam! Do you see it? Crouched behind that hummock.

– No . . . Where!

Cy began groaning and jumped up into the air again. This time he remained in view and came stumbling towards the lady. His bare feet were filthy with mud and his hair looked like a bird's nest. She was standing stock-still as if she knew a hunter had her in his rifle sites and she must freeze or perish. Cy roared and spat a potato skin at her. She obliged him with a scream.

– Shooo. Shoo, you nasty, smelly thing. Get away from me. Go on! No, wait, wait, is that a boy, is that a poor little boy under all that disgusting mess?

The boggart turned around and ruthlessly showed her its bare backside. Behind her Jonty and Morris were now helpless with laughter. The woman screamed again and lifted her skirt and began to totter speedily over the moor back towards the town. She was still screaming when she reached the promenade. Suddenly Jonty was running after her.

– Bugger it! Hey, missis, the shilling! Stop, you haven't paid. You owe us a shilling. Tell everyone you saw a genuine boggart and who showed you . . .

From the next customer the boys made sure to take payment first. The resulting sherbet was delicious and did a fine job of ridding his tongue of the terrible taste of un-scrubbed potato, but Cy was certain that he could still smell the shit on himself for the whole of the next week, even after several baths, and that guests in the hotel were covering their faces when he leaned past them to ladle soup from the tureen into their bowls in the dining room.

When the local boys tired of acting as tour guides some of them would try to outrun the Bore for bets, that sweeping tidal wave created as two Atlantic currents, one from the north of Ireland and one from the south, met up and converged in the direction of Morecambe's shore. Cy, having a healthy respect for the sea, which had casually robbed him of his father, considered this scheme to be ridiculous and foolhardy in the extreme, did not mind saying so, and would not participate in any wager. The Bore came in faster than a grown man could sprint, let alone a penny-pinching stump-legged junior. It was one of the fastest tides in the British Isles and on more than one occasion every year lifeboats were sent out to collect a drowning soul who had underestimated its maritime throttle.

Morris Gibbs's older brother, Terrance, was perhaps the most fortunate of all the youngsters in town trying to make some pocket money. He had been wading around barefoot and dredging cockles from the sandy rocks with his father and Morris out on the Jacky John Skears one day when he trod on something wriggling and writhing and he found the eel. The Eel. Not just any eel, for it took all three of them to yank the beast from the sand hole it was hell bent on squirming into. It was a monster, a creature that rivalled all the sea-devils and sturgeon and Greenland whales and curious, unnamed specimens ever tossed up on the shore for unsuspecting Morecambrians to find. It was the granddaddy of all eels. The struggle to catch it was for many years to come a frequently told yarn in the Gibbs home, Mrs Gibbs remained ever sad not to have been able to dice it up and have a preposterously large spitchcock fry, Mr Gibbs adding inches to the beast with every retelling of its capture, not to mention fangs, prehistoric spines and red eyes made of rubies. As legend was soon to have it, Morris's dad had been busy with the pronged rake that day while Terrance was emptying bucketloads of fish into the cart. Morris was giving the silty-covered horse her nosebag of oats and adjusting her blanket when Terrance let out a yell so loud both brother and father thought he'd stepped on a Portuguese man o' war. The eel was coiled in a puddle of water in a depression in the beach next to a boulder, trying for all its slippery life to make that boulder a shield above it.

Terrance had already begun to wrestle it out when the two came over to help. Thus ensued a battle of Argonaut proportions. Boots were dug in. Sludge was shovelled out. Waists were grasped and hauled. The Gibbs men finally prevailed. It turned out to be sixty-four inches long, and nineteen inches in girth, the largest eel ever found and recorded in Morecambe history. For the whole summer long Terrance took it round the pubs and the promenade and charged a penny a look at the creature, concertina-snug in a large glass jar, which had once held Edmondson's pickled eggs. Alive or dead it was hard to say, but the eel impressed many a man and distressed many a lady that summer. By the end of the season, much to his younger brother's envy, Terrance had enough money for a brand new shining bicycle from Lancaster.

~

The sand-bred citizens of the town seemed born with a sense of what might make their fortunes. If there was a tale to be told or a whimsy to be shown or a skill to be extorted, very possibly only the Lord God himself could put a stop to it in Morecambe Bay. In summer, copper coins shuffled through the pockets and purses of townsfolk faster than they could be counted by the tellers in the bank. Professional entertainment was bigger business still, and on the occasions when he and Reeda were invited along by guests of the hotel to the shows Cy marvelled at what was on offer inside the pavilions and gardens, what strange and exotic talents could earn a decent wage. There were male impersonators and jugglers, vaudevillians, dames and geishas, ghost train operators, acrobats and circus ringmasters. Grease-coated-throated men ate fire and then drove home in brand-new cars. At the monkey castle blue-bottomed primates swung from the rafters and chattered loudly amongst themselves while the crowds bought and tossed them nuts and peel. Miss India Rubber, contortionist extraordinaire, could put both legs behind her shoulders so her backside was cushioning her skull and then walk crab-like from the stage of the Taj Mahal to the end of the western pier and back again – she would patrol through the crowds after the show with her live boa constrictor, letting it sit on the shoulders of dare-devil boys and girls for another extra penny from their parents. It was rumoured that she was so wealthy she owned a flat in the city of Manchester which was home to not less than one thousand poisonous snakes and spiders imported from the Amazon. Fat comedians with cigars in their mouths shook the bellies of the visitors with gags about mothers-in-law and brothels. And there was that favourite rude old chestnut as the curtain went up to commence every show:

– Where are we all tonight, ladies and gentlemen?

– More-cambe.

– And is there more come here ladies and gentlemen? Ooh sorry Sally-Ann, that's a bit naughty, isn't it?

Short of a visit to the towers or the museums of London, and within the bounds of imagination and reason, there was nothing more thrilling and funny and silly that turned a profit to be found anywhere outside the chuckle-creased corners of the bay.

~

In March of 1917, sometime between the hours of ten and eleven at night, a faulty fuse sparked on the western pier, inside its most majestic building. The little smoulder gathered strength and in the strong sea breeze it spun into a persistent glut of flame. Then the fire, suddenly very confident, spread to the ground-floor ceiling of the structure and lay upside down across its rafters. The great pavilion of the Taj Mahal went up in a blaze the likes of which the town had never seen before. The golden dome of the building shone in the darkness as reddish flames leaped upwards from the wooden strutting of the deck. Within twenty minutes the fire had created a bright Pharos of light to alert those not yet abed and to wake those who were. Cy pulled back the curtain of his window. He'd been reading when an undefined patch of light, out of keeping with the glare of the streetlamps on the promenade, caught his eye. His mother at her window saw wings of orange curving up the sides of the main dome, mimicking its shape, tormenting it with the authority to destroy it. Both ran to the front door, knocking awake their guests. An opportunistic buzz quickly went through Morecambe. It soon reached the back end of the town, those properties without a view of the fiery pavilion, through to the slums of Moss Street and the train station, all were invited to the show.

The townsfolk and the first of the season's visitors made their way out of their houses and hotels and down to the beach, awed and hurriedly, as if late for the performance, though it looked in no danger of finishing before time. They came fully dressed or in nightgowns and slippers, rolling rags and winkie caps, caring nothing for appearance, drawn to the scene as if hypnotized, swaying quickly but thickly, like the frantic slowness towards the end of a strong dream. The tide was low, the entire mud beach stretching out for the spectators to take to like the apron of a stage. And take to it they did, thousands of people, standing close together on the sands, watching extraordinary light floating out above the bay. The wooden walkway to the pavilion had become a burning road above them, an almost biblical vision some said, and others passed that thought along.

Fire itself would have been incendiary beauty enough for one evening. But then, it snowed. First it snowed lightly, a flake or two on the heads of the bemused onlookers, like winter waving a handkerchief from a distant carriage of the train taking it away. Somebody close to Cy in the crowd cheered, presuming the snow would extinguish the blaze, as if one tear could put out the fire of a tormented heart! Then the wind turned, switched tracks, and brought with it an entire fast batch of plump snow, a blizzard in fact. Those in undergarments and long shirts shivered and reached for spouses and children for warmth, and some reached for convenient strangers. Those with rotting chests wheezed and coughed but did not go inside. Reeda's consumptives benefited from her foresight and blessed her as she handed out a stack of woollen blankets. Cy found Morris Gibbs in the crowd, for his red hair seemed like a portion of fire itself in the light, and he pulled on his arm. They walked closer to the blaze, so close Cy could feel his face changing texture, crisping, broiling. Behind him Morris had hiked his jumper over his head for protection from the heat and was looking through the neck of it so the scope of his vision could have been no larger than that seen through a penny slot machine. The fire leaned slightly to the right, at an angle appropriate to the wind. The snow blew fast to the right, arced upwards, fell, was chaotic, then resumed its course. Cy looked up. Oh. The snow. The snow was on fire. How could that be? Though he had mastered none of the sciences yet in junior school, he understood that the two elements were seldom in cahoots, let alone conjoined. And yet it was so. Fire and ice. There above him. The brilliant snow moved like thousands of migrating, flaming birds across the sky, flocking, reforming, conflagrating. It was like meteors swarming and rushing on some swift and undisclosed passage, riding the rapids of the cosmos. Or like being spun with his eyes open in a circle on a clear night except that he was standing still and the sky was whirling of its own accord. It was like pieces of a mirror being smashed in the heavens, in a fury of narcissistic disappointment. He was ten years old and dizzy with amazement.

– Look at it. It's beautiful, Morris. It's beautiful.

– It is at that.

And the two boys stood watching the impossibility of the entire western portion of the sky alight with burning snowflakes. When the dome finally tumbled it did so without grace. It sucked into itself the way a drunk finally gives in to stupor and folds inwards to the floor. The noise of it crashing down one hundred feet to the shore below was equally ignominious, it was the uncontrolled groaning of something large and restricted becoming uncharacteristically mobile. Though the fall looked to be an implosion of sorts, an inverted tumble, at the end of its descent it altered shape to thrust outwards. The crowds on the beach gasped. A flush of warmth moved past them, as did a small tidal wave of sparks and fireworks.

By this point Cy's mother was looking for him. She had not liked the way in which the fire had leaped and streaked along the sand with the pavilion's collapse, chasing after the stray wood it was intent on devouring. The faces of those watching the show were orange and shadowy, even her sicker guests looked momentarily healthy in the warm aura of the blaze. Those in the front row, closer to the volatile mass of cinder-spinning, roaring timber were only black silhouettes, and she could not see the one belonging to her boy. By the time she had reached the Bayview Hotel and checked that her guests did not need any calming spirits or rubs for their smoke-agitated chests, her son was already home, drinking milk in the kitchen with Morris Gibbs. His cheeks were blown red and his eyebrows were thinner than she remembered. And he had the look about him of a laudanum taker after a purchase. Lit up, let out and satisfied.

~

The next morning was Easter Sunday. Even for such a holy day the churches of the town were unusually packed for the morning services. Many had not felt at all comfortable with the previous night's events, and were comforted even less by the image of a burning pathway leading to a fiery temple which had been presented to them. It was interpreted by multiple citizens on a personal level as possibly being prophetic, an indication of what might be awaiting them upon their deathbeds. Caring little for damnation or days of reckoning, all the boys of the town went down to the wreckage of the pavilion to ferret around. It was now a huge pile of debris that the tide had been in and out over, extinguishing any residual smoulder. Some were climbing on the blackened heap, others rooting through the rubble looking for treasure, fake gold-leafing from the roof, tapestry from within the ballroom. After serving breakfast in the hotel Cy slipped out and went down to the beach. He walked about with his hands in his pockets, kicking bits of decking and bricks, tarnished tiles. The lads around him were excited by the proximity of destruction, by the fact that something formerly so grand and spectacular was now demolished. A strange exuberance and exhilaration roused them and they shoved each other around. Their behaviour reminded him of Reeda's comments about the present ugliness abroad that much of Europe was well and truly engaged in. She often said to him over the top of the morning paper that there was a certain pleasure for some people in violence. She said you could still hear it ringing in a few of the ones who came back from the war, and in those running the affair. Men especially suffered from this disposition, she informed him frankly and unapologetically. As if some were born hollow and there was a hole cut in their hearts that produced music when the breath of spite and madness was blown through them.

Cy looked up at the greyish March sky. Not a hint that it had once swum with flickering schooling light remained there. The fiery winter storm was gone. It seemed right that out of such beauty should come such awful devastation, he supposed, the things of the universe being equal and linked, like birth and death, his life for his father's. Fee Lung, the Chinese magician who played in the pavilion every Friday night, was standing by the desecrated spire of the dome, now half-buried in the sand, shaking his head. He looked over at Cy and smiled pristinely, solemnly.

– Yes, yes, all is gone.

Next to his polished feet, half hidden by spoiled wood, there appeared to be a stringed instrument of some kind, smallish, charred at the neck, perhaps a violin that had miraculously avoided being consumed by the flames. Cy pointed to it and Fee Lung stooped to retrieve the charmed item, bringing it out from under the wreckage like a rabbit from a black top hat. The Viennese Orchestra had been booked to play in the Taj Mahal that very evening.

Beauty and destruction, thought Cy, now there's a trick.

~

His mother was right. War was a peculiar thing. It suited some and sullied others. It combed the region thinner of its men and provided conveyor-belt work and wagon-driving skills for women. Loved ones were lost, new loves were found. Soldiers arrived and marched on the prom, soldiers disappeared and died at Ypres and the Somme. Mrs Gardner of number 42 West Street claimed a widow's pension for her deceased husband, then married to become Mrs Burton, until Mr Gardner arrived home on one leg and off she went to court for bigamy. Many families retired to Morecambe when husbands and fathers returned from abroad, having faced the worst that life could offer they were now content to live in the cheeriest place they could remember, and new houses were built to accommodate those coming in. The Tower, incomplete and scarcely rivalling those neighbouring structures it was supposed to rival, was stripped of excess metal for the war effort, rendered skeletal, though the dancehalls still made a roaring profit and provided funds for the returning wounded, and the picture houses boomed, providing a shadowy haven for potentially doomed couples to explore inside each other's clothing while they had the chance. In people's eyes there were strange lights that Cy had never seen before. Often it was a sad luminescence, weary with grief, light in a minor key, like the death-glow of the moon when it's left behind in the winter day sky, stranded long after night has departed. Sometimes, as in the eyes of the White Lund women, the lights were new and budding, as useful as fresh stars emerging against a world of blackness. Then the stars went out when the girls were told their sweethearts would not be coming home. It was a time of light and dark, of good and bad. The war gave people purpose and it also brought them pain. Either way the town came through the troubles with remark- able resilience. It wept for the unfortunate, then gathered itself up and in a spirit of continuing humour it told a joke or two. Reeda said to Cy that Morecambe was needed more than ever in these years. And perhaps escape was the best prescription for the nation's suffering, a way for the north to keep up morale. For those used to scraping by with very little money and holidaying cheap at the seaside resort the pinch of the war was no deterrent. Reeda's consumptives were unfit for any kind of duty and were as faithful to the Bayview as ever. There may have been more day-trippers to the coast and fewer boarders through the years of conflict, but by and by the income of the town remained the same. Though the war changed something in folk slightly, Cy could tell. When people made mention of it, it was never certain what they would offer you. If asked they could be enraged or sullen, broken or mending, hopeful or raving. So for a time he had the feeling the ground was never quite firm beneath his feet.

～

The quicksands of Morecambe Bay took the lives of a few unsuspecting beach-explorers and visitors every decade or so. They lay out to the south-west, beyond the town itself, and when the tide went out they formed in a quiet, saturated strip that could pull down and swallow a whole adult body in fifteen minutes or less, like an egg in the muscular throat of a snake. Once swallowed, bones could crack like the egg's shell under pressure and the body cavities would be invaded by thick wet juice. The heavier the victim, the quicker the death was how it went. The beach was a fateful combination of rock, pebble, river-borne silt and mud hollows, which could create vertical sand tunnels and crusted-edged bowls of considerable depth. A nasty liquid conspiracy between trickling eddies and the ebbing tide resulted in some of the worst and most dangerous traps on the whole of the British coastline. When a tourist was lost, or a local went missing, the first place the police constables looked for them after Moss Street was south-west of the harbour beach. Local guides would bring the uniformed men out on to the perimeter of the quicksands to assess the possibility of those ravenous hydra sand-mouths having claimed another victim. Drunks had a habit of challenging the quicksands when they were losing at life. And they would lose again, lose their last rum-reeky breath, and complete their demise. Sometimes the sucking holes were not that deep, they were deep enough to kill and drown and crush but not to consume fully, Morecambe Bay itself being partial to a little comedy, it would seem. And a hand or a whole arm would protrude from the surface as if waving to the search party, as if the sand predator had eyes that were bigger than its belly. Immune only were the dirty, grey, juvenile swans that waddled out flat-webbed over the mouths of the beast in search of worms and flapped extraordinarily powerful wings to lift out of the grip at the slightest indication that the ground was beginning to take them.

The younger children of the town occasionally played a game called quicksand in the school playground, where the pretended execution of one of them was always tragically improvised. Some of the older, bolder children from the town formed lines out on the beach during holidays or weekends and the bravest of them all would step out into the treacherous jaws of living sand until the pull began to frighten them, then they would yell and get heaved back to safety, out on to the dry, stable, trustworthy beach. Almost before the children of Morecambe could understand the English language their parents told them about the perils of quicksand. How, if caught, they should remain absolutely still and not struggle, that made it worse you see, just scream for help, scream and scream until rescue came. And they were taken out across the vast, empty, sealess beach at low tide and shown that portion of the shore they must not venture on to, where there were shiny looking patches of smooth sand, which differed slightly from their surrounding canvas. Scream and scream for help, the parents said.

But every so often a child from Morecambe would actually wander out on the beach at low tide where they should not go, perhaps collecting shells or rock-pooling, perhaps under the spell of the brewing fog that rolled in from time to time, and they would step through a patch of live sand and not step out again, and they would struggle because it is human nature to fight for life when it is being taken, and nobody would hear the screams and come to help even though it had been promised. Only the cold, disdainful Irish Sea would hear the calls and come up to investigate, that fickle arm of the Atlantic Ocean which had in part set up the trap. In it would rush and smooth over the strange, lumpy, depressed portion of beach with the wet scuffled tracks and the trenched handprints. Smoothing it over like glass, as if complicit in the murder, as if further employed in the conspiracy to get rid of the evidence. And the child would join the company of a few others inside the tightest, sludgiest, densest of bellies. And crack like an egg the child would go, and thick wet sand would seep into his mouth and ears, setting him in the last position his limbs could move into. And out would come the search parties and the guides and the police when little Charlie didn't come home at teatime. A scarf would eventually be found, or a glove, a shoe, a fishing net, too light to be a decent meal for the hungry sand and so it was left above ground, moved around by the sea, and brought up to the piers by the police sergeant to be recognized by a now hysterical mother. Then the game in the school playground would start up again in earnest and the shrieks of panicking children would echo over to Charlie Jessop's house on Royal Street, where his mother would be looking at a photograph of her son, whom the wretched Morecambe quicksand had made eternally seven years old.

Cyril Parks had been up to his crotch in it before, with Jonty and Morris holding his outstretched arms. The theory was that since he was the tallest of the three there would be more of him to get pulled down, and more of him left sticking out to grab hold of and yank back out. Height was a surprisingly versatile argument for being the first to undertake experimental practices, Cy noticed.

– Go on, Parksie, those great long legs will hit the bottom before you drown.

– Aye. We'll not wander off and leave you.

It was amusing up over the ankles, sort of tickling and soft. Cy laughed to his friends and said that it was grand. But then the sand began to work faster and after a few seconds his knees were gone and it was not soft any more, it was cold and wet, like a big, pillowy tongue up his trouser legs. It was nasty. There was an unmistakable feeling of being swallowed. Sucked on like a lollipop, like the bigger boys said Lucy Willacy, the headmaster's daughter, had done to their dickies but not as nice, he assumed.

– What's it like now?

As ever, Morris and Jonty were keen to know the exact details of the experience. Cy didn't reply. It was like being buried, he thought. Like swimming in Lyle's Golden Syrup. Like amputation of his legs so that he suddenly felt shorter, a good deal smaller, and he could not say with certainty that he had toes any more. He got to just past his knees and said to his friends enough and to pull him out. So they tried pulling. But he kept going down, he did not start coming up. The sand had opened its monstrous gullet and begun its gurgitation. Mid-thigh now, he lost his balance, swayed, but was unable to adjust the position of his legs and he tipped over to one side. His left hand was caught by the sand and sucked on. He dragged it out, covered in a new, gluey brown skin.

Then panic, panic, panic was all Cy felt, getting quicker in him and bigger. He was stuck. Too stuck. He was being eaten. Jonty and Morris had him by the shoulders and arms and were jerking at him but he was still going down. He tried to talk and started stumbling over bits of speech, rambling about nothing.

– Mam's cutlery . . . she'll bust us over the chops . . . I . . . I . . . want to go, come back, Dad . . . Lu, Lu, Lucy, then if I don't . . . of God, oh God . . . Ah, ah . . .

And the ranting was replaced by yelling. He was low enough to feel the compression of sand on the end of his dicky and it was not a marvellous sensation in the slightest. He was now half-wearing the beach.

Morris Gibbs bent suddenly and put a hand over Cy's mouth.

– Shut up, you idiot. Undo your trews. Quick sharp, eh.

– What? It's not funny Morris, it's not –

– Aye, go on and do it. No time to explain. Cy . . . Cyril. It's all right.

Cy fumbled with his buttons and pulled his breeches down until they met the wet sand.

– Now. Try to point your feet down. Like standing on your tippy-toes.

Morris's instructions were surprisingly calm. Cy looked up and found that the eyes regarding him were utterly placid. His friend was wearing an expression that Cy had seen before somewhere, on a face under a moustache, in an old photograph on the Trawlers' Cooperative Society building wall. It was the look of knowing the sea, come what may. And it suddenly gave him comfort. So he pushed as hard as he could without really feeling his ankles move and took a deep breath.

Morris was counting.

– One, two . . .

On three the two boys heaved and wrenched and Cy slowly came up, peeling out of his trousers and his shoes as he did so with a loud sucking sound. The boys landed together in an untidy heap. They stood up quickly and looked back at the puddle of sand with the shed clothing inside. The vacated legs were squeezing together, shrinking in, and were full of mucky-looking water that was being displaced upwards, out-wards, and filtering back through the sand like awful digestive juices in a stomach. Cy blew out a great lungful of air.

– Well. Bugger me sideways.

– Not on your nelly.

They walked back over the beach towards town, laughing about the predicament they had escaped. Cy's bare legs were cold in the fresh breeze, he was careful to tread lightly as he walked, pulling his feet up quickly from the sand, for the sensation of his toes sinking down even a little, that closeness of damp pressure to his skin, was sickening now and made him feel light-headed. It was an anxiety that would never quite leave him. After the quicksands he could no longer sleep with the blankets close about him, boggarts under the bed or not. And if he happened to saturate his garments in the rain or the river or when he was dropped off the pier by the boys at full tide, it would never remain on his body long enough to dry and release the flesh beneath it from its clasp. He'd rather go stark bollock naked through the town than feel that terrible tight claustrophobia again. Morris Gibbs and Jonty Preston, though, were quick-thinking devils, and friends for life.

~

It was when the war was pulling its hardest on the continent, when Europeans were streaming hither and thither from their smashed-open homes and villages and fields like ants from a disturbed hill-nest, and official letters to mothers and wives were flowing with regularity through the letter boxes around the bay, that another wonder was bestowed upon Morecambe. If not for harmony's sake then for counterplay. The pavilion fire of that same year was all but eclipsed by this new and celestial beauty. Aurora Borealis. The northern bloodlights.

It was not the crowded spectacle of the fire, nor an occasion of mass mesmerism, with all seats sold out for the performance. It was to be a private show. The town had long since known that it held one of the best positions in the country for observing this display, the tourist leaflets listing local attractions and entertainments made great mention of it, it was almost as compulsory a feature as leaving Blackpool off every local map and out of every visitor handbook. Aurora was not a stranger to the bay, for all her being the classiest act around. She was not the rarest sight, though many may have missed her that night, coming unannounced and under a dark cloak as she always did. Cy was almost sleeping when his mother knocked softly on his door and entered. Her face was softer than he had ever seen it, her eyes contained light stolen from every scrap and corner of the room it seemed, so it was dim about them, so at first his mind went out to thoughts of witchery, to her capabilities of subversion and collaboration in the parlour room. As if some sinister rite of passage bequeathed him was about to take place. Perhaps he never left his slumber, and his dreaming memory deluded him into his coming vision. But she took the covers back off him, reached for his hand and led him to the window. And fatefully he went with her.

Outside there was nothing but a red sky. Red long past sunset and long before sunrise. Red of an impossible hour. Red, and behind that struggling green, and behind that trapped and gentlest white. It was light that had neither the impatience of fire, nor the snap of electricity, nor the fluttering sway of a candle. It was light that was nature's grace, unhurried, the slowest, seeping effulgence. Lesser and greater than all light. Blood of the sky.

Cyril Parks left himself then. Perhaps it was the solitary quietude of this occurrence, which was kept under glass for they did not step outside to applaud Miss Borealis, though she was intensely lovely, or his condition, resting on the swaying anchor of sleep, ready ahoy, soon to be sent down to the depths and so susceptible to any form of sublimation. Perhaps it was holding his mother's hand at the window as though she were a guide, neither witch nor widow nor angel at that moment, but simply a guide on the wasteland sand of the shore, and when she took her hand softly away from his he felt arrived. Perhaps this is what ended that first part of his life. He stepped out of it willingly. And for all his remaining youth and curiosity, the full store of energy set to keep him beating on until it finally wound down and fluttered out in his heart, he would have taken death right then, under Aurora's beauty, and gone happily, knowing he had seen the last and brightest of all miracles.

– The Kaiser and the Queen of Morecambe –

Where one confusion ended two more were sure to take its place, wasn't that how it went? Soon there was to be an entirely new batch of contentious issues to wrangle with. Life's next riddles may well have stemmed from Cy's discovery of the *Pisces vaginales* in a science book during a weekly biology lesson, given as always and as it was currently being, by Colin Willacy, headmaster of Morecambe Grammar School. The *Pisces vaginales*. It certainly had a funny ring to it. It had a funny shape to it also, there on the page, like a mangled anemone. Every Wednesday afternoon, prior to rugby, the class of boys was required to locate within their natural-history textbooks a fish native to the British Isles so that they could then march down to the bay's shore, attempt to find the selected species and sketch the blighter into their notebooks, for Headmaster Willacy was quite the practitioner, favouring the methods of field research to classroom dissertation. He also possessed a boisterous, cane-happy left arm and a good aim for catapulting loose objects from the blackboard shelf at chattering individuals, but that was by the by. Star-slubbers, flukes, ink fish, barnacles, rays. The marine choices were many. Top marks were awarded for a successful find, which seemed a little random and circumstantial to Cy, though he made no mention of this theory. And if success was not to be had they were to draw whatever God may provide for them that day, as Mr Willacy forthrightly put it. The beach and God provided artistic and scientific bounty only when either felt moved to. They also provided a startling collection of oddities from time to time, items not grown within the nurturing womb of the ocean, but fashioned in the factories of smoky towns, delivered by trains, bought in haberdasheries and

56

market places, then lost or discarded near water channels only to end up gallivanting right around the coast before arriving at Morecambe. Old shoes, pots and pans, gloves, bottles, pieces of motor cars, rubber devices with ambiguous functions. None of which carried any merit if it was drawn. Cy had a decent artistic hand. It was perhaps his finest talent, other than distance piddling. Since a relatively young age he had been able to copy an object from sight or memory, exact to its edges, true to its dimensions, faithful to its proportions, so he did not mind these excursions to the beach so very much and was largely keen, even when the bucketing rain smudged his charcoal and the strong wind flapped his note-book out of his hands.

– Sir. I've found mine. The *Pisces vaginales*. That's what I'll hunt for today.

– What's that Parks?

– *Pisces vaginales*, sir. Recorded at Morecambe Bay in the eighteen hundreds according to the book. So called because it resembles the genitalia of a woman. What's a genitalia, sir? Sir? It says here that they contract tightly when touched and emit a liquor like that of a vagina in coy . . . in coy . . . in coitu . . .

– My room, Parks! Immediately! The rest of you, on with your study. In silence. And if I hear a word . . .

Cy was marched down to the fusty, book-strewn office of Colin Willacy where all castigations and lectures were issued, and where, it was widely rumoured, the headmaster took a wee drop of port daily around about lunchtime. If you licked your hand before Old Willacy had a chance to whip it with his cane it didn't hurt so very much. It still hurt, but was less likely to redden up and blister and smart all day. However, it turned out there were misdemeanours that did not warrant a caning. Much to his surprise and relief Cy did not get birched for his fishy transgression, though the headmaster paced about the room a good while before making this clear, giving Cy ample time to prepare his appendages for the onslaught of stinging wood. The old man removed his mortarboard and ran a hand lengthwise through his thinning white hair, smoothing long wayward strands of it along the dome of his pate. He adjusted his chalk-stained gown about him.

– Sit down, lad.

Willacy had never called him lad before. He was a funny old codger, with foibles and eccentricities, like insisting Cy write script with his unnatural right hand not his natural left, and a recurrently weepy, pus-crusted eye when it came to the examination period, but this term of endearment was a new one to Cy. He wiped his palms on his breeches leg and sat.

– Now, Cyril, I'm going to tell you this because I know you are without a father and it is a father's duty to inform his off-spring of such matters. I do not fault your mother for her neglect, indeed you've arrived at your inquisitiveness and speculation reasonably early it seems; then again you are a rather . . . tall fellow for your age, but, she shall not be blamed for ill preparation. However, we cannot have you running around declaring vulgarity to the world. That would not do. I shall try to be brief and I shall try to be frank.

Being brief and frank were not two of Colin Willacy's strong points. In all fairness, Cy was of the opinion, he did not get off lightly. It was quite possibly one of the worst punish-ments he had ever received, and after a dire, meandering, inclusive speech containing every loathsome aspect of a curriculum Cy had no inclination to participate in, he left the headmaster's quarters, pale and visibly shaken, so his pals were at first convinced he had taken the birching of a lifetime. He probably would have preferred a caning. The incident did not prevent him from sharing his new-found knowledge about the school yard, since he was now in possession of some remarkably formal terminology, some remarkably extensive slang words, and some remarkably modern con-cepts – Mr Willacy was, after all, a thorough teacher. Within a week several new rhymes had been introduced to Morecambe's school yards, though Cy sincerely maintained, whilst getting severely caned, that he was the author and distributor of none of them.

– French letter, French letter, on the spot, there's nothing better.

– Fishy fanny, fanny fish, won't you make a funny dish.

So it was that another mysterious world creaked open its door for him.

~

That July they were all treated to Gaynor Shearer's obvious nipples, seen like broomhandles through her bathing suit as the chill wind off the Atlantic puckered her skin and the skin of all the other Bathing Beauties lined up on the promenade. They were in the midst of a four-day carnival in anticipation of armistice. Decorated horses and carriages had made their way through the streets in the parade, streaming with banners and leaving snowy trails of paper confetti in their wake. The beauties were officially daring to bare more than had ever been bared before. Had any of the Tory councillors been present at the pedestal that afternoon there may have been a swift dismantling of the exhibition, coats flung over scantily clad bodies – which would not have been entirely unwelcomed by the girls for the air was not a little nippy – and a general sense of spoiled fun. As it was the Bathing Beauties were not interrupted and they posed bravely on the platform, hips at hourglass angles, and with lunatic grins on their powdered faces which were in actuality jaw-locked grimaces of discomfort at being exposed to the elements in such a savage fashion. Cy and every other come-of-age lad in town of such proclivity marvelled at the show, which was nice and naughty at once, and stirred a new ingredient up in them, like batter which would thereafter coat every desirable woman in their lives. He came home immediately after the show and disappeared into his room, eyes a little fazed, gait a little obstructed, so that Reeda assumed her son to be sick with excessive eating. The affair was destined to become one of Morecambe Council's annual pet peeves and one of England's best-loved, male-melded, seaside-resort traditions. And though Gaynor's were not the only nipples on display that day, they certainly were the most pronounced and most persistent and she was crowned queen of the first ever Morecambe Bathing Beauties competition.

On the third day of the carnival there was an ox roast on the prom. A beast from a nearby farm had been slaughtered and roasted on a massive medieval spit. It was set up on a pole resting between two trestles. The strong meaty fragrance drifted across the piers and through the streets, rumbling stomachs and suggesting to the whole of Morecambe that just around every corner was a gorgeous oven-warmed dinner. It was high season and the crowds thronged about the town, queuing for almost a mile to buy their ox sandwiches. Reeda Parks and her son had been helping the butcher carve and distribute the fare all day with the help of two other ladies. It was up to Cy to wrestle as best he could with the monstrous bottle of HP sauce, getting as little as possible on each sandwich – though it was a tad like riding a bicycle downhill without a handle-bar for steering or brakes for stopping – before one of the women whipped the bread together and handed it out to the next in line. Lomax, the butcher, a striped-aproned giant who seemed completely suitable for the task of slicing up such a carcass, was carving furiously and great portions of shredded brown flesh fell into the catch tray below, where Reeda and the others would retrieve it in accordance with the customers' preferred tastes, lean or gristle or crackling. The butcher's patter never tired, and never altered.

– Lancashire or Yorkshire, sir? Meat or fat? Lancashire or Yorkshire, madam? Meat or fat? Lancashire or Yorkshire sir? Meat or fat?

By the end of the afternoon if Cy never saw an ox sandwich again before departing the earth for more clement climes, or gruelling, furnace-like ones – he still had not ruled out that possibility – it would be entirely too soon.

≈

The boys were cutting down an effigy of Kaiser Bill from the flagpole hook in Pedder Street ready to burn him that evening before the dance when Cy first got a whiff of what was to become, later on, his profession of choice. Though at the time, had this been revealed to him in Alva's crystal ball or via some other tarot table, it would have seemed pure madness, he would have scoffed and laughed and asked for his carny-thieved jiggery-pokeried pennies back. But that was all to come.

Pedder Street was narrow and winding, one of the older parts of town, with moss on its walls, three churches nestled into its corners and a length of small, sunken-windowed, three-storeyed dwellings with sooty chimneys. It also contained some houses and businesses of ill-reputation, the Professor and Madame Johnson for example, spiritualists with the capability to reunite you with the souls of deceased loved ones and occasionally the departed infamous – communing, it seemed, was a bit like an open telephone line, you never quite knew who you might find on the other end – something Cy's mother was vehemently against, and there were also houses where it was understood that many women lived at once and many gentlemen visited. From this end of town Cy could just about hear the clank and boom of rust-dead trawlers and German U-boats and submarines being dismantled at Ward's Ship-Breakers and the strains of mendicant music being played by the blind fiddler at the old harbour. There was no political choice for stringing up the Kaiser in this particular street other than a convenient metal crooking from which to play out his demise and ridicule by hanging. Being still the tallest of the three, and therefore having the extra reach, Cy had climbed up the nearest building with a pair of garden shears to hack the villain loose. It was a question of balance and stretch, out-manoeuvring gravity, wielding the shears while slumped up the crumbling bricks, bandy-legged like a frog. Inelegantly, he held his arms out and with a quick snip removed the Kaiser's bulging nose.

– Take that you daft little Prussian.

– No time for that now, Cy. It's a shilling per hundred candles lit along the prom if we hurry.

– All right. Hold your horses.

There was a funny noise coming from the window on whose sill his foot was resting. The sash was cracked open a fraction and Cy could hear a buzzing like that generated inside a beehive when the workers are about to swarm. But it was less of a bumbling, husking animal effect and more the uniform drone of man-made apparatus, like a dentist's drill. The sound was captivating. There were voices also, men's voices, one of which was substantially louder and more commanding than the other. He leaned against the wall and tried to listen in to what was being said, while the boys below him waited, shuffling their feet.

– Get on with it, would you, you great string bean?

– We haven't got all night, nosey-Parker.

Such was the strain of his eavesdropping that Cy was having trouble balancing. He adjusted himself clumsily on the sill. It was at about that point in the proceedings when there was a telltale tinkle of glass pane being broken and the buzzing ceased and the cracked window suddenly slid up. A careless boot-toe, he had over-stepped the platform! A woollen-capped head arrived at the level of Cy's foot. Two hands with colourfully stained fingers then came out on to the window ledge, one of them grasped Cy's boot firmly, as if snaring a hare, and the man in the wool cap turned to look up. His eyes were a guttering glacial blue and unrelenting. They were as pale and transparent and fire-cold as a flame leaping out of a mineral-grained log in a grate. Eyes that you wouldn't want to have to out-stare in an argument, thought Cy, that would make you feel like quarry in a dispute even before a word or curse was spoken, and he returned their gaze, spellbound. The vessels were large and round, containing bad emotion and amusement at once, indications of a personality that would travel the length and breadth of its own deficiencies as well as its redeeming traits, though the former seemed much more likely. And as the eyes observed him upwardly, there was something else to them too: not exactly shock, for here was a man probably not put into such conditions easily, Cy read of him, but soft-surprised cognition. Cy felt a strange perception also. As if some mutual knowledge of the other was casting itself about them. As if both their graves were simultaneously being trodden over. Cy remained perfectly still, partly in sympathetic curiosity, and partly because there did not seem to be another course of action which would not involve an untidy jump from a fair height with the open shearing blades, perhaps leaving one incarcerated leg behind on the sill, and uncomfortably stretching recently evolved and endeared parts of himself he wasn't willing to stretch before he could wrestle free. Then there might be running and quite possibly a sound leathering from the pursuer if he was caught. After a few quiet, canny moments the eyes waned, the stained hand let go of his ankle, tapped his boot three times, and disappeared. The head retreated and the window sash banged shut, dislodging the remainder of the fractured glass pane. Jonty loud-whispered up to Cy, his hands cupped about his mouth.

– Get down. Get Kaiser Bill down. Hurry up, we can't stop here. He's a left-footer and a gype.

– Who's a left-footer?

– Shhhhh! Mr Riley.

Above Cy another window suddenly opened and the figure of a man leaned out. He had a knife. Cy peered up as best he could without becoming dizzy and losing his footing. It was the same man as before, though he now seemed annoyed. There were keen gestures from his arms and irritation stacked along the veins in his neck. Moving swiftly he sawed through the roping of the Kaiser's gallows and the doll slumped to the ground. The potty Hohenzollern helmet rattled and spun on the street and rag intestines burst out through the grey uniform. Without a word the window shut, slicing down with a final shucking sound like that of a guillotine. The boys hastily departed Pedder Street.

Afterwards, walking back along the pier and towing the Kaiser behind them in a barrow, Jonty told Cy and Morris that his dad said Mr Riley was an undesirable papist with a disgraceful occupation, who bought dead pigs' heads from the butchers and took them home for ungodly purposes. Morris was not impressed at all.

– So, my mam eats fish cheeks, she says that's the best part of the fish to eat. And sometimes the eyeballs, raw, she just picks them out and pops them in her mouth like aniseed balls!

– No, not to eat, you great pillock, to practise on, on the hide, with his needle. His mucky needle. He's a scraper.

– What does he scrape?

– Don't know exactly, father won't tell me, but I know it isn't nice.

Apparently there was more pointy ministry in the town than just Cy's mother's. When he got home Cy told his mam about the Kaiser, about Mr Riley and the pigs, hoping she might be able to clarify the situation.

– Well. I doubt very much whether Lomax would let go of his pigs' heads to anyone, love, Catholic or not. Otherwise he'd not have any sausages to sell on Thursdays.

– Do we know Mr Riley?

– I know of him, love.

– What's a scraper?

– It's a man that does tattooing. Your dad had a tattoo on his shoulder. Lots of men of the sea do. Sort of like a club badge, though it's quite a personal thing.

– Why was he not mad about the window pane? Why did he help us cut Kaiser Bill down? Is he a radical?

– Oh, goodness knows. Perhaps Mr Riley is a Bolshevik, son. I believe there are a few around.

Cy did not mention his feeling of déjà vu, that grave-robbing look between them of retrieving a body they both had some loon-moon claim to. It was as if the man had recognized him. It was as if he had been expecting him. That's how the eyes had seemed.

There were times when initial introductions were so vested with something other as to confuse and distract and entrance both parties, Cy would realize later. And only further into relationships when you knew the person better, and their place in your life became clear, if there was love, if there was hate, if there was deepness of any kind, only then did you understand that the embers of meaning had been present all along and glowing since that first moment you laid eyes on them. As if you already knew them before you came to know them. As if some rift had bent time.

~

Eva Brennan, on the other hand, gave him no such early forecast that she would trample on his heart. Life had been ticking along just fine until she stepped a dainty foot through the Bayview's door with her mother and father two years later, lent like the weather, like the bright borrowed days in the northern counties that early guest season of 1920. She was the loveliest thing Cy had ever seen, beside Aurora Borealis and Gaynor's nipples. She was fourteen. She was blonde. And had freckles on the backs of her arms. She didn't have tuberculosis. Her mother had made her a flower bonnet to wear in the Easter parade, with blue cornflowers in it that made her eyes seem darker and sadder. In the citrus light of the spring bay parade the hair on her temples had an aura of something fairy-spun. For three days Cy tried to tell her that he liked her by giving her an extra large helping of cabbage at dinner, and hanging her coat up on the stand whenever she came in. She always smiled at him. As if curious and waiting.

When he lay in bed at night and thought of her two rooms away his legs and chest ached, as if he'd spent the day on the school's pitches at the bottom of a scrum, and his now basally controllable cock rose, bowed, and rose again. There was only one thing for it – he would have to enlist the help of the boys in order to woo her. Jonty had had more experience with girls, being not averse to handing out his mother's beauty potions in the school yard and having kissed two at least for payment to the best of Cy's knowledge, which was two more than he ever had. He invited his friends over to formulate a plan of action. Morris said he would rather go fishing than watch anyone fumbling with a girl, and that Cy could hook her *Pisces vaginales* if he wanted, but he himself fancied a nice flounder for his supper. Morris hadn't quite got the hang of girls. Jonty was only too happy to assist.

– Does she have big bosomers?
– Biggish.
– Bigger than a bee sting?
– Yes.
– Marvellous.

On the last day of the Brennans' seaside vacation Cy and Eva and Jonty went for a walk along the beach. Jonty was always good for getting people talking. He could talk the hind legs off a donkey. It was low tide and Cy was determined to find a shell or two to add to Eva's collection. He walked down to the waterline keeping his eyes peeled for a worthy specimen – something she could put on her vanity dresser when she went back home to Yorkshire, and she'd remember him and write him letters glancing up at it, pink and glazed inside with the light coming through it like thin bone china, sitting next to a hairbrush spun with her blonde hair. And she'd sign her name with an X at the bottom of the page signifying their first kiss on the shore at Morecambe, shortly to be undertaken. So peeled were his eyes between bubbled seaweed and smooth shingle, that he drifted off away from the other two as they chatted. So peeled were they that he missed their abbreviated courtship, the giggle of innuendo, the not-so-accidental brush of hands together as they strolled, the sharing of an ice-cone – trailing tongues along the paths made in the vanilla cream by each other. When he looked up, finally defeated in his search for a suitable love-token, he could see them standing very close together. And Eva put her arms up round Jonty's neck, and gave him the kiss that was supposed to be Cy's. Every bone in Cy's body let go of its neighbour and clattered down inside him to the sick soles of his shoes. It was as if somebody had taken a wrecking ball not only to his skeleton but to his porcelain-baked, sea-delicate, pink-lit aspirations as well. When they were done kissing Eva turned to Cy and waved, then tickled Jonty in his ribs, and she went alone back up the beach steps to the prom and then back to the Bayview Hotel, where she packed her suitcase full of bonnets and shells and that afternoon left on the train to Yorkshire with her parents. Cy would probably have been too tall to kiss her anyway, Jonty informed him as they sat on the bathing pool wall later that day, even if he had got round to it, and his you-know-what would have likely bayoneted her in the stomach.

~

There were to be other kisses for Cyril Parks, with girls of varying statures. He drank extra milk for mending his weakened spirit and bones and put himself back together. He forgave Jonty, who hadn't known the whole truth of the matter, he insisted, and bit by bit Cy acquainted himself with the messy, mistimed, warm and wet-patched world of court-ing. But Eva Brennan had done her part and remodelled his anatomy, if for no other reason than she was the first to break him. His bones felt still a little weak, as if once having been dislocated from each other they would never again bear quite such romantic weight. And he stopped riding the toboggans and the wooden coasters in the fun parks of Morecambe, not being able to take pleasure in the sensation of being boneless any more, the feeling of having something falling out of him, like hope falling down brittle as calcium dust to the empty shore.

~

Boggarts and eels and bore-running behind them, the boys found part-time employment around the town so as to be able to help out at home, purchase tickets to the pictures and chips from the kiosks. Cy got a job after school and on Saturday afternoons at the print shop on Strickland Street. The printers was owned by Reginald Greene, who droned on about the war and how he'd never sleep another full night for the perpetual ringing in his ears of explosions, and how his wife was as cold as a fish when she moved past him after his return and that he might as well have perished in the bloody trenches for all she cared. Greene paid him enough to keep him amused at weekends and some went to his mother, which gave her a proud look every time an envelope was handed to her and she would mark it up in its own separate column on the page of her weekly accounting log. Then she would produce Stanley Parks's old curved pipe from the kitchen drawer, pack it with tobacco and have a smoke. Cy was never sure his mother truly enjoyed smoking for she sneezed frequently as she partook and her eyes watered. The act seemed more compulsive and obligatory than a pleasurable habit, but he knew better than to question it. Reeda had her ways.

The work at the printers was decent, straightforward and repetitive, giving him a chance to develop his artistic proclivity and perfect his lettering. There was something satisfying about surrounding bright paints with fat black borders. There was something pleasing about blocking and keeping colour. It was a nice job. And for a time he felt well suited and well spent in life. Aside from the wrinkling up of girls' skirts and shortly thereafter the wrinkling up of their foreheads in protest, the tedium of Greene's curmudgeonly company with its nocturnally repressed urges, and the occasional cauliflower ear or black eye received while flanking on the school rugby pitches, if there were years in his life which he would call smooth and peaceful and easy it would be these. Even so, at the back of that thought, at the bottom of his memory, in the rafters of his mind, he knew some alternate state of being must soon exist, a converse influence, that which weighed down the rusty pan on the darker side of the scales to balance its shiny partner. The things of the universe being equal as they always were.

~

Eliot Riley swore he was the first man to try graduated black shading and make it work, though Cy would hear that claim repeated in the booths of Coney Island a decade later. Riley could create an illusion on a flat surface of skin. The things he could do with black ink and shading on flesh were quasi-magical. He was an engraver, like William Blake. He was a sculptor, he was a Bernini, had Cy heard of Bernini?

– No.

– Well what in God's great name is being taught in the school these days if not the finer aspects of art, sonny?

– We did draw fish on the beach when the war was on.

– Fish on the fucking beach?

Riley had him cornered by the bait and tackle shop, next to the printers in Strickland Street, in the late afternoon drizzle. Cy knew it was him, the face and eyes were unforgettable. He had a visage that was photographic, not attractive in its looks but memorable, bringing back images of it during previous meetings with a flash of the brain's bulb and the fizzle of recollection like burnt celluloid. It was a face that was architectural, having a structure that was soundly constructed and defined and heavily employed, as a bridge that carries too much traffic. His skin about the scaffolding of bones was smooth and opaque and olive, as some of the Welsh or southern Celts will have accompanying dark hair. He was unshaven, as blue-eyed

69

as a Siamese cat, and apparently not one for conventional conversation. He slapped Cy's hand away as Cy tried to turn up the collar of his coat against the fine rain to prevent it from blowing into his ear, and continued outlining what was some oddly mannered work proposal. This apprenticeship was a fucking honour, Riley stated, if he wanted it, if he was visionary enough to see it. He said his own technique and style were dimensional in a way others would kill for in the industry. Likely kill for mind, such was the game he played. And if Cy spoke of these skills out of turn to anyone, after being taught, if he got loose lipped in the pub at weekends, he'd pay for it with a hiding such as he doubted the boy had had since his father passed, rest him. Cy did not mention that he'd never met his father, that the man had been dead long before Cy's backside had been ripe for any kind of hiding. If any of Riley's designs made their way down to any of the other tattoo shops in town, particularly Larrikin Harry's, that cheap tuppenny scraper on Lowther Street, Cy would be held directly responsible for it. And get a hiding. Genius, and make no mistake, Riley was a genius, was to be protected fiercely as a knight protects a king, did he understand that concept? With a bit of luck Cyril Parks might learn a thing or two about honour along with tattooing. If he wanted the apprenticeship.

– I've got a job, Mr Riley.

One eyelid flickered down and up on the whiskered face of the man like an insect stalling in the air. Making him look threatening, delinquent even. Riley let his jaw go slack, the too-big tongue swelling out in the rain. Perturbed, Cy looked away, into the window of the novelty sweet shop opposite, to escape the madman's stare. There was a sign in the window that Cy had made which read 'World's first lettered rock'. Underneath was a stack of white sugar tubes with 'Morecambe' written through them in red. Then a booming, spitting laughter erupted from the man, splattering the left side of Cy's face, interrupting his distraction and drawing his attention back to Riley.

– Right, you do lad, you do, but it's about as useful as a mickey in a nunnery.

The laughter was an erratic feature, which Cy would become used to from his future employer over the years, though he would not become any more astute in predicting it. He looked back at the man, found that he was now grinning with his large top teeth resting on his full lower lip. Eliot Riley was dressed like a buffoon, with an old long-tailed suit and a white smock shirt underneath it, a woollen hat – the one Cy had seen appearing from his window during the Peace celebrations – and woollen gloves. It was as if he'd visited every charitable church sale and flea market in Morecambe and been donated each item separately.

– Look, lad, it's too bloody cold to be standing about out-side in the pissy weather getting gout. What say I take you for a jar and we discuss this thing further along in comfort. It's a Dog and Partridge day, I think.

Riley put a hand on Cy's shoulder and propelled him down Strickland Street where the wind, coming in off the great bay strengthened and propelled him back. The lights along the promenade did little to brighten the street. The tail end of autumn was lashing and extinguishing all pauper attempts at illumination. They rounded the corner onto Marine Avenue and were roared at by the arguing marriage of sea and sky. Riley wrestled the door of the pub open and shoved Cy inside. Cy had never been into the Dog and Partridge before, he had not in fact made it into any of the town's drinking establishments. It was more maritime sea-dog's haunt than gamekeeper's sporting inn within, and it was just after four o'clock in the afternoon on Saturday. There were only a few brave customers, most were safe in their homes if they were sensible, the rest straggling back from the cancelled races. A man was wiping the bar down with a cloth, he nodded his head to Riley when they entered, in cursory greeting. The windows were rattling in the November gale. The floor was swept by stealthy, nautical gusts of air that sloped in under

71

the gap of the door and through the loose panelling round the window-frames. The whole bar seemed buffeted. It was like being inside the creaking wooden bowels of a ship, while its gaff and staysails were broadsided by a forceful swell. On the walls of the room were old photographs of local fishermen and paintings of schooners. Cy wondered if his father was among them. The bar room smelled of smoke and hops and chowder. Not wanting to seem unaccustomed to such sur-roundings, Cy removed his cap and hung it on a peg on the wall by the door. Riley kept his woollen hat firmly on his head and they sat at two tall wooden stools alongside the bar.

Riley insisted on a drink before work, every day, as Cy found out during this first hour of the man's company.

– To relax the hand and oil up the humour. Men like humour from a tattoo artist, to put them at ease. Lesson num-ber one, cut up the tension before the skin, sonny, that's a free lesson 'cause you've not give me an answer to my offer yet. Two pints please, Paddy, best make it ale for junior.

The barkeep served them and continued wiping. Riley paid for his own drink and jerked his head to the side towards the barman for Cy to take care of his own payment. As luck would have it, Greene had given him his wages that afternoon, so he was not short of money. He reached into his pocket and set several coins on the bar, not knowing how much the cost of a drink was. The barman took his due and left the rest, a tug of a smile pulling at the corner of his bearded mouth.

– First pint a man imbibes he should have paid for off his own back with wage from honest work. Eh? Isn't that right, Paddy? Paddy Broadbent, Cyril Parks. Oh, and listen lad, call me Riley. Eliot was my mother's worst idea. Cheers.

– Cyril was my mother's worst idea.

Cy attempted some humour of his own, being somewhat nervous about the man's company and about venturing in to his first ever pint of ale.

– Don't bad-mouth your mam, boy. She'll not take kindly to hearing about it.

Cy's damp, fledgling banter dried up. Riley made him uneasy and charmed him at once, and it was a hangman's charm of the kind that keeps the crowd nervously enthralled. Cy might have left earlier than he did but for the man's compelling combination, that and the sense he had stepped across a threshold with this individual, which joined them in a rebels' pact of some variety. Four drinks into the afternoon Riley's lessons were expanding, philosophically, and Cy was feeling a very dull and blurrish head on him, trying to keep up with his employer's pace. The trade was changing, Riley insisted, wasn't what it should be. Some bad characters were getting in on it. He didn't elaborate on what exactly constituted a bad character, and Cy was left wondering what murkier levels lay beneath Riley himself who elicited notoriety for his faith and his founding, and who had a reputation of practising his craft on the severed heads of farmyard animals. It was those without a calling that Riley scorned, those for whom the profession was about self-inflation, braggery, and big-man's sport, those who relished the coarse top coat of it all. They were scrapers, scratchers and scoundrels, he was an artist through which anomalous human messages were conveyed.

As stout gave way to spirit, Riley proceeded on to personal matters. There was no way Cy should consider him a father figure, that was absolutely clear. Not unless his mother could be brought into the equation.

– Fine legged woman, your mother, I saw her at the fishmonger's last Thursday buying cod for her guests at the hotel. A good ankle on her. Oh, yes. A fine woman.

Spitting laughter from the man. He went on with the conversation again, while the room sailed out to sea a little further for Cy and he swayed on his stool. No. Riley did not need the obligation of a son, not even a part grown-up and useful one. This was business, open and shut. He had seen Cy's work at the printers, his hand was fair. Fair was flattery in his book, he'd say no more than that. Riley thought it unfortunate and somewhat foolish not to bestow upon the world his extraordinary gift when he passed away, at this juncture the man left off for a moment, crossed himself profoundly and then in reverse, kissed the back of his wrist and took a lengthy swill of drink. He'd been considering an apprentice for a time now. Found one, potentially. That was that. Death did not scare him, by the way, no. All death would do was secure his place in history as the considerable artist that he was, the way Van Gogh's life was celebrated after he'd lived it out in poverty. Had Cy heard of Van Gogh? And as far as he was aware he was not up for that prize soon, he did not have a dicky ticker, nor a tricky dicky, spitting laughter, so there was little rush in the matter of bequeathed craftsmanship and genius endowed. Cy should find himself some patience, maybe by the summer he'd be ready to help out with the barrage of holiday-makers wanting tattoos, oh yes, barrage, for his was not a slender occupation. And Riley was ready to teach. Because there came a point in every man's life . . .

~

The offer was not illustrious. Not overly tempting or pitched all that well. At this point, Eliot Riley hadn't entirely sold Cy on the profession. He still had not made it clear exactly why Cyril Parks was his chosen target and Cy was not informed that Riley had visited the print shop on Strickland Street a couple of times when he was absent with no apparent motive or request for work. What had caught Riley's eye initially were the bold designs on the wooden signs that hung in the windows to advertise Greene's service, painted by the boy. The renditions of high- and low-skirted women holding cigarettes, joker faces, bubble lettering and scrolling borders. He had loitered about the shop front, several times, flicking through scripts and letting out the occasional grunt. The work was very good. It described an illustrator who had both imagination and dexterity of hand. He'd seen the boy working through the window, a long loose shank of a fellow, scruffy and soulful, but careful with his ink in his rolled-back shirtsleeve. And he remembered him, remembered him climbing up the shop building, remembered the look on his face, grey-eyed and ash-bark-whittled, like his mother's. It was a risk for Riley, that surveillance – Greene had seen him in Hagan's Manufacturing in Lancaster on occasion when both were purchasing supplies of ink, knew him for what he truly was, not the sign painter he professed to be because there was only one in Morecambe Bay, though Greene had thankfully not made mention, suppliers could get shy in their support of the tattooing industry, or downright vicious. Discretion aside, Reginald Greene would not want him in the print shop. That would suggest appreciation, friendship, or secondary distribution of ink – ink, the only thing Eliot Riley and Reginald Greene had in common other than a masculine set of tackle! Their difference as great as collaborating with the living compared to working with the dead. So Riley had waited for the busier moments and was quick about his perusal of Cyril Parks's work.

Eliot Riley knew he was not popular with many of the businesses in Morecambe, which frowned on the seedier aspects of the town in which they were located, nor the Council, nor the sanitation department, for similar reasons. But that did not alter the fact that in summer the crowds flocked to his shop, the way they flocked to the pie rooms and the ghost-train rides and the ballrooms, wanting to take home an altogether more permanent holiday souvenir. Something they could call their own and never have it taken off them. He was just as much a part of the town's leisure and entertainment features as the other businesses, and sometimes made better money.

Then the last Saturday of November 1921, a handful of years after meeting the lad, he decided to make his move. He wasn't sure why he chose that moment over any other. Maybe just because the boy was getting taller and older. Maybe just because he was passing him in the street. As Cy was locking up and leaving work, Riley collared him and said there was a better job for him if he wanted it, better than blocking in signs and calligraphy and being forced to produce insipid, uninspired art. And he took him to the pub where the boy spent near on all his wages on ale and listened to him talk.

Outside the Dog and Partridge two hours later the wind had calmed, having lost the spouse's quarrel with the sea, and it was replaced by a gentle roar inside Cy's ears from the merry passage of drink around his body. Riley took hold of him and suddenly became serious. The drawbridge lifted in his face, he clouded over, and he seemed to Cyril, through a pair of eyes that were for once in his life not truly well behaving, incredibly angry. The man appeared thunderous with concentration and premeditation, as if some kind of vendetta were in operation. It was the look of a bully about to strike. The look of a man closed up sentimentally from those he faces and about to pull a trigger. Perhaps it was the broken window, thought Cy, perhaps that was what this meeting had really been all about, though it seemed a little unfair to be holding a grudge this long and Riley had made no mention. He'd seen a pocket full of coin and not claimed compensation.

– You have until eleven o'clock tonight to give me an answer. I've someone coming in at ten if you want to see what it's about. Won't take me more than an hour. Eleven Pedder Street, door with the split lock and the Jewish looking lights in the window. You know it? Yes, you know it.

Cy nodded. Something about the length of time Riley said his work would take gave the scenario an official feel, gave it credibility and made Cy nervous in his stomach, as if a doctor's appointment had been scheduled, as if he were about to enter the rooking parlour room in which his mother worked with Mrs Preston.

– Ask for me if someone else answers. Don't take guff off any of them. This is important, boy.

And Riley placed his hand around the back of Cy's neck and seemed to tighten his grip on the hairline.

– This is important, boy.

He said it again, quietly. There was the manure smell of stout on his breath, and pickled herring. For a brief second Cy thought the man might be about to kiss him on the forehead with his large lips. He held very still. Those eyes looking at him! Desperate and dying blue, like the top of the sky when the sun is sinking. Then Riley released him, stood back, untucked and pulled up his painter's shirt and exposed five inches of gut sporting some of the strangest compositions of ink that Cy had ever seen. He was bright like the skin of a tropical creature, like he was half-lizard. And then the man was gone, arched-legged up the wet, leaf-blown street.

～

Cy almost didn't go. There were taut fibres within him that told him to stay at home, stay put at the Bayview after supper, go to his bedroom and read or sit with his mother at the kitchen table, which always made her happy. He should find the boys and throw stones into the sea. Anything other. He could not eat much of his dinner, being fairly well filled with ale from the afternoon, and as he forked the kale around his plate he remembered the blue-fascination of eyes, and the profound words, hearing them as well as if a light chanting curse had been laid upon him. This is important, boy. He had an inkling that within this choice there was one path, flat as the promenade, which doubled back and led somewhere he had already been, and another path that led somewhere high and low and haunted, like the trail alongside Moffat Ravine, where land fell sharply away and black space opened like a channel to the underworld. Or like one of the wending tracks on the Yorkshire moors by his Aunt Doris, which led away to nothing, and only sick animals or werewolves or madmen would choose to take them. And he'd a sense that if he saw Riley twice in that same day it would mean consent, it would make it certain, because Riley was a strong whirlpool of himself taking others in, because he was conviction. And while

77

his manner was tawdry, the ink stains on his fingers were so very oddly compelling. When Cy thought of Riley it felt fated, like water was already tunnelling past him. Some rip current had already taken him, and he was going without fighting. He was going. Not to say yes, for he didn't think he would, not to say no, because he was not sure refusal was yet ready in him. Just going.

It was a ten-minute walk to Pedder Street, give or take, having climbed from the washroom window out into a liver-brown night whose character made his belly turn. The town was mostly empty for the weather and the season. The waves on the shore were moderate, though fortified by darkness and imagination they echoed louder than their size. But the bricks and the gutters and the slates and the car wheels seemed precise and clear and absolute to Cy during the late walk, and owing nothing, as if electricity had lately passed through his body. His hands were deep in his pockets, and his tall body was hoisted backwards and forwards like a spinnaker by the breathing sea. His shoes loud against the pavement. Yes. He was going. Not in keeping with nor against his own will, just going. Past the creaking wooden fairground rides in the park – the spindle-some tumbling teacups and the Ring-o-Rounder – which were laid up for winter, and the empty toffee-apple stalls, past the Alhambra picture house and dancehall closed for the night and past Professor and Madame Johnson's where they held communion with dead husbands and wives, ancestors, impending progeny and walk-ins, the lost souls of unreconciled lives. Until there were the droll Hebrew candles in the window, there was the door with the split lock, and there was his heart hammering a knock on it to open.

～

How long had it taken? How long for him to be convinced he would learn that intimate and colourful language? That folk-ish tongue, spoken in symbols and essence and tokens. It took no longer than twenty minutes. Twenty minutes to decide a life's journey. Twenty, for a rapid, press-gangless signature, acceptance of an invisible king's shilling with its obverse decreeing he would join the ranks of the town's eccentric subculture, and stand to attention and salute Eliot Riley. Such a small portion of life, and yet so filled with energy, force, momentum. Cy had told nobody of his plans to visit Riley, not quite knowing how to express the man's appeal, nor describe his own curiosity, his sense of being summoned. He spoke of it to no one, though he passed by Jonty's house as he walked the streets and he could have pebbled his window and held a conference about his intention, and he had crept past his mother's room while her lamp was still shining and he knew her ear was always willing and her heart always open. But he went alone.

Cy arrived at the building on Pedder Street and knocked on the door, which was opened by a small, hatless, catgut-looking man who said nothing, and he came into a cold parlour. There was one other man sitting on a chair there – two more chairs were empty – his cap pulled over his face and he was leaning back, with folded arms, as if sleeping or laid out to rest dead in an upright coffin. But the walls, the walls were more than living, they were full and lost under black-bordered colour. It was the inside of a kaleidoscope. It was Aladdin's cave, a store of pirates' bounty. Pictures and motifs of dragons and angels and Christ and bones and flowers and hearts and weaponry hung from the walls. A curtain separated this room from another, or another section of it, and behind its tatty covering there was that noise, that noise again, like mechanical workers in a beehive, a determined machinist's hum. The faint smell of antiseptic or spirits was in the air, some-thing medicinal, like the waft from the bottle of witch hazel his mother had dabbed his cuts and scrapes with as a boy, and along side that Cy detected another fragrance, pleasant, female, ill-fitting, which he could not quite determine.

– Mr Riley? Sir?

79

The wasp-motor noise stopped and the curtain was drawn back sharply on its metal rings. There stood his potential employer, wearing his careless, navvie-wedding garb, wired needle in hand, looking like the sanest man in the asylum. Something had changed about him. His eyes had shifted focus. He looked quite calm. More at ease than Cy had ever seen him look before, at least of the two occasions that he'd met him, perhaps because now Cy was in his lair, on his common turf, and the host knew balls to brawn that here he was king of his own country. His broody, intense presence seemed now to be more self-assured swagger than the displaced arrogance of the bar and street.

– Late. Inside, lad, sharpish. I'd about give up on you, you little bugger.

Cy glanced at the two young men in the waiting area, who were watching him, the sleeper now awake and out from under his hat, unsmiling, bored or prejudicial or curious. There was a sense of vague challenge about them, so Cy knew right there and then what kind of environment this profession was surrounded by or founded on, what kind of landscape would be denied or chosen that night. He moved past them into the back room and the curtain was drawn screechingly closed again. Inside it was much warmer. This half of the room contained a coal fire, which was gently smoking. Damp rags had been hung about it and the enclosure felt soft-boiled like a warm vegetable. Humid, like Cy imagined the tropics to be. A man was sitting reversed on a chair, with his legs on either side of it, and he was gripping two wooden handles fixed to the wall. A cigarette holding a long, strained orange tip came from between his lips. He was naked from the waist up and sweating profusely. Above his belt was a patch of highly irritated red skin and inside that was half a hooded cobra snake, red, green, black, and yellow, its tail beginning along the slight depression between muscle and spinal column, the finished body coiled round a dagger that ran the first length of his backbone. Cy could tell that the hooded neck and head would be drawn to the right of the dagger's handle, there was a pale grey stencil mark there to indicate a border, at the point where the opposite depression became a flank. On the table next to Eliot Riley and his now-quiet tattoo equipment were four vials of ink. Riley gave him a look that told him he was expected to behave himself, though what behaviour was warranted Cy did not exactly know, probably humility, because he was now inside the monarch's personal chamber. The man straddling the chair looked at him also, a hooded look of pure, unadulterated, knew-his-own-venom superiority.

Eliot Riley began talking then, a speedy flow of vocabulary, which wove jokes into stories into opinions into questions.

– . . . I'll tell you this for nowt, when the lucky bastard woke up and her sister was there as well, what do you think he said? 'Susan I've always said your family was a good lot,' he said, 'but I can't for the life of me remember where I put that fucking ring just now. Perhaps the pair of you can remind me.' And then her and her sister top and tailed the fella . . .

It was performance talk. Talky-talk. Some of the best Cy had ever heard. Like the vendors on the promenade selling wares to the hustled masses, but better, detailed, tailored, or as if a many-tongued demon had possessed the teller. And Riley was sweating as he talked, almost as much as the man in the chair was sweating. A bottle of open whisky on the floor between their feet. Somewhere in the midst of all the dialogue the electric hurring noise switched back on and the needle was inked, lowered down on to the snake's decapitated body and it began to do its work. Riley dipped his needle, scratched the back, and wiped the surface. Over and over. All the while looming the conversation, pausing to let his customer reply if he was going to, using those words to complement his own swarthy, rough-thread tapestry. Dip, etch, wipe. Talky-talk.

– No more whisky now or you'll bleed too much.

Dip, etch, wipe. Talky-talk.

– . . . in the alley and he had her legs round his waist and he was giving her one when she said she had to go. You know, go. So he said he dropped her and she went right there in front of him, said she didn't care . . .

It seemed that Riley had almost forgotten Cy's presence. Until, about five minutes into the work and mid-snake-muscle, he glanced back and gestured with his head – an impatient jerk to the side for Cy to approach. Then what Eliot Riley did was bring Cyril Parks in very close to the lower back being tattooed on the chair while the customer gritted his teeth and continued sweating. Cy saw fine lines being set in under a slight wash of blood. There was close black hatching, diagonal upon diagonal, done in a way to cheat the eye into a shadow, into artificial dimension. More water than blood was the leakage really, a strange combined fluid that reminded him of something else, the Bayview's discharge basins with their wet-farmed contents. The customer's knuckles protruded yellowy from under his hands' skin as he gripped the wooden railing, which creaked a fraction under the strong fingers. Riley paused for whisky. After ten more minutes the customer stood wearing art. The snake and dagger flexed on his back, weeping a little as he bent for his shirt. The man had added to his body in a way that was brave and timeless and beyond adornment. No argument Riley could have made in the street or the bar would have been more convincing and he had known it, and Cy knew then why Riley had wanted him to come see, why it was important, boy.

– It'll bleed a little colour, give it a day or two of rest. Now, it's not a wound, so don't treat it as such. Don't bathe it for a while, give it a chance to scab up. Don't soap it 'til the scab comes off and don't put pure cotton right against it 'til it's dried out. That's important, it'll wick the ink out, make it duller. And listen to me now. Let that scab come off of its own accord! If you're not happy with the lines come back. You will be, but if not come back, I'll work you right – if the scab's been messed with, mind, I'll know and there'll be no alterations done free.

Riley's words sounded half wise-man's lecture, half witch-doctor's ramble. And part scold, and part commandment. Then he glanced at Cy and asked the man to stay on for a minute, he needed a witness so this ludicrous goggle-eyed boy wouldn't have him arrested for perversity. The customer nodded, took a permissive slug of whisky and rolled the tension out of his jaw with his hand. Then Riley stripped himself out of his clothes and boots, until he was completely naked, and he stood proud and unfocused like a glass-eyed, taxidermy tiger at the edge of the jungle. Except he wasn't naked. He was tightly dressed with ink. The section of gut seen earlier that day had only been the tip of a vast and ornamental iceberg. Riley's good, smooth, Welsh-looking skin appeared not to have many borders remaining on it. He was an assemblage of abstract patterns and cartoon images, reptiles, birds, dragons, like a fishing net cast into the ocean and catching a bizarre school of fantastic objects. Black lines courted and controlled colour, right up to the hilt of his genitals. His elbows, the backs of the knees, every raised plateau of muscle was taken. He turned his arms as if twisting two invisible dials in front of him for Cy to see the complete designs ringing them. The left arm contained some kind of Eden, the right was as full of animals as Noah's ark. He lifted a leg and along the sole of his right foot was a passage of writing, the words too tiny to be read. Cyril Parks was speechless. He had never seen a living thing so camouflaged with art.

After he had dressed his painted, taproot body and dismissed the customer, for he had already taken payment from him prior to starting, Riley claimed every piece on his body, either by design or executed by his own hand, and he made as if to cuff Cy's head when the enquiry was made, more in earnest than jest, how and by what contortion exactly Riley had managed to tattoo the rose garden blooming down his back. And true to the brash assertion of being a three-dimensional master and genius that Riley had made on Strickland Street that afternoon in the rain, one or two pieces had tried to step outwards off his naked body, right off his body into life. Like magic, like an illusion, or a trick of light, or some other unspecified miracle, one or other of which, that night in late November, according to Cyril Parks there seemed to be.

∼

Reeda was not overly pleased to hear about the prospect of her son's new apprenticeship. In fact she simmered hotly while she spoke like a pan of broth left on the hob too long, her words beginning to stick together. He was fifteen years old. There was his schooling to consider. And his after-study work at the print shop. Eliot Riley was definitely a drinker, she knew that to be true of him. Those partial to drink were hiding faults and dishonesty, they were sloppy souls, even the ones with pleasant manners and fine noses. Reeda Parks was an honest if occasionally private woman who did not appreciate those with untidy dispositions. That Reeda had noticed Riley's nose, and that Riley had commented upon his mother's ankles did not pass Cy by without first clipping him like a buggersome fingernail on the back of an earlobe. Her answer sounded dangerously like a no.

– Is it because he's a left-footer? Is it because he's a Bolshevik?

Catholics were generally less tolerated in the predominantly Methodist town than any other denomination. Jonty's dad for one would not entertain them at his table. Nor humour them with conversation at the pub. It was assumed that there was something belligerent about stray papists in Morecambe, and though his mam had never seemed to judge one way or another when it came to matters of religion it did not mean she was without discrimination. Anybody remotely liberal in Morecambe was considered to be a Bolshevik, and about as remote to the affection of the town as Russia itself.

– No, love, it's because it's a difficult trade.

The curious part was that for all the bits and pieces of argument Cy had stored up in preparation, how his dad had had a tattoo as she herself had told him, how he just liked seeing the colours go in, how it gave him opportunity to use his best talent, how Mr Greene at the print shop was a boring old coot who left his hands too long on ladies elbows and made them uncomfortable, it was Reeda herself that changed her own mind during the course of the discussion the following Sunday morning. First she insisted it was not a good idea. Next she began to dwell on the profession of tattooing itself, in relation to her own, the difficulties, she wouldn't wish them on anyone let alone her own, but for herself she could justify them. Cy suspected that his mother was alluding to her secondary profession undertaken with her silent partner Mrs Preston rather than hotel managing. Then she became defensive, and from that empathy, part pride, part fool's pardon, she gradually spun a web that caught her.

– It's not that I don't approve of the trade, for all its oddness. And goodness knows I should comprehend an odd profession. I cannot say I don't. But sometimes what choice have we? Life conspires to plant us in the funniest of gardens where the trees need an especial form of tending. We are all here to serve one another, Cyril, after all, and some serve in stranger ways than others, but one without the other we are made the poorer. There's room for all kinds of folk in this wide world. You're old enough to see that now, that what I do is necessary. Mr Riley, well I'm sure he has his incentives too. It's a most unusual calling, those who go to him are sent for very deep and mysterious reasons as best that I can see. And I suppose you're old enough to make your judgments as you will of him also.

– So, you're saying I'm grand to do it.

– I'm saying someone has probably got to do it.

– Me as well as anyone?

She came around to it like a person slowly developing a taste for bread and dripping because that's all there is left to eat in the kitchen, or like a dog, finally defeated in a frenzied circle by its own tail and slowing and realizing then that the tail it was after all along was already in its possession. Until her decision was reversed.

– Though I'll be wanting a word with Mr Riley first, if you'll pass that on to him. Yes, Cyril, I'll be wanting a word with him. Oh, Pedder Street! I swear on all things true and holy if you put a foot inside Professor Johnson's looking for the spirit of your father I'll honest to goodness wring your scrawny neck. He's where he should be, and not hanging around trying to . . . make contact . . . or whatever it is they say!

Mesmerists were Reeda Parks's least favourite type of people. She was very much in contempt of that kind of penny-stealing, preying on the weaker soul, charlatan's act. Manipulating the bereaved and lonely was not only a shabby way to make a living, it was a moral disgrace, she said. Neither was her son to have anything to do with it. And with that Cy received the only condition to her endorsement of his new profession that his mother would issue.

~

Eliot Riley was a blaggard but he knew when to trim the excessive fat off the edges of his raillery. Face to face with a steel-eyed, dyed-in-the-wool, straight-and-narrow-peddling Reeda Parks was one such occasion. Nor was Riley well suited to unwavering, tedious sincerity. Instead of bluff or sombre, he settled for a compromise of personality, nearer to streaky bacon than a flabby or lean cut of behaviour. He had called at the Bayview at Reeda's behest and was being poured a cup of her strongest tea. Cy sat on a sofa next to his mam as she saw to the cups and saucers, her best rose-patterned china no less, and he distributed the buttery crumpets. She'd insisted he comb his hair and wear his school tie, which, given his new insight into the trade he was entering, seemed not unlike polishing a shovel to carry muck. She herself was rouged. There was a string of pearls about her neck, and a workwoman's headscarf hid her thinning hair, suggesting she always went about the hotel's upkeep bejewelled and made-up like a lady. Riley had on the usual combination of derelict smocking and turn of the century gentleman's suiting, but the tips of his boots looked buffed. The woollen hat was firm about his ears. It was a most peculiar tea-party, as if several mismatched elements of fable had been stuffed into a magician's box, thoroughly shaken, then evicted. There was something slapstick and pantomime and overly choreographed about it all, thought Cy, like one of the more farcical shows in the pavilions.

– Eliot.

– Reeda, my dove. It appears your boy wants to learn the annals of my craft.

Eliot? Reeda? He wasn't aware the two were on such informal terms. The town was small but locals were, in general, candid about their friendships and allegiances, yet here was possibly another of Reeda's covert associations.

– Yes. So it would seem. And what, in your opinion, is to become of his schooling?

– He'll finish it, I'll not hear otherwise, and Reeda, pet, I would suggest you let him do so. I've no room for a simpleton at my shop, getting under my feet and fiddling with machinery, not to mention annoying the customers. He's not exactly sharp as a brass tack now.

– Be serious, Eliot. I won't have him disadvantaged by this.

– I think you'll find him well advantaged if he comes to me. Not only will he learn himself a craft, a craft I say, Reeda, and a good one, he'll learn a thing or two about the wider world.

Cy began to feel rather like a platter of star-gazey pie, scooped into pieces and distributed around the table. His mother straightened her back.

– Yes. That's exactly my concern. You're not to take him drinking. You're not to . . . harden his edges either. And, I need to ask this of you Eliot and I'll ask only once, this is an . . . independent offer, isn't it?

Riley's eyes flickered briefly over Cy, who had lost the thread of the conversation.

– Reeda. You know what sort of man I am. Don't you? Yes, love, you do. I wouldn't be here in your pretty sitting room eating your delicious crumpets if you thought of me what your tone implies. He has the skills necessary. That's all. Call it . . . a happy coincidence. What can I tell you that you don't already know, love? He'll be well looked after. Made as firm as any man must be, and not a hinge or bracket firmer. I'll not say the wage will be anything to look forward to in the beginning mind. But that's the nature of an apprenticeship, isn't it? Which brings me on to my next consideration. He's learning bugger-all at school. I quizzed the boy myself not a week ago and he's sorely lacking in a nobler knowledge. Do you know the lad had never even heard of Leonardo da-bloody-Vinci? Eh? Eh? Hogarth, Rembrandt. Not a noddle. Michel-bloody-angelo! Masters, all of them. Passing their gifts down to the next generation through which honourable system, incidentally? The apprentice system. You can't have a craftsman doesn't ken these things. It's like having a magistrate doesn't know the law, then where would we be? The poor lad's been disadvantaged already Reeda. Sorely disadvantaged.

Here Cy's mother appeared to be stumped, which was a rarity. Riley was winding himself up into a tame fury over the apparently criminal and substandard education at Morecambe Grammar School. His enormous pale eyes were in a cultivated temper, insulted and assaulting, and Reeda reached and tugged the hem down on her skirt. He was leaning towards her with one arm resting on his leg, his teacup tipping at a hazardous angle. She had pitifully little with which to counter his mock academics or his advancing eyes or his rhetoric. Cy wanted to pitch in that he did, in actual fact, know who Leonardo da Vinci was. Just not Bernini, who hadn't got a look in to the conversation that afternoon either. But it did not seem to be a three-way conversation, if it had ever been intended as one.

– Well, I'll have a word with Colin Willacy . . . perhaps something can be done . . . and I'll mention your concern . . .

– No, Reeda, no! You'll not! I plan to teach the lad myself, don't I?

∽

Sanctity of the body, and of the mind which was housed within it, did not exist in Riley's rooms, that is to say it existed only within the scope the man himself deemed suitable and sacred. Nor did respect for lackeys and flunkies exist. Nor was any former knowledge of anything much useful. Tattooing was a dreamscape type of world, where strange occurrences and dark-wrought ideas, if not normal, were almost commonplace. Within number eleven Pedder Street hideous, painful, often screaming regurgitations of human skin went on. A month in and it seemed to Cy that he was an explorer summiting only the foothills of a bizarre and primitive island. There was the grinding of sharp implements into dart-like points, which would be soldered to a drive shaft, the grinding of pigments to mix with alcohol, the grinding of both aspects into frail swathes of skin, and the grinding of the bossy expedition leader on his nerves. Because Cy was made to feel, almost every day, like a blundering idiot with all the handy skills of a caveman wielding a flat rock.

– You ground the needle down too far, it's bloody useless. This coil burnt out too fast, you didn't fit it properly. There's too much powder in my ink solution, mix it carefully, part by part like I showed you, we're not running an artists' retreat here lad. You'll be going to Lancaster for more supplies docked out of your own wages if you keep this malarkey up. Come to think, I could fancy one of Donaldson's oatcakes right about now. So, off you toddle.

Wages? There had been no wages.

– How will I get there?

– Shanks's bloody pony, sonny. You've got legs in working, haven't you? Go on, lad.

89

There was one aspect of the trade that Cy managed to conquer immediately. The odder, danker, gorier ends of physicality had been presented to him and reconciled at a tender age, so the actual tattooing process did not bother him, and if Riley was impressed with one thing it was the boy's ability to stomach the bodily indelicacies of the profession. Not that he ever voiced it. Riley himself was utterly unperturbed and unaffected by blood, gore, and odour. If there was one similarity between Riley and Reeda, one thing they had in common at root, it was their indiscriminate ability to tolerate the organic human body.

Customers were bullied into stripping, often half naked – Riley wanted to see a whole canvas before beginning a work, placement within borders was vital. Ladies were included, though if he was doing a titty-job, or hip work, requiring them to expose breasts or certain vulnerable areas below the waist, he'd instruct them to bring a friend along with them for the appointment, as witness to his proper conduct. All flesh was capable of blood and sweat, female flesh included. Riley found no reverence in it the way Cy still felt a little awe, and a little flex at the front of his trouser, if he was behind the curtain while a woman had her skirts gathered up about her while Riley manipulated a tight plane of skin on her inner thigh and punctured it. Women were an occasional distraction for Riley, each one resulted in another portrait somewhere on his own leg, if there was space, and if they were worthy – worth usually being defined by them terminating the relationship, not vice-versa – and he would produce a drunken little verse to wish them bon voyage when the affair ended. Helena Skeet, barmaid at the Dog and Partridge on nights when Paddy Broadbent was a little worse for wear, was one such muse.

– Over the coun-ter, she might let you mount-her, but then in the morning, there'll be no more whoring, and it's off to the doc-ter for warts on your cock-ker . . .

Riley enjoyed working on a woman's form no more than a man's, it seemed. It provided as difficult a landscape as any to pave with ink. He enjoyed them in his bed only for as long as they did not truly know one another.

His teaching methods and lectures started well but always seemed to descend into petty opinion, as if his top half was gentrified but below the belt-buckle he was all rogue, and couldn't help spoiling his better part.

– Now, while lacking the indulgence of manly hair, though you're not always guaranteed that up north here lad, ha-ah-ha, there are often more internal fatty parts in women, I call them bitty-bags, you can call 'em whatever you want. Like a little purse of water and you've got to take care around them 'cause they can dilute pigment or throw off a line. Especially arses. One thing I will say, they often take it better than a man. Pain, that is. Probably the residue of tolerance left over from when they were all bloody witches and got stoned or burned or drowned for it, eh lad? Never tell your mother I said that, by the way.

People were made up of shit and piss and phlegm and bits and pieces of experience. They were either in possession of the ability to tell a good joke or lacking it; he preferred the former. What Riley excelled at was his profession, his art. And art it was without question, Cy had seen that when he came initially into Riley's tatty little room, twenty to eleven at night, with a mind to consider the strange employment proposal. Or at the very least ask the strange man to leave him alone and stop accosting him after work. There was something about the way Riley's wrist broke no more than a fraction when holding the gun and his hand glided with authority, as if being pulled by a magnet in the elbow, not dictated to by the fingers, exerting more pressure over muscle, less over patches of loose skin, to produce an absolute uniform line, that left Cy unable to reconcile the skill with the man. It was remarkable that someone so flaccid and bawdy could then be so intricate and precise.

Riley's own arms were exquisite. Even the older fading ink remained tight in its rivers. Riley explained that he tended to them with lotion daily, the way others would shine silverware with polish or wax a car incessantly to keep that heirloom conditioned. It explained the strange out-of-place fragrance of the shop. It was lady's Nivea lotion. Floral and sweet smelling and, what's more, expensive. He had that good, smooth, olive skin, complementing his dark hair, at least that which protruded from under his permanently worn woollen hat and prickled his chin was dark. The skin provided a very good background for his luminous modern frescos, none of which showed below his wrist cuff, or above his shirt collar, those were the borders of his craft. But under his hide it was another story, it was a soul half blackened with some kind of loathing and scorn. Eliot Riley was a drinker, Cy's mother had been right. And he was a poor drinker. One that let the demons of the bottle into his head when he tipped it back, demons that went about unloosing all the trouble they could find stashed in the catacombs of his mind. Every tragic thing that had ever happened, every self-doubt, every delusion, freed itself from bondage and revisited him when he drank.

Perhaps he had something of a Welshman or a Celt about him after all, some dual identity, a dispossession, a longing. Inside his rooms was his private, celebrating heart, outside a dislocation from his self-determined red and black and rich green legacy. He was a man split in half, as if he had been born in two, and the pieces appeared not ever to have been joined as a healthy whole, for they vied constantly with each other. At work he wore the expression of a man consumed, whose trade dealt with expression, and minutiae, the exploitation of details and colour perforation. And he loved the bi-tonal beauty he could give people. He was unconditional that way. His eyes sang in concentration when he went to this half of himself, ink was the natural language of his heart, he could not be more in the throne of a motherland when he took his equipment in hand. Then he was bard-like, king-like, god-like, waging accurate and beautiful war over the bodies of those willing to allow his definition and rendition of beauty.

Oh, but it was a strange land to be ruler of, violent, sexual, bold, uncompromising, subversive, curious, and oftentimes tasteless to others – the middle-upper classes, the Tory councillors, the snobbish businesses, who all said it was not art. What he did was not art. Outside the antiseptic, illustrated room on Pedder Street there was the Eliot Riley who was frowned at in the street, challenged in bars, named by the press as disreputable, and of his own inebriated volition was morally redundant. A man of yellow-blue, ale-driven eyes, of vomit on a Saturday night and untimely, sour-spitting laughter that quickly spoiled the mood of those in his company. He was the product of a damaged religion. He was the devil-sick Catholic about town. Cy would be taken to the pub before or after work and treated to the man's poor taste and his public indiscretion. Other men came and went as public house acquaintances with a passing interest in what he did for a living, or wishing to borrow his reputation for their inferior needs, but they were finally sickened by him, and abandoned his presence for good. He was wicked, he was pernicious, and he infected others like a noxious spill.

Riley was the only man Cy knew to find humour in the pieces of flesh found tidily wrapped up in newspaper and smudging the print at the bottom of Moffat Ravine, the only man to laugh out loud when the news reached the town that Dr Ruxton of Lancaster was finally hanged at Strangeways gallows for the ghastly murder and butchery of his wife and nurse, to the blessed relief of the entire nation.

– What's black and white and red all over? A Moffat Ravine newspaper. Get it, get it? Read all over . . . He probably found them together eh? Doing the Queen Victoria shuffle. Daft bugger should of joined in.

There were absurd and treacherous and dark elements to be found in people that Riley could understand and even be amused or thrilled by, where others could not fathom their existence, and had to rely on standard judgments – it was horror and sin and evil and lunacy in the world. And Riley would simply call it truth, truth, as true as any high achievement, love or God or beatific goodness. One without the other was a falseness, he said. Humans were black and white with too much red blood inside, just like that Moffat Ravine newspaper.

He was a vessel through which these messages passed, for better or for worse. What he pulled out of people and drew on them was as varied and degenerate as it was honourable and illuminating. On his walls were warrior signs and heads with swords clean through them, women on their knees bending naked towards men's cocks, next to Christ on his cross, the scales of justice and doves with olive branches. From all the world's distilled meanings, from the chaotic jumble, Riley located human totems and gifted them to their patrons. A man was his soul of a lion, his courage. A man was his profession at sea. A man was the flag of his nation. A woman was her dead child's name. A woman was her ability to use her body for pleasure, or her inability to ever truly expose herself because she had had a black brassiere tattooed on her chest. A woman was as abstract as the abstract spiral on her back.

It did not take an age to come to know these things of Eliot Riley. And so the first time Cy happened across him with his friends, drunk and beaten and raving on the central pier, his slurring madman's words were not completely senseless. Jonty and Morris looked on with horror and confusion as the indigent, broken-looking man raised one arm and called out to Cy.

– Boy, come here. Listen. I'm a fucking midwife, boy, that's what I do, spread their fucking legs open and I catch their little babies and all their shit and blood from pushing and they never even bloody know it . . . hahaha . . . they never know they're birthing themselves, a fucking midwife I am. I am.

– What the bloody hell's he on about, Cyril? Come away and leave him.

– Got to get used to it, boy. Got to get used to the shit and quim. Smell's not so bad after a bit. Oh, we're all soaking wet with it, yes we are . . . hahaha . . . you little buggers too, you fuckers with your mammies' clean hands on you . . . and your bright hopeful ideas . . .

– Go on home, lads, I'll be all right. I'd better stop here. Mr Riley has a condition, see, it comes in fits. Go on now. See you tomorrow.

Cy bent down and began to lift his employer to his feet. And Riley smiled at him, a pleased, pitying smile that was wetted by the tears from his eyes and the effluent from his mouth, a smile that was both moved by and derisive of this complicit new comradeship.

Before long Cy could see that Riley was torn in two, he was Janus-looking. Perhaps it was the humanity of his craft that allowed him this quality, this taking or leaving of life's mucky mire as well as its lovely sandy beaches, the ropes strung round both poles. Perhaps he had come of his trade well-fitting with a character already formed and suitable, or perhaps the trade had made him. Of fowl and egg, Cy would never truly know which had arrived first.

Outside the shop, in life, Riley was a failure. He was society's satirical, ugly cousin. He drank, offended, was loud, misunderstood. None could see him at work, and if they did they were too busy undergoing what was painful to notice his sudden clear eye, his steady hand, the hymns of his singing heart. So he turned this wrong territory in on himself, knowing that outside he was an unwelcome conduit, become dislodged from the one room other than a confessional box where the souls of men and women could travel freely. He went without that minister's identity. He went too far, got obstinate about his courtship of living wrongly and loudly and creating effrontery. Where Reeda milled the good of life, he harvested the ill and took it to market where he shouted out his wares. He believed deeply that he did not like himself, and he liked others less. Just as he did not like the environment of unpainted flesh, and normalcy, life's plug of decency that tried to stop up the devil's half of life. And he lived as if trying to siphon out that darker portion, with alcohol, with banter, with bad habits, bad politics, bad language, obloquy, anguish and despair.

– Not that I would, love, with a tuss as big as a cathedral my organ's play would seem too small. Set me up again, Paddy. What do you mean you've called last orders? I never heard, and what with Miss York Cathedral here you'd think there'd have been an echo.

All with suicidal desperation, if in hitting rock bottom that useless, disliked and disliking half of himself would abandon ship. Around him he created a mentality of a wet, wintry self-defeat. There were the brawls, the complaints, the lasting rivalries where Eliot Riley never came out the winner. He was barred from six public houses in the town for his conduct, had tried the patience of Paddy Broadbent on more than one occasion. He was notorious. But in his rooms he could embroider the human body with beauty and he was glorious. His reputation for it brought men and women in from as far afield as Belfast and Nottingham, Stirling and Glasgow, by appointment in the winter and in the summer months they queued outside his door. The brighter part of the man kept them coming, kept them coming back so that he could dress them in new, perfect, custom-fitting clothing. Give them their lasting souvenirs. Give them their natural markings. Give them a picture of and for themselves.

The two halves of his soul were split, one great and dexterous, the other destitute and murderous. And only Cy knew both for what they were. Only he could see the both sides, as he worked alongside the man in eminence and walked alongside the man in disgrace, and saw him love and saw him hate. And very early on in knowing him it struck Cy that there was something absolutely suiting about Eliot Riley and Morecambe Bay. Both were tidal and schizophrenic, two seasons right, two seasons wrong.

~

– Don't even bother asking when you'll get a go, sonny Jim. You'll pick up a needle when I say so and not before. And first off it'll be on those sticky celery legs you own, sunshine, not a paying customer.

It was no privilege and no honour working for Riley in those first months. And there were no civilized lessons about the great artistic masters as promised to Reeda Parks over tea and crumpets. Riley liked to talk about himself and he liked to give opinions. And he liked to show off. He was a freehander. He could gather a piece of linen skin and mark it with ink confidently if he chose to, without any preliminary work. It meant he could veer from the standard flash and boost his reputation with inventiveness and charge more money, but it also gave him a vastly engorged ego. If he saw the potential of it in Cy, through the bold designs in the print shop window, he passed on not one word of the prophecy. He was old-school, he said, proud to be it. He abhorred gimmicks, sloganeering, all the mock-surgery stuff, the laboratory coats, stethoscopes, the monikers, the aliases, Doc, Captain Red, Painless Andy, though he understood the need for rapport, for entertainment during the procedure, which was a different matter, and he delivered it nightly. He could pinpoint a proclivity for discrimination or the style of comedy a man preferred and would arrive there within a minute.

– What about these votes for women, eh? There's a reason they're going to repeal prohibition in America, isn't there? There's a reason drink is needed over there again now. What say you? Eh?

There was often so much bluff and showmanship present in the room that the customer would be hard pressed to dwell all that much on the scratchy sensation bothering them. There were stories told about whores and virgins and fights, about acquaintances caught short of the law, about the man he had been taught by, Black Percy, who had beheaded another man with his father's army sabre right before Riley's eyes. Riley had come through an industry that was as colourful as chintz, that was wholly self-sufficient and home-skilled, where equipment had to be constructed by the individual tattoo artist, handmade from convenient objects, electric doorbells, drills, industrial drive mechanisms, factory parts, medical quills, everything was bent, filed down, soldered and fixed. Ink had to be acquired under the guise of another profession, but established contacts could then be trusted, he told Cy. It was useful to know people at warehouses, scrappies, repair shops, and hospitals – Riley recommended going down on the nurses. Coils could now be bought for the machinery, mostly meant for other trades but easily adapted, though he continued to fashion every piece to suit his tastes wherever possible. And so would Cy learn to, so help him.

The man took him on a tour of every tattoo artist in Lancaster and Blackpool and sent him round the ones in Morecambe solo, window-shopping, to see how not to do it. If there was anything different to be found within it was not the designs, which were derivative, it was the men who ran them, somehow modern in their dress and criminal in their demeanour, compared to Eliot Riley, half seadog, half aristo-crat groom, the atavist, who most days, working or not, donned the dull black morning jacket, the woollen hat, the gloves with the finger ends cut out. Where the others embraced the ritzy persona of the profession Riley might have been the original mould of it, the genuine article.

It was a constant battle to keep the stone room warm that winter, the air was drawn out by the grey slurrying sea in the bay down at the end of Pedder Street, which seemed to heave out any heat from the building on its long retreat to low tide. Cy spent much of his time fetching firewood from the beach for the grate, so Riley could save money on coal, feeling demoted and cheated out of the warm comfort and the dependable clack-clack of the big press in the printers. Riley insisted on warmth for the customer section of the room behind the curtain, he had a thing about working on warm skin. He said it was better to get it into a temperate condition, it became readier to receive colour. There was the added frustration for Cy of being taught how to engineer all the fiddly equipment and getting it endlessly wrong. Piece after piece was rejected for being ground poorly, soldered at the wrong angle, botched and buggered and wasted. Riley often tossing them back into the box of metal parts without so much as a proper glance at the workmanship, judging it already shoddy. Had he wanted a career in mechanics Cy would have gone to work for a motor company or as a fitter at the foundry, he often thought to himself bitterly. There was, however, not a pig's head in sight, much to Cy's relief.

In February of that year, Riley had Cy begin his practice on his own cold, goose-pimpled shin, surrendering a leg, as he'd been informed he'd have to. And he'd also have to make a little visit to pay his respects to the primary creators of the trade. So it was tap-tap-tap on his shin with a bamboo block and a hammer, Riley slapping Cy's face when the pain got him teary and his concentration lapsed and he dropped the equipment, saying no more. He would learn the traditions, from beginning to end, and respect them, bellowed Riley.

– Now pick up that fucking mallet, boy. Or get out.

It may have been the electric age of needles but tattooing was as ancient as the mummies being pried from their sarcophaguses in the Egyptian desert, and if chiselled ink was good enough for the Pharaohs, it was certainly good enough for Cyril bloody Parks. Then, milliner's needles lashed to a stick, leaving thick rivers of colour, destroying a white leg with black practice. Oh, the bastard was old-school all right.

In addition, there were the personal comments, which the man took no great shame in making.

– Your problem, lad, is your natural inclination towards silence. Get it out, sonny. You're too dour, you need to perk up a bit, find some character. They won't credit you for just the ink, lad. Besides, the ladies do not like a dullard in their beds – how many have already fallen asleep under you, eh lad? Or on top of you for that matter. Or are you still a novice in that regard? Don't tell me I'll have to apprentice you in that field too.

Sour, wet laughter.

– Look. A bit of self-examination and melancholy is all right later on in the night, with a drop of something to accompany, but in front of the customer you'll have to perk up, do you understand? Work on your patter, I can't let you loose on the summer crowd if you're going to bore them into a coma. Zest, lad, zest! And get yourself greased up properly by a woman!

Such was the disappointment and frustration of the commencement of his apprenticeship. Countless times Cy nearly put down what he was carrying, firewood, needles, cartridges of ink, and left the shop on Pedder Street, never to return. Countless times he curled a fist up at his side and wished to God he could let it fly in Riley's general direction. Countless times he found the shop closed and empty and he'd have to search the streets for Riley, only to find him stained and stinking in some corner. And he'd lie to his mother that Riley wasn't drinking, that Riley didn't need him as a crutch to limp home with, and that he wasn't up half the night on weekends tending to the lush, making him oversleep and late for school on Monday morning, that Riley was a kinder tutor and that of all those great artists now known to him, Michelangelo was his favourite painter. Michelangelo. A name pulled out of thin air one day, to assure Reeda that everything was all right, that he hadn't taken a wrong path, that he wasn't lost and inches from the edge of a cliff. Though he had only to watch Eliot Riley at work on a customer, see the true colour finding its way into skin, and he felt all the antagonism and resentment absconding. Because from this brutish man could come humane and brilliant art.

~

– Are you feeling ill, love? You've a paleness to you these last few days.

– Oh, no, I'm grand thanks, Mam.

– You've not quarrelled with El . . . with Mr Riley, have you?

– No.

His mother put down her washing basket and placed a hand on his shoulder.

– Because that would be a shame.

– No, I'm just tired.

– Well. When I'm weary I tell myself if I can manage just one more chore for the day it'll be one less to do tomorrow. Of course it's funny, there always seems to be an abundance of chores and they never get any fewer, do they? It's a bit like a bottomless well, so you just have to keep working. Folk can be like that too, Cyril. It's what makes them so infuriating and it's what endears them to us. Your father could drive me to despair and ruination with his forgetfulness of the milk lid and his silly ideas about who should sit on the Council and who shouldn't, depending on if they wore a skirt or long trousers.

This was the first time he had ever heard his mother venture a criticism of his father, a remark that was less than a noble memorial of his exemplary character. Cy turned to look up at her. She seemed nervous but also relieved.

– Lordy, look at the time. I must get on or we'll be wearing wet woollies all week. Perhaps you'll tell me about it later on, about what you've been doing and how things are shaping up.

~

The summer of 1922 was to be a summer of disappointment, with little else for Cy to do than continue sitting mixing ink and filing needles, fixing electro-magnets and springs to the best of his ability and taking money from the customers. And not even enough scant pay to get him to the picture house on Saturday night to see Charlie Chaplin films or Marnau's stoddering vampire, with Morris and Jonty, who would sub him the ticket price whenever they could, but had no steadier or more generous income than he did. They couldn't understand Cy's interest in tattooing. They couldn't understand it under all his disappointment, his giving up of drawing – for Riley didn't even let him hang up his good designs in the shop, though he had made plenty, nor when he was not free-handing did he let him trace the acetate stencils, print them with charcoal, Vaseline a back and leave a preliminary mark for Riley to finish, like a proper apprentice blocking in compositions for the master. And they could not understand Eliot Riley, with his scowls and his songs, his bear-baiting sneers and his never certain behaviour when they came to call for Cy. Had he fought in the war? they asked. Is that why he was such a bastard, is that why he had become so impossible, because he had some kind of battle shock disorder, like the twitching men returned to the town in 1918, who from time to time fell to their knees and howled in the streets of Morecambe? Was it mania? Was it depression? Was it both together? The boys were stumped for any other reason. They could not fathom Cy's loyalty to this villain. They were befuddled and afraid and unable to relate to the man. For who in any right mind or any leap into a madhouse limbo could understand the workings and breakings of Eliot Riley?

∼

When Reeda Parks's breast began to invert she knew, in that portion of her heart where the tightest-bound and least-admitted of all secrets are kept, that her time had come. She watched her nipple retreat for five days, she became quieter and less certain of her work, leaving cupboards open and pastry half rolled. There were small pains in her body that she had not taken seriously before, had not let bother her – in her wrist, her abdomen, her upper back. Now they took on meaning. But she hadn't seen it coming, she hadn't seen it coming, that was what made her lean to the wall on which

she had leaned after the deaths of the ideas of so many children, and weep. She took the time to observe her tall son
across the table when they ate supper together, noticing his
high forehead, the untidy locks of hair around his collar – he
hated visiting the barber and would never let her cut it, and
how his Adam's apple moved in his throat when he swallowed, triangularly, like the corner shank on a steam-train
wheel as it begins to piston. And how she could tell when he
was thinking hard on something because his lips sometimes
ghosted over words without realizing what they were doing,
or he suddenly snorted or laughed out loud for no good reason. And she thought about how she loved him, all through
herself, like muscle that held her up without her even feeling
it. She visited the doctor and a surgery was planned, but
within weeks it became apparent that there was little could
be done, they couldn't cut her back far enough, she was a
blighted tree that had a cancer close around its trunk. She
would not remain in Lancaster infirmary. She wanted the
Bayview, where she could take the last of her life, so she
could end it where she'd always made it. And she would take
the opportunity to watch the pleasing motion of bay, that
enormous living clock that had always been at the back of her
when she worked, like a long, daily two-swing pendulum
clock. She would open the window in her own room and let
the sea's breath invigorate the air around her, she did enjoy
the cooler weather, there was a rousing, wakeful quality
about it. As if clarity had been restored after the muggy,
yawning heat of summer. There would be her Cyril. With her
breast gone and her body faltering she would need to finally
and fully wean him off her care.

He was destroyed only in so far as all young men who
lose their mothers are but will recover. Before she left for
the hospital he wouldn't let her see his face, keeping it
pressed into the crook of his elbow on the table for an hour.
As if to take it out and let his eyes notice her new paleness
and tiredness and the determination of her belief in her

mortem-lot would be to admit her fate himself and say he gave it blessing, which he did not, he did not.

– They've got to cut the fly-walk off me, luvvie; if it doesn't go the whole loaf will turn bad.

Finding somewhere within her another of her knell-captured allegories, another of her boiled-down for stock metaphors. It was September's end. A full blustery September with water along its edges at night and a wet blue colour to its days. The town and bay were rushing along under a painter's oil-stroked sky as they always did in autumn. The guests were all but gone, Reeda had finished another summer season, and to her credit everything was in order. She adjusted her books, summarized them, did not make a budget for the winter. It had been a fair summer, there was money enough to set Cyril up in a way that meant he could soon provide for himself. The bank was informed of the discontinuance of mortgage. Hotel furniture was sold off. There were no stacks of sheets brought out for mending, nor was a list of winter repairs for the hotel made. She went in for her already failed surgery, spent an agonizing week in hospital during which Cy visited every day, and she came home draining fluids through piping in her chest and unable to lift her right arm. She let her son rally round her, knowing he needed to feel useful. Then she summoned Eliot Riley, who took one look at her lying drained and smeary as an empty bottle of cream against the pillow and fell about weeping.

– Take your hat off, Eliot, and close the door. And I truly hope you've sobered.

– Of course I'm sober, woman! What do you take me for?

Cy was not in the room but he could half hear Riley in his distress, hear the serration at the pauses of his brittle, cuttle-fish sentences and the use of his mother's name over and over: Reeda, Reeda. For two people who saw each other infrequently as they did, their meetings were actuated, senti-mental affairs. So that again Cy wondered if there was not some old abandoned, rusted chassis to their relationship, down under all the growth of years it might lie there still, hidden, even from them, but obstruction enough for them to clang their feet on when they came together. Perhaps in a time before his father, though Cy felt sure his mam would have told him back when he first asked to be Riley's lad if there was a personal history which meant the employment proposal was improper. Towards the end of the discussion it was Reeda who did the talking and Riley listened. Her tone was matter of fact, occasionally she broke off, for her pain came intermittently, like the occasional taller waves in the bay that threw boats upwards and off their charted course. And he could make out one word that she repeated. If, if, if, so he knew there was choice somewhere in the matter.

As he left the Bayview, Riley walked past Cy without a word of consolation. Without a word at all. As if his own grief invested in the loss of Cy's mother prevented him from such expressions and inclusions lest he break down again. His demeanour was that of an emoting ham, the theatrical pathos of a fan leaving a tragic opera. Like he was wrapped up in the misery and felt it more than even Cy, the son, who was dwarfed and discredited by such enthusiastic mourning. The minted eyes had swathes of red and grey about them. His big lips quavered. He had sympathy only for himself. Not for the first time Cy wanted to yell out or run his hand along the table crashing through objects and creating infernal noise, to assure Riley he was not invisible, not insignificant, actually. Riley was a sentimental, discriminate-hearted, impossibly rude and selfish man.

~

Reeda had written to her sister Doris, informing her of the situation. She arrived a week later, smelling of old lace and apprehension, and Cy was sent to meet her at the station. Doris scuttled about in the Bayview kitchen, pasting food down into something manageable for his mother, and she read her articles from the *Visitor*, about the bus which had crashed through the prom rail to the shore killing three passengers, about which of the town's prostitutes had been arrested, as if Morecambe was a venue somewhere across the country, not a place just outside the window. Reeda's hair thinned to the point where she kept a headscarf on her at all times like a clay-baked caul. Her limbs and organs began to fail her, one day she simply could not get out of bed, and Cy was once again required to empty basins of waste – her bile ducts sent into frenzy, her lungs like blighted branches, her bowels leaking. There was more and more blood in her waters, as the cancer moved further in. And there was a lot of pain, times when his mother cinched in on the bed and held her breath for long minutes, before releasing it and panting dryly like a heat-exhausted dog. Her grey gunmetal eyes went out to some place stranded between the conscious oracle of her ill fortune and a bed-of-nails of sleep. The doctor called by with stronger medication for her to take, and when she refused it, saying she would not waste her last hours and days with red dreams or a mouth too cottony to speak, her sister ground down the tablets and mixed it with her broth, asking Cy for forgiveness as she did so. As if he now held the map to Reeda's mind, and might direct them in their search for a rational, befitting, governed end. As if his complicity might unkill her thinking, suffering death.

She wanted her son. When everyone else in the room became a stranger, she wanted him. To sit with her if he would, and remember her with a measure of sweet and a measure of savoury when it was over, like all well-prepared dishes both parts together made the other complementary and better. Her words quick now as if she wanted them expelled, as if they were her deadlined duty and not to be relished or appraised as a glass-blown object passed gently between hands and turned over.

– One without the other we are all made poorer. Remember that of all of us, Cyril. Remember it of Mr Riley. He is what he is and he's more a mirror than any man you'll meet. We did our bit, didn't we, love? We did our bit here.

He did not know which pieces of life she was speaking about. He didn't know but he took her hand as she had once taken his to lead him to the blood-lit window, and he wished for a white horse on the shore to see her safely through the mist. Then, after four months of struggling, her death grew and hatched one night from the repeating, withering body and she was gone. Reeda Parks, in all her graceless, earthed and ordinary wisdom, was gone.

~

The Ladies of Leeds arrived the day of the funeral and laid flowers on Reeda's grave, dressed in long, out-of-fashion skirts as if for a royal funeral. Cy had not seen them since his youth and did not know his mother was still in correspondence with them. But he remembered their complementary, stirred-up faces as they filed into the Bayview for her wake, and washed the dishes and made Doris feel uncomfortable. That night they each lit candles on the promenade and joined hands. They were tearless, resolute. There was something martial to their movements, a quality of drilled and synchronous ceremony beneath their ruffles, like the softest military salute. It was the second of March, in 1923, and one of the ladies came to Cy and passed him a candle as he stood by the Bayview door watching the gunner's flames pinking up the ladies' hands. This day, eleven years ago, she said, London rattled and shook with the sound of rocks and sticks breaking Parliament's windows, and though she wasn't there, your mother's heart was one of those rocks, like the rocks that will one day smash all the prejudices of her country.

~

She had said he would have to make a choice – go with his Aunt Doris to Yorkshire, if he wanted, or stay with Mr Riley, who would take him in as boarder and apprentice, if he

107

wanted. If, if, if. And there again was that forking road unfolding and dividing, and him knowing there was a route of moderate, well-put-together living, or a way of life bitter-sacrificed and bitter-gained, of damning and enlightening direction. The path of shallow passing, or the path that cut right through him – the path of Riley's influence and Riley's needle inserted like a catheter into the deepest soul chamber of him, into the worst and best places of him, which would never be removed, or if it was scar-tissue would for ever keep the channel open.

So when Cy got as far as the brown moors of Yorkshire on the train, and heard the reeding wind again across the rock formations, he kissed his Aunt Doris goodbye and thanked her, then got off at the very next station and bought a one-way ticket back to Morecambe Bay.

– Salvaging Renaissance –

– Michelagniolo di Lodovico Buonarroti, who became known to the world and its dog as Michelangelo, was born in 1475 and died in 1564. That made him eighty-nine years old. Not a bad age for a bugger back then. Now, there wasn't a lot the man couldn't do, which was quite common for that period. Not like today, where men just sit around with their cocks in their hands waiting for a job to come along, and only being skilled enough to mortar brick or dig out coal or count up taxes, one at a time. Depression or not, lad, it was harder back then, so I've more respect for what got done. No, this was a different time. When men could set to on any task and get it done. So Michelangelo was a painter, an architect, a sculptor and a poet. All things relevant to our trade. Some say Leonardo was the tip-top-tradey of that period, and fair play, he wasn't a village idiot, but the truth is Michelangelo had a calling and was his own boss in a way none of the rest were, even while he took work for bread and butter. That's why his painting got all long and stretchy, and not everybody's cup of tea. He had something go through him towards the end. Let me tell you, any man that sees it in himself to paint the hand of God is something a bit special. Now the thing to remember about Michelangelo is this; he'd a bugger of a time getting blue paint. Just like us. It was expensive back then, see, hard to manage, and it was only used for very special things, like our Holy Mother's robes. If there's one thing we could do to live up to Michelangelo, it's crack this bastard riddle with blue ink. Speaking of tea, what say you pop upstairs and put the kettle on, lad?

There were five colours in the tattooing pallet, and a limited archive of symbols to cover the spectrum of life and death.

Five colours to capture all the joys and sorrows of the world and hold them down against a piece of body. Red, brown, yellow, green, black. Five colours to say everything that could be said. And what Cy suddenly wanted, more than anything in the world right then, what he wanted was that missing blue, primary and resistant to the trade. Blue that was unstable and misbehaved when left in skin. Blue like the sea that had taken his father. Blue, for his mother's sake, and for the true colour of every bereaved and bloodless heart when it is collapsing.

～

The rooms above Eleven Pedder Street were cold and small, claustrophobic, like a cell or priest's hole. Riley was not one for warmth but he was neat and he was tidy, which came as a surprise to Cy when he entered the domain. He had never been upstairs in all the time he had been warden to Riley and carted the drunk man home, preferring to leave him in the parlour downstairs or at the front door. Things were put away, stacked, or folded; washed at the sink the cups were shining in the bleached light of the kitchen as they dried, and there was a row of eggs on a dresser shelf as concise and uniform as a squadron. Or perhaps Riley was just deficient in acquiring domestic items, for the place was basic in appearance: chairs, table, plates, sink, bottles, food in stages of decay. And on the mantelpiece of the ever-empty fireplace were the skulls of several birds, hook-beaked, cranially fissured, delicate and predatory. A statue of the Virgin Mary stood on the very corner of the mantle as if any moment she might topple off, as if she were being tested in her balance or her own faith. Her hands were folded together in prayer, her head was bent and it seemed she was in fact looking over the precipice to the floor below. There were one or two other objects lying about, nothing distinguished, old art history books with splitting spines. The place itself was like a still-life painting. In Cy's room, the room that Riley had prepared for him, was a mattress on the floor and four empty wooden vegetable crates to hold his possessions and clothing. There was a small window, from which the metal hook that had hung Kaiser Bill could be reached. A paint-peeling ceiling. Separating floorboards. It was monastic, it was bare and minimal, and he could not help but feel that he had stepped back in time to some artistic, suffering vault, which was appropriate to his new situation. There was an awful feel to the place – like it had been, for quite some time, waiting for him.

It became apparent that Cy had finished with school. He was sixteen, and Headmaster Willacy was no match for the law and logistics of Eliot Riley, for all his insistence that the boy had brains and should be allowed to continue. It became apparent that he was now a full-time employee and that in that one about turn half way to Yorkshire he had sold his soul to Riley. For better, for worse. He was not heckled for being late to work, for walking back to Eleven Pedder Street with his suitcase in hand a week after he was due. Riley had expected him to come after they boarded up the Bayview, just as Aunt Doris had expected him to come with her after they lowered the body of his mother into the ground, but there were no repercussions for his hiatus. He had given assurance to neither guardian of his plans, in truth he had not really spoken to anyone such was his grief. Riley simply opened the door and stepped aside and let him enter, and on his first day back in the shop, he proceeded with the first of his customized Lives of the Great Masters lectures. It was long overdue after his promise to Reeda, and came now as if in compensation for her death, and it had more than a note or two of personal fabrication and fiction to it. Though this one slackening of the bit in his mouth and the bridle would be the last courtesy Riley ever paid Cy. Ever after, he woke him with his morning pissing and his coughing. He woke him with his nocturnal smashing and his cussing, the occasional sound of his voice joined with another, its pitch become more female, as he grunted and groaned. He berated him for every minor fault and fumble at work. He made him skivvy to his every whim and fancy. He was unfair and cruel and tasteless with his comments. And he began to infect Cy with his maelstrom temperament. Cy found his shouting voice and the terrifying beauty of fists against a surface when the gates of control and reason are unhinged and the hooves of thick-packed, red-eyed beasts come thundering out. He had to concentrate, harder than he ever had in school, to tease out splinters of fulfilment and sanity and peace from the arrangement. And all the while he missed Reeda, missed her unmitigated kindness and her simple reasoning, the salve of benevolence with which she soothed his raw troubles and loosened the dirt of life that might if left untreated infect his spirit. And God, wasn't life just lonely without her!

It was awful not to be in the Bayview for the first few summer seasons, with the sick but happy crowds. It was like being shown an amputated leg that had once held up his torso. At times he found himself automatically walking in the hotel's direction, and he'd have to stop and remember his mother's death and turn back on the way he had come. It was strange to pass by the graveyard and think of his mother, put away there, like her extra linens in the autumn in a dark cupboard. Betrayed by the soft air, which didn't save her. There had been something certain about turn-over and survival at the Bayview Hotel, whether it was his mother's financial acumen or her loyal guests or her ability to pin the bottom of the world up with her ethics and her tolerance and her mulish, working-woman's patience, he did not know. Tattooing, as he came to understand it, was an altogether more precarious vocation and style of living. There could be no advertisements in the *Visitor*. There may have been more people around in the summer but there were no set seasons when it came to the compulsions and treasons and decisions of the human brain to change its packaging, to disguise its appearance or release its imprisoned identity. A man or woman had to refer to the discrete almanac of the mind to find those changeling cycles and tides and magnitudes, and arrive at the needle's end of his or her own accord. Impulsively, erratically, naturally. So, now and again, other supplemental jobs had to be found. For Cy in hotel kitchens, dismantling fish heads and filleting spines from smoked bodies at the Trawlers' Cooperative building with Morris, even sweeping the aisles of the theatre in the Alhambra on Saturday and Sunday mornings. Riley had his own methods for breaking even, some of which were legal, many of which were not. The least reliable source of income was his gambling, on horses, on hounds, and even on cockfights held in farms around the region. The most dangerous were his excursions with Paddy Broadbent to the city of Liverpool for unspecified purposes, which resulted in frequent scars and injuries though tired jubilation observed upon their return.

And the most remarkable, though if Cy thought about it perhaps it was somehow fitting, was Riley's skill for training hawks. He was a part-time falconer, hence his penchant for displaying bird skulls like pieces of art on the mantle. Some family connection or learned relative had granted him membership to this singular game-keeping guild. He had in his time worked at three manor houses in the district, and one in East Yorkshire, riding with the aristocracy as they searched the moors and estate lands for hares and rabbits, and that employment opportunity seemed always to be open, so Cy guessed it was highly specialized. Business needed to be consistently bad for him to do it as he would need to spend guaranteed time during the juvenile months with the bird, weighing it on the leather wrist strap, fitting the tiny ankle brace, easing the hood and helmet on and off the bird until it trusted him to do it without fighting the darkness, during which period trade at Morecambe could suddenly pick up again. And Riley did not like these employers. He scorned their birthrights, their repressions and what they represented to the common man while he took their wages.

The outcome of breaking the outer layer of the bird's wild nature was by no means certain. Rather than cooperate a bird of prey could will itself to death, Riley told him. They could be the stubbornest buggers, he said with admiration. He took Cy along with him just once on such an excursion. The lord was away from his manor and Riley brought his apprentice down to the mews. He put on a heavy greasy jacket and instructed Cy to be as quiet as he could. In the cage at the outskirts of the estate was a peregrine falcon, which took to Riley's arm and sat blinking at him, razor strength and precision to its beak. It was as if the tidy, blue-winged bird was no more than an extension of the man himself, when he was focused and sharp and all instinct and energy travelled the length of the arm to one keen and cutting point. Cy felt it was wrong for him to be so close to the creature, it was of another world, defined by the remote levitating laws of a different dimension, and the falcon-gentle also knew this. A shrill cry came from it, like a woman being carved up within her. Its tongue like a beak within a beak, hard and melded and traced with pollen dampness like the lock stamen of an exotic flower. Riley stroked the bird and it turned to him with a look of coy and marginal tolerance. Then he showed Cy how, when you split open the compacted droppings of the bird, you might find tiny rodent skeletons and bones as soft and pliant as feathers inside. And there was something between them then, a lull, like the lowest tide of the year, or a sense of human archaeology. For an hour or two Cy felt untrammelled by loneliness, he felt a sympathy with the man, and his solitude lessened.

~

But always there were the times of seizure, when thoughtful doctrine and moments of kindness or enlightenment were lost. Times when the man took back every decent thing he issued. Like the sea coming quick up the shore, opaque and silty and fouling, to retrieve its temporary leavings. Cy was no longer just an associate, just an orderly who collected the wandering drunken madman from the piers and alleyways of Morecambe, he was not indulged with satisfactory distance any more. He was Riley's Boy. He was implicated in his behaviour. The stories that went about town, that bit at Riley's ragged temper and fanned the flame of belligerence within him, now included Cyril Parks – he was the antidote to all the venom, the one they'd come searching for to talk the man off a half-beaten body and retract the knife nicking a throbbing jugular, or to help Paddy carry the purpling, moaning body from the Dog and Partridge to the rooms above the tattoo parlour, and sometimes to fetch the doctor when Riley was pissing blood. Cy was the tidy, busy suffix by name and then by nature, the coda at the end of all the stories. The story of Riley drunk at the carnival and livid, overturning a float carrying rice-throwers, sending children flying, because the drains of Pedder Street were blocked up with rice and Riley's pipes were overflowing so he had to see his own shit, he had to smell his own shit, and it was too close to something in him or of him to simply clean it up without roaring down the culprits and blaming them for his stench. And Cy had to talky-talk the mothers away from their pri-mordial fury over their children's injuries, for they would have lynched the goading, unrepentant Riley, torn him into shreds, he saw it in their faces, had there not been a grey-eyed boy between them, like a single, durable ash tree between two quaking mountains. The story of the fire in 1925, that took away the central pier, a slow fire this time without a helpful blizzard, that meant the looters could first charge through the abandoned buildings over the sea and help themselves to what the owners couldn't carry, and Riley and six other men sat drinking beer as fast as their oesophagus tunnels could convey it to their stomachs in the Pier bar. Then just Riley, daft with alcohol and alone, pouring another glass of ale as the fire crept past him on the counter, singeing his jacket sleeve, until, hearing that some skinflint idiot was left inside the now-prodigal inferno, Cy ran in and screamed murder at Riley and called him Eliot and hit him for the first time in his jaw to get him to follow him out. Jack-Frost eyes couldn't quite decide whether to pummel his lackey for laying one on him or shake his hand for the rescue operation as the pier collapsed behind them, so in the end he did neither, just stared at the boy. The story of the General Strike in '26, when Riley made a point of shutting up the shop, politically, with a banner hung in the window, while all the other businesses scabbed the order, and he went about the town like a proletariat crusader unhooking the horses from their trams and throwing their bells into the ocean, until he was arrested for being a public nuisance. The bail money spent from the sum that Reeda had left her son was never recovered by Cyril Parks from he whom it had saved. And it was more than any wage the man had ever paid him.

∾

The art lessons, if they could be called such a thing, had no formal structure and no chronology. They had decidedly rip-rap foundations. They came whenever Riley felt like sharing his wisdom, axe-hewn from history and varnished into hard fact-like items by his own resinous, sap-seeping philosophy. How Raphael faked his genius, fooled the world with his too-posed, too-pretty, too-poncy figures, the more refined and idealized he got the more he gave back what the Renaissance had recovered from the Dark-Age graves of mighty empires, namely the accurately imperfect human anatomy. How Dante Gabriel Rossetti went grave robbing to retrieve some poems he had coffined with his lover, because art and desecration were as close as an incestuous brother and sister. How Rembrandt painted his portrait face from adolescence into death and wasn't afraid to show just what an ugly bugger he had been, because ugly was simply beauty in a place across the river. How Courbet, Gustave Courbet, now there was a rabble-leader, there was a people's hero, armed with undeni-

116

able talent had won his way into the most prestigious gallery in his native country and shocked the whole of France with his masterpiece, *The Stone Breakers*, as well as if he'd laid his castrated tackle in a dish before Le Salon. How Edouard Manet had put a slut along a sacred icon's bed, posing her with symbols of her wayward cunt, how he'd cut the child-bearing hips off every woman in artistic memory to say that she was pleasure without responsibility, how he'd made a whore out of faithful, chaste tradition. How Caravaggio had painted the portrait of a poor carpenter, possibly his own father, and dared to say that the son of God was surrogated to this old, this broken-bodied, callused-handed worker. And there was Blake with his mutative, folded-together mind and his temporal visions and his careful illustrations of heaven and hell, of tigers and lambs, the opposing hemi-spheres of humans. These were the things of art. Taken by the rich from the poor, but a poor man's currency no less. They were beautiful and they were malignant and they were the things of genius.

~

There were always fellows hanging around Riley's studio. Men and boys drawn to the base intrigue of the profession, that which it represented, the disreputable image. They were males on the cusp of maturity, or just past where its borders were considered to be, those who wanted an endorsement of their manhood, their tougher qualities, and so they sought out models straddling the rawer end of society with which to affiliate themselves, from which to draw estimation, or perhaps identity. They would last the duration of Riley's tolerance, or until his curt humour, his abuse, became unworthy of the thrill of association with the town's best and most infamous tattoo artist. Until the myth of butchery and colouring skin was exploded for them or until professionally damaged flesh was no longer violence enough and trouble took them someplace new.

At heart Riley was a solitary, and though he was open to flattery, to appreciation of his showmanship, he did not require crowds to conduct business. In each of the other shops in town similar hangers-on might have been found; they amplified and reinforced the proprietor's ego, his position as noncomformist hard man. They might be turned by the owner's hand or barking command and aimed at potential troublemakers, the inevitable brawling, like the big dogs employed to guard the fairground rides from thieves and travelling gypsies out of season. But at Riley's they served no such purpose. There was little titillation for them beyond the art. The curtain remained mostly closed when Eliot Riley was working. He himself waded in to any turbid situations, to break up fights, to threaten those angling for a scuffle, he did not need mercenary goons at his disposal. But he let the young men sit, two or three at a time, in the outer rooms of the building. For reasons that Cy could never completely grasp, his employer's shop became host to a variety of scar-faced adolescents and potentially rough young men. Fighters, energetic loafers. Lads not unknown to the local constabulary and the courts. Dirty-faced, unshaven and hatless, they hung about. They had hair that suggested the slip from maternal care, or conventional pride, or employed and codified appearance, into near poverty and reckless self-opinion, the absence of standards. Occasionally an old seadog hung about for a week or so too before the character moved on to another out-of-season coastal town where obscurity and initial pity would bring him luck, drink, and while the vagrant was there Riley might be generous with a quarter-bottle of rum in passing. But the youths were always a guaranteed feature.

In this matter Riley displayed an uncharacteristic flexibility. He was not one for gangs or social gatherings, least of all those to which he was centrally located: it leached too greedily the black soil of his integrity. He was by nature a separatist, contrary, one who cut away from crowds in opinion, often for the sake of belligerence itself. Cy knew his own relations with the man to be in all likelihood a fluked and fashioned attempt to preserve what slim achievement or prowess the man saw in himself, ego clambering up from the chaos of his personality. For Eliot Riley, without his equipment in his hand, found his own company barely agreeable. Neither did he aspire to surround his too-often failing esteem with doting minions, as if for reassurance, those who might raise him up as the emperor of an underworld they gloried. He did not need these man-boys. But for the ill-bred idlers he seemed to find reserves of uneasy, almost familial permission. Some nights they were rewarded with the best of Riley's banter, his winning bluff, an inclusive, Faginish greeting.

– Now then, my lads, what've y'got for me tonight?

To which there would be a chorus of eager, earnest reply. A fledgling effort to win the man over with a tale about some kind of injurious endeavour.

– Not a lot, nowt, not much really. Garry got his hand cut in a scrap with a fucker from Lancaster.

– Did he now. Well isn't that a pretty story?

Other times they endured Riley's pettiness along with Cy: a thrown vial of ink if business was slack, staining what was probably one of only two shirts belonging to the recipient, or silence, his empirical reducing of them all to the level of furniture.

They mulled about smoking and looking at the walls as back after back, shoulder after bicep, became coloured and etched to the sound of a motorized needle. Drinking was only permitted behind the curtain, from Riley's stash, not in the waiting area. They knew this rule and did not break it. While the back room was kept warm, the outer room which passed as a waiting area where the flash adorned the walls was cold. Cold enough to dissuade all but the hardiest, most persevering from loitering. It was almost as if temperature was a test for endurance and admission. At any point, Riley could clear them out with a few curt words and that elaborately flickering eyelid. There was never any denying his potency within his own rooms, though the boys must have known he was not consistently god-like, was mortal in the public houses and bar rooms of Morecambe; they must have seen him softened on the tarmac and wooden piers of the towns at weekends. Stripped of swagger and royal-ruffian demeanour. Stripped of his money-clip and his clear vision in one eye for a week.

Eventually they did not try to woo Riley with tales of bravado to elicit admiration, affection or for qualification, a right to be present, at least not by a second or third visit when they knew it to be useless. Nor did they try for camaraderie with Cy, he was a lesser being in the scheme of things and as there was little paternal investment shown by the owner towards him they must have supposed that he was not a means by which to infiltrate the greater man. So the boys would sit shivering and smoking in twos or threes, staring down clients that entered the studio as if they were sub-demons on the periphery of Hades, whose purpose was no more than to create a gargoyled atmosphere, more watchful and implicit and slightly unpleasant than it was a genuine threat. Many were already tattooed, and then better worked on by Eliot Riley, often displaying substandard, rough marks on their necks and hands so that Cy knew they had been to other less fussy and capable tattoo artists. Or they had tried to mark themselves, the self-inflicted rudimentary efforts done in school detention rooms or in the company of other street pals, during youthful misadventures. When they could afford it, and sometimes when they could not, Riley tidied them up, redressed old wounds, drained septic injuries, and added newer, doctored motifs, all the while scolding them for their past errors. There was something to be said for their loyalty to each other. If one lad was employed his wages might furnish a mate with a fresh tattoo. And though Riley was a stickler for payment, with these boys he often worked on a system of exchange and barter. A bag of tools for the scythed grim reaper or the death-before-dishonour badge. It was a relationship Cy found hard to comprehend. And only Riley might accept payment in kind, for Cy to consider it with any of his school friends was out of the question. Morris and Jonty were permitted in to the studio only in the capacity of paying customers, an opportunity which they never took.

The hangers-on arrived a few hours into the evening, alone like strays or in their small packs. If they were drunk they did not show it. If the curtain was left open they would watch the needle when Riley worked, entranced, as if it sewed the very secrets of virility and aggression into the skin. They browsed endlessly through flash, sifting through it for the best, death-maw images. Their conversation was amateur, imbued with the pressure to impress each other. Or it was lazy, lackadaisical. Eventually the dynamics within any one group would alter. Tension fermented. Habits and the haunt grew old. New thrills were required. A fight or a weariness with this association or a graduation into higher crime would see them gone. Or sensing that things were on the turn, like milk about to curdle, Riley would one night unlock the door and when the boys came by he'd stand in the doorway and refuse them entry, bullying one by grabbing a collar at random and throwing the brawny youth back into the street. As if lit by the sudden grounded rage of an abusive father. By then the group had accomplished the discredit it had set out to gain. And they were granted recognition for the anti-merits of such an inclement alliance by the community. By its nicer end, the authorities and toffs and round circles of the town, the ladies' auxiliary, the big hotel owners, who considered them not unlike maggots in an infected carcass.

~

Cy had gone from a life of female, maternal company and influence to something thoroughly male and, as if to signify that, Eliot Riley tattooed a ship on the chest of Cyril Parks with the name of his dead father along the rigging. The piece was completed in one long and painful sitting, as if it were another test set up by Riley. It was as if the man could not bear to inscribe Reeda Parks's name in death, just as he could not quite validate his affection during her life, and he became bristled with anger and refused when he was asked to by her lad. And so with the use of mirrors and patience and sheer will, Cyril Parks wrote Reeda's name on himself permanently one night as soon as he felt capable of doing it justice. If he'd ever had any perspective on the female brain, thanks to his mother, within the following years he felt he'd lost it. Cy marvelled that any women made it through the door of Eleven Pedder Street, let alone stayed put in the waiting room until it was her turn in the chair. But they came, endured some crude and saucy confrontations in the waiting room, and often gave as good as got. They came not infrequently either, that was one of the best kept secrets of the industry, that the inches of female bodies walking around in the street were as colourful as they were under their slips and girdles. They chose smaller motifs than their male counterparts, in discreet places, their thighs, their bellies, their lower backs, which would never be shown naturally in public, like a man's tattooed forearm when the sleeve was rolled back for toil, or the pride of a sailor's knuckles. For them the matter was entirely personal. Only one or two were bolder, full-body tattooed, women from the circus when the carnivals rolled through Morecambe. For the others it was flowers and swallows and the names of lovers. They were guaranteed proper handling. Riley, for all his boorishness about the town enjoyed the professional respect of those who valued his skill. He was known to be a safe-scraper. And they knew that once their clothes were off, behind the curtain, there was no danger of impropriety with the man unless they wanted there to be; he had about him the air of someone so imbued with the minutiae of his profession, as with a doctor, a solicitor, a business man, that the weight of it grounded him, and won the genuine confidences of others. For this and other tradesman's foibles, the frequent exchange of ink, the sterility of needles and rags for cleaning, Riley earned the reputation of a purist, strangely professional in an industry not truly applied to the snobbery and expected comportment of corporate, higher-class society. So that while his sloppy drinking habits and his loud bombastic mouth earned him the title of fool and drunkard, his skills, his standards, afforded him a constant supply of clients, including ladies in their heels and hoods, felt hats, crinoline petticoats, boas and brooches and occasionally in fox fur wraps.

But oh, they were hard to fathom, and Cy felt remote from them now. They were creatures of extraordinary endurance and unpredictability. Riley was right, they could smile through the treatment as if it were no more than a loofah brush massage. As if having marched straight to the shop from their covens. They were not as inclined to grip the wooden wall shackle for their discomfort as the men were, externalizing pain. Instead they held their own hands tightly, as if intent on retaining the sensation, their bodies became continuous units like the symbol for infinity. Their reaction to the work done on them was as varied as it could be extreme. Tears, hysterical laughter, absolute silent obduracy, quiet lunacy, resolve, sudden terror, mania, lasciviousness, sentiments from all the filler layers, all the fuller levels between defined emotions, like the white pulpy substance found inside the tough green skin of a split reed. A man would not do it that way, he would be happy, blasé, angry or bluffing something. So there was always that sense, that feeling that the female customers were closer to the mystery of the trade that Riley maintained was sacred and central. Nor could Riley crack them in his personal life, for all his keen eye into the caves and fissures of people's minds, his forcipial ability to guide out an image or symbolic rendition of their traits if they were stuck or stalling amid the flash.

It was at the Pedder Street parlour that Cyril Parks graduated from the blue-balled frustrations and unconsummated altercations of sexual prelude to the real thing with women. Some of them came into the shop with their loins already aflame, and either he or Riley would be offered their rumps on heat if there was enough privacy. Some considered it essential gratuity. They came to have fire drawn on their white bodies, or flowers around their nipples, their nipples extended pinkly like rose petals across the breast, felines crouching near their vulvas. The hints of coitus. There was that aspect to the profession. The graphic, creamy rich slick of it, its spermary and ovum character. Marine life on an inner thigh, a snake resting coiled on a buttock or slithering into the shadow-crease of a bum. The base symbols of fucking, the vividly erotic. Some women came to inscribe their risqué nature on their bodies, to elicit wanton behaviour from the viewer or to declare their own, and they would desire Cy afterwards, being already mostly naked, being ready for more than the needle's entry. The last scratch of pain leaving behind only sore proof of lust as it departed. Some of them wanted to see it through to the gasping, shuddering, juddering very end. So there was sex like gauze to cover their colourful wounds.

– Do you know what this swallow means, darling? Can you guess it? Well, I'll show you. Take your trousers down. Come on, you'll not be sorry. That's right. Well, look at you, all truncheon meat and no helmet, constable. You better sit for this, hadn't you?

Or they would take his hand and place it between their legs, wait for his response, his eyes complying, then they'd mould his cock into a pleasing shape like potters at the wheel, glaze him hard with the spit of their hot, kiln-oven mouths, so that he was in a state where they could use him. And some of them he liked, over and above the sucking and screwing, and he would have courted them were it not for the rigmarole of having to introduce them to his boss, the certainty of his malevolent interference. Riley, at his lewdest and most sordid, said not to be fooled by caresses and kisses, polite and tender exchanges, the lick of a tuss and the sweet discovery of that spot which got both parties banging together like shutters in a hurricane. He said that some women just liked the bite and the tear and the spite of tattooing and of coupling, that it was pain which got them wet and wanting. And if Cy was going to handle these ones in the parlour when Riley wasn't around, randy and mucky and germ-ridden as they may be, he'd have do away with shy passes and gentle thrusting and considerate loving. He'd have to slap them and grip them and fist them and turn them around dog-mounted to blunt himself in, or put it in their arses.

Though they came less often than the men to Eleven Pedder Street, females carried with them intrigue, life's oddest embolus in their blood, and they undid the work's simplicity. Cy tried his best to wind his way through the skein grounds surrounding them but often felt lagging and lost.

Once, there was a woman crying at the back of the building after her work was completed. Riley would not comfort her. For whatever unsympathetic reason, or cruelty, or voyeuristic detachment, he did not feel like he had enough invested in the situation to warrant it and he did not approach her. Instead, he went about cleaning the ink vials and left her be to soggy up her handkerchief with grief and snot. Human canvas could never be relied on for rational behaviour, especially not the female variety, Riley always said. She was sorry she'd had it done perhaps, thought Cy, that tiny black-red rose flower above the navel. A thumbnail's length above it, Riley's broad, stained nail the measure. Her face was all bunched together and full of concentration, as if crying were a matter that should be attended to with effort and determination, as if she was making herself do it. This Cy had never understood, whenever he'd seen it in women. They could turn to it with passion and dedication. The quality of adamant self-destruction at the back of it unsettled him, the way that people would risk against themselves, double up, self-destruct. For it seemed a betrayal of the worst kind, and he always felt he should try to stop the rebellion. Whether it was out of pity or penalty, he knew you only had to have your dying mother take your hand before taking the hands of weeping women became a reflex action. Not so for Riley. It seemed he felt nothing at all and he could watch the upset of others for hours while smoking, like being at the cinema. Or maybe one part of him was mentally slapping their hysterical faces. Cy had heard a few of the women Riley brought home with him reduced to this condition, their furious wailing seemed only to intensify through the walls when met with his executioner's insensate reaction, his void of emotion, his catatonic stance. Then there was the smashing of breakable objects if something portable could be found to aid their performance, as if torment increased in volatility until it was met with the proper appreciation, as if that was a given emotional equation. Like upping the stakes in poker until a hand was called. And Cy could sympathize with them, could he not, for all the occasions he himself wanted to roar at Riley to be more human when met with his outstanding cruelty, as human as those who had shaped Cy's life so far and set the kindly standard.

But this one woman, now flowered just above her belly-button, and still open-bloused so that her quaking belly was seen, seemed so strangely broken open when it was done that there were vast spaces of confusion Cy could not cross. And she was Riley's customer, and it was the big man's shop. If Riley could not go to her in comfort how could he? Tired of the noise, or perhaps impatient for the next customer, Riley finally spoke to her.

– Stop it. No need for all this fuss. You're just being silly. Stop it.

Her eyes and her shaking head said she could not.

– But of course you can. All you need to do is stand and pick up your overcoat, love, go home and pretend it never happened. You'll get used to it. Look, you've a mole almost as big under your tit and there's that mark up above your fanny that looks far worse! What's that from? They operate on your tubing?

This was Riley's tenth commandment argument – thou shalt get used to it. Thou shalt not pick thy scab was number one. The other eight were entirely changeable. New drama-

provided marks became old at some stage and ceased to offend, or to shock in the mirror. Surgical scars, by the onset of old age, were as familiar and bodily incorporated as a limb. The stretches of childbirth, like the lines on a brow, were simply mementos indicating the passage of life. Silky-looking bullet pools – there'd be a few of those in the shop, the business drew a crowd that was not unacquainted with attempted murder – were only a little bigger than vaccination scars or strawberry birthmarks. Tattoos could be briefly upsetting. But eventually they became ordinary components on the human anatomy. People went through life like well-handled jugs, collecting chips and scrapes and stains from wear and tear, from holding and pouring life.

Perhaps jolted by the man's indelicacy, the woman started talking.

– Wednesday I'm to be married. This Wednesday as a matter of fact.

Riley was unimpressed.

– What kind of silly day is that for a wedding, love?

– Oh, I know. They're busy Saturdays until Christmas.

It was Sunday afternoon. Still disaffected, Riley nodded, probably thinking she'd be accustomed to it by her marriage day. The woman's eyes had finished leaking but remained thick with water like bottle bottoms.

– It's funny, isn't it? How you might put something break-able in a place where you know it'll likely fall. My husband will like it, the tattoo. And, I didn't want him to. That's the thing of it. I didn't want him to like it.

Then, composed, she stood, picked up her overcoat and left the shop. Wishing what exactly never happened Cy did not know. This trade, he thought and not for the first time, was located at the darker end of town in many more ways than one. And in the event of being stumped by human obscurity, he decided, you just had to let it pass you by.

≈

Then one day Cy held the electric needle in his own hand and before he knew it ten years had passed by him! Ten years of Eliot Riley. Ten years in a storm of his behaviour and without the safe harbour of his mother. He had eventually stopped growing taller. He had learned to fight and evict brawlers from the vicinity, and to negotiate with the enemies of his employer. He had been enjoyed by women in the back room of Pedder Street, had seen some of his friends marry and produce children, he had become older, had become firmer, he had forgotten the exact face of Reeda, he had not visited the photograph of his father. And he could not remember what his first ever sold and paid for tattoo had been a picture of. A dragon. A butterfly. A heart. It didn't matter. The shop now had neon lights around its doorway, to attract passers-by, though still no signs or monikers or gimmickry, for Riley was of an older bent that did without the new jive and jazz-coat trappings. It was in any case well-known that there were two unrelated freehanders working side by side behind separate curtains within. Like partners without equality. Like father and son without the intimate connection. But two freehanders under one roof. Now that was a rarity. Amid all the professional rivalry and the slander and the battle of one ego and one reputation raging against another, in a trade where tattoo artists still acquired sheets of images subversively from each other and crossed out the designer's signature for their own, such collaboration was rare indeed. Eliot Riley had never suggested he move on, perhaps liking the position of authority of being the Pedder Street shop owner, and still the one they truly came for. And Cy had never chosen to leave, though he had the skills to set up on his own and frequently he had the bloody-minded will to do it.

He had grown to love the scent of skin. The way it told him something of the person in the chair. Their basic character, their occupation, their choice of artificial perfume spritzed on to that flexing medium with which he worked. The smell of skin was like the smell of an oil-primer. It signified the beginning of art. He had one leg entirely dedicated now to the hunt for a blue ink that was stable, he had messed up the appendage so badly under Riley's duress that it didn't really matter, his vanity was abandoned, and it became smudged and smeared with broken veins as pigment after pigment proved impossible to use. Twice he had mildly poisoned his blood, his ankle bone becoming manky with sores. The challenge of blue ink had become one of his inherited frustrations, passed down from the man who'd taught him how to paint, and how to hate, and, in conjunction, how, for his own sanity's sake to save any piece of gilded faith or instrument of celebration from the wreckage of the relationship that he could. At the start of every illumination festival, as the gales blew the bulbed garlands out to sea, Riley would say the same thing to him with an aggressive humour.

– They won't be asking us to switch on the lights this year, will they boy? They won't be asking us to put on our ties and dinner jackets and make a speech and throw that switch.

As if at every annual cusp Riley was giving Cy the opportunity to bow out from the underbelly operation. Or as if he was confirming Cy's position at the helm of first-mate to the captain of a perpetually sinking ship. There was something unnerving and continually harrowing about the man's embrace of pessimistic forces, how he thrived on conflict and ugliness, the malodorous aspects of life. Riley continued to manhandle people, to drink, to fight, even as he got slower, more pitiful, and less able to find ways to make other men want to challenge him. His hair greyed under his woollen hat. His good skin wrinkled. But his hand remained steady, and if he missed alcohol in the daytime his body did not show it by jerking and shaking when he needed it to be still. It was the one thing cherished by him – it was his saving grace. His redeeming talent. It countered his sooty mania. Until the inevitable happened, the inevitable opportunity of one long-time rival and his pals, from the bar or from the business, it was never clear, found him drunk or got him drunk and alone and took him to the old abandoned blacksmith's stable out near Moffat Ravine, waited until he was sober, so that he would be clear with his fate, and laid his right hand on a table. Then another of them produced a claw-iron from a bag and showed it to an ever-resisting ever-raging Eliot Riley. And then he used it. Five gavel hammers for Riley's guilty life. Five falling claw-iron pistons for his shuttle-bust fingers. Five colours to the pallet of the tattooer's spectrum – black, red, yellow, for the bruises which took off every nail, above every shattered bone which grew back crooked, green and brown for the gangrene infection which took off his middle digit completely. So that his crippled hand would never hold his equipment with enough dexterity to use it ever again. So that his saving grace was damned.

≈

But first Cy got the needle in his own hand. It happened one morning soon after Reeda's death when Riley was sleeping late and heavy from the night's drink, and as Cy was leaving the shop to buy bread a man asked him if he could have work done, and he accepted. He was tired of being told every time he got close to being an artist, to being a fully working tattooist, that some slip, some invisible flaw, some bloody unidentifiable cruel mystery of a failure had discredited him, made him ineligible for promotion, that he had failed Eliot Riley. He was tired of being filled with impotent anger and confusion, or sulking upstairs, tired of the snide, petty arguing, which always ensued from Cy's failed examination, which the master thrived upon, flaring up to it like an itch that's scratched.

– Well, I was going to let you start next week but you've blown it, lad. I had it all planned, you would have been sitting over there, happy as Larry, with your own kit. You've nobody to blame but yourself.

– What did I do wrong? I did fuck all!

– You know what you did. And if you need telling, that just proves what a stupid article you truly are.

Cy brought the customer inside, took the money, and prepared his body exactly as he'd seen Riley do a hundred times. He coloured in his first black-bordered image, bottom corner up to top so as not to smear the transfer, working in a small pool of ink, steadily, interpreting lines beneath it. And how the needle sang when it was put on someone else's body! Like a tuning fork struck against a piece of wood. An entirely different melody than that made from working on his own leg. And his mind rushed out to all the aspects of chromatic nature, and came back within the image he was making. Whatever that image had been that he didn't remember, but he did a decent job and the customer was happy. And by the time the man had put his shirt back on Riley was awake and downstairs and watching.

– About time you started pulling your weight around here, lad. Wondered when you'd get your finger out of your arse. Next time use your own chair, that one is mine.

– I don't have a chair.

– Well best you get to the scrappy's and buy one. Gun purrs like a cock that's shooting, doesn't it?

And then there was another tattoo and another. And fairly soon the electric singing was a familiar song. He went from standard designs to freehand images, though he was only permitted to work if Riley was out of the Pedder Street shop or there was more than one customer waiting at a time, like a young lion guarding a den when the alpha male was away.

What never changed was the voice within Cy's mind in the moments before he began working, in the brief interval between the removal of clothing from a piece of flesh, administering the cleaning fluid, the grease, and the tactility of human against needle, during which time he would ask a simple one-word question.

– Ready?

And in that small portion of time he was really asking many things. He was seeking, one final, crucial time, an endorsement of the metamorphosis, for which he was in part responsible, and the customer was in part responsible. He was waiting for their signature on a contract they had drawn together, before he also wrote his own in ink. Because some did get up and leave the shop, right at that moment. And some had their faces fall half way through the procedure for they hadn't truly decided. He might not even always vocalize the question, he might just have assumed they were hearing it, considering it, but always that small amount of time was set aside, an escape route out of the prison, a burning walkway from the flaming pavilion. On the outside it seemed to produce tension, that period of impending discomfort being so very quiet, and Riley continued to berate him for it, saying what he needed to do was talk the customer into comfort.

– Doesn't matter if you've not got one interesting thing to say to them. Make up a story. Tell a joke. Saying nowt to them is like not having songs sung at their funeral or not having a toast at their wedding! Bad form is what it is, lad. It's just not done.

But it was a doctrine of Cy's religion, it was his own brand of ceremony. And oddly, there was no real silence in those moments. Not inside Cy's mind anyway. In those seconds before he started, strange little hymns of thought chorused through his brain. Words that were a last-minute warning, words that were encouraging, or applauding. Like testimonies for those writing their histories on their bodies, because there was no better place for those chapters to be written. For those taking the insignia of the country, who were made of their nation. For those catching the name of the women they loved, who would love her in some permanent way always until they died or forgot her. For those selecting war armour, who would have conflict around them until they were too old and weak to lift a fist and their banners were meaningless. For those destroying and recreating themselves. For those bringing to their skin only that which their heart was capable of making. For those becoming a cipher of meaning. For those being reborn, selecting the organs of their lives, unravelling the probabilities of themselves, and turning away from their invisible, ether-blank souls. So frequently his mind said these things that in the end even he began not to hear it. He just let the silence tell it.

~

Often Cy wondered about the night of Riley's assault, when his mind and faculty were murdered, for it marked the beginning of his death. Cy let his imagination go out to the possibilities of what occurred, he let it haunt him. There might have been a morning hawk above the ravine when the men held him down, moving with some kind of patience through the pale air, a calming tipped-winged movement above him, something to focus on as his eyes came out of their distorted vision shortly before they began. Like a piece of his spirit having got free. Those slow-waking hours between last orders and daybreak, as he waited for his abductors to take of him whatever they were going to take, his throat eventually becoming raw and hoarse with protestation, may have been the most acutely aware hours ever spent by Riley, when he suddenly noticed details like the smell of burning as the dew came on to the moor, or the rings under the feet of insects in an old barrel of water, treading as if with secret knowledge of the water's masonry. And he might have noticed how a man's face in barbarity will show traces of compassion even though it is already determined in its fulfilment of cruelty. Or he might have dulled himself away from reality, like some could under the needle in the chair, that numbing oriental style of slumber. Until the sensation of the claw hammer on his skin and bone came, like the purest thing Eliot Riley had ever felt in his life. It might have been purer than even electricity, Cy thought. Riley may have passed out more than once with pain and loss of blood on the four-mile walk back from the scene of his sick trial, his hand doubled in original size and screaming its condition. Cy would never know these things for sure, for he was never told what occurred. All he knew was that Eliot Riley arrived home shortly after the milk had been delivered on the doorstep, with the face of a dead man and his arm strung up inside his coat, looking like mince, looking like tendrils of riverweed when it was revealed. Then he sat down in his wooden chair and fell asleep. As if sleep was the next best thing to admitting defeat.

~

It took almost a year for Riley to finish dying. After he was sentenced by his assailants, abused, and exiled from his profession, he willed himself dead, like a bird in a cage that will not compromise its nature. He went about it methodically. He would kill himself with drink and depression and starvation. Half a bottle of liquor past possible human consumption a night. As little food as physically manageable before hunger sent him mad and ratching like a badger through the kitchen for scraps. All the melancholy he could summon about him, to eat away at his mind. Where once he had given pathetic assistance to Cy and Paddy when they half-carried him home, shuffling his feet, grunting for them to stop so he could vomit, now he was a dead-weight that often had to be dragged along the road and pavement. No more useful than a sack of potatoes. And if they weren't careful he'd leave his head back and choke on his own sick and Cy would have to grope about in his soupy mouth for his missing tongue. There were times when the washroom above Eleven Pedder Street was such a mess with blood and shit and vomit and all three together that Cy wondered if the man had been swallowing his own needles, like Chatterton with his lacerated lunched-on poems in his attic. Again in his life he would have to remove the stinking, revolting waste of a suffering individual, like a nursemaid, like a bloody nursemaid. Not even false hope in the air this time, nor his mother's noble acceptance. Just long, meaningless, suicidal death. Riley often stayed in his bed until the late afternoon, would not even answer if Cy knocked on his door. He lay bent round on the mattress like a baby under an old blanket, his breathing slower than any human lung should endure. Cy would try to get him to eat something, anything. A biscuit. A piece of cheese. He tempted him and tried to trick him into it like he was a fussy infant. Where once he had crept around him with cups of pacifying or demanded tea, now he trod heavily, bringing fresh brews in the hope that Riley would put something into his thinning, reddening body. Occasionally a sentence here and there in response, so Cy would become hopeful, if there were words issued there was part of a brain left over to see reason. If he had enough passion to curse, he had enough care to live.

– Leave me alone, boy. Can't you see it, you fucking imbecile, can't you see it's all over now? I'm sleeping. I'm sleeping. Go away.

Still a lad, still a boy, to Eliot Riley, though Cy was well on his way to thirty. Though he played the youth, didn't he? The tenderfoot, the loyal subject and the looby, as if to give the man his position back, restore him to his throne. He would try to get him involved with the trade again by asking foolish questions, whose answers he already knew. Where was the best place to store ink pigment in the winter so it wouldn't spoil? Which was the best manufacturer to go to for the liquid black? As if he had forgotten his monthly trips to Hagan's in Lancaster for the last ten years. Were brass or steel coils better for the new electric motor? The photography shop was closing down and selling off its goods, did the boss want him to get whatever old dry-point celluloid they may have left over for stencilling material? There were never any answers. Just a slammed door. A room empty of dialogue. Blue eyes paling and melting and dissolving against skin, like a glacier mint in a mouth.

He drank. Night and day, Riley drank whatever he could get hold of. When there was no money and Paddy wouldn't serve him, for his own good, he stole bottles from shops. Or he went with groups of comrade-desolates around the slums of Moss Street to sup on rot and pauper's brews. Even the alcohol spirit solution in the cupboard was taken so that it wasn't safe to keep it, and Cy had to blend powder with distilled water to make his ink. And he was left thinking, thinking about a time when Riley had informed him, with crude gusto, that in this craft any solution could be used to dissolve and bind pigments – blood, spit, a woman's juice, semen, piss – it was an ancient, resilient, inventive industry.

The customers still asked for him. His reputation did not cease to exist just because his will to go on without his loved and soul-fortifying profession did. Cy would have to explain that he was retired now, resting upstairs, unavailable, the way he had first lied about Riley's fits to Jonty and Morris, and for it he would often lose a sale. What other honesty could he give them? That the man was dropped down in his own waste somewhere around the town, body parts foul like a gutter, crevices stinking of built-up dirt, and his mind no cleaner than a septic tank? That his once good, colourful Welsh skin was busting open with rag-ended capillaries and his hand was a disabled stump? That he'd become one of those desperately exploding men who mumble and yell at folk because they can't or don't want to speak clearly, and if let wander in that direction he would put his four-fingered hand on the train tracks because he was that bloody determined? That he was already dead, that he was already rotting? No.

Here was a young fellow working in the parlour of the greatest tattooer of northern England and the master was not around. There was something treacherous and suspicious about it, something not quite right. Together they might have tattooed the top of their country's masses, alone he was implicated in some crime, or failed venture, and was suddenly without reputation. A ventriloquist's wooden dummy without the speaker. For it seemed Cyril Parks could only live in Eliot Riley's shadow if the shadow of his master still lived also.

~

It was a life completed by the last sour joke of Eliot Riley dying on April the first, appropriately bad-humoured until the end. But it was not plain old-fashioned dying, not passing on as a natural last function of the body, or being triumphed over by a disease like Cy's mother had been, that would have been too simple and not had enough of a bastard's composition to it. He got hold of something rank and poisonous that would sit for a while in his gut removing its lining and then making him pour blood up from his mouth like a fountain. It was bleach. Ordinary washing bleach, of the kind that kept white collars white in the nicer houses of Morecambe Bay, the kind that had cleansed the Bayview's tuberculosis basins. He'd gone from wine bottles in pockets and a bad charm to his philosophy and swagger, to caustic industrial solvent that robbed his body of its ability to clot blood and its ability to stop heaving. By the close of it there was enough blood in his room to mop the floors with. Enough to paint the sky with. Most of it not in any basin, for Riley was twisting and writhing on the floor and unable to control his sickness – the regurgitation of every evil thing that was in him, every drop of loathsome emotion that spewed forth like an exorcism. And when it was gone, so too would he be, because hemispheres cannot live one without the other, for those born in two parts, black and white hearted. So his final empty unequal peace would last but a few minutes. He made it home from wherever he had taken his terrible potion and up the stairs before the demise of his body really started, so that he could have Cy see him, and hear him as he spoke more words than he had said all bitter year. With the last of his blue eyes and his fat-lipped mouth he said that finally something shackled had been removed from him, like the manacles of Socrates before his hemlock execution. And though in great pain from the holes being punched in his stomach and in pain from his tattered life, there was at last a deeper absence of agony in him, which was a pleasure for knowing well the other. Between great choking mouthfuls he gave his soft departure, as if to a son he'd always wanted but never had it in him to acknowledge, making his potential to beget and brook and love apparent, making it impossible to wholly hate the man, making it impossible to ever take his catheter needle out.

– Good lad. Good lad. Shop's yours now. Left to you, officially. You'll be grand, if you stay by the sea. That's the trick, we're meant to be by water, folk like you and me. No more than a stone's throw from her. She's our muse, lad. She smells like a woman in your bed when the rain hits her, did you know that? That's where you'll have them put me. Out at sea. Make me a promise, make it your word. Out at sea. You've your mother's eyes, lad, you've her eyes.

And Cy didn't know if he was weeping for his dead mother, or his dead and dying fathers, or because there was just death in the red room. Or because it was over and his ship had broken free of the rocks and was miraculously still afloat, even though the captain was strung up in the crow's nest with his throat slit wide open, and not a soul left on board knew how to sail.

~

The body was released to the authorities and then claimed back by Cyril Parks. It was a remarkable body, for all its ruination and its infiltration with drink, the sagging skin and sorry legacy of abuse. There were whole worlds and stories written on it. It was as a piece of polished heather root or something that had been kept in the ground and under the force of heat and pressure of many ages had become gem-like. And on the sole of the right foot, in tiny curving script, was the poem, not recognized by the undertaker but recognized by Cy as he had taken Riley's boots off on the bed when he lay still, flooded with his own rust-red waters. It was the only time he had removed the man's boots, though many, many times he had wrestled his fully clothed, limp body into positions where it could be left to sober. And on this last, post-mortem occasion, with his hands trembling as they untied the laces, he had needed to do it, to make the episode formal, a proper Maundy gesture amid the squalor of the room. It was a poem, which Riley had fancied as meaningful and had stolen as a possession of his own. Like the books in his rooms, like the dissembling ideas of art with their approbation of only the most controversial agenda.

> *Tyger! Tyger! burning bright,*
> *In the forests of the night,*
> *What immortal hand or eye*
> *Could frame thy fearful symmetry?*

And wasn't that about right for the fucker, thought Cy.

The body was wrapped and prepared for burial at sea and it was taken out on a chartered fishing vessel into the Irish Channel and dumped overboard without ceremony as the sun was setting, so that Riley, with his Celtic looks and his split identity might have found his way into some ancient Gaelic paradise by accident, if God and the Devil were not quick enough to settle the dispute over him. Cy leaned on the side of the boat and watched the sunset on the waves. What had his mother told him as a boy in her spinner-woman nursery-time way? That when the sun went away its light never went out, it only went to Ireland, and then it went to America, and then right around the world until it came back in the morning. And it was some kind of lamp for all lost souls to follow. So he watched it leaving, turning a slow red corner of the earth, the sky above it pale blue and doomed with intensity before it shut down, like Riley's eyes. Behind him somewhere was Morecambe Bay, with its strange long tide and all his life's history. His home. The place that had shaped him from its sand and clay. The place that had set him up well in the first half of life only to make room for his faltering and to allow his tumble in the next half. Because wasn't he fallen? Wasn't he as lost and low as he could possibly be? Like one of the ragged souls of Reeda's fables. The boat wallowed gently in the current for a time, then began back to shore. And at that moment Cy did not want his home, majestic or malfeasant, he would have renounced it gladly, and paid all the money he had ever owned and a tithe on all he would ever earn to have the fishing vessel come about and head west in the wake of the sun.

Late that night he took a drink at the Dog and Partridge with Paddy and toasted Eliot Riley, though neither of them spoke beyond that of the man lest his recently departed spirit become blackened with the pluming particles of ill-thought and defamation. Paddy reached behind the bar and pulled out a bottle of whisky and poured a dram for Cy, his first proof liquor ever. The fumes were as wretched as the taste but he took the contents of the glass whole.

– What of Cyril Parks next then? Get yourself a pretty missy and raise a brood? Will you be able to cope with all the trade this summer?

Cy shook his head and shrugged.

– Well. You could become a travelling man. Find yourself a circus to join. See the world. Send me some postcards to put up in the bar and impress people with my connections.

– Is the world a better place than Morecambe then, Paddy?

– Well, I believe it's bigger. And there are no doubt fewer donkeys. Some people say it's a small world, of course. But, I wouldn't like to have to paint it.

≈

The next day Cy locked the door of Eleven Pedder Street and took a train to the city of Liverpool, then took a hire carriage out to the docks, where he met with an acquaintance of Paddy Broadbent behind the dripping dolly crane. The woman sold him counterfeit passport and papers and permits, rolling the money received into the handle of her umbrella and never looking Cy in the face. Then he bought a third-class ticket, with the last of Reeda's money, on a ship bound for America.

≈

The *Adriatic* was a four-mast, four steam-engine, Harland & Wolff built monster. She'd run the Atlantic for twenty-five years since her Belfast birth, ferrying immigrants, cargo and the wealthy backwards and forwards to the new world, when she wasn't vacationing in the Mediterranean, and she'd seen every kind of weather. She'd held Russians and Polish Jews, Lithuanians and Czechoslovakians, who first made passage through the North Sea and took a train to reach her, and thousands of Irish Catholics who took steamers from their native ports to Liverpool docks. She held oil, and coal, the belongings of many nations, and occasionally lowing, bleating cattle. The rich luxuriated in her polished dining rooms, or the indoor pool, the Turkish bath, while the poor were sent down towards the lower decks, near her two propellers, where the noise of her motion was mature and continuous. She was the last of the Big Four vessel quartet run by White Star liners, a fine old lady retired in her later years now to the summer transatlantic passage. In May of 1933 Cyril Parks boarded her, one year before the Cunard–White Star merger, one year before she would be laid up permanently then sold to the Japanese and broken up for parts. To Cy she was magnificent, simply because she was whole and moving. He'd seen so many battered, wrecked and ravaged vessels out at Ward's Ship-breakers – they looked like noble prehistoric beasts bonded and tortured – that the *Adriatic* was miraculous in her capacity and condition. At first her groans and internal knocking and the noise of her robust metallic sashaying left him uneasy, for it seemed that parts of the structure were unhappy in their bolted proximity with each other and were trying to separate. Then it became apparent that she was simply living, her sounds became the music of a giant iron body, breathing, digesting, beating, and it was comforting. The wake behind the ship was tremendous, like Moby Dick spouting water through a blow-hole. Almost three thousand passengers doing seventeen knots had their hats tugged off by the ocean breeze when they came out to grip the railing, to bid farewell to the continent slipping away behind them, or to play shuffle-board on the middle decks. They were citizens of a small city floating out to a promised land.

There was work for Cy on board the ship, more work than he ever imagined or expected, in the third-class cabins and the sailors' quarters, many wanted motifs done, to celebrate new beginnings, or finished struggles. And with both of these sentiments Cyril Parks could certainly sympathize. In his suitcase he had his equipment and four books of bound-together manila flash, Riley's designs cut down from the walls of the shop and his own never before displayed pic-tures. Each page was dedicated to a certain theme, skulls, hearts, lovelies. That which had covered the walls of the par-lour could now fit in a large pocket. He set up a little station on F deck where they came to him and waited their turn, browsing through the notebooks, often pointing to a tattoo without knowing the English word for it, writing the names of loved ones down on scraps of paper so that he could spell them out with unfamiliar letters and etch it through a heart. So that left-behind wives or sweethearts or daughters were not so very much forgotten.

The *Adriatic*'s sailors went in for women, patriotism, and souvenirs. Codes. Their codes were precise and adhered to as men of the navy, there were rules at sea, similar to those which would only permit a soldier to wear a medal if it had been won in service. There were anchors for crossing the Atlantic, turtles for passing the equator, and dragons for being stationed in China. Often barnyard animals on the balls of their fists, which was an old, old tradition that still prevailed, animals that liked to keep dry and would scramble out of water quickly in a panic should they need to. Roosters. Pigs. It was ugly flash, but Cy was nobody to deny a man his superstition. The men followed strict, professional qualifications, would not have a mark done without having earned credit for it and they wanted to assure him of entitlement with stories of voyages as he prepared and stencilled their shoulder.

– When I crossed to the Cape with Blue Flue we hit a storm so big it put us back a week. A week I tell you, in this day and age, isn't it madness. The thing would not let up. Not that I'm complaining, mind, I thought my number was being called. Waves bigger than Cader Idris, I tell no lie.

It was honour and accomplishment. It was a maritime record like a ship's log. When Cy first apprenticed with Eliot Riley, Riley had told him that he'd been tattooing so long he'd even done a few *hold* and *fast* tattoos on the knuckles of old-timeys on sailing ships and clippers. As if he'd been born before the age of steam! Riley could have shipped ice to the North Pole though, until he got too drunk to make feasible his lying.

The shop in Morecambe had witnessed its fair share of naval customers. They were the old uncles and true souls of the industry, perhaps the rational explanation of Riley's riparian assertion that tattooists gravitate to water. Here on board the ship there were old retired navy boys, who had sailed with the empire's fleets since before the war and during, who had come back to the country with the decorations of the world, Japanese love-dots and *ukiyo-e*, traditional south hemisphere markings, and now they couldn't stop dressing up their skin. They came to him and filled up the last little pieces of clear flesh with ornamentation. Some of their existing work had even been done using a woodcut technique with the ink chipped and rubbed in, but with all the vernacular skill that Cy had not possessed when Riley demanded he do it to his own leg. These tattoos were primitive, effective, beautiful, in his time at Morecambe he had even seen some done on faces, Maori moko style, though Cy knew that took a man who had lost something of his country to the different one, as if he knew his blood was journeying wrong and he was trying to find its source. The old sea-travellers who had collected foreign marks were exotic, alligator-skinned men, men who had passed through a spiritual threshold and met something sacred head-on in the delirium of pain. They were strong,

143

strong in their discomfort, strong in their minds, men for whom the tapping of ink blocks into skin might in their heads become the beat of a song, clung to like a chanty to get them through the strenuous endeavour. It was true engraving, disparate at the edges so you could know it was a deep art, deeper than it needed to be for permanence – the colour and the scar coming together in something ritualistic. This was the most painful method of tattooing Cy knew of, and he knew of it all right as Eliot Riley got him to begin his training that way, raking off skin on his shins with that piece of blacked bamboo and a mason's mallet, not sixteen years old and already scarred up like a battle-torn soldier. Having to hammer ink down on to his bone before he got anywhere near the helpful electric needle or exaction. The pure agony had him hating Riley, hating the man for the pedantic devils within him, the humiliation of that initial pedigree, and for crying in front of his master who had knelt with his hands pushing down on Cy's feet, roaring at him to continue when the pain got too much, slapping his face softly like he was a blathering girl. Yes, he could respect these men, these sailors and travellers who'd seen the method through to the full torso pattern, black nippled, with knots of red along their hipbones and thighs, backbones crackling like the spine of a lizard. Because the pain was immeasurable, the blood loss was fantastic and any infection could be lasting, occasionally deadly if it wasn't treated quick enough. Sailors had sometimes come into Pedder Street with whole stories on their backs, right down to their calves. Maps of where they'd been without the need for countries, or seas. There were the markings of Japan, New Zealand, Fiji. He would try to decipher what had been put on them. He would pull away a shirt and sit and smoke a cigarette and interpret them, respectfully, before he started adding anything else.

~

Open ocean was a reflective, ponderous, dangerous place to be. A place of sickness and cabin-fever and contemplation, where it was said a person might meet up with their own self at a central axis travelling from another set of coordinates in life. There was something about the swollen surge of the sea that set the mind free, gave it a queer loose balance and direction like a compass riding on gimbals on the ship's bridge. So that time spent alone seemed amplified by significance and conversations with fellow passengers, while often very welcome, could take on prematurely intimate or confidential proportions.

– Afternoon to you, Mr Parks. Looking a tad vexed today, if you don't mind my saying.

– Hello, Harry. It's a long way back now, isn't it, England? Will we miss it, I wonder?

– I should think in the end we'll manage without her. I'll not miss the Scrubs, which is where I'd be residing presently if it were not for the ingenious garter of my good lady. Just a shame she missed the boat really. I'll not mention her name in case the authorities tackle you anon about meeting me in the middle of this old stone boat called fate. Still, I'm sure America has its fair share of ingenious women.

– We'll keep our fingers crossed, shan't we?

Luckily for Cy, and perhaps because he had inherited his father's sea-legs and nautical tolerance, he suffered from neither the sickness nor the fever. But he did fall into thinking, fell into the condition with heaviness. Or a great, weighty thinking fell on him, like a piano slipping its fastening as it was hauled up a building and landing on his head. Either way they met. In his slim bunk at night, to the churning purr of the engines and the ruck of propellers through dark water, in a cabin of twenty other snoring men, his mind went out to the things that had formed him and been farmed from him. In the deep baths of the washroom, with the soapy water mirroring the sea's external motions, he could lie for hours and be oblivious to the minutes that passed, annoying the steward who had others queuing for the facility. As he dressed the bodies with ink stolen from the Captain's helm or the first-class lounges, he thought of his life, its gains and losses. He thought of Riley and his mother. There were memories like artefacts, half-there and jagged, suggesting a shape that was apparent but unfinished, as if misused or harmed by something, or waiting to be completed. At the rail of the *Adriatic*, outside her glassed-in walkways, salt-water smeared like the windows of the Bayview, with Riley's lyrical rain on the waves scented strongly like a woman in the throes of love, and the deck made slick and slippery, he leaned looking out with his face on his fist, as if stopped in time in a position of self-battery. The whole Atlantic surface was like a blue and white tablecloth to the edges of nowhere for him to lay his memories upon like dashed apart, salvaged crockery. And he thought about who he was and what he did and why.

What was it that had drawn him to the occupation of painting flesh, of permanent living art, and had kept him there through all the shit and shovel of Eliot Riley? What was he that he went to it and stayed put while the gentle humour of Morecambe evaporated around him in all but the tattoo barker's showroom comedy? There were times when he could take no more from the man, no more abuse or inclusion in his province of mind, his wretched damaging honesty, the butchery of esteem, and he could have smashed Riley's head against the wall like a turnip until his sneering voice stopped once and for all. There were times when he had looked at his dwindling bundle of money and got as far as the train station. Then turned back. Where was the reward for all that masochistic persistence and endurance? The dispatching of his youth. The decay of his happy childhood. The reluctant temper that was made unobstructed by following the big man's example. What was it about the trade that was day to the night of Riley? Suddenly Cy wanted an answer. Without it he was a piece from the past in the ruins of a decade. But like the bawdy pauper king himself had once told him it was

146

impossible to pin down the exact appeal and beauty of their folkish profession, butterfly-captured and gorgeously open for all to see. You couldn't find the marrow or the quick of it to suck out, or set a flame to the wick of it and illuminate a room. Tattooing was like being called by a siren song, or the music of the spheres, impossible to resist, impossible to explain.

– Ask any one of us, lad, the good ones, not these buggers who do it for show, and we'll all give the same answer. Why do we do it? Don't fucking know.

No, he could not find the degree of precision that his own hand delivered during the colourful transformation of others, to explain it, to explain his own part in it, though he tried hard with his knuckles on his cheekbone and his hours at the deck rail. His trade was about conveying meaning, about visual abbreviation, an indication of what elements a creature was comprised. Like the red hourglass on the black widow spider. Like the fangs and poison and claws and stripes found in nature. It was a non-verbal language. It had inherent meaning. How many war signs and symbols had he tattooed? A thousand, more? How many predatory markings designed to elicit terror, how much hostile camouflage, how many death banners, daggers, skulls, slogans, how much battle pride?

Then there were the signs of sex, the big-titted women, the kitten girls, the exhibition of body parts, the twists on the spigot of breeding. Rude puns and come-ons. And there was love. Love in all its forms was boiled back to the red heart like beef to stock. All those hearts he had been commissioned to render. Heart after heart after red, red heart. Fat and full with *True Love*, with *Mother*, with *Anita*, with *Josephine*, with *Clara* inside, pierced by Cupid's spindly arrows. Or broken, cut into two, torn open, *Deceived* written through the separated sections so that there could be no mistake as to why the damage had occurred. Such scars of emotion that would never heal! Or they would heal through his intervention, by being made secondary in ink. Because he could give pain a shape, and he could place it. And always the customers wanted to tell him about it. Their stories that had deserved an indelible memento. He was a funnel through which confidences and lives passed, became pigmented. His was a position of confidentiality, a tailor cutting round the balls of society, he would fashion the essence of a person, their experiences, into quick information or codification on the body where henceforth the public could read it from them. That was it. The tattoo was a jump too far. It was implicit. It was explicit. It was utter intimacy, intimacy with the whole basic fucking, killing, loving world. These were the prime colours of the life, were they not, the original three, and human beings simply mixed them up into civilized hues from there.

Riley had been right. Underneath all the rambling philosophy that went nowhere, that made Cy want to curse at him for such pretension, there was one thing the man had seen. He had seen people stripped bare, he had reduced them down into an essence, to experience, who they really were – angels and demons and lovers and everything strung in between. He cut them back and went from there. He seemed able to do it, to pull a picture off a wall, personalize and tattoo it. Riley had once told him that it was not those big titties on a bare arm that offended, not farting ladies, nor a marked face. Tattooing was on the black side, yes, not because it dealt largely with the rougher working classes, not because it meant that sex and danger and opinion got put about in pictures on people like a rude proclamation. The boldness of it wasn't liked often, granted; the tattoo might even be considered ugly or primitive in itself. That counted towards their trade's bad reputation, but it was not solely responsible for it. The matter of public disturbance was not as simple as violated flesh or visual shock. What had the big man said?

– Tattooing distresses those it does, lad, because it's as generous as a whore on her birthday. It's human art that you can't peel back off the human or put away in a dresser drawer. It's an unselfish trade, is ours. I'll tell you what it is, it's personal socialism, lad. Everyone's included, everyone gets to look in to a person and share them, like what they see or not. It says here I am, shit and come and all. Nationality, how I like my women, what does it for me. Just like a bullet hole into the guts and bowels. Oh aye, and I'll tell you this, lad: a tattoo says more of a fellow looking at it than it can do of the man who's got it on his back. And people don't like each other half the time, they don't like each other's opinions or lives, they don't want to sympathize with each other, they don't want to share, so what they do is shoot the messenger. You and me. Scapegoats is what we are. What we do is in bad taste, they say, oh, it's not artistic. When what it really is, is people like to keep each other strangers until they've judged. You remember that.

And Cy had not understood it then, thinking it just polite society's snobbery, and thinking Riley a bag of talking shit, he had not really understood it until now, here, ensconced on F deck of the *Adriatic*, tattooing perhaps his five-hundredth ruptured heart. And the man on whose shoulder the heart was coming was sitting as silent as stone, with tears running down his face for the woman he had lost and left back in Warsaw or Prague or Moscow. As true to the image as a shadow to any dimensional thing. Suddenly Cy knew what it was all about. He saw past the red ink going into the skin. He saw through to the core of what he was doing, how he bestowed uncompromising communication upon the world, how he brought forth self. How he translated experience and identity into colour and shape. How he caught the echo of a person and engraved it on to them. How he functioned as the artistic hands of others, redundant in choosing subject maybe yet imperative in its delivery. That was the strange and impossible core of it.

Humans had gone well beyond the red hourglass and the simplicity of natural informative markings. They had evolved, complicated life, refined it, and lost touch. They had tried to push back the basics, the cruelty and poison, the seeds and urges, the nurture and beauty. The potential to love and kill, having loved and killed, the need to rut, could not be an initial introduction any more, set on a shoulder like a swarthy badge of life. Yet some would have it that way still, they would have the ordinary speech of identity, the colours of their landscape, that which they had in common with the rest of the human beings of the world, and Cyril Parks was just their scribe.

Eliot Riley was gone. He was contained by death, finished, and his life's picture had become clear. Who he was, a drunk, a bastard, a master of ink. Blue eyed in Cy's memory, brilliant and awful, loved and hated. The only flesh-and-blood father he had ever known. He was the definition of Eliot Riley, and he had left his mark. Like a force of nature, like an earthquake bending a river, a volcano scarring mountains with lava or lightning striking tree bark. Like a tattoo on Cy's life. And only then, with the understanding and realization, through Riley's own death, of that which the man had tried to convey alive, did Cy's apprenticeship to him truly end.

~

– These buggers are open books.

Riley had once said this to Cy as another Ribble bus-load of drunken Scots arrived one September and spewed forth its cargo on to the promenade at Morecambe. The air had been cool that day and the sun seemed hot only when it reached Cy's bare arms, as if not having done much work in warming up the space between. One of the passengers had clambered down the bus steps and gone to the railing at the edge of the seafront parade. He pissed off the platform as if standing at the public urinal while drinking from a brown bottle at the same time.

– Open books. But they know who they are. They can tell you with a punch or a stiff cock or a few words exactly who they are and where they come from. Take a country away from someone and it firms up their notions. Tells them what they want to be and what they don't. Makes my job easier, son. A lot easier. No dawdling about deciding on a tattoo. They know what they want and why they want it.

– They want rampant lions and the St Andrew's cross, no doubt, or Rangers colours, eh?

Cy remembered he had said this somewhat smugly, thinking himself capable of a certain amount of discerning and prediction after a year's apprenticeship. The Scots were singing a song about virgins in Inverness, happy to have arrived at last on their annual holiday. Riley had been walking away from them but at this remark he stopped and turned back to Cy.

– No. No, lad. I paint hearts. And I paint souls. That's what I do.

Back then it had seemed a ridiculous thing to say. Too much like the great Eliot Riley on a flight of fancy, getting wordy and profound, trying to make Cy feel like the village idiot again. But the comment stuck with Cy for some reason, perhaps because it sounded good, the sound of the words themselves had a note of quiet percussion to them, unlike Riley's usual loud and boasting bluff, or perhaps just because aspects of the man were like burdock that got on to you and sank in. And Cy remembered what he said that afternoon. And then one day, years later and half way across the Atlantic Ocean, with a country lost from sight behind him, an old life scuppered and a new one about to be launched, it became true.

PART II

– Babylon in Brooklyn –

Coney Island lay colourful and flashing and ready for revelry under a dull coat of inclement weather. It was a slow day, with pedestrian business responding to the greyish skies overhead, the glitz and hum of the parks seeming all the more stark and garish for the lack of visitors to justify their existence. The mazed walkways, the decorated blinking gateways and turnstiles into the fairgrounds were almost deserted, the rides and the shows were quiet but for their own character exertion. On days like this the whole place gave the gimcrackery impression of a bright and showy and useless thing, or a clown vigorously juggling for empty rows of seating in a circus tent, primed and pathetic and somehow futile. Coney's beach could seem as dire against the damp and drizzle as it could be inviting on days of clear sunshine. The sand looked logged with water, heavy and turgid. The Wonder Wheel in Luna Park was turning through the mist, providing a view of nothing but cloud for the few in its carriage seats, perhaps a stray patch of the city in the distance where there was an opening in the fog. For the past half hour Cy had been chatting with the hotdog vendor opposite his booth in the alley, smoking cigarettes, passing the time under the rattling, dripping awning of the meat stand. The grease-aproned man was stirring up his sauerkraut with a spoon and complaining half-heartedly about trade as if for something to do rather than with earnest concern.

– Half my stock will go bad if I can't boil it by the week's end. I'm going to have to ditch it with the fishermen for bait, the fish really go for the fat see, chicken bones too, go figure, or I end up eating fifty a day myself and I ain't that hard a worker. Nobody will put up with old meat these days, not that I'd serve it mind with those sanitation chumps breathing down my neck. Listen, you come back when you leave and take a box of bratwurst home with you. Hate to see it go to waste. You gonna take off, board up early?

– No, no. I'll hold on a spell. Never know, do you?

– Nope. Never know what they'll hand you down here. Hey, you gonna do my Rosie over sometime? Her tits are beginning to fade. Gotta have those red tits! Old Grady Feltz did a good job on her for one of them navy yard boxer guys, and blind in the eye and wearing that damn patch and all, but she's beginning to go a little at the chest. Her and the wife, I love my wife but you know what I mean. She's my lucky charm, my Rosie, got to keep her looking sweet and shiny, right?

– Come on by later if there's nothing doing.

Some of the other tattoo artists did not bother opening on wet days at Coney. For Cy it was a different matter – had he closed up shop in Morecambe on every poor day he would have lost two-thirds of his business or more. Besides, there were those who felt an urge to come to him on broody, over-cast days, or the rain would pull them in off the boardwalk and beach to the inside venues past his place of work, and they might be struck with the inspiration to get tattooed. Sure enough two men were walking up the narrow avenue with caps turned slightly down against the first mention of rain coming in off the Atlantic and when they got to Cy's booth they paused to look at the bright, fluttering walls of the small hut. The vendor gestured with an uncooked sausage to him that he had customers and better go. Cy ground out his cigarette under his heel and approached the men, his hands in his pockets, his stride long. And without a moment's hesi-tation the brassy polished voice of his profession left his mouth.

– Grand day, gents. Seems this is fine English weather we'd be experiencing here. I knew it wouldn't take too long for it to find me hiding in your great country. I suppose my old missus must have sent it as a present for our happy parting. What'll it be for you? I can see you're both men who know your minds, which means you know you want the best and you've found it. Your girls' names with a red rose perhaps, in keeping with this fine English weather, eh? No better way to say you love 'em than their name on your shoulder. This one here's a beauty. A prize-winner, I'd say, perfect as any from the King of England's palace gardens, am I right? And since it's my national weather day I'll work you both for two dollars and the King'll think you stole those roses right out of his garden from under his nose.

The patter of rain, the patter of the trade, it was as easy as that now, when he wanted it to be, when he switched to a higher gear in his brain. It was as easy as starting anew in another country and introducing himself as a brighter version of what he had been.

The men continued looking at the flash. A bulb was flickering on the sign festooning the doorway. Cy reached up and moved it in its hub and it calmed its erratic light. Underneath that was a painted sign that read 'The Electric Michelangelo, Freehander, Antiseptic treatment, Crude Work Removal, No Tattoos under 18 years of age'. There was a picture of an artist's palette with a paintbrush resting on it underneath the lettering. Cy's hair was tied back with a piece of black ribbon, and in his left ear was a pearl, as if he were a character from another century. This was his life now. This was who he was.

One of the men seemed more serious than the other, examining the pictures lengthily while his pal chuckled at bare ladies and grinning, horned faces. Cy turned his attention to the first man.

– Sir, you look like a boxer to me, am I right about that? It's in the shoulders, if you'll pardon the interpretation. What do you say to a champion middleweight puncher right along your back and your name alongside it? What's your name, sir?

– Eddie.

– Nothing fits on a man's back better than his ability to fight, Eddie. That's a talent to be proud of. That lets other men know the situation right off the bat. Repels the rivals. Keeps the public informed, you could consider it a service.

Eddie shook his head and started talking, softly, a little embarrassed.

– I'm not a boxer. Glass jaw, see. Do kinda like the Dodgers though. Gonna take my kid when he's old enough. Been going since I was six. My old man took me, back then there was Dazzy Vance, that guy could put 'em past a hornet's tail, had this funny little wait before he pitched. Sweetest right armer there ever was, my daddy used to say. Saw Ol' Stubblebeard pitch back when he played, before he took to managing.

And there was the in, the doorway into which a professional boot tip could be inserted. Cy himself had never stepped foot through the gates of Ebbet's Field, he had never been amid the almighty ballpark cheer, though he'd lived in Brooklyn for several years now. But he could walk into any drinking establishment or bakery or butcher's in the district, in the entire borough, and there would be daffy Dodgers talk, so all he had to do was collect pieces of their history and recent programme along with his bread and his meat and beer. Cookie Lavagetto, Al Lopez, Van Lingle Mungo. These were names he could produce with confidence in a conversation to gain a local confidence, like a handshake between allies. The feuds, the players, the shares bought and sold and inherited and disputed. It was revered territory, daily exchanged Brooklyn currency, one of the glues of the people. There were those that believed in the heroes and ghosts of the game so fervently that even the curse of Charlie Ebbet's grave which had struck McKeever down was real to them. And this was how Cy worked the crowds. He had learned to tease out a splinter of interest in a customer just by working loose its tip.

– Brooklyn Dodgers, best team in the country right now without a doubt, though I'm no expert I'll confess, more of a cricket and rugby man, but anyway, I'm sure you know the business. What with Camilli coming in from Philly, and Grimes at the helm, and who knows more than Grimes let's face it, those Giants won't stand a chance. Teach Fat Bill Terry to have ever asked if Brooklyn's still in the league, eh Eddie lad? Teach them all another lesson.

Eddie's eyes got a glint and a luminescence like the unshuttering of blinds in a dim room. He took Cy by the elbow and leaned in.

– You know they got Ruthie coaching first base too this season, don't ya? I seen him play last month, that exhibition game for the night-lighting. Oh, he's still got it, he may be the same age as my old daddy woulda been, God rest him, and I ain't saying forty-three is old, but oh brother is he a slugger. Why, those lights light up the ground like something holy . . . like some kinda holy thing . . . like I don't know what . . .

The chuckling friend pitched in a comment suddenly.

– Hey. Get this mermaid here, Eddie, she's a beauty. Yeah, I like her, Eddie; c'mon take that one. Look at her on that rock, like she's been swimming all day and now she's resting, well, she's a sweetheart. I like the way her little tail tips up. And her cute little pout. She has a flower in her hair like one of them hula girls! Can you get that green of her tail just the same when you put it on a fella?

– Green as you see it on the page there.

Eddie wasn't sure he liked the mermaid being pointed out to him. He furrowed up his brow while his friend tried to convince him. He was a browser apparently, not an impulsive man, he could have talked about baseball until the sun went down and came up again without getting tattooed. The perky mermaid did not compare with the Dodgers by any measure, but Eddie's friend would not let the idea drop.

– Hear that? He's going to make her just as cute. See, with the little dip at the top of the tail, you know what that's like. C'mon. What's the matter with you, buddy?

By now Eddie was shrugging and backing up towards the entrance of the booth and Cy could see that if his friend kept it up, shoving the idea over to him like a helping of vegetables he didn't like and didn't want, he'd lose interest in the meal altogether and the sale would be gone. Some men were like children that way, they had to be guided to an outcome or they'd waste the day on nothing but idle play. And in the business every sale counted. It had been a slow week for mid-season. The rain was cool, autumnal, and premature in August. A quality of it brought to mind Cy's hometown. Poor weather could give him a slight feeling of edginess, a sense of struggle, and he would put more effort into his sales brag. Then, the very next moment, Cy was remembering, clear as a bell chiming inside his head, his mother's rusting Tate and Lyle sugar tin with its pennies at the bottom that blackened up and stuck together with old damp sugar close to the end of winter, close to the last of them, and how she'd make him shine them with polish before he went out to buy potatoes and beetroot from the greengrocer. Reeda Parks had possessed her own style of pride, pride in the ability to provide for her fatherless son with money that shone and looked newly handled. Even if she had walked the pier with her political plate collecting naught but laughter and buttons and fudge from the bathers and holiday-makers and gathering unfavourable reputation among the women that ran the guest houses in Morecambe Bay. Even if she had emptied the basins of consumptives like a maid and did not object to the wet slush of their diseases. Cy hadn't thought of his mother in a while. But now he was suddenly remembering too the way she would write out in pencil in a little notebook the budget for the months of October through to March and she would be pleased with herself if there was money left over after any one week, but she would never spend it, she'd just carry the surplus over into the savings from the summer. Hatching a line through the dates, adding half-sized numbers to the next portion of the notebook, faintly, gently where she usually licked the lead tip and charcoaled darkly, as if the numbers were precious and fragile because of their diminutive status, their ghost life as money. She never once spent beyond what the small sturdy pencil marks dictated she could spend, and so if the price of pork rose at the butchers they would eat fish twice a week instead of loin, if the price of fish rose they would eat oatcakes through the winter. That kind of caution must have been hereditary, or it infected Cy where the consumption didn't. Either way, he could calculate how long the money from the work of the last twenty customers would support him here now, if they proved to be his last twenty of the season. He realized that if he let his mind focus through the numbers, he could work out what percentage of summer income the two customers in front of him now represented, should he make the sale.

In any case the men seemed to have reached an impasse in the discussion while his mind had been wandering. Eddie looked downright sulky while his friend had an expression of pinched impatience on his face. Cy turned to Eddie's friend. He was a handsome fellow, with his cap on at a jocular, upturned angle suggesting that he was a man prone to humour and chaff.

– And what might your name be, sir?

– Richard Samuel Bender.

– Now then, this one I could do for you, Dick. I like to think a man can find the right woman in a crowd, by instinct if you will, and you went straight for her. Eddie's loss, he missed her and she's a beauty, but you picked her out. Better not to give her to another chap, she wouldn't appreciate the hand-off, eh? You picked her. Like you knew her. The amount of times I've seen that happen with a design you couldn't count. But there's something to it in this trade. Oh, yes. There's something to it all right.

– Well, by God she is a little darling! It's why I went for her.

– Oh, she is at that. I painted her up from scratch, there's not another mermaid like her at Coney, and if there is she's stolen off me and I'll take it up with the thief because I wouldn't sell her on as flash. Some of the others are standard.

She's not, she's an original, see I've initialled the piece in the corner there, and if you look at her closely you'll see my shading. I had a feeling somebody would choose her today would you believe?

– Dollar you say?

– Two dollars for two I'm afraid, Dickie. Freehand they take a little longer, and what with this rain set to clear up this afternoon I'll be hard pressed to take less for the time. It gets busy quickly and if I'm stuck under-priced and out of time, well you understand that, being a business man right? But certainly, when Eddie's chosen his tattoo, I'll do the pair of you for that price, two for two. Not another freehander down here, and with that fine shading you know where that you pointed out to Eddie you'll be wanting her done properly, I imagine. And if Eddie's changed his mind, and there's no crime to that, it happens that a man comes here on occasion and doesn't fancy what he sees or gets a bit shy, and there's no harm to it I say, well, then maybe just a dime extra, she is after all the siren that called to you.

– Siren, huh? Hey, I like that, like in that story with the sailor, that's what I'll tell people when they see her. She called to me. C'mon Eddie, you heard the man, what y'gonna get? We came down here for you, so don't go getting stiff on me or you'll lose us the deal.

Cy handed Eddie a manila book with the page open at the sports section of flash, telling him to take his time, or, if he wanted, the designs could be changed to suit him. In the middle of the page was the Dodgers' logo.

– What do you say, Eddie lad, get yourself a lifelong season ticket? That's a true sporting fan.

An hour and a half later the two had bled a little into his cotton rags and had gone through a simple, colourful meta-morphosis, and he was two dollars better off. He told them to go and celebrate with an onion Polish, they should have worked up quite an appetite. He watched them walking back up the street a minute later in the rain, demolishing their food, shirts un-tucked and loose off the skin. They were slapping each other on their sore spots, blown up on the adrenalin of having passed through a gauntlet of minor pain and being in possession of motifs they would tell others were meant for them. The sausage vendor saluted him and he hung the mermaid back up on the wall. She was crisp around her curved edges and high-breasted, with a true green tail and red along her fins. He hadn't lied. He had drawn her from the imagination, she had been one of his first designs, and she'd sat in between the pages of a book in a cupboard for a decade when Riley wouldn't put her up on the Pedder Street shop wall. Now she was on display, with the salty sea air surrounding her. And as Cy thought about it, putting her back amid her oceanic sisters, he hadn't lied either when he called her a siren.

~

Women and fish. It was a presumptuous and runic combination. There were some tattoos as obvious and simple in their symbolic identification as the red-flagged danger in nature or the colours of a nation. Sport was one thing, a contemporary religion to the masses, hearts and flowers were easily deciphered. Women and fish entwined was another thing altogether. That association had something instinctual to it, something primal, buried in the psyche. There were at least three dozen subtly different female fish icons in his booth – bare-breasted, bare-bottomed, arch-backed lovelies, with curved hips and hair rippling like the waves below them. They were reclining or pert on the wall, drawn riding on scaled creatures like lovers, joined with them, and gripping the harness of a whisker or gill or a reptilian tongue like a bridle on a horse as they rode, like hair on a man beneath them, the better with which to steer him. And they stirred men up, stirred up that savant batter within them. They were provocative and sultry and saucy. They were the women of the sea calling to sailors, they were finned beauties, slipping from shells, aphrodisiac as oysters. There were traditional mermaids, green tailed and cheeky, females with the lower halves of them become aquatic, human legs joined and sealed by scale, by soft, femoral meat-muscle. So that they were cuntless, or maybe they were all cunt, like their parts had been turned inside out and were spreading down their legs, melting over human limbs, becoming overt genital tails. That was all the mermaid symbol was. The sex of her. A reduction of image to the essence of what made a woman different. Then there were fish with women's faces, women shrunk into their own symbolic parts. They were the *Pisces vaginales*, like that troublesomely aptly named species in Morecambe Bay for his interest in which Cy had ultimately taken a caning. Men had wed the two aspects together, and made them aesthetic. It was worship of the liquid territory between their legs. It was the smell of them. The way they were scented – it was their brine, like salt made inside the human body, that reek of the sea. And it was the feel of them inside, slippery, like fish-tail. And it was the taste, you could taste the sea in them, like in creatures manufactured by the ocean. All the slippery pictures of that deep wet place had men drawn to the tattoos on the walls like sailors to the come-hither songs of mermaids.

The designs had become perfected over the years, since delirious sailors had first spotted them cavorting off the bowwave or blowing kisses to the departing stern. Those voluptuous chimeras sheathed in scales. Men had eventually reduced it down to that passion, that desire for the place, that symbol of her, and the ones that chose the flash wanted to put its rudimentary marker on their flesh permanently, like the wet smell of a woman on their skin after she lifted off them. It was permanent intimate homage, a venereal badge of proclivity. It was eternal sex. When they looked at the mermaid they knew what she meant, somewhere in them, not very far down in the subconscious, was that knowledge. And Cy knew what it meant when he drew mermaids or naked women straddle-riding sea-serpents. And Riley had known all along and he'd said on more than one occasion that the reason women cried so readily was they were too full of salt-water like the sea, and he'd even put the notion of it in his dying speech. And if some men didn't admit to knowing the derivation of the She-Fish image which they instinctively liked best on the walls of Cy's booth, and paid him to transfer on to them, their cocks would know it and nod a little when, after the colour healed and the crust came off the tattoo, there she was in all her glory in the mirror, bright on the shoulder, top half woman, bottom half cunt-fish.

Some days it was abundantly clear to him that men were truly still mesmerized by women, obsessed with their defini-tion and their difference, and that all he was doing with his ink and his needle was recording the history of the female sex through the symbolic vision of another species.

∼

When he arrived in the greatest city on earth Cyril Parks still had with him most of the designs from the shop in Morecambe, and he would soon collect new ones in America that would adorn the summer booth or be bound in books for customers to flip through. Walking down the steep gangplank of the ship he had over three hundred designs and variations on designs, all told. He was going to be the Electric Michelangelo. He was going to be his own master. He was going to renew life, taking the best of the old and making it modern. Other than the copious flash, he had fewer possessions than ever though, it seemed, and if he tried to remember what he had once owned, those things that had been kept above the Pedder Street shop in old crates or in the Bayview Hotel on the windowsill or under the bed, his mem-ory failed him, produced small black voids. In his scramble to get away he had brought almost nothing with him, he had left behind as much of his old existence as he could.

He was now the falsely legal resident of a new country, his mind went out no further than his current situation in ambition, and he still was not fixing himself down with gathered material weight, not in the way that Reeda had positioned cups in her cupboards over the years, pictures along the walls, and manifest pieces of herself throughout the hotel, nor the way Riley marked his territory with eggs in a row, the last structure of skull of the birds he trained, put on his mantle like objects of art, and his thick, possessive handwriting in his vagabond books.

The apartment in the building into which Cy moved was swabbed clean and raw and it was scented of sparse, woody emptiness like the deck of an antique ship after disembarkation. It had a chair, washing facilities, adequate space and acoustics that elaborated on tales told by the daily lives of other residents. He came to it unremarkably, indiscriminately, via a contact provided to him by the cousin of a friend of a man he had tattooed on board the *Adriatic*, and that was the way of New York City, a million corresponding pathways could open up from one handshake, or a meaningful cigarette shared. The building was located in Sheepshead Bay, a provincial town of Brooklyn not far from where he would soon work, a place where he could watch the fishing boats to-ing and fro-ing in the harbour, or the cranes on Emmons Avenue winching construction material on the banks, and where children sold clams and paper-wrapped fish by the water's edge or out of wooden shacks. By the shipping lanes, in the district's restaurants, there always seemed to be unassuming music being played, accordions and flutes and stringed instruments rhyming with each other, and it was a place of labour and banter and bustle. He paid a rental deposit to a tiny, old Sephardic Jew, a lady with hands warped and clawed and folded over like dead bird's feet, and with spinning, white-blind eyes, and he was given a key. She put a limp talon to his chest in welcome.

– For the dead before you here, bless this place. For the lock, turn the key against good sense.

He unpacked his suitcase, it contained five shirts, two pairs of breeches, some shaving soap and his tattoo equipment and he took several long walks around the vicinity. He had a little money left over from the work on the ship, but he would need to find employment soon. And so he set out to explore the options. There were fish markets along the wharf and grocery stores that sold the foods of many nations, shore diners, chop and chow mein restaurants, barbershops and tackle huts. Bridges were being built and cobblestones were being uprooted to widen roads. When he looked into other dwellings in the neighbourhood he could see economical furnishings and delightful attempts to bend possessions into art, normalcy into creativity. Or perhaps there was in this country a new, incidental aesthetic to a coat hanging on a stand, a hat hung on a peg, the mosaic made against the wall from shadows of items on a table reaching too far, which he had not been aware of previously. The big houses on Lundy's Row contained beautiful stained-glass fixtures that warmed the faces of their inhabitants. He enjoyed looking in people's windows, he liked it even better than the infectious, inclusive conversations of neighbours on their stoops and in their gardens across the borough. It gave him a sense of serendipity, that here after all were other humans living in proximity, coincidentally and fully, and so for a time he was able to borrow the density of their lives to fill in his whittled-out own.

The building where he lived was old by local standards, not as old as the brownstones further into the district, but it was already shambolic, as if used thoroughly by its successive residents. Its bricks were crumbling and spreading apart, and there were several long fissures in the dull marble of the foyer floor. The structure seemed as if it had once been quite grand and rather than keep up with the times it had gone gently the way of a stubborn aristocratic decline. Harder times had come its way with the influx of more and more immigrants, lowlier tenants with menial occupations had moved in as nicer buildings along Voorhies went up. It had been divided further into smaller units, as a government under pressure, and yet the building held on to a proud grace, and its tenacity did not go unnoticed by Cy. It was built five stories high in the shape of the letter H and at night there was cinema in each corner of the structure made from the light of lamps projected on to the wing walls and the casters of people, revealing the contents and dramas of each living quarter opposite. Cy was granted access into the lives of strangers as they went about their evening business, before they drew the curtains. A kiss as two silhouettes met, a soup tureen placed in front of an elderly man, an ironing board pulled out, fastened, and a bottle of starch set upright as laundry was attended to.

Not many of his neighbours were known to him, beyond what habits and transactions the echoing pipes and slamming doors conveyed, the calls to each other in the hallway – Hey, Larry, get me some coffee, dark, twelve sugars – and the nocturnal cinematography generously provided. There were intriguing pieces of evidence which hinted at who might live inside. Letters in the foyer mail slots told him their names. Bierdronski. Vellum. Mr and Mrs Berger. Odours came from under the doors, cooking, cigar smoke, even the rich smell of the English countryside was detectable some days outside one of the first floor residences, number 104, and every time he passed by Cy paused momentarily, confused, enchanted, perhaps even a touch homesick for God knew what bucolic portion of his nation. Once he had even stopped a few minutes in the corridor, determined to define the fragrance. He bent close to the apartment door, closer than he had been to it ever before, close enough to qualify as a rudeness. It was a sweet ripe smell, stronger for his attendance, that was redolent of the marshes and the moors and the outer lying land around the bay. The scent of newly turned fields and useful earth and livestock. Inside there was a faint shuffling sound, but as you could never rely on the building's erratic acoustics for authenticity, he was unsure if

the noise was actually coming from the chamber beyond his
ear. Then he heard a masculine snort, as if somebody inside
was very sick with a deep chest cold. There was the rasping
sound of a person perhaps breathing with immense difficulty
just on the other side of the door or perhaps rubbing a beard
along the wall, almost next to his ear. But he did not knock
and introduce himself.

He had been brought up in a hotel, where it was not necessary to form lasting relationships with the inhabitants of a
place of residence, even though some had left lasting
impressions on him, the consumptives with their wrung-out
hope and Eva Brennan, who was the first girl to have drawn
her name through his heart. Guests were no more than
briefly fostered children, to be fed, washed, kept tolerably
warm and entertained on funds provided. In truth, after the
close-kept treachery of living with Eliot Riley, his
inescapable, random tyranny, the perpetual evidence of his
sickness and the availability of Cy as whipping boy, nursemaid and verbal punching bag to his landlord and boss, he
was glad to be alone now and remote, with a simple new
identity of his own choosing.

$\sim$

There was a moment after he first came to the continent when
he began to question the truth of what his trustworthy eyes
conveyed, America unravelled, and for a short time reality
departed, threw up its hands and marched out of the room.
The moment passed, but it may have weakened his grip on
the ordinary, the way Eva had weakened his disposition for
love, and if he thought back to it, it may have led to all the
strangeness, the dreaming and the madness that would occur
during his time in the new world. It was a moment that he
assumed all newcomers to the city must have felt at some
point or another, for who could sustain a calm pace of breath
or look up with an unimpressed eye or speak with a blasé
tone in unwavering consistency and unaffectedness in this

place? Who could get used to the set and the stage of the ongoing play? Such banality was impossible even for a lifelong citizen of New York, for whenever it felt the urge, the city itself and all its boroughs could toss up a curiosity or a peculiarity, or kilter out a hitherto unnoticed detail, or create a marvel of fiction or of fact right before the eyes to remind its residents that this indeed was New York, lest that absurd fact be forgotten, crucible of miracles and violence and spectacular wonder. These were the moments that defined the city. They were the waking dreams of a never sleeping metropolis.

Cy's first New York moment came only days after he had clutched the deck rail of the *Adriatic* as the tugs brought her in. He had been pouring water into the sink to wash his face one evening in his new apartment and on the brick wall opposite, slightly below his window, there was suddenly the magical shadow-house show of one of the lower apartments. A strong light at the back of the room was illustrating its contents, the shapes, and the occupants. The black profile of a woman walked past across the screen of bricks, her hips and breastplate and hair illustrating gender. She might have walked downstage but for being kept within the flat dimension. Her movements were restricted, lateral, and she was busy. She was carrying something soft that slipped in small pieces from her arms, clothing perhaps or gauze, like the filaments of an enormous blown dandelion head. In the vacuum of space all he had to go by, to differentiate by, were the textures, thickness and pronouncement of shadows. The woman dropped her load and disappeared into the black wings. And then she was followed by another puppet, something impossible, something from a pantomime. A horse moved onto the stage after her. Its cameo head tilted, paused. He could tell immediately what the shadow was from the length of muzzle, the triangular skull, the almost human brush of an eyelash. But it must have been some kind of accidental invention cast by debris and objects positioned one on top of the other, books, a vase, and something organic like coarse hair, a flower perhaps or a plant, lit from behind like a lie and moved. Just a trick of the light and a liaison between the contents of the room, or an illusion, the way children fake their hands into animal silhouettes when they find empty white pools of light or useful sunshine on the playground floor. There was equestrian stillness for a long minute so Cy could almost persuade himself that it must have been some kind of trick, simply chanced items stacked up on the shelf and misunderstood. But then the muzzle tipped up a fraction, the ear rotated half a degree, the animal bent its head to the floor and came up with the soft substance in its muzzle, which must have been hay.

– Well, I'll be a monkey's uncle! Less donkeys, more horses, Paddy Broadbent!

Any doubts Cy had, evaporated. There was a horse living with a woman in an apartment in his building and Brooklyn was as hopping crazy as a bucket of painted frogs.

The terrain altered. The lamp dimmed, and the horse was gone. The illusion vanished and any strange city secrets went with it. Next door's shadow theatre concluded to no applause, just Cy's slack jaw and his blinking grey eyes, the end of his first foray into the screwy possibilities of this realm. He brought water in his hands to his face, dampened his long hair where it met his neck. He would never again be sure that he could rely on his eyes, as he had relied on them for years in Morecambe Bay, give or take a picture of blood, a drop of drink, the odd little white lie. Because here, in this rubble-some, rimose city there were actual anomalies in life. Because below him lived a horse and a woman who blew around like a dandelion stalk in the breeze. He laughed out loud then and it sounded hollow in the sparse apartment. He had become for that moment a lunatic, delusive, he had become one of life's apostolic madmen. In rural England, people concentrating hard on the paths over moorland as they drove carts and motor cars occasionally swore they had seen a black panther cross in front of them, or an Indian tiger. And they believed it ever after, blindly, and they would always search for spoors whenever they passed by that spot again. There was one supposedly roaming around by Moffat Ravine, a beast of the moor, sabre-toothed and with fur that was mottled exotically, living right alongside the native sheep and rabbits, though Cy had never seen it. He had come to a new city only to find that it contained all the indistinct chaos and divergence and eccentric myth of the old world he had left behind. The same batty behaviour of its citizens, the same colourful prankishness and thunderstruck chromosomes. He had been met with it convincingly. And then he knew it. He could expect no easier life here, no clean slate, no simpler version. There would be no more clarity or charity in this land of new beginnings than anywhere else he had known.

~

For all the city's obscure adaptations and unclear reveries, for all its urban confusion and impacted allegories, Brooklyn did have one uncomplicated feature. It had purity of light. The early morning and late afternoon light was appraisingly referred to as being like that found in a Dutch master's painting. From the prehistoric-looking bridge and Williamsburg at twelve on the clock face, around the borough past the border with Queens, Canarsie and the residences along Jamaica Bay, to Coney Island at the half hour, Fort Hamilton and back to the mouth of the east river, and in all the neighbourhoods converging on the dial-pin of Flatbush, something radiant and luminous could wash over the streets and the great parks and the tall, tight-packed headstones of the cemeteries, enhancing the buildings and making shaded areas seem more profound. Or rather the light did not come from above, but Brooklyn seemed able to imbue itself, generating the energy of illumination from within. It was a quality as self-produced and collaborative as the smell of the cuisines that wafted through the streets, and for many it represented the very magic of the place. That distinctive, shining character. Brooklynites would disagree about the best month for this light, the way museum-goers argue about the best portrayals of the masters, more for mild academic exercise than from a necessity to produce the definitive answer. Some swore by November, those of a melancholy disposition who enjoyed the hue of opal along the pavements, the glimmering quality of it on the stoop railings like the glitter along the edges of carving knives and scissors after they had been brought out by residents and sharpened by the blade grinders who came round in carts ringing bells. For these people the late fall light reflected as sombrely as the atmosphere of mournful memories belonging to so many of Brooklyn's residents. Some said the weeks in spring were most lovely when the light woke up and had newness, silver-air, and potential, making mirrors of the standing water in the roads – that period around which Cy had arrived first on the scene. For those, it was the light of amnesty and hope, complementing the eyes of free and living souls. In these early weeks Cy loved to walk through the district for this very reason, the reason of light, when it seemed he was travelling through an expansive, expressive painting. Upstairs, Eleven Pedder Street had also seemed painterly, but so devoid of joyful illumination. It was a still-life, a place of inanimate objects assembled with meticulous and menacing care, and washed over with tension. It held its breath.

Here Cy would walk through the market, a few blocks from his building, when it was winding down, with stray cabbage leaves blowing on the ground, the clink of glass going back into a crate and it was as a working studio, where artists and their renditions were juxtaposed. A last attempt being made from a persistent huckster at a sale, a discounted rate for the last of his fruit with its waxy, polished appearance.

– Ten cents for a dozen, nickel for five, sir? Sweet as honey, crisp as ice.

He liked the raucous and rarefied arena of Brooklyn, the glossy look of old women hanging their washing out in long jowls between buildings, and the quartz faces of children playing marbles and hopscotch in the mud roads, swapping baseball cards on the sidewalk. Brown paper bags in the gutter could seem purposeful as they drifted along and the fishing boats cast tussled shadows on the water like a breath of wind through wheat fields. More than the baseball and the cooking, more even than the religion that blessed the Judaist congregations, the light was the binding ingredient of the place, like water in bread dough. It was the spirit of Brooklyn.

～

He was procuring his first batch of ink from a pigeon-filled, paint-peeling warehouse in Gravesend when he met Arturas and Claudia Overas, husband and wife who made up one of the most famous partnerships in all of Coney Island. With his usual caution and subterfuge Cy was selecting his products when he noticed a large Teutonic looking man with hairy blond cheeks following his progress around the suppliers. The man was considerably larger than Cy and apparently quite comfortable with staring down the gaze of others for he made no bones about his optical inquisition. Uncomfortable, and unfamiliar with his surroundings, Cy finally went to pay for his goods and was reaching into his pocket for money when the fellow strode up to him and punched one fist into his other palm. He addressed the cashier in English, which seemed not to be his most comfortable language though it was still used emphatically and with speed, like a swing in a park too small for the backside of a grown child.

– This man must not pay these prices. Give this man my good prices.

Suddenly nervous, Cyril Parks attempted to extinguish the interference.

– No. I'll pay what's marked up, thank you for your concern. I'm sure that's fair. Just ring me up as is, please, and I'll be on my way.

He had no wish to draw attention to himself and the blond man was not assisting with his attempt to be discreet about who he was and what he needed the supplies for. He turned to the man accosting him with an economy of aggression, hoping not to further provoke a conflict with him but knowing that a vacuum of defence could potentially extend the exchange, may give the loud, uninhibited stranger licence to toy with him. Cy was tall and always had been thus, it was advantageous in his profession, but the man in question was another foot clear above him. There were more lashes around the eyes regarding him than he had ever seen on a person, man or woman, and the coiled mustard growth on his cheeks almost reached his nostrils. The open neck of his shirt revealed a great crop of chest hair. In complete contrast to the knots and whorls elsewhere on his body, the flax on the man's head lay perfectly straight, without so much as a hint of a kink to it, giving the distinct impression that there had been a civil war of some variety on his anatomy and the hair had divorced into two opposing autarkies a long time ago.

– Hören Sie! You must not pay these prices. They are for other trades. We take smaller quantity, better quality. We are the same, we are similar breed, I can tell that by your . . .

Here the man pulled an expression of mock surreptitiousness and hunched his shoulders. He looked affected, exaggerated, like a silent-movie villain.

– . . . your old habits. Never mind what is kept under your shirt. But here, it's OK, just buy your ink. You ask for what you want, exactly, and you get, my friend! Yes, in America!

– Look. I'll have to ask you not to interfere, I'm not sure what you're talking about. I'm an artist. Freelance. This is for lettering work on . . .

– Oh, ass-shit! They don't care what you do! Do you care what this man does with his ink?

The cashier shrugged, assessing Cy over a bottle of Coca-Cola with mild attention and one lazy, fizzing eye.

– No, of course not. He has four Abbildungen by me no doubt if I tell him to remove shirt – Arturas Overas, best tattoo artist in all of New York! My friend, you must get big balls if you are going to work here, understand! Otherwise they put you on a boat back to wherever you have come from, or into a bag of bricks in East river! I try to help you in this regard.

Still unsure of the protocol for tattoo artists in this country, Cy was hesitant to give himself up so easily. This man was obviously trying to set him up, ensnare him in some kind of trap that the warehouse management were no doubt privy to. Tattoo artists, if that is what this man indeed was, were notoriously competitive and inventive when it came to bettering a rival, or planning his demise. Cy knew this as well as he knew his own shoe size.

– Look, if it's all the same, I'd rather not have you shouting about this. I'd rather you minded your own business in fact. I'll take this now and I'll pay what the marked price is and if you'd like to finish this conversation outside I'll be happy to oblige.

– Have it your way. My wife is waiting for me outside also, she does not like the smell of glue and paint, it gives her headache, perhaps she can talk sense to you, crazy englischer Dummkopf. She is a beautiful lady, an angel, my Claudia, probably killing all the men that try to steal her from me while I am gone. Ja. I will see you outside.

With that the man left the warehouse. Cy sighed, paid for his supplies, looked for another exit and upon seeing none followed him through the warehouse doorway. Beyond it not one but two mastodon giants were waiting for him, for the man had been joined by his female equal.

They were a stalwart, striking pair without a doubt. Both were well over six feet tall and possibly weighed an equal tonnage. The great blond interferer was standing flirtatiously close to his wife – a megalithic woman with bright crisp orange hair and heavy, smudged black eyes. She had on an oversized dress that covered most of her body but Cy could make out the undeniable black borders of prolific tattooing on her wrists and through her nylon hose. She had the knuckles of a boxer and the defined muscles of an Olympian. There were veins in her neck that were like the roots of a tree plunging up against soil. Between the two of them they could have reduced him to mash and gravy in a very short amount of time, he was certain of it, for he was Lilliputian in comparison. His thoughts turned to flight, he could drop his wares and out-run them, but they were blocking the road, his only avenue of escape. He suddenly remembered his careless foot on a smashed Pedder Street windowsill held tight by an ink-stained hand securing it at the ankle, and he knew once again that running was the foolhardy choice. The woman turned and spotted Cy.

– Turo. Is this the English man?

– Ja.

Arturas gestured to him. It seemed he had inflated his pectorals further still, perhaps having found a convenient tyre-pump in the vicinity, and he had his knuckles resting on a thick belt holding up his trousers. He looked like a legendary woodcutting champion of yore.

– Come, come. Sit on this wall. We will speak now.

Cy hesitated, then sat. The woman lowered herself down next to him and placed an arm around his shoulder. The weight of it was extraordinary – and it seemed to possess a serpent-like grip of its own that felt not unlike Miss India Rubber's boa constrictor when she had draped it over Cy's shoulders and arms as a boy, a squeeze so powerful that it paralysed the body and made it ache until the thing was ready to release its tension and move off. The arm itself smelled incongruously of talcum powder.

– Good. Now, I try to do you a favour as my brother but you refuse to accept. You take the advice of Arturas Overas and piss it into the gutter. No matter. We will see to it that you learn. This is my wife, Claudia. She is my assistant in all things of life, as I am hers also. Now that we are introduced properly, let us begin.

Cyril Parks closed his eyes. This was ridiculous. He was a grown man who had diffused many a fight in the Pedder Street parlour and the public houses of Morecambe Bay, on behalf of a man highly qualified to provoke them. He was adept at negotiating peace, it came with the job and the association, and he had even put in a good performance for fights that he could not escape. How had he so readily and stupidly walked into this situation? It was useless to think of victory or apology. Instead he thought of Riley's reedy red hand when he had staggered back from the smithy by the ravine. He thought of brown-red discharge in a basin, fish guts in the Cooperative Society building sliding down conveyors into buckets, and he thought of the weeping scar along Reeda Parks's chest.

~

They were carnival folk, who had come to America fifteen years ago and had since travelled the country extensively with fairs and shows and circuses. They were Germanic people originally, comprised, it seemed, of every powerful myth and mettle available from that heritage. Arturas was a tattoo artist, not a bad one, although not, as he claimed, the best in New York. Cy had met men as big as him before, but his bride was a colossus such as he had never seen. Born with exceptional strength and size, she was not ridiculed for either by her kinfolk, nor by her village in the Erz mountains, so that by the time the rest of the world was ready to set upon her in fear or familism for her lack of classical female form she had been convinced so thoroughly of her magnificence already that she did not doubt it. Criticism and cruelty bounced off her hide like hail from the rump of a prize ox. Her heart was good, her body was capable, her mind was sturdy and possessed of no more frailties than any other well-bolstered human brain. What the world saw as freakish and a spectacle, the incarnation of a creature from a dark fairytale like the Ogre's daughter, her loved ones saw as fantastic and spectacular, the work of an inventive and benevolent God. If there was hair on her chin by puberty it was because she was blessed with more than her fair share of that chemical which made humans miraculously strong. If she began life able to pick up heavy objects where her brothers could not and box grown men at the village fair, she only went on to refine her muscle, to train her limbs to perform feats industrial machinery heretofore had the exclusive right to undertake. In the mornings and evenings she would squat and thrust and lunge and curl iron in her arms. Occasionally she would bleed herself before taking exercise, letting out the ichor through a puncture or lesion in the crux of her elbow or knee so that the engine of her heart would have to work twice as hard with less of its fuel, but this was a discipline in her mind and it would only serve to make her stronger in the end. So she embraced her lot and strove to perfect it.

And Arturas loved her, loved her deeply and truly, that much was abundantly clear, since they first met at the local market and he watched as she hoisted home a calf on her shoulders. Arturas was a strongman who lifted weights above his head in a circus that had come to town, he wooed Claudia, convinced her family to let her accompany him as his bride – the money was good, his love was noble – and for a while they billed themselves as the only husband and wife strongman and strongwoman team in the whole of Europe. Within a year Arturas had popped the cartilage out of his left knee and torn several ligaments on a poorly executed clean-and-press manoeuvre, so badly in fact that the joint remained herniated and he would never be able to hoist barbells professionally again. With his leg packed in plaster he was doodling with his wife's lipstick on his cast and wondering what to do next – he did not want to leave the circus – when he struck on the idea of body art. Claudia was all for it and said she would become his living canvas. He tattooed her top to toe and together the two of them travelled about, awing the crowds in Europe and America. Carnival life was suited to them both – they were restless people, prideful and expressive. When the circus dissolved they stayed on in America and went to the one place where people of their ilk were more than welcome. That throbbing, pustulous, inflamed amusement-industry boil on the backside of Brooklyn.

They had been at Coney Island for eight years now, the longest either had lived in one place since they left the village in Germany. When she was not lifting her petticoats outside his parlour on Stillwell Avenue to show the self-portrait of her husband on her thigh, or displaying her form in the human picture gallery of Luna Park, Claudia was hoisting pewter balls in her outstretched hands, or turning over vehicles like a tornado, or hurling ingots and faggots and scaffolding over twelve prostrate men to the gasps of the enthralled public.

~

Cy opened his eyes to see the enormous pair smiling kindly at him. The thing he had to understand about Arturas Overas, he was told by the subject himself, was that he was not one for all the competitive tussling and ruffianry with others in the same profession. It gave him bad indigestion and a spastic colon, a griping of the guts such as bad clams will provide. He worked in a place that was a tattooist's paradise. There was more work there than an additional ten artists could manage. And if more artists came, more customers would follow. The more cows, the more milk produced and the more milk produced the more people would drink the milk, said Arturas. It was good for business to have more cows in the herd. When one was milking, all were milking. This was Arturas's interpretation and philosophy regarding the tattoo trade and, after the thorough, huff-duff style of warfare to the industry in Morecambe, it was a bold new concept to Cy. The man placed a big hand on Cy's knee.

– But are you good, my friend? Or are you, what is it they say, are you rinky-dink?

Cy's heartbeat was still erratic. His shoulders ached from the constrictor arm.

– I work freehand. I have for over ten years. I apprenticed with the greatest artist in the north of England.

– Excellent! Then I was right. I am always right about such matters. We were meant to meet, my friend, do you not agree? And what is your name?

– Cyril Parks. Cy.

– No, your other name.

– Oh. The Electric Michelangelo.

It was the first time he had spoken of his new identity, the first time he had rechristened himself out loud.

– Aah! It is good! It is very good! Not as good as mine. I am the Black Baron. You like it?

How had Arturas known what kind of man he was, Cy asked, back in the warehouse when he had tried his best to conceal himself. Claudia was the one who replied. She had a beautiful soft, basso voice when it came to speaking of her husband.

– Turo is a very sensitive man. He will watch the spider in the bathtub for an hour to know if it is poisonous or harmless rather than squashing it without asking. He has a sense of life, of joy and pain. He is my bear with a thorn in his paw and his tongue in the honey pot.

They told Cy about Coney Island. There were booths that could be rented seasonally and upwards of one million visitors swarmed through the fairgrounds and parks every weekend in summer. One million people, could he imagine such a thing? Sometimes you could not find the boardwalk for all the people on it – you just had to assume that it was there, said Arturas. It was the chosen place for the likes of them, full of the wonders of the world, the ingenuity and curiosity of man, and hotdogs, delicious hotdogs.

– Ah, yes. With the onion and ketchup along the top, just enough for tasting each bite. Geschmackvoll! And, my friend, wait until you see, there is the fourteen-inch frank made for two people to share.

He leaned over and kissed his wife and she patted his

cheek. There were good friendships that could start with almighty confrontation or terrible prejudice, Cy would learn.

~

Coney Island, as it turned out, was Morecambe's richer, zany American relative. A fat, expensively dressed in-law with a wicked smile and the tendency, once caught up in the mood, to take things too far. The family resemblance was there for displaced Lancashire folk to see upon arrival if they cared to. Both were made up of a multitude of interdependent entertainment cells designed to remove a person from the dimension of ordinary life. Both sat sublimely and noisomely next to water, defining themselves in relation to the sea. Had anyone with latitudinal skills measured the direction of their gaze, the two resorts probably faced each other across that vast and busy piece of ocean water – give or take a small land mass positioned in between, Manx and Irish populated – like a pair of gargoyles, one smiling cheerfully, the other laughing maniacally. Both purveyed a bawdy sense of humour when it came to the indelicate human body, with its gases and growths and ganglions, and both acknowledged the desire of its inquisitive mind to be shocked and appalled and entertained and mystified. Cy had never heard of the place until he arrived in the country, until he got into the slipstream of immigrants flushing through the massive borough city of Brooklyn, but when he got there it seemed like fulfilling a prophecy. Within weeks, he had secured a rental tattoo booth on Oceanic Walk, one of the honky-tonk alleys that ran through the catacombs of amusement facilities at the Island, only three hops, skips and jumps from Coney's boardwalk and beach. It was a good tip from Arturas and Claudia, and a natural progression for Cy. He went where the work was, because he had been born of that peculiar seaside-growing odd-fruit-bearing family tree, because he was sired from that dynasty. Looking back it was as simple as that. Go to America, make up a name, aim for the ringing, singing, screaming, teeming water's edge. There was a sense of graduation to his life now, as if he had found the doorway to another level of the same happy, haunted hotel, the same colourful house of torture, the same quarantined wonderland, where the insanity of the population was just brighter and more intense and extended, because it had the freedom to be so, because this was America. The Electric Michelangelo belonged, Cy sensed it. Because Coney itself was like the work of his moniker's original, towards the end of his life, when something went vain and vivid in his brain and the result was a painted world that was past real, surreal, mannered from psychosis and all the more poignant for it.

~

And if Eliot Riley had seen Coney Island, what would he have thought of it? What would he have made of the madness? It was a question Cy returned to for some reason as often as he returned to work at the booth down the roads from Sheepshead Bay. As often as he saw the turrets and columns and big wheels and the Cyclone rollercoaster tracks rising against the sky, looking out of the train or trolley window as it moved down the Brighton Beach line. Maybe Riley was the centre-pin by which he judged all engineering and all ideas of craft and social reckoning now, having eclipsed his mother in that regard, he didn't know. But the big man's ghost seemingly could enter his head as effortlessly as water left the clouds over Morecambe and entered the sea, three thousand and more miles to the east. Cy's memory could summon up a fingerless-gloved hand agitating the stubble of a chin, and a voluptuous mouth above it that was flatulent with corrupt and folkish philosophies, and judgments and jibes, faster than it could bring to mind the faces of his new acquaintances. Riley had left his mark all right, just as Cy had divined on the *Adriatic*. Cyril Parks had the sorry residue of the man's opinions and bander-snatch politics and inappropriate, spitting laughter like constant drizzle in his mind, for all the escape of death and nations left behind.

Coney Island. By the decade Cy reached it, it was on the way down, sobering up from its early-century glory when even God had paid his entrance fee amongst the hatted masses and ridden the rollercoasters and giggled at what animation he saw and marvelled at the bizarre golems and part-animal-humans on display that he himself had botched during their creation. When he had joined the ogling crowds at the base of Golgotha rebuilt to watch the nails of entertainment sink in and the centurians rolling dice for the profit of robes. But still, to the present day, the Island churned and rattled and tipped over like a fat girl in costume for the public to be titillated by her privates. Cy could sense the decline almost immediately after his arrival – the atmosphere was like coming late to a party where the hullabaloo had built and perhaps peaked and though it was still loud the partygoers' eyes had begun to glaze. It remained a fun place, in a frightening and enticing way, but you knew that troublesome events would soon happen, that stories would later be told about all over the city, accompanied by grimaces and winces and scars.

There was the perpetual hum of electrical rides heard from the train carriage several stops away. The dull scream of voices, the insulated booms and hoots and toots of barges and cannons and carts. Fountains of metal scaffolding erupted on the horizon dropping stomachless couples on fast parachute rides to the ground, fortune machines spat balls out through their mouths so you could know what was coming your way on behalf of God or Ganesha or whatever celestial benefactor or patron you chose. A cacophony of technology was employed to make people rapid and exhilarated. Steeplechase made Morecambe's ghost train look like a caterpillar crawling beside a great wooden and iron python. Cy could not believe the construction when he first laid eyes upon it – people were bent over horses that rushed along undulating tracks as if being sucked into the mouth of hell on apocalyptic steeds.

The massive parks whooped and hollered and honked and echoed with the hubbub of customers letting off steam. Women had their skirts blown over their heads, if not by the strong coastal wind on the wide boardwalk, then by air pumps in the Blow-Hole, a theatre full of mirrors and vents, while men had their bottoms paddled mechanically to the delight of recently molested onlookers in an amphitheatre. There was the buzz, buzz, buzz of adrenalin everywhere, from the loss of gravity on the spinning rides, to the awe-invoking tattoo guns and the shrieking commotion over the freaks, the spectacle of a three-headed cow. Voyeurism was key to any attraction, because Americans at leisure wanted to witness something to take away thought and replace it with emotion, they wanted beautiful smut, a punch in the gut. There was that pivotal ocular quality to anything on offer. The devouring eye.

And Cy found himself having to bind and fortify himself with British-borrowed opinion so as to remain firm on his feet, tolerating the place perhaps only up to what would have been the limit of Riley's credulous mind, an imagination which had more elasticity than most of those owned by his compatriots. For there were nasty things on offer at Coney, worse than basins of blood and jokes about ejaculation, worse than accidental sewage and the double-jointed torsion of per-formers. The parks fizzed with rough energy and raw spirit for all the nice hats of the visitors and the tidy rows of black motor cars parked in municipal lots behind the enormous pavilions and arcades. Riley would have appreciated that spirit. He had possessed a taste for the absurd, the rotten apple of entertainment, the wrong side of the brain. And he could have appreciated the awful individual eccentricity of each and every attraction. The whimsy, the grotesque, the bizarre, it was Sodom's own wicked comedy room where mule women and savages sent the crowds into a frenzy of disgust and gaping mortification. Riley would have said there was more honesty at Coney than in the Bible or any other spiritual verse, because it read the stupefying human soul accurately at both ends. It was no wonder he had never gone to confession in all the years Cy knew him, as his faith decreed he should; it would have combed out what balance deviance in the man provided and he would have keeled over on to the priest. People wanted to laugh and to loathe, it was simple nature, he would have said, pointing to the freaks as they tumbled and crawled about on stage, hermaphrodites in fishnet and conjoined twins, the horrors of the body become biologically lazy or gone wild. In the freak shows you could have anything, any dark nightmare from the mind made real. And there was the slam of bodies against each other for the sake of fun in motorized carriages, the rowing bark of sea lions in pools, babies painted with pancake make-up on the walkways, with spikes glued on their heads like Liberty herself. Row after row after row of old Russian men took to the plateau of sand behind the domes and palace turrets of Coney and out towards Brighton Beach every morning, bending and stretching in exercise before taking to the water in the milk-churn light of eastern daybreak. If Cy got there early enough in the day he'd see them swim out like suited penguins and return to the shore flapping off cold blue Atlantic water minutes later. It was super-sized seaside mayhem.

This was Morecambe of international proportions and inconceivable wealth, it was Morecambe gone putrid and suffering without any of its former inhibitions, as if the Tory councillors had packed up their belongings and documents banning distasteful shows and left town, taking their collective prudish notions for ever with them and leaving the occult industries to ferment and sprout and run amok. Here there was far too much attention to detail, far too much gruesome investigation into what would titillate and far too much anarchy of demeanour, and it blew Cy away as if he'd placed a gun to his head and squeezed the trigger. As if this truly was the nation's purgatory, where any prurient display was advocated, any misdemeanour was acquitted, any sin suspended before a hopelessly hung celestial jury. Or would that have ultimately trumped Riley, taken away his role as contrarian and endorser of all things repellent as well as alluring? Would it have sent him into a sulk of scorn and fury that his brilliance and humour and ornery distinctiveness would be lost in low-level mediocrity in a place like this, lost in the shuffle of New York's terrible versatility, its many pinnacles, its deco skyscrapers and baroque muses? What was one more drunk amid the clutter and spill of human bodies and empty bottles on the Bowery? What was one more tattoo artist in the parks that were already filled with electric masters? What was one more harlequin soul in such a vast double-diamond-edged circus? What was one more crucified saint or criminal on an already stained and overcrowded Calvary?

~

When the *Adriatic* slid in past Manhattan to Ellis Island Cy might never have been more malleable in his life, never more able to dictate self, and Riley's ghost might have been exorcized then and there, put asunder, had his apprentice concentrated on that possibility instead of surrendering to incredulity. New York was a dream of architecture and vertical economy, of uncompromising coexistence. Suddenly everybody at the ship's rail had offered one another cigarettes, needing some kind of filter, some kind of method to take it all in, compressed tobacco was the easiest and only filtration tool available so they sucked away at smoke, though some drew out cameras to put a lens between them and what was too much. Cy would never know the city, he thought that moment as the boat blasted her arrival, not the way he knew the back streets and districts and the tides of Morecambe Bay. It was a squall of urban settlement, a storm of existence coming closer on the horizon, and he gripped the deck rail tighter, dizzy with what he saw. He would have to find some corner of it to huddle down in, it was all he would be able to do. Compared to the impending city, the water on which they were afloat seemed to be the only stable thing. Suddenly he wanted that old-timey's *hold* and *fast* written on his own fingers so that he could keep himself from going overboard, tumbling back-to-front and headlong up the tall buildings with the glass reflections telling him he was falling in many ways, up past windows and spires and skyscrapers and up past height itself, up through the sky and out into space. New York was the sacred centre of all pilgrimages, the big catcher's mitt for every nation's Diaspora. And Cyril Parks did not even know why he had come!

The Polish man next to him at the rail, on whose shoulder he had tattooed a heart not three days before, was laughing with tears in his eyes, like a child tipped too far into uncontrollable hysteria and his laughter had become something else, another emotion, unstoppable and debilitating. Cy put a hand on the newly decorated shoulder and the Pole placed in turn a hand over Cy's stained fingers, his laughter finally tapering. And the two of them held on.

But where had Europe been when New York went up? What had Europe been doing? Hunting for old-fashioned ideals like a shell on a beach while behind its back something enormous was happening? Fighting wars and remembering old grudges while abroad a fairytale land was being fashioned? Who had sold the Americans those magic beans that when planted would grow a city overnight, crushing myopic imagination upwards as it grew so that visions elongated and defied limit? Or what old peasant had boarded which creaking wooden clipper with those beans in his tatty coat pocket centuries ago, stolen from the garden belonging to the last mad emperor of some tiny dying country, to create this impossible new world?

∼

The stretch of seaside carnival on the southern lip of Brooklyn was the biggest amusement park on earth and for several asylum-spun years Cyril Parks would be one of the cogs of its summer machinery. It dedicated itself to invention and intrigue, hedonistic indulgence, freakery. Unlike Morecambe's pervasive tipsiness, its summer loosening of national character, the gently crude insight into gross anatomy, Coney Island offered up inebriation with startling dexterity and precision and for a time it could predict the vulgar thoughts of the masses like a mind-reader, responding with tailor-made surrealities and rides which were pure stimulant. Like Eliot Riley, who could unlock a sense of humour in a customer, and play on it to make his money, Coney could hypnotize the crowds with their own sensual fantasies and squeamishness made external. If they feared the dark they would be inserted into a pitch-black chamber and shaken. If they feared perversion some cage or dank oubliette would produce it. Specialization was everywhere, from the sculptor who carved out wax moulds of famous people and painted their wet eyeballs living then destroyed them over a fiery grill, to the variform deformities of the abnormals once imported from every nation in the world by the legendary Gumpertz, now limping about the parks and breeding with each other. Sword-swallowers guzzled blades, fire-breathers spat flaming rings, twisted females were pierced on beds of nails, shrunken heads hung from walls and adorned pikes, wrongly made people were revealed behind curtains of shame. The sick and the sinister abounded. The crowds could choose their indelicate pleasure or poison. They came, they paid, they saw, and they were entertained.

In England there had been the sense that if a man found two sticks on the beach he could incorporate them into a magic trick, children would laugh at Shakespearean fools, jokes were repeated and eventually formulized, the striped tents on the beach grew dirtier each year and their tears flapped in the breeze, but it was what you did come summer, it was tradition. It was as if the funfair carnival business itself was a deliberate step behind the collective British humour or that humour was a happy caricature of itself, belonging best in cheap hotels and prom pavilions at the seaside. Cy's hometown was, for the workers of the north, a harmless, farcical, if slightly uncouth associate, that was met with once a year and who could be relied upon to get merry and fall down, providing a laugh or two, but doing no lasting harm. Perversities were hinted at, nudge-nudged about with an elbow in the side. Things never went too far.

The Island on the other hand was absolute consumer-driven modernism, it was in-vogue anthropomorphism, a swim through the guts and entrails of the world. By the start of every season the repulsive and the breathtaking had regenerated itself. New monsters were found, new tracks spiralled. Money would come from somewhere, some mysterious new location, even after rainy summers or failed business endeavours or massive fires. Paint was fresh and the sideshows were ready to excrete their freakish wares, new rides appeared annually, at the cost of tens of thousands of dollars and bought from the World's Fair, to take people to the moon or to the bottom of the sea, to give them artificial magic environments. And the place revelled in near-perfect macabre entertainment, as if the juice of wacky Victorian society had been stewed up and injected into a Promethean American creation, a new world Moulin Rouge, a blaring creature that was concentrated along a two-mile strip of beachfront on the tip of the hipbone of that most fantastic city ever conceived. Coney could have outdone the rest of America's oddest finds had she pried them out of her vast corners and put them together in a room. Cy could stand at the entrance of Luna Park and forget which direction his booth was seven years after first squeezing his business in. He could walk the corridors and never become accustomed to what he witnessed within, the boggling acts, the sickest tracts, the mucus and prolapse and fistula afflicted.

What was the essence of Coney Island, he often wondered, sitting on the train approaching the station. What was it exactly? Horrific proof that the Victorian era could not invoke and conjure the black soul of the Gothic and eternally suppress its darker energy with mere cages of ornament and primness and order. Proof that it could not tinker around with salivating, mechanical wolf-heads, musical skulls and pictures made from human hair and not be opening a terminal crack in Pandora's Box, a vile vessel containing utter subversion of good behaviour, bodily curiosity, the peculiar viscera of Adam, Eve and all their deformed, stump-legged children. Proof that when the Victorian age collapsed under its own weighty ideals and detail, the dark varnish peeled off and stood up on its own, ghoulishly, and that weird spectre did a clatterbone jig right into the next century.

Cy had heard it said that twenty thousand light bulbs blew out on Coney every day – he himself lost one every month or so. In the first decade of the new century it boasted to consume more power a week than an average American city, and when Cy got there it had only added to itself after the sporadic fires that from time to time took down its magnificently housed attractions. Perhaps it was the smell that characterized the place for Cyril Parks. Not the perspiring adrenalin of its customers or the popped corn, the fry of meat and potato knishes, Nathan's nickel hotdogs, not even the grease on the runners of the newly refurbished Steeplechase, or the salty sea air on the skins of the customers. Other seaside resorts had those qualities, Morecambe Bay had those qualities. What characterized Coney Island was the bitter, slightly sulphuric odour of lights popping, of electric energy being fundamentally used up and escaping from behind glass.

≈

The day that Lulu died was the day Cy knew with certainty that the place itself was also doomed to expire. Something had belly-flopped hard and was smarting. Some vital ingredient of the Island was curdling. The management was killing one of the park's elephants. It turned out to be blasé amusement, for all its hideous effort. The beast, normally gentle, had accidentally killed a man, backing over him while avoiding a speeding vehicle on the road so that his chest and legs were crushed, and his bones made themselves known to the world through his flesh. Lulu was usually found wearing tassels and twirling batons in the Luna circus. She had spent years carrying excited children in a woven basket on her back. Her execution was advertised in the papers and Cy did not truly know why he attended it but he did so. And he was sorry that he did, sorry with himself and his disgraceful curiosity, and sorry for Lulu, who must have known from the way the eyes of humans had changed from kind to cold when they regarded her after she felt the delicate crickle-crackle of skeleton underneath her foot, that she was no longer loved. And then Cy was sorry for Coney Island, for its maliciously disassociated behaviour and its fate. Lulu had been, at one time, a very popular attraction. She could stand up on her hind legs and balance a person on her head. She could kneel and turn tricks with balls and hula-hoops and blow peanuts into the crowd, catch them in the gripping tip of her trunk when they were thrown back. Nobody seemed to care that the twenty-year-old mascot of the circus was condemned, except for her trainer who was restrained in his house that day and eventually given a sedative by a doctor to prevent him from harming himself or anyone else in an effort to save her. Nobody else shed a tear when the switch was thrown, and maybe that was not so very surprising.

Because the place was going down the tubes. Because it had begun to stink. Because there had been a reduction of reactivity to stimulus lately, for it seemed even in the new world with its distant limits to freedoms, you could only go so far before nothing worthwhile and appealing was left. The people had become unimpressed, like devilish abusers who were filled with ennui, they had molested entertainment, consumed it and driven up their tolerance for being entertained, they wanted bigger, they wanted better, more muck, more magic, and they were not getting it. Cy could see it in the glassy, unblinking eyes of onlookers when Madame

Electra took to her mains-fed chair and hit the button, and he knew just what they were thinking.

– So the broad likes to sizzle, so what else is new?

And when Swiss Cheese Man threaded metal hooks through holes in his body and was hoisted up on cables into the roof of the tent where he performed, the applause was staccato, bored. There was a disinclination to ride the chutes more than once, children used to run back for another go, and another, and another, now they whined to their parents for candy instead. Things changed accordingly and rapidly. If a ride didn't appeal and make money it was dismantled. It was out with the old, in with the new, and nobody wanted to put a hand to a brow and squint down the road to the future to see where the artificial replacement would end, at what point there would be nothing left to consume. It seemed that every day when Cy came to work there was something being packed away in crates and something else being unloaded and bolted together. The Island's thrill was diminishing year after year. Movies were now in vogue and cheap and a step further out into an abstract world where fantasy was less touchable, less refutable, wires were less visible when people flew.

As a reward for their dissatisfaction, the public had been given new and more shocking shows, spineless children in wicker baskets, human beings born as if through a washing-mangler, things Cyril Parks, with his moderate sensibilities, had trouble reconciling. But the worst had already been seen and there was not the strange anthropology of Nature's Mistakes any more, which had once educated and delighted New York's citizens, it was simply perpetual titillation, sickness for its own sake, the search for a high. Dreamland itself had burned years earlier and the original dreams of the place were still being eaten by the flames. Gone was the noble entertainment model. The crowds had become hooked on the salacious, that feeling in the stomach, that rush. The once-great inventors and builders of the Island had died or were bankrupt, now the place was reduced to the mere business of fake-freakery and fast metal, the give-them-what-they-want theory. And the crowds knew it. And the workers knew it, and they knew the crest of the wave could not last. It was why everyone talked quickly and at cross-purposes to each other about work, not answering questions about new routines or costumes. It was why the dwarfs in Midget Land grew suddenly concerned with their bank accounts and their retirement plans.

Coney now had all the desperation of a mistress high on some cheap substance, eager to please her lover, terrified and motivated by the knowledge that he was becoming less interested in her charms and she could no longer instinctively guess his fetish or cavort to his wishes. So there was a sense that, although things continued at an alarmingly intense level of savage entertainment and consumer demand, the full-steam-ahead status quo could not go on. If Coney was the city's whore, the city's narcotic escape, the desperation of her sexual effort was climaxing in some unimaginable and deviant and tragic way.

And so Lulu's death became more of a thrill than her life. And it disappointed. The circus management charged ten cents entry to see her demise. She was led into the ring she had been led into so many times before and though it was not the man she was used to having lead her, she still went. She was about to kneel and begin her act when she felt unfamiliar copper coils placed around her two front legs but she was a trusting animal and she did not protest. She lifted her trunk and showed her crinkled lips to the audience, expecting a cheer. Cy looked around. People were chewing on roast nuts they had bought from a vendor, picking sticky pieces out of their back teeth with their fingernails. After a few seconds of massive voltage Lulu's hide began to smoulder and her eyes rolled back. After years of service, one wrong back-step over a passing pedestrian and she was no better than glue, or four hollow umbrella stands, no better than the profit she represented. She made no sound, not even the bleat of a smaller animal, her mouth was paralysed and unable to vocalize what she felt. But Cyril Parks knew what she felt, or at least he knew in part what she felt. That rigid, disempowering energy that makes every fibre in the thing it touches a slave to its command, that white-hot possession. He knew from Mrs Preston's electro-therapy head-gear. Except that Lulu had no friend to knock off the switch when she had taken her fill of electricity, the courtesy that Jonty and Morris had once paid him. Her quivers seemed not to match her size, and to Cy that marked the tragedy of the event, the pathos of it – that muted quality, which ultimately failed to please the audience, for their gladiatorial thumbs remained down. Her death throes were just subtle ripples in her great grey body, small ruffles on the vast surface of skin and along her ears. Her trunk straightened a fraction, her softer parts began to blacken. She must have died before the power was knocked off, for she did not stagger and sway before slumping to the side when it was finished. Her life popped. She dropped. She went out immediately like another of Coney's bulbs.

There were a few 'oohs' and 'aahs', a cough or two at the unpleasant odour produced by the execution. Then a grumble swelled through the big top, as multiple unkind comments about the show were made.

– I expected her to explode! Brought a hat in case of a mess. You ever see a squirrel catch a stray current? Those things 'splode like firecrackers!

– I rode her when I was a child, you know. If I'da known she was a killer elephant I never woulda let my Pappy lift me up on her. When I think how close I musta come to . . . well, it don't bear thinkin' about.

– Phew-ee! Smells kinda like liver-mush frying.

Cyril Parks put his head in his hands and rubbed his eyes. Then he softly addressed himself and the grizzling crowds.

– Lancashire or Yorkshire, sir? Meat or fat?

Perhaps only the final show, the death of the Island itself, would give the public a fix large enough to sate their habit, so that the dome of whitish light consuming the horizon on the edge of Brooklyn one night or week or month or decade in the future would once again and for one last time have meaning to it, validity. And until then the desperate carnival would continue its spluttering, groaning wind down. And Cy would just have to choose his moment to bow out.

$\sim$

The booth on Oceanic Walk was tiny, and looked more like a cupboard for fishing equipment or brooms than a place of business. It had something reminiscent of that section of the Pedder Street shop behind the curtain that separated browsing customers from the union of artist and canvas, a private enclosed realm. It was located at the scaffolding base of the bobsled ride so the wooden walls rattled and shook when the carriage whooshed past and occasionally flash fell down and had to be re-mounted. Cy usually arrived in the mid-morning and unboarded the booth, stacking sections of wood against the outer wall. He had overlaid as many pictures on the inside as possible and there was room for only himself and one other person to sit or lie down. There was a power outlet, a bright overhead light, and a drawer for extra equipment. And that was all. But he needed no more. On busier days he would try to have his customers line up along the alley, past the hotdog vendor and the shooting range, so that they were kept busy with frankfurters and targets while they waited, past the dental practice with the huge, floating, long-rooted molar on its sign and down to the cigar shop at the end of the Walk. But the crowd would inevitably curl round the booth's doorway, breaking up its queue to watch the proceedings and he'd have to instruct them not to push in.

– Back up there. Watch out sir, if you spoil this gentleman's work he'll no doubt want to spoil your face. Back up now, ladies and gents. Mind the door. I must have some room.

And again an orderly line would form, and again it would disassemble. Some of the other parlours and booths had hired a bouncer to keep the crowds organized. It made only a temporary difference. Customers were curious to watch the work being done, they wanted to see the proceedings as they got to see every other marvel in the fair. So they came and they pushed and they looked around the heads of others and tried to fit into the booth itself. If someone had rolled back the roof of the booth on a turn-twist key they would have seen them all jammed together, like sardines in a tin.

∽

In the first half of the twentieth century, every budding tattoo artist worth his salt on the upper East Coast gravitated to the Island or to the Bowery to get apprenticed or to get ideas or to gain notoriety. At Coney tattooing was the fine art of the place. Like a portrait painter recording noble faces and mansions for posterity's drawing room, the tattooer was a cheap, modern-day equivalent. Arturas had explained it thus, on the wall outside the Gravesend warehouse.

– We are the poor man's illustrator. We bring art to the working-man and he has a picture gallery of his own, like the mansion house or castle is his body. It's beautiful, yes? We do good.

Cy would rent his summer booth for several years and through the winters, when Coney quietened down and became foggy and forlorn and empty, he'd work from the back room of a barbershop in his neighbourhood owned by Den Jones, an old black man transplanted from the America South. Den Jones would have him when trade was slower and the rides were unplugged and the parks shut, when only the maddest of the mad and the indestructible members of the Polar Bear Club took to the sea, but hair still grew in Brooklyn and people still bought tattoos. The off-season work was pleasant, a tidy arrangement. A kid named Joe ran a shoe-shine pedestal outside the store, so they could charge two-dollars all round for a cut, a shine, and a tattoo. The smell of citrus pomade and foam and wet gamey hair was

197

comforting and Jonesy always had the radio tuned to a station with good old-fashioned tunes, or sometimes the Yiddish station if the waiting room was full of old Jewish men. Things slowed down. Customers sat around and chatted about the ponies and their dreadful families and second-storey guys flummoxing the authorities. The frenzied pace of the summer froze like ice on the sidewalks. In the barbershop there was no need for the incessant patter and haggling and tense brokerage for the benefit of the customer, like with Coney's masses. In terms of professional barkery the year was peaks and troughs, feast and famine. In any case Cy was used to turning it on and off, and used to seasonal work, he had grown up with that structure to his life, and to him it was as natural a change as the weather. Come October he transferred his pictures to the walls of the backroom in the barber shop. Asiatic eyes, hourglass girls, dragons erupting from nowhere, the new pieces with all that New York style and colour – there was a now a trend for heavy black bordering that gave new designs, variations of the standard, a sharp, comic-book, cartoon feel. Cy would wander through into the shaving parlour when he was not busy and listen to the stories told by Den Jones, good-humouredly resisting the man when he tried to coax him into the chair to trim his unkempt locks up off his collar. He got the sense that old Jonesy liked him just for the ambition of wanting to take away his long hair.

– Look at that crazy mess on your head, no wonder no lady ever steps up to greet you. You look like some damn nineteenth-century throwback, do you know that? Well, it about gives me the ju-jus, truth be told.

Occasionally the police would come round and make their presence known. Cy had not the strength of numbers to defend what was seen as slightly wrong and slightly freakish here as he had at the Island, which was left to its own devices, or maybe the barbershop set-up was still too controversial an enterprise, mixed raced and cross religioned, it was never made clear. The cops did not seem to want anything other than to stride around the place examining things. Once they removed his equipment and did not bring it back, saying something about a sanitation check, blood diseases and infection control. Rumours had been flying around New York since Cy's arrival on the scene about a total ban on the trade that was coming, though nothing had been publicly announced. It did not matter, in New York what was outlawed was often still as available as what was legal, he had quickly found. He apologized to Jonesy for the inconvenience, offered to leave, but Den just laughed and shook his head and told him to cut his hair. Cy got hold of new parts, a drive shaft with a trapdoor mechanism, which made cleaning easier, there was a network in the city which provided most everything a person could want for, and he continued decorating bodies.

So the cops came back, and they fiddled and they stared. The younger ones seemed to fixate on the equipment Cy kept in the back room, staring at the vials of ink and the needle head as if intrigued that some people would allow others to stick them in a way that was not medical, as if there was a perverse sexual aspect to it and he was not right in the head. One or two would sneak back later and have work done, usually flags, military symbols and motifs, with names fixed accordingly to them. There was never anything theoretical like justice, nor the essence of an idea. But they seemed calm under the grating needle, as if enjoying the thirty-minute trip into the underworld and the brief freedom from authority, even as its trappings were printed on their arms. The older police never came back. They were tired overweight types, with swollen ankles and tarry coughs. They did not need to bunt confederacy or discipline or any other system of control. They had it under their skins already.

～

It was at the barbershop that Cy met Henry Beausang, another Southerner. Henry was a talker and something of a nuisance to Den Jones, frequently unable to pay for haircuts, and taking up the revolving chairs for an excessive amount of time while he slept. By some fluke of charm or chancery he managed to wheedle his way into Den's affections and was able to fast-talk him into a line of credit no other customer was permitted. It could have been that they were born in the same state, Georgia, not fifteen miles from one another, and they could reminisce about local dishes and gossip about old scandals. Or it could have been that here, in New York, a friendship was possible that might still otherwise, south of the Mason–Dixon line, have been disallowed. They bickered and they squabbled but ultimately they got on. Henry worked nights at the psychiatric hospital on the Avenue as an orderly. He was small and handsome and quick about the eyes. He was also a merciless, dedicated, unrepentant drunk.

Henry's mild curiosity about the tattoo artist in the back room soon got the better of him and one day he slipped through the door, which was off-limits to anyone not under-going work, and he went unnoticed for fully five minutes while Cy concentrated on the handle of a sword. The customer noticed him first.

– Your apprentice, I presume? He's a shabby fella, huh? Needs a trip to the steam room.

The hum of the machinery stopped.

– Excuse me? What apprentice?

Cy turned to look behind him. At the back of the room was a stretched bow of a man, leaning too far to one side as if he had run hard and had a keen pain in his ribs. He had a vaunt-ing smile and hooded eyes.

– Why, there's nothing to it. A chile could paint as very well.

– Excuse me?

Cy had been squatting across a chair and now he stood, gained some height, not in a truly threatening manner, but the intruder flexed upwards himself like a startled cat or as if in mock response. Usually nobody slipped in past Jonesy but

200

he must have been using the restroom or had gone out on a quick errand. Cy put down the equipment he was holding, carefully. The stranger stepped untidily towards him, waving a hand in front of him like a cop directing traffic.

– Whoa there. I don't wanna hafta kill you. Jus' came in to see, to see. Tha's all.

The smile doubled in size. There were scars on the man's face, like those of a boxer, fat paunches of tissue and thin-cut lunulated marks along the bone. Cy realized the man was drunk and jumpy – a strange combination, usually there was a slurred, diffuse aggression to the anger of drunks, not focus, so perhaps another narcotic was acting as an energetic bedfellow with the booze – and he was quite possibly very dangerous. There was something about American confrontation Cy did not yet know how to navigate, not in the way that he could comprehend the butch inebriated combat, the smut, and the easily classified sober quarrels of his compatriots. It often had qualities of recklessness, wildness and inexplicability that made him nervous and uncertain of his ability to handle the protagonist. This man had an imagined capacity to fight that went well beyond the borders of his physical form, a vain-glory, that much was obvious. Something in the foreground of his eyes revealed that a message had been sent down from his brain informing him that he was completely invincible, and therefore fearlessness was the natural order of things. He kept touching his breast pocket as if tapping a weapon stashed within. Cy suddenly got the urge to finish the sword, he wanted to finish it if he was going to fight or perish, he didn't want to leave an unfinished piece of work. He sat slowly and took up his needle.

– Do you want work done?

– Naw. Not me, sir. Not on mamma bird's baby. Haha, you're an Englishman.

– Yes.

– Well I'm a Frenchman by history so that about makes us equally and thoroughly bad, now don't it?

Cy pulled his braces down over his shoulders so they hung at his sides, he unbuttoned another fastening on his shirt and bent back in towards the sword. The drunk crab-stepped closer in. There was a smell of alcohol on him that had been passed through the skin and mixed with sweat. It was a distinctive odour, like the smell of a man not far back in Cy's memory. Alcohol fumes in the air and the sense that he was being scrutinized sent a shiver through him. But Cyril Parks continued as he had always continued under pressure. With a steady hand. Red on the sword's hilt. A broad border of black to keep it from spilling. He switched needles. Yellow blade, yellow blade. The hairs in the pores on the customer's arms were blonde and dark at their tips, as if he had very recently travelled into old age. Around the delivered ink and under the wiping cloth the skin was beginning to inflame. It took ten minutes to finish, ten minutes of full concentration, slow internal time, with Cy half-believing he would, at any moment, receive a bullet or a blade in his kidney. When he looked around the strange man was sitting cross-legged on the floor sleeping with his chin touching his chest – eastern-god style. Cy leaned over and gently reached into the man's pocket for the weapon and instead pulled out a hipflask of bourbon.

Den Jones stuck his head round the door.

– O Lord! That no-good kid bothering you? He don't sleep when he gets off work so he falls asleep wherever he is through the day like a damn stray cat. Starts drinkin' the minute he leaves the hospital, like he'd rather do that than get some proper rest! Henry! Henry Beausang, wake up and brush off your pants seat and drink some coffee. Black coffee.

∽

After the first winter at the barbershop they might have been considered friends. Cy took to Henry in a quiet, reserved manner, and Henry's enthusiasm saw little restriction in the face of a tepid foreign temperament. Henry began to re-sell stolen hospital gauze and needles to Cy, at a cut-rate price that was all profit to himself. He even 'borrowed' an old hospital steam sterilizer, which Cy used to keep his equipment sanitary, saying it had been sitting idle in the store room for all the years he had patrolled the dull, grey umbilical corridors of the asylum, and it may as well be put to use. For his part Cy inherited Den's role of benefactor, giving to Henry what money he could spare if his wages had been taken from him in a brawl or he had spent too much that month on liquor, lottery slop, or whatever else lit him up, leaving not enough for rent. When word got back that Henry was in trouble or badly beaten, Cy would arrive on the scene. He was well versed in the skills of salvaging drunks. He did it because, after a decade with Eliot Riley, it was second nature to him, the way a person trained in medicine will be the first one to administer aid if a passer-by falls in the street or burns their hand, the way Reeda tended her consumptives, year after year, from habit. Or maybe there was something else that made Cy do it, the idea that Henry was somehow a redeeming version of Riley, younger, hopeful, benign to others if not to himself.

The first night of many that Cy carried Henry back to his own apartment, not yet knowing where the other lived, and put him on the floor to sleep off his stupor, he realized that his new friend was barely out of his teens. Henry was well banged-up, his cuts had begun to congeal and needed cleaning before an infection was sealed in. Cy took off the torn shirt that had grime on the collar and cuffs, removed his bloody vest and found underneath a small boyish chest, with only a few adolescent hairs on the breastbone. He had taken many more blows to the face than to his body in his life it seemed. So there was prolific damage and false years of ageing above the lines of his clothing. He put a blanket over him and a glass of water within reach. In the morning the blanket was folded neatly on a chair, the water glass was defiantly full, and Henry himself was gone.

A routine developed on Henry's weekends off. There was one Saturday repetition like a nightmare that kept on recurring in which Henry flirted balefully with death and danger. Somebody would come to get Cy at the barbershop or at Coney, depending on the season, to tell him Henry Beausang was sick-drunk behind the train station again, or by a bench in the park. Tipped over into the dust and haemorrhaging from a beating he had just taken by men he had tried to swindle or resemble or call the bluff of or God knew what other transgression. Cy would leave his work, a bird half flying across a bicep, and he'd go down and get his friend, hauling him back to somewhere safe. He'd put his hands on the ribs that weren't broken and place Henry into a part balance, part lean, then he'd throw the weaker, dislocated shoulder back into joint. At this Henry would wake up enough to laugh at the sensation, making his face beautiful, desperate, and foolish. And then he'd realize what the sudden jolt against his torso actually was, and pain would arrive. He would jump back livid so Cy would have to mind his feet quickly out of the way or Henry would be tripped down in the road again. But by then the drunk was awake and upright and could stay there to be helped home, singing and rejoicing like Riley never did.

Every Saturday that Henry did not have to work a graveyard shift it was like clockwork exploding. He was lighter than Eliot Riley, made of skin and bones only, and polite in his position of helplessness but that was all that could be said in favour of the situation. Cy would chide him, scold him, tend to him, and would end up finishing the second tattooed wing of the bird later for no cost to the annoyed, abandoned customer.

– But why does he do it, Den?

– Why does any drinker do it? He's got devils in him that are too slippery to catch. Carrying around a lot of family disgrace in him too. He comes from a wealthy family, Baptists every last one. Now I know that ain't in your understanding

Cyril, but take it from me it ain't good. Let them down bad. He was married once to the daughter of some rich cotton tycoon and did that lady a disservice so bad his mamma about threw him out of the state of Georgia. Him and his best school friend were found together embracing like husband and wife behind the bandstand at the reception. See, Henry married is like a chicken taking up with a hog. Half the time it ain't a fight he's looking for. No sir. Those men don't beat him because they know what he can't do to them, they beat him for what he's willing to do. But I ain't no-one to judge. We've all come to this city carrying suitcases full of history, and that's the God-honest truth. That boy might have been born on third base but he sure as shit ain't scored a triple.

∼

Then it was back to Coney Island after the cold damp Brooklyn winters of working on men with wet flecks of fresh cut hair on their skin. In the summer he'd unboard the dusty booth, re-dress it and work along with the sounds of hurtling coasters and carnival barkers. Henry would come by and laugh at the shows and say the hospital had nothing on this place and he'd drink in the bars on the alleys with Cy, faithful and persistent and less likely to jar, or as if he just felt happier alongside the Coney crowd.

The artists tattooing around the parks and the avenues of Coney Island were mostly very talented, the good mechanics of their trade, inheritors of Chuck Wagner's legacy, of bold-coloured, heavy-bordered symbols. Wagner himself came down for vacations to Coney and would stick his big plum-nose into the booths from time to time. The shyster copyists and dross merchants lasted only a season or less before fading out of the façade, before being kicked out, not being able to compete in such a skilled industry. The talented prospered; Arturas had not exaggerated the volume of work. There was something genuine about the artists amid the artificial stimula-tion, something older, timeless, a lasting appeal, like scrimshaw placed alongside the plastic novelties. They were at odds with the tricksters now lining the freak tents, who passed by Cy's booth in costume at midday before the matinee shows, with glued-on ears or dyed skin, self-made freaks instead of those with genuine birth debility – the ichthyosis sufferers, the bearded women or armless children with teeth as strong as pliers who had in the past reigned supreme. The truly old-school terrible, like the Human Fountain, a man with water pipes forced under the skin of his arms, which led down to his finger-tips from where the spray would be ejected like plasmic geysers into the air, had become lost among the mass of counterfeit sensationalists. Freakery was now the means to a quick buck, where once it had had something bizarrely disciplined and formal if brutal about it – like the mad-dog children yanked from the woods of Idaho and pitied by civilization, or the Human Fountain himself, meticulously cleaning the pipes under his raw skin each evening to prevent infection – that was professionalism at its highest. Cy had once had a strange conversation with the Human Fountain about cleaning solution outside his booth, they were curious of each other's equipment, and he had been left full of admiration for the man, who seemed at once so normal and yet so extraordinary.

– I used to just use salty water but if it's not the right temperature the salt will clog up. I like less chemicals. Have you tried a tiny amount of ammonia or white spirits when you clean your gun? Vinegar may do as well, though. Obviously I don't have the pleasure of steam or I'd cook like a wonton!

– I find bleach will work also but it needs to sit. There is so much movement to these new pieces that the ink gets everywhere. I like to dip my quill often, so to speak. Call me old fashioned.

– Oy. The days of old fashioned are no more, I fear. Some days I think I will have to take out my own spleen to get a cheer. Me, I have to bring fluid through my pipes every morning, regardless of a show, otherwise I'm asking for trouble, I'll get made a mess of. An hour or more every time, and people say you have no skills, you are just a joke, you aren't marketable! Now it's just like eating or washing my face, I guess; I do it without thinking.

Tattooing was the one culture at Coney that had lasted over the years, and remained credible, arresting audiences in their tracks. It was something that could be done to the watching, yawning, masses that included them, a sensation actually felt by them. That was the very nucleus of its longevity – inclusion, involvement, connection. Where other shows now missed the mark, tattoo artists struck the bullseye time and again, allowing customers to self-customize, to tailor their own ride, and they brought them the physical sensation and the realm of suffering and beauty which was sought. Reputations were hard fought for in New York City but, once achieved, they seldom were demolished. The lone female tattoo artist on the Bowery, Minny Hendry, was as admired for her hand-poked work as she was ridiculed for her anomalous gender within the profession. Cy had not a bad word to say against her, he had seen her daintily executed designs, and he imagined Reeda clipping him round the ear for it anyway. There were still prickles between those in the industry at Coney, tongue-in-cheek rivalry, to goad the crowds, but trade was good enough to support all the booth artists. Sometimes Arturas would stop by Cy's booth in the late afternoon or evening and shadow-spar with him.

– How many today, my friend?

– About twenty. Twenty-five.

– Hah! Rinky-dink, I knew it all along! Me, I work over fifty as usual. So tonight I buy the beer for you, since I am still best and richest artist at Coney.

Cy walked in to the Island with the lucky dice of the free-hander, he knew that particular skill carried anywhere, it was his best card to play, doubling the prices from the offset. He could lie on his back and paint a whole body, did not need any more than a needle, some ink and a muse. Some of the others had copied the model of Arturas and Claudia, and they had women that were decorated from head to toe, wives, girlfriends, even sisters. Other scrapers had partnerships with big, obese girls of no relation, carnival women who no longer grossed the public with mere size and needed new disfigurements, additional attractions, to remain useful in the Coney community where they now felt they belonged. Some weighed in at five hundred pounds, their glands all out of whack, and they had special boxcar transportation arranged for them to get them to the Island. Pictures got shipwrecked under the waves in the oceans of their rippling skin.

Cy lit up his booth with colourful signs and stark bulbs and convoluted claims of brilliance, as did the others, and he wore the hair of a Renaissance master and had a pierced ear. But he did not need to go to the trouble, it was merely in keeping with the costume of the place. Riley would have scoffed at him, informed him that he was a sell-out, a bootlick and an idiot, the sheep in wolf's clothing. But he did not care. If he wanted to he could remember that Riley was dead, even if the voice lived on in his head. Come mid-summer the crowds swarmed around the doorway of his establishment, drawn away from the screech of the Steeplechase horses on their metal tracking and the gasps inside the circus tents and the stomach-less laughter of turning upside down in the Loop-O-Plane, drawn to another kind of intrigue. They peered in between each other at wall-to-wall flash and watched him working and for once they were hushed, listening only to that notorious, serious sound – the gamma purr of the electric needle.

~

Varga Oyster Bar was no Dog and Partridge, but for Cyril Parks's habitual presence there it was a sort of equivalent. There were initial similarities; a menu that served a variety of fishy dishes, which ultimately all came out looking and tasting the same, a constant greasy smell of seafood in the air even when the kitchen fryers were not blasting clams or whelks, shrimp or oysters into crisp breaded cinders, the mismatched wooden furniture that had over the years picked up a faint slimy, sticky sheen, and it was frequented by a selection of regulars who were well-known to each other, visiting players and inevitable strangers. There was a gaming section to the bar, which had achieved a certain local infamy for its cerebral dexterity and its violence, and an outdoor beer garden mostly used for the purposes of courting, sobering or ending a dispute the quickest way. There were squabbles between punters and occasional brawls, merriment and banter, times of quietude for contemplation or the perusal of bad fortune, and the chance of a little look-see with a member of the opposite sex if the planets were in lucky alignment. And that's where the similarities ended.

Varga caught Coney's off-work crowd. Brighton Beach's weary old Russians wandered into the gaming room from time to time, strung-out drunks stumbled through the threshold, as did Brooklyn's braver souls, or occasionally a curious city resident who had heard an odd rumour about the proprietors. During the years that Cy worked at Coney Island and for the previous six, Varga had been run by a pair of Siamese-twin sisters, Mary and Valerie, who bore as little resemblance to Paddy Broadbent as chalk did to cheese. The sisters were joined at the waist and hip, and though they shared no organs and separational surgery would have been relatively simple for them, having missed that opportunity at birth owing to poverty and rural location, they remained of one entity, moving quick and coordinated around the bar to clear dishes and glasses. Their dresses were specially made with four sleeves and one full skirt, though it was not until they lifted a hem that their condition was revealed. Until then it could have been assumed that they simply walked in an exactly matching pace butting up against each other. The bar often ran on the system of good cop, bad cop, Mary being of the softer disposition and Valerie the tougher – there was trouble for those who would court the former for they would have to go through the latter, and Valerie was not one for romance, she was intimidating at best, able to oust even the meanest element at closing time and send the bums limping from the establishment smelling of a bucket of well-aimed fish guts. The Sweet and Sour Sisters, Cy called them, and on nights of failing lucidity he had even offered to tattoo them accordingly on their bosoms. For all the sticks and stones and taunting and teasing of their youth, the shame of adults to be handling them, and the knowledge that only two decades earlier conspicuous abnormals had been kept in cages with orang-utans in the Bronx Zoo, they were remarkably well-adjusted, fearless and very enterprising ladies.

They had worked at the Island's freak shows back in their youth, having been brought in from a small town outside Spokane, Washington, by Gumpertz's cronies, before retiring from circus life to a steadier profession. They took their ample money – having been paid a double rate of course and bartering only ever single rent at Coney's hotels and hostels, and bought a little space which had once been a chop house on Jones Walk, near the boardwalk, where the dish of the day was never certain and the alcohol was compulsorily served over ice. They timed their exit well, only a short time before the World Circus went into an irreversible decline at the insistence of even the larger, poorer crowds that they were becoming apathetic towards freakery and acrobats, and the pin-heads and Spider Boy and Cobrina were shuffled out into the unforgiving world of unmutant humanity.

Varga could seem like the wrong side of the looking glass. The punters were deformed or used to handling lions or too small to reach the bar counter while simultaneously boastful of their oversized ding-dongs. They had remarkable talents that they were not opposed to flouting. They could be extremely heavy drinkers and if Cy was out with Claudia and Arturas, whose simultaneous capacity to hold liquor well exceeded his own, or with Henry Beausang and his unholy sponge-like liver, he often ended the evening in a very sorry state. There were nights when everything within the sticky walls was a blur of wrong operation, like the subconscious product of a surgeon's trickling syringe, like a laughing-gas lullaby. Life at Coney could seem surreal and endgame at the best of times, but coupled with quantities of drink the labouring brain dissolved, leaked out through an ear canal, and a world of ridiculous inner sense found its escape. There were nights of stripteases and oyster-dances, dare-devil asphyxiation and fish-hook eating contests, nights so stupid that Cy thought he might wake up the next morning in his bed in the small rooms above the Pedder Street shop having dreamed-up America like the epic hallucinations of a coma, and Varga was the candied cherry on the iced bun of it all, the red nose on the clown. Sometimes he thought he might even bolt upright in his bed in the Bayview Hotel, ten years old again, having to shake away sleep, shake off the ether-like stupor, and he'd get up and go into his mother's room and find her sleeping in her headscarf. With a hand on her shoulder he'd wake her and tell her about the strangest of dreams he had just had, and she'd smile and say that the slumberous arms of Morpheus were curious, curious things, and that yes, America existed, and one day he might see it, though she doubted she ever would.

∾

Chess was Varga's passion. The bar ran midweek tournaments that were dangerous, florid affairs. Tuesday and Wednesday was the topsy-turvy weekend for the workers at Coney who were otherwise kept busy Saturday and Sunday with their shows and professional roles when the rest of New York wanted relaxation and fun. On these uneventful days they took their break from the jaunty, vulgar entertainment world, shut down their bodies and their rides, and became just normal folk with leisure time. Some went into the city for their own entertainment, the art of the museums, the excitement and invisibility of walking amid the thronging masses in Manhattan. Brooklyn absorbed many of the workers back into its massive corners where they sat out on stoops and gossiped about the Island, scrubbed costumes clean and hung breeches with tail-sleeves out to dry. Corporeal deformity and mystery were packed away. Ordinary speech was made, and love; sleep was enjoyed, vigs and bills were paid.

It was never clear how the chess tournaments got started, it was simply understood that that's where they were held. Mary and Valerie themselves did not play the game, and the tournaments had been running before they took over the establishment. Since Cy had first started coming to Varga there had been chess gatherings. The game was not played as he had always imagined it to be played, in the drawing rooms of nice houses between fathers and sons, in the expansive high-ceilinged rooms of European manors and estates, to polite, white-gloved applause. It was played viciously and inconsiderately. With expletives and bets. Legend had it a player had been stabbed in the gaming room of Varga over a debate about the origin of the game itself. One man had said China, his opponent maintained India, tempers frayed, a knife appeared and things got crazy. The fight was barely a fight at all, just one sharp stroke that punctured a lung, and Mr China was carted out feet first only two theoretical moves away from the first check of the game. It seemed that intellect and bohemian temper were not exclusive features in Varga. No watches or sand-timers were employed to keep the proceedings moving along – though if a player was taking too long to make a move the opponent was permitted to use psychological tactics as encouragement. Inciting comments, provocative gestures, cigarette smoke blown casually in a face. Frequently the tournaments went on until the early hours of the morning, or into the next day. Riley would have said that it was a canny contravention, the game of princes and goddesses had been well and truly bastardized by a proletariat rabble. Those who did not play often observed the games, catching their breath when a rook swept away a bishop, clearing an open weft-ward path to the unprotected king, and adding to the already flinty tension. If the noise of the audience increased, or news of a queen's gambit broke, it passed along the rows of spectators, and new onlookers would be drawn from the other rooms, squeezing in to the smoky gaming arena. It was said more games ended in an argument or a skirmish in Varga than with capitulation or a victory move. That was just the way things went.

There were no two chessboards alike in the bar. They had arrived on the premises from various locations, other incarnations, foreign countries, having seen the world in all its brilliant and bustling and beggarly wonder. They had been sold on markets and in boutiques and in tents and bazaars, or had been made especially for royal children by master carvers. They had been saved from plundering empires and looted from ransacked museums. There were smoked glass boards with polished pieces, others made of varnished wood, pink and cream ivory, jade, woven straw and slate. There was even a bronze board that weighed as much as a human head, with a hole in one corner where an emerald had been pried out.

Players were amateur professionals and minor celebrities from Coney, from all over the city and beyond. Local champions attended with regularity, vying over the top spots. Occasionally a flamboyant character would turn up and draw the attention of the locals, an English shire-man who wore a top hat to compete in because he said it brought him luck, and a Russian who had come over for the world tournament in '39 and had heard bizarre tales of the Coney Island chess-wars and wanted to see them for himself. There was once an ex-congressman, a motion-picture star, a duke, an African chief. There were the old Europeans who played chess in Prospect Park in the day under the shady trees and in Varga at night, who would not allow their photographs to be taken if they won. There were carnival workers and the inventive, sequitor-minded children of the circus. And then there was Grace.

– The Lady of Many Eyes –

Grace had solemn eyes that were territorial and displaced and dark, like the eyes of the children from eastern Europe that had, for the last two years, been arriving in England in droves on the Kindertransport. She was perhaps twenty years too early for those trains and there might have been eyes like hers all over Brooklyn that had arrived there by some stray, unorganized miracle, by their own dogged mobility. Her eyes said that she also arrived young in a foreign country, or on the cusp of two ages, that time when life can be so easily hindered or so easily accelerated at the bidding of a catalyst, holding the hand of someone who may or may not be her father, a man who disappeared into the crowds of the great city shortly after the boat docked and the official checkpoints were cleared. The eyes spoke somehow of abandonment and resolve, and about a new name, eclipsing and clumsy and Christian, which was designed to cancel out bitter history and give her peace but didn't. They spoke of adoptive parents, early efforts to learn a language that fitted in her mouth like a wrong shape, triumph, for she was determined in that as in all things, and other languages picked up in waiting rooms and on street corners and with the exchange of money. They said something of failed immigration procedures and a leap to the underside of the city without a second thought because she would not ever go backwards in life. And they described how the taste of her homeland's traditional foods was not quite the same in America, not quite, there was a subtle mistranslation. But when she heard violin music on Brooklyn's Yiddish radio and those sad male voices lamenting through apartment windows and inside restaurants the city suddenly seemed like a familiar local graveyard, inhabiting the ghosts of her never revealed nation and she could grieve.

There was an important secret about New York that Grace found out one day, very early on after that brave leap from one civilization to another, lying on the sidewalk with blood coming from her nose and legs. She took a guess at universal human kindness and spoke a very old and very reliant word to a stranger. And a woman she didn't know spoke the same word back to her and helped her up. The secret was that if the city tipped just so against the light you could see a fine web between corresponding human hearts throughout it, like a spider's web revealed in the grass on the steppe in the morning dew against the sun. It connected all paths and all peoples with a frail strength that could be traversed if you learned how to move that way. And she learned to tightrope it, like a little spider from home to home, from neighbourhood to neighbourhood, delicately between native tongues and histories and cultures. And the beauty was, if you turned and looked behind you, perhaps you would see that you had spun a separate strand along which others could then follow, adding to the web.

Cyril Parks swore that he saw all this in Grace's eyes when he first met her, in the spring of 1940. Beyond that he could only speculate, for she never spoke of an abandoned town's name, a river indicating the border of two countries on a map, a family crest or lowly shack, or which cruel twist in Europe's fabric by which cruel empire, monarch or army general's hand, had wrung her people out.

Her own troubles travelled down a long way into her, became mature in her voice like something that has churned and changed to a different substance after much motion and time. She slipped between identities, slipped the nets of conversations which would eventually trap her and pin her down. Her heritage was American, it was all she would ever say, slipping the country on like a large overcoat to cover her native dress. She knew the Polish butcher to affectionately call him Tatusiu, she knew her local synagogue Rabbi, the

Italians, the Ukrainians, she bought bulk-sized bags of oats and rusk from the Jewish bakery at trade price. She knew the recipe for the pogácsa which the Hungarian mothers baked in ashes for their departing sons. She would send the men and women and children of southern Brooklyn to Euginio, Oceanic Walk's resident dentist, saying that he was her uncle, she washed her dresses and headscarves alongside the black women that were domestic servants and the Japanese women and the poorer Jewish daughters at the great concrete and iron sinks of the washhouse because amongst the steam and suds gossip and songs translated into community. In the meat-packing district of the city she exchanged money with middle business men. Most people presumed her to be their own, emancipated but choosing to remain associated, and their presumptions simply made it so. It turned out she had the bad temper of every nation, showing it sporadically and viciously, and she could curse profoundly at anyone of any offending nationality as she could also console and toast and bless. She may have known the songs of the Saracens and the secrets of Cleopatra's maidservants with their cosmetic confidentialities, the great kings of the Middle East, and every carnival cousin in Russia for all anyone knew about her. Her soul might have been loaned by one of several supreme or subordinate beings. She may have owned the petrified heart of Icarus and the charred harness of his blackened wings. She took to Coney like an otter to the shining, reedy river, had worked there for several years before Cy came to meet her. Those who knew her were not surprised by her choices, though this did little to undermine the irrevocable misfortune of her story.

~

They were neighbours. It was four in the morning and Cy was suddenly in possession of some new information regarding one of the tenants of his building – the one from 104, with the doorway smelling of the countryside. Her name was Grace. Her eyes were dark and productive, there were traces of auburn in her dark locks lit by the streetlamp and a piece of straw was sticking up from a roll of hair by her ear like a fashion accessory. She was a remarkable woman, he would soon find out, having a mind that went out like a rider on horseback to meet an enemy, both courageous and negotiating, but ultimately loyal to her own side. Both parties had been on their way home, walking away from the still riotous, still inebriated Island. Cy liked to walk at night when he was tipsy, it gave journeys a mythical feel.

As he passed by the small park several homeless drunks were sleeping on benches, or shuffling about in the undergrowth. The atmosphere was gestational and insect, creatures in the trees and bushes had woken up after winter from their larvae pods and were making music on their wings and hind legs. The bats above were intent on their business, flailing through the sky towards the presence of water or blood. Unrecognized species were stirring in black corners of the park, cruttering, scuttling, ratching. It was a night of city wildlife, it had something living and restless about it. As if it was ready for her entrance.

He did not meet her first. He met her horse, drinking furiously from the fountain at the entrance of the park itself, drinking as if it would drink the source dry. It was not startled when he came upon it. It turned its head in the water so that one profoundly placid eye could watch his approach. He had not seen a horse this close since leaving England, not even in the circus at Coney – the tiny, pig-like horses that the midget police department rode. This was a horse of quite larger proportions and in the dim light he could see that it was black, black-brown, or at least dark enough to look like a horse-shaped hole in the slightly lighter street. In fact, as he got closer, he found it was enormous, and it wore no bridlery or tackle. Warm with alcohol and enchanted by the irregular urban vision he moved towards the animal, which then stopped drinking from the old mossy font and raised its head. It snorted gently. It had obviously been positioned in his path for the sole purpose of improving upon his misty, bard-like composition. What better than a horse, the oldest and most trusted other half of ancient human-creature partnerships to petition his imagination? While dogs ran wild on the plains and in forests, horses were carrying warriors into battle, they were tilling the land and guiding pathfinders across perilous sand.

– Hello, boy, what are you doing out so late at night alone? Where did you come from then? Did you break out of somewhere, clever boy? Did you jump over a ten-foot hedge?

He put a hand up to its muzzle, rubbed where it was softest, where it felt like a piece of brushed muslin. The horse nosed his ear, snorted again and tugged on his long hair with its dripping, bearded mouth.

– Oh. He likes you.

A woman stepped out from behind or underneath the beast, it was not immediately clear, as if from a doorway in the massive creature, and she ran a hand along its lower flanks with familiarity. The gesture stated that this was her horse. She was obviously the owner. Like a lightning conductor she grounded the current of the dream and it brought him round a little from his reverie. She was in any case the antidote to his flight of fancy, her attire was much too plain and modern for one thing. She should have had on a cloak or shawl, something ethereal and medieval, and more fitting with the black horse at night, but she did not. Rather than being elfin or sprite-like she was dressed in a knee-length skirt and leather laced shoes, a plain blouse. There was a coat folded neatly over her arm. Her hair, but for the straw, was tidy, combed and pinned quite fashionably. It was as if she had of late finished typing documents in an office. Mostly it was her manner that evicted the gentle flocking thoughts in Cy's mind. She had definition. Her hand on her hip and the cock of her head described a psyche impartial to flowing robes and the lore of women in inoffensive or precarious situations. She seemed to change position every once in a while and then hold very still. Her eyes, even in the inadequate light, were each a litany of struggle, strategy, and survival. Cy spent a good few moments reading her life's history in them and then he pulled his hair free from the horse's mouth.

– He's yours?

The woman nodded, her eyes narrowing.

– Mine. I have a horse, but it's a secret past this street here. I thought perhaps you suspected, living so close by. Perhaps we can be quite noisy, coming in and out as we do? And the building is . . . indiscreet. Señora Ubago is blind but it is amazing what her sources tell her.

Her eyes again shifted inwards a fraction while she waited for her answer, as if in assessment, and they reflected a sickle-shape of streetlight. For a moment she had the look of a lawyer laying down a verbal trap for a witness. Or a fox up against a loose board of the chicken shed. Cy stared at her for a moment, not comprehending what she had said and distracted by all that was unrestful and then focused about her. A small gong sounded in his head, neither alarm nor warning nor accompanied by a voice calling an all clear, but heraldic of something, something. She made him want to shake off the haze around his brain and in his present condition, a half bottle of hooch the happier, it was not an easy thing. Evidently his vexation and slowness were easily interpreted.

– You live in my building. Second floor. The Electric Michelangelo. Works at Coney, drinks in Varga, doesn't play in the tournaments. English, northern. Doesn't mind Germans. Doesn't mind drunks. Doesn't say much, unless he's had whisky and is arguing with ghosts.

She had just reduced him to his basic existence, and addressed his foibles. It was a touch disconcerting, this ability, particularly given that he knew nothing of the woman in retaliation. He suddenly felt very careless, slovenly, and as if he had, ever since disembarking from the *Adriatic*, been observed closely through spy-glasses or by shady, door-way-concealed officials without his knowledge.

– I'm Grace. This is Maximus.

– Oh. Hello. Actually my name is Cyril. Cy. So where do you keep him? Does the building have stables?

Grace tipped her head to the side for a moment. The horse was nosing Cy's unkempt locks again.

– He really likes you. He likes your hair, he thinks it's his feed. He lives with me. He's my guardian, better than a dog. I can put him up against a door when the invaders arrive.

– I don't really understand. Lives with you where?

– Prosze. In my apartment, Electric Michelangelo, where else, have you seen the mess in the storage rooms? Not always, but sometimes it's necessary, there is not always room in the circus stables. And I don't like the way he gets treated down there. They can be cruel and stupid. You cannot put a horse in a stall next to a snow leopard or a lion. They do this and they wonder why he kicks down the door and tramples the side of the enclosure. Fucking idiots. He could have broken a leg. Poor Maximus.

Her expression did not allow for any doubt that she was telling the truth. And then the last of the thick, addling smoke blew away and Cy remembered the shadow-box menagerie below him on the wall in his first week of residence. And the fecund, agrarian smell in the hallway outside 104 was identified without the use of forensics or snooping guesses and given its correct label. Horse.

– Good Lord! I thought so. I mean at first I thought I was quite mad to imagine it – I thought I was being a dozy article. It has bothered me since I saw his outline, I'll confess. How is that possible. Is it allowed?

– I told you, it's a secret past this street right here. Señora would telephone the butchers if she knew. I tell her it is the paprika in the stews that smells strong, since she cooks only rice what can she say? But back there the whole world knows. We work in Luna.

– I won't tell a soul, you have my word. Bloody hell, nobody would believe it anyway.

The conversation became momentarily cloudy again.

– So there's no man?

– No man?

– In your apartment? With you? With a chest complaint, a cold? An old man, perhaps your father?

– An old man with a cold, no I don't think so. Just Maximus, but he has no cold. He had a cough last month. I gave him camphor oil in his hay, it seemed to work just fine. He's better now, aren't you, Maximus?

There was a matter-of-fact tone to her voice, an austerity, and yet it also had a quality of bemusement, not exactly sham presentation, but an internal humour, as if either option were available as evidence for the listener and would be upheld in a court of law. And there was the trace of an accent, at least her voice morphed convincingly through several accents, Slavic, French, Hungarian, more like a child raised by multi-lingual parents than a spoiled girl in a playhouse dressing-room trying on different personalities along with her costumes. And yet, right at the very back of the voice, like indistinguishable static noise on the radio, there was a note of preservation, it was an accent that had been held on to delib-erately when it could have been discarded – perhaps kept alive because of her chosen proximity to first-generation immigrants, perhaps through sentimentality or pride. She was watching him now, and occasionally glancing at the horse by the fountain. Her brows were dark but her face was pale and vividly sloped, with prominent, Tartar cheekbones. Cy could think of nothing else worthwhile to say. Following the recent disclosure, he felt small talk would be a meagre offering. This woman made him want to be very sure of himself, to stretch his brain an inch more and grasp what was going. And in that sense she was magnetic, pulling on thought and concentration, bringing him to her without moving herself.

He accompanied her home. Or perhaps he was himself accompanied, he didn't rightly know that night. Maximus was immaculately trained, it seemed; he followed Grace with the click of her tongue, passing patches of grass that a less well-behaved animal would have dropped its head into and locked its neck. It appeared there was no need for a rein or a bit. Their conversation seemed to Cy to be serious and effortful and somehow a failure, though the next morning he could remember nothing of it past her name, the bold whimsy of her keeping a horse in her apartment, and the image of her turning somersaults on the animal's back in the Luna circus. He remembered wanting to ask her if the horse was housebroken and not finding the courage, thinking it a frivolous thing. At the door of their building she removed her coat from her arm and under it were four hemp potato sacks and four lengths of string. She clicked her tongue again and Maximus lifted up his rear hind leg. Grace put it between her legs and between the pleats of her skirt. She fitted a sack over the thick unshod hoof and tied it on. This was repeated for the remaining three hooves – the beast was utterly compliant and on the last hoof Grace took out a blue-handled pocket-knife from her skirt, unhinged a tool and scraped a stone and some debris out of the depression. It was obviously a well-practised manoeuvre, both parties knew it by heart. She opened the door, took a look inside, gestured, and both Cy and the horse entered the old marble foyer. To his amazement the horse moved almost silently down the corridor, stepping high as if over small streams or boulders with each forward motion. Grace turned a key in the lock of her door and the horse ducked its long head as it went inside, into the darkness, like a pit pony entering a mine. She turned to Cy and before he forgot all about the details, he was aware of a small line at the top of her nose where her brow met in an expression of fortification and the humour lines surrounding her eyes. In the dim hallway her irises were so dark they seemed pupil-less, deep, vertigo inducing. There was a languid, sombre curve to her bottom lip. He could find a loveliness to her face as he looked at her that was underlaid with something aged and earnest. She was compelling in a way, and he wondered if he should perhaps lean in and kiss her, he was drunk enough to warrant it. He was about to when she made a sound under her breath, a murmur of enjoyment which also contained marginal dissatisfaction, as if she was tasting a spoonful of soup and trying to decide which ingredient to add next. Then she spoke.

– Yeah, anyway. I'm going to come and find you soon, Electric Michelangelo. I need your help with something. I think the time is right for a change.

She offered him a smile, and then she closed the door. He waited politely for a moment and then turned and went up to his apartment, walked to the window with a chair and sat to watch the brick wall opposite. Sunrise was a few hours away, it was deathly dark, and if Grace was still up and about with the lights on he might see her doppelgänger puppet again, acting out a simplified shadow edition of what she was doing. After a while he felt too tired to focus his eyes. Dually, he was certain that somewhere below him in the building was a woman who would never yawn and drowse, she would either be fully awake and wary of all her surroundings, or unconscious. He opened his window and blew a kiss to the empty brick wall. Then he lay down on his bed and slept off the incident of meeting Grace like it was balanced on the back of a black stallion galloping away from him or balanced on a temporary filament of night.

～

The next morning the apartment was cold from the open window and the rain which the daylight had brought with it. Before waking he had dreamt a succession of rapid, gritty dreams, his mind slipping and jamming from the leak of hard alcohol into his brain, flickering through meaningless images in photo-frenzy, stuttering like the heavy strobo-scope projectors in the Tunnel of Terror at Coney. With each misfiring shutter came another epileptic reel of pictures, of him running and ducking to avoid being skewered and torn apart by a giant crochet pick, him trapped in a sunken sub-marine at the bottom of an underwater canyon, its blue emergency lamp pulsing. At one point he woke only to find he had been telegraphed to another dream where his room was on board a train rattling along the edge of a mountain pass, Carpathian steep, with the tracks about to tip over, and he panicked to think he may never be restored to truth-ful existence. Finally it was the sound of the rain that woke him, like the long dark whispering hair of a woman being pulled across his ear. Soothingly.

Cy lit a cigarette in bed, pulled up the covers and tried to rub away his sore head. He thought of Grace. The sharpness and discordance of her had faded – the lawyerly intonation, the knife, the snappy dialogue – leaving an unformed image that could be fashioned into a smooth idea of a woman he might like to know and possibly touch. She was beautiful through the hair and mouth and eyes, he remembered. With the vague look of Salome about her – he had seen the dancer in a painting in one of Riley's old art books, pale and dark and intent, John's severed head behind her on a tray – perhaps if Grace held herself that way or let down her hair? She was undoubtedly clever and wilful, which was, if he was honest about it, nothing short of arousing to him, and he just plain admired the fact that she managed to house a horse in her room. The idea itself was baffling. That she got away with the covert dressage was brilliant. He had a sense that he liked her, very much, and not so far away from that prospect was the notion that he could love her, perhaps. He shivered, huddled down further in his bed, listening to the brickish drip of water outside the window. He could love her. Couldn't he? There was the potential. There was the rub. It was unclear if this was truly a resolution in his mind or simply an acknowledgement of a lesser kind. Perhaps, he thought, it is only ever a combination of the two – as if holding open the door for an ancient creature taught to enter with bound feet. It felt like another strangely exotic moment in his life, the pairing of Grace and love, not dissimilar to the day he had agreed to be Riley's lad, within half an hour or less of seeing Riley at work, of seeing the man's own magnificent coloured body. Maybe it was even as ludicrous as that first sighting of Eva Brennan, with her English-garden eyes and her freckled arms, when his heart came undone. That feeling of being befallen, of something preordained and unavoidable and uncontrollable at work, like the diaphanous flutter of Fate's lungs, the sluicing of its digestive system, its marrowy brewing of new blood.

He lay in bed for a while with a headache from the previous night's drink and a dry throat, looking at his ceiling and thinking back over the years of encountering women. He thought of the way he had set an affair in motion between Jonty and Eva, whom he had loved when he was thirteen years old. And after introducing them he had watched them first kiss on the pebbled mucky beach of Morecambe Bay as the tide was going out, feeling something heavy collapse down through him to the ground. He could remember that sensation as clear and awful as if it had happened only yesterday. Eva had left him romantically vulnerable, he liked to think, and that's why he had avoided love ever since, even if he had been with a few women in the parlour of Pedder Street after his needle had finished on them, their breathing fast together, their bodies aching and after a point coordinating. But it had been so long ago, that original offence, that the face of the girl he held responsible was gone, and only the feeling of damage remained. Now he was the true keeper of the experience. He had wanted to preserve it as Riley had kept his tattoos fresh and bright with Nivea lotion, because it seemed a meaningful thing to do. And in polishing it up like a brass fixture he had worn it down to its hub, until it was nothing. Eva could no longer be conjured up to explain his aversion and trepidation in matters of the heart. She would not suffice as an icon of pain and disappointment, her ghost, her sign could no longer be used convincingly to hold him back.

Since her, his mother had passed away, and though it had not been his choice to love Reeda and there had been no catastrophic disqualification of her love for her son, it was a wrenching emotional blow to lose her in the end. From that he had healed. It had been a less personal loss of love. Riley had scarred him up far worse with his fanatical abuse, he had opened channels in Cy that meant if he wasn't careful to keep them covered or pursed closed, the unstemmed passage of fury and scorn might occur, the overspill of reservoirs on the darker side of him. Riley had made him want to hate and fight, he had shaded Cy in. For a full decade the big man had been an excuse for sabotaging potential relations – he could not court with Riley as a manipulative joker in the deck, a scathing father who would tell a girl about her cunt over a cup of tea and a slice of cake. Dwelling on it he knew there was now an absence of a male plan-foiler or a symbol of female loss to propel towards an affair in order to avoid it or break it. There was nobody but he, alone, to ruin love. And now there was Grace, Grace with her dark eyes and her qualities and her horse.

He rose from bed and poured a glass of water and drank it. Then he drank another and refilled his glass. He felt hollow in his torso. Spacious. And nervous to be thinking about that which he was thinking. There was a strong presence in the room and he turned round suddenly to look behind him as if having caught sight of another being, but nothing was there, just a rumpled bed. Then he had the definite sensation of something moving on the periphery, just out of sight, waiting at the edge of him, restlessly, treading between memories, between his ribs and lungs, and nudging softly at the vacant chamber, knocking very timidly. Wasn't it always a question

226

of opening doors? His mother and Mrs Preston behind the sororal, screeching parlour door? Eliot Riley on the other side of number eleven Pedder Street? The blue cabin door at the top of the gangplank walkway up to the *Adriatic*? A key in the lock of a door in America that turned the wrong way? His heart was empty now and something of a mystery. And so one rainy spring morning at the start of a new decade he lifted the latch, opened it, and let Grace in.

≈

After that she seemed to be everywhere, but nowhere convenient that he could talk to her or put in his eyes an expression that would inform her of what was on his mind. He saw her riding down the boardwalk on Maximus, seated high above the throngs of people, all the strolling couples and the sugar-smeared, skipping children, the men in straw summer hats with canes and the ladies perspiring against mink in the rolling wicker chairs pushed by young black men. She was in costume, with a suit of sequin and a comb of purple feathers in her hair. She was standing up on the horse's rump bare footed, rising and falling steadily as he moved, dropping circus flyers to the pedestrians below. He tried to attract her attention but the crowd was too thick and noisy. Later that day he closed the booth for an hour and went to watch her perform in the circus. He had not been since witnessing the demise of Lulu, had sworn he would never return, but it seemed to be a mitigating motive. To loud trombone music and cymbal clashes the horse cantered briskly into the tent then round the ring with his tail held out while Grace swapped her feet with her hands on his back. She was strong, lithe, well constructed. But the face under the make-up seemed not to be hers.

Mornings and evenings he would pause outside her doorway, wondering if he should knock and ask her a question, something pithy and impressive, or ask her to join him for a drink. She seemed seldom to be home and when she was he often heard other voices in her rooms and shyness prevented him from announcing himself. And always, night after night, he would watch from his window for the silhouette theatre of her life to appear on the wall, her shape cut out by light like a paper chalked shape from a seamstress's pattern. As if even the cast outline of her was enough encouragement for his affection to grow.

At Varga he watched her play in two Wednesday chess tournaments. Ordinarily he would not have bothered to observe them, he was not terribly fond of the game, and he knew only its most basic arrangements and rules. He preferred to sit at the bar counter and pass idle conversation with friends and new acquaintances, or simply soak up the atmosphere, sitting quietly after having barked and intimidated and prattled on at customers all day long. But now he stood against the doorjamb and twice watched her make it to the final round, and lose. She was apathetic towards those contestants that she beat, barely offering a handshake lest it distract her from her prevailing concentration, and almost spiteful in her mannerisms of exasperation when they stalled on the last few moves, crossing her arms, pinching the bridge of her nose, knocking on the table top. She was a player of tempo. She kept her own pace and lost patience if it was interfered with. Habitually she would touch the base of her neck when she played, the spot at the V of her hairline. When she was finally put out she was enthusiastic towards her victor, as if in unforeseen admiration of the competitive skills that had ousted her from the proceedings, but her display seemed to have about it the marked kiss of an impending assassination. It unnerved Cy, this lack of graciousness in winning and the fire in her eye that kindled over defeat, the passion of the high-duel. There was something backwards about it, arse over tit as Riley would have said. And indeed like Riley she seemed to thrive on certain conflict where other humans tiptoed on eggshells around it. Her voice rose in argument in the gaming room as readily as did the voices of others. But he did not want to liken her to Eliot Riley. And so quickly he put the similarities out of his mind. The observers liked to pass comment on the gaming and offer analysis of strategy. There was a strange thrill to their voices, a muffled equivalent to the screaming elation and post-match autopsy of a ball game. From this Cy gleaned snippets of information about Grace's game and translated them into personality – he realized he could question strangers about her with it seeming to be no more than topical or sporting curiosity.

– Who is she playing tonight?

– Sedak. She has beaten him before. Then if she goes through she'll meet Torlione who won last week.

– How is she doing?

– Bishop, three pawns apiece. She'll take the rook next. Running round the queen as usual.

– What do you mean?

– Girl's weakness is her queen. She won't ever gambit, surrenders far too many pieces to protect her, leaves the king thin, priorities out of whack. Cost her plenty a game, I'll tell you. Means she has to suffer twice as hard on the back end defending double, especially as it's her favourite long attacking piece. Can't have it both ways. Quite a common eccentricity, of course, but sentimentality always has a price. You play?

– Not really.

– Here's the trick. You watch her – watch her go after the other queen like she's got a fire under her hood. That there is the giveaway. Keeps her for a reason, see. And if queen takes queen chances are she won't get taken – there'll be cavalry. All of a sudden, Boom! Lightning down the passageway and it's the only risk she'll take with her. Beautiful to watch, that spontaneity, that charge, makes my night when she does it.

– Got a thing against her own kind, do you think? Bit of a harridan?

– Bit of a hellion. Got a thing against the best fighter, got a thing for disabling the heaviest weaponry. Someone like Torlione or Sedak will get scrambled by her eventually on a set-play, if she gets clear. Real tough to pull off that style, then again so was any war that went the wrong way. Little Joan of Arc, I call her.

– Is she a genius?

– Nothing to do with it, buddy. The formal mathematic play is a given here. They all have memories like elephants. Past that it's all about being fearless. And lady luck.

A conspiratorial voice chipped in from the side.

– She sleeps with a black queen under her pillow I heard. Spooky woman. Brrrrh.

Cy and the commentator turned to see who had elaborated so audaciously on the discussion. It was Claudia. She winked at Cy and laughed, her orange hair bobbing.

– Oh, hello Claudia. Do you know Grace?

Claudia nodded, emphatically, still laughing. Then she suddenly became serious and paused to collect her thoughts. Cy fancied for a moment that she might have had a tear in the corner of the black explosion of powder around her eye.

– Ja. Of course, who does not know Grace! She is my good friend. Sie ist meine Königin.

Claudia had a secret that only Grace knew. She was obsessed with the baby incubator exhibition at Coney. She could not keep away from it. Outside there was a painted sign that read 'Little babies who came before their time', and there was a note that the youngest surviving infant to date had been born after just twenty-one weeks of pregnancy, though there was no formal medical verification that Claudia knew of to substantiate this claim. Cy had passed the place often but never been inside the show. He disapproved of it. It was one of the more extreme and less tasteful enterprises at the Island, a macabre maternity ward. Beyond the unseemliness of the place it also disturbed him on a sinister, childhood level, for it brought to mind the strange work of his mother, all the children of her unmaking, all the undone babies of

Morecambe Bay. And even though he had long ago reconciled what his mother had undertaken as a sideline profession, he never went inside the exhibition, just in case all the sick infants within stood up in their cots and waved to him, intent on delivering messages from their ghostly British brothers and sisters, in the manner of Professor and Madame Johnson.

The show brought Claudia sadness finer than any requiem or any gravestone or anything beautiful or sorrowful that she could think of. On afternoons when she wasn't working with her husband or rotating on the platform in the Human Picture Gallery at Luna, she would go off by herself and pay her dime and linger in the corridors of the exhibit. Looking into the room of plastic sheeted cots, where the city's poor mothers brought their premature infants in the hope that they would be taken and saved, somehow miraculously transformed from the translucent, purple-limbed, bulging-eyed creatures they were into normal opaque, pink, brown or white skinned babies, like the children of fully termed mothers. Then, eventually, they would cry normally, tears of participatory complaint and appetite, not fatality, not like ratsbane-screaming rodents, but like hungry, healthy mammals eager for the breast. And their white drenched eyes would grow coloured telescopes to see the world.

She would stand in the greenhouse hallways, very, very still. She would watch the women dressed as nurses, she did not know if they were actually nurses, in stiffcaps and red-crossed aprons, thick medical shoes, drifting through the room on the other side of the window and monitoring the babies, patient as gardeners in a mushroom factory, gentle in amongst the planted glass beds. Claudia watched with bird-quick eyes and a worried forehead. She watched for the roll of an all-white eye, or for tiny purple hands to reach up and grasp the air – a sign of life, a sign of hunger, a sign of hopeful brain activity. And then when there was movement she would knock on the divider and point and point until a nurse's attention was raised and the starched woman would move to the baby, smiling. Claudia watched for the mice-fast hearts to beat a little slower, a little less furiously and more privately behind their skin. There were tubes that she did not understand. There were suckling procedures that tugged at her own breast.

Claudia had miscarried six times in her life and Arturas did not blame her, even as she was confounded by her own body and wept for not giving their love issue. He fixed their dead children's names to her mighty body in black ink, like eulogies on a mausoleum. Though her magnificent, vital anatomy seemed it should allow for the breeding of a hundred robust little warriors, she had not once brought a foetus to term. Six half children in hospital dishes and in the roadways of Germany, of New York and Florida, and lately in the powder room of Varga. Six small babies with tails like tadpoles, with whole souls like bright bubbles as they left her. The doctors said it was unsafe to try for any more. It was unsafe to try again, they said. Her womb was tipped, her womb was now unstable, her womb was very faulty. She had control over all the regions of her body, its power of gesture, its constantly increasing muscle, the coloured skin wrapping up her brawn. But in the secret hidden valley of her reproductive system the rebels still burnt down houses, strangled children and the rivers ran red with blood.

So Claudia watched the little babies in the Coney Island incubators as they raised their purple, webbed-together fingers in the air. And she was not alone. New York's bereaved and grieving mothers came by the dozen to see the show. They came in the weeks after delivering stillborn babies, unbeknownst to their husbands, or in the days after apnoea or asphyxia had absurdly robbed them of their infants, paying their dimes to enter, which in turn paid for oxygen and milk and sterile warmth and profit. Some came to donate breastmilk, sobbing all the while. The women came to see the babies who had just and so survived, who were made of terrible colours like rust and rose and cardamom, who were raw under tiny handkerchief-sized blankets, no longer than the palms of their mother's hands, but somehow living. It was a quiet exhibition, except for the croaking of a baby behind the window, and the occasional breakdown of a customer. But there was drama to the delicacy and frailty and the tenacity of the all-too-early lives, and specifically appealing drama it was too, as with every other Coney Island exhibition or ride or show, it hit the corkscrew nail on its tilted, twisted head. It was a show mostly women came to see. And they, and Claudia, loved and loathed the tiny babies, jealous and tender at once, because they were seeing miracles not granted to them, because these were children that were still closed, like mushroom caps, or sprouting bulbs, and their lives were hanging in the balance. There was love and pain and longing in the air, filling the muted exhibition corridor with something thick and enriching like fertilizer in soil, as if the pungent, solicitous emotions of the women might open the premature, closed children, and somehow help them live.

The women, similar, united, but oblivious to each other, came to watch the babies grow and fade into colours more befitting healthy newborn infants, they came because their own were dead, closed and red, and would not ever fully open or fade or grow. Or they came to watch them die, for fairness' sake, to reassure themselves that God was even-handed with his rescinding of souls. Sometimes the nurses would find a baby lying too still or too struggling, going from red to blue, squeaking through the tubing like a mouse, and they would smile, and very calmly lift the baby out of the incubator with white cotton gloves, as if to hold it, or comfort it. And then they would remove the child through the back door to a room beyond the view of the spectators, perhaps to see a doctor, and it would be absent when they reappeared, smiling, always smiling.

Claudia was incredibly patient. Claudia always waited. When a baby was removed she would linger all afternoon for the nurses to bring the infant back. They hardly ever did.

Towards closing time she would finally slump to the wall, and her body would rumble with thunderous weeping, her eyes smeared black from the wetted shadow, the hairs on her chin dripping with tears, and the veins in her biceps standing stark and tense with suffering blood. She became known to the staff of the show as the grieving giantess.

After five months of this routine the management of the baby incubator exhibition decided to put a ceiling on the amount of time allocated to the entrance fee. It was considered unhealthy for some women in particular to spend all their time in there, too tempting a self-destruction for hysterics. They could not be relied on for self-regulation and the discipline required not to torture and torment themselves. Also medical costs had risen, more money was needed to maintain the exhibition, they said, so now a dime would only get an hour. Claudia did not care. Her muscled tattooed body made her plenty of money, as her husband's ink and needles made him plenty of money, so there was more than enough to support her obsession. She revolved through the rooms hourly on her day off, repaying, weeping, repaying, weeping.

Grace always knew where to find her when her husband did not and she was missing. Grace could be relied on for discretion, she did not tell Turo why Claudia could not be found. They let her into the show for free, knowing she was there for the sole purpose of removing the weeping whale and not, in any case, daring to demand payment from her – for she had that look of Sonderkommando to her: detachment, appallingly intrepid workmanship. She would follow the wailing to find her friend collapsed on the floor. Then she would take the big, barbell-callused appendage, which had the astounding capabilities for hurling iron for the crowd's enjoyment, in her own small hand. Claudia would pull Grace close and cradle her on the floor, holding her in her strong arms, and crooning.

– Kleines Baby, kleines Baby, zu klein.

And Grace would allow the psychotherapy and she would soothe Claudia's crackling orange hair if she could free herself to reach, and make her promise not to come back any more. It wasn't good for her, she said. It was as salt in an unhealed wound. Not come back, Claudia would repeat, but then the next week she always did return.

~

– And why is it that you ask about my friend?

Cy shrugged his shoulders, smiled at Claudia and turned back to watch Grace at the chess table. She was leaning far back on her chair waiting for her opponent to move his piece, with her hands on the table top, her fingers splayed out and lifting erratically as if she were playing the piano.

– No reason. I thought perhaps I . . . it's not important. She lives in my building. I only recently found that out. She seems to be quite an extraordinary person. It's sudden, but I thought perhaps I might quite like to, well, to learn to play chess. I never have.

He felt Claudia's hand on his back, pressing along his spine. She forgave him the lie.

– Good. Don't let her teach you, though, she'll spoil it for you. And don't listen to the rest of what you hear. It's not important. She is just a person who knows about many things.

~

Three weeks after they met by the fountain Grace came to see Cy at his booth. A small midweek crowd had gathered, rowdy military boys, looking for relevant undertakings on their first official days of leave. Six or seven uniformed young men were waiting for their tattoo, the same dagger stencil for each of them, sharp up on its bloody tip on six or seven shoulders. All were gauging by the face of the first man on the stool – the smallest of the group, a blond, pockmarked chip of a lad – how it would be to get the work done. They had all taken their shirts off at once, solidarity in preparation, they said. Cy could smell the cheap, army-issue soap on them, the sweat and the scent of unwearied leather. Stiff army fatigues had left patches of dry irritated skin on their bodies, and were it not for their obvious excitement to be soldiers he could have ascertained simply from the telltale bands of eczema around the waist and cuffs and necks that they were newly signed. The skin could always be relied upon to provide information – battery, disease, scars over failed organs, souvenirs from assaults and from pubescent conditions, race, combined race, sustained dependence on alcohol, diet, and the marks of love, old and new, good and bad. Other than the superficial damage caused by the chafing uniforms they seemed healthy, their bodies were firming, becoming refined, and adjusting to a regime of less sleep, hard drills, economy of food. They would be broken only to the point where they would become good soldiers before eventually being shipped off to Europe, he guessed.

The noise of their voices rose when Cy started work, a swell of bravado to address the streak of colour being set indelibly on the youth's shoulder. It was a ritual of no return that always elicited jeers, jibes, cheers, or laughter from groups of men who were taking part in the ceremony together. The boy began by taking the line-work well, on the verge of a smile, seeming more relieved that the discomfort was manageable than proud of his pioneering accomplishment. Then the smile turned into a half grimace as the needle nicked over the same red dripping patch again and again for the full deep colour of the shading. Sweat came on to his skin and blood, so that there was a time when rendition and reality were one and the same. His muscles began to quake uncontrollably.

– Oh! Easy up there. That's not good, kiddo. Steady as you can, steady as you can. It's honestly better if you don't clench that hand.

Cy wiped up the fluids and gave the boy a chance to catch his breath. The others, beginning to bore or hunger, strolled shirtless over to the sausage stall. They had been suspicious of Cy when they arrived, they hadn't trusted him to freehand them or hadn't had the extra money for it. Or perhaps it was just his profession that worried them, made them skittish, he was after all the bogeyman. But he'd spent so long wading through the muddy bog of disapproval that he was beyond its reproach and could not separate out the various components any more. His long, trussed-up hair was too obvious in contrast to their similarly shaven heads. They were based upstate, outside the city. They must have headed out to Coney for the sole purpose of getting tattooed, having heard that's where it was best or easiest or cheapest done. It was early in the day when they arrived, and already they were planning the rest of the excursion. One of them addressed Cy with gusto.

– We heard there was Chinamen freaks and Negroes with plates in their lips and tiny pin-head men down here.

– Is that right? Well, go to Luna Park and catch a show. All the wonders of the world in there.

Cy had taken money from all of them before starting the first, so that they would know a contract had been agreed upon. They liked this, it added to the sense of brotherhood. He had locked it in the metal box and put it in the counter drawer behind him. With his friends having briefly deserted, the blond's mouth was now belying him his pain. His thin upper lip was riding high on his two front teeth and gums. Cy paused his work and leaned back to light a cigarette. He wasn't one for encouragement or sympathy usually but today he felt generous.

– Try to think about something else, lad. Let your mind wander along. Talk it out if you like. But relax, it's easier. It'll pass through you better.

For his advice he received a look of sceptical disbelief. The boy wanted only for it all to be over. Cy shrugged and lifted the needle back into position, placing the cigarette in a comfortable corner of his mouth.

– Try to think of those things that make you fall asleep. So you are no longer really in your body.

Both men looked up. It was Grace's voice. She was standing at the entrance of the booth in a tobacco coloured dress. Cy lifted the needle off again, smudging the frail black stencil a little as his pinkie passed over the traced image. Smoke stung him sourly in the eye and he removed the cigarette. She had one of the bound books of flash in her hand, was browsing through the skull page with a finger moving from one skeletal orb to the next, as if testing for ripe fruit. Her eyes moved to Cy for a time and she observed him with jurisdiction, as if he was in the wrong place somehow, intruding on her interaction with the man on the stool. He thought at one point she might be about to ask him to leave. Then she looked back at the soldier.

– What did you say?

– Nothing ma'am. I didn't say a word. It was you who talked to me.

– Don't you realize that soon you're going to have to be able to put your mind in a box and bury it in the ground and remember where you left it? Otherwise you're going to lose it, one way or another. You can practise now, this man here will help you, he will oblige you with some pain. So do it, think of those safe things that make you sleep.

She was a bully. She was either a bully or some kind of blunt, combative angel, too concerned with issuing warnings and reinforcing weak spots in the spirit of her wards to waste time with pleasantries. She repeated her demand. Hearing a single female addressing their comrade the other army boys came back to the booth with mouths full, wiping splashes of ketchup off their bare chests, and they wound up their noise to declare their presence. Had they been walking round Central Park or the Upper East Side they would have tipped their hat at an unescorted woman and stood back off the sidewalk. At Coney there was licence to depart from the polite rules of etiquette. It was a flophouse, a brothel-style place for

satiation, or like a music-box populated by performing characters who defied regular social ordinance, beings who
slipped into the chained sack of the underworld with a key to
the lock in their teeth, they knew the deal, so why bother with
courtesy, why court the whores?

– What's that, lady? Sure, Donny, what d'ya do before you
sleep – think about that buddy, just don't take your hat outa
your lap when you stand up.

The friend was rocking his groin back and forwards in a
quick motion to much laughter.

– Margie! Helen! Oh, Fraaances . . .

Grace turned to the man behind her. She smiled.

– You'll see. You'll also be trying to get away from the pain.
Look at you, so fresh in your uniform, you think you understand what it is to fight.

– Well I have an idea, but why don't you inform me,
colonel.

– Let me tell you then. They tie the tubes off in your stomach with small metal clamps before you die, so that your shit
can't come out of the bullet holes while the priest reads last
rites. It's not possible to have a priest vomiting over a dying
man because of the smell of guts and food turning into shit,
you see. Have they told you what the most common injury
is in the war? It's your brain. The war punches an asshole in
it and whenever it feels like it, it fucks the asshole. Always it
feels too small, like it's tearing open. You're never going to
get used to it – like a virgin will make herself stronger and
stop bleeding. It always hurts when the war fucks you, but
you know it's rubbing on a place in your brain that you can't
control so you're going to respond like you want to be
fucked by it – maybe you'll beat your wife when you get
home or put your fingers in your little daughter, put her up
on the table and make her dance for you in her mother's
shoes and pearls. And when the war is done fucking it
comes, this stinking mess, this juice just like your own, and
then the children of the war will live in your brain too. Even

when you're an old man with your polished medals, all bent over and can't get hard and smelling of piss, sometimes the war will want to come back and fuck your brain in its asshole. All your life. Or until you put your gun up to here and pull the trigger. Yes. Yes.

Only the noise of the bobsled chicaning on its runners and the screams of its jubilant riders and the creak of shutters and signs leaning into the breeze on Oceanic Walk could be heard in the ensuing quiet. Grace was still smiling, broadly now, with her finger pointing to her temple like a gun barrel. And it was a terrible smile, terrible for the lack of psychotic characteristics, for the peaceful crescent moon it made of her mouth while the words escaping it had been rank. Cy could smell the tide coming in four hundred yards away, though he was holding his breath. She removed her hand and nodded again.

– Yes.

– Jesus Christ! Alrighty then, missy, no need to get crazy. Why the hell did you have to go and say all that for, anyway?

The young man turned to face Cy, to find out where his allegiances lay.

– This your girl? 'Cause, she sure is a swell lady. A real charmer.

Cy suddenly breathed out as if he'd been struck in the stomach and winded. The torque of the situation amazed him. Where had it come from, that sudden capsizing squall on a slightly choppy ocean? Grace was like a dripping tap that had broken its seal and flooded the kitchen. Oh, she reminded him of Riley, she did, who at the flick of a switch could become overblown and would attack the most insignificant foes with his thorough, histrionic rage, crushing them like a steamroller over a blade of wavering grass. He could only think that one of the soldiers had hurt her, touched a nerve as if something hot had been put on a cavity-brittle tooth. Perhaps she had been an orphan of the Great War?

– Look, lads. If you've got muck on your arms I strongly suggest you go and wash it off down at the beach so it doesn't go into the bloodstream. Go on now. Your money's good, you're settled up, I'll not mess with you. Be about another ten minutes here.

He put a little northern into his tone. It meant nothing to them geographically, of course, he doubted if they had even heard of Lancashire, though the short, peaking syllables spoke universally, put obvious obstructions into the conversational landscape. He was annoyed with the crowd distracting him from Grace and annoyed that the soldiers had brought this mercurial side out in her. And he was disconcerted by the way in which Grace herself could call into question everyone's conduct simply via her presence, by the generous and offensive way she spoke to complete strangers, and her lewd and razing wisdom. The youngster on the stool was getting edgier by the minute. His pals had just been told to clear off and they were disappearing down the alley. He had only half a tattoo. And he did not want to be left alone with Grace, who could very well be disturbed in the head, and a tattoo artist who was possibly sympathetic towards her dementia. Nor did he appreciate the news that skin needed treatment his had not received before tattooing.

– Hey, buster. Why didn't you tell me to do that? You didn't tell me to wash up. This sanitary? This gonna get infected? They gonna have to cut my balls off?

– Don't worry, I'll cut 'em off myself if you don't stop jumping round like a snared rabbit. Dicky an' all. Hold still, lad, or you'll have a dagger that looks like the captain's missing mate and a needle sticking out the other side of your arm. It does not say Septic Sid on my sign, does it?

The humour-threat was Riley's stock in trade. Cyril Parks had instinctually flipped through his memory for a response to losing control of the situation and he had found Riley's split personality, his ability to wed two strong aspects of his character together for professional purposes. Comedy and Ferocity. These two were the husband and the wife of presentation in the tattooing industry, Eliot Riley had told him on more than one occasion. The old ball and chain. To control the crowds there was no better combination than gruff and foolery, for they book-ended any form of disorder or trouble, and there was disorder and trouble a-plenty in this trade.

Grace put her small hand on Cy's shoulder then. The lightness of it calmed him. It was the first time she had touched him and it felt like the passage of light. She passed a sheet of folded paper between the wires of his equipment to the counter next to the coloured vials. Moving through the air past him, she was fragrant of unperfumed skin, the scent of her undisclosed origins or the smell of the weather.

– If you can copy it I will come back tomorrow morning. Eventually I want many, everywhere. All over, if you can do it. You'll know best how to place them and the rest of how it goes. I work at three o'clock. Maximus will be with me. Can he be tethered to the booth, do you think?

– Only if he doesn't drag us all into the water or start eating my hair again.

She smiled, harmlessly. The storm in her had passed, if ever it had been a threat.

– I'll bring some mints. It will distract him. You'll be in Varga tonight? You'll tell me if it is at all possible?

– Of course. Though I'm sure it will be. You did say full body? You're sure about that?

– Sure. Until I am gone, poof, no more.

She watched him work, gently and ruthlessly with the implement, the way passers-by would linger and watch him. It was an artistic procedure after all, the way painterly hands moved with premeditation, leaving behind a trail of ink, and it could be oddly subduing and soothing. Or perhaps she was hypnotized by the sound of mechanical embroidery as so many others were. Her eyes were slow over his hand for a moment or two, he could feel them there, and he was pleased that she stayed on and pleased that his hand remained adept. He felt suddenly proud of his work, prouder than he ever had before. He wished he could stop work and talk to her, perhaps to reassure himself that she was only very fierce when under threat, but there was the rest of the group to consider and the bright sun in the alley would mean more crowds later in the day. He took small glances at her in between attending to the smears on the man with a lint rag, catching only portions of her body in his peripheral vision, corners of the brown dress at her hip, dark red hair pinned back off her recessive face, abstract pieces. Of the things she said there were always references to other more important matters, it seemed; she was never far from sermon. She reminded him of Morecambe's councillors and ministers that way.

The soldiers came back from the sea, two of them were soaked through after having been thrown in, and they loitered beside the booth, keeping a moderate distance from Grace. She had acted like an astringent on their free-flowing bravado. Or perhaps the cold water had sobered them. Whatever the sedation, they had simmered down a little now. But as Grace walked away one of them looked up and whistled after her. The whistle followed her walk for a few paces, dribbling wet on her calves and heels, a last attempt to better her, or a last flush arrow aimed at her composure with a message tied to its shaft saying she was still a woman after all, and this fact alone had drawn the man's bow. She paused, turned, walked back and stood in front of the largest man with the largest smirk on his face, interpreting him to be the whistler. He sucked in his belly, blew up his chest with his lungs, expecting a bitter pass, a strike to the face, blushing chastising, the usual gender haggling. Cy was about to stand up and intervene when Grace put her thumb in her mouth, licked it, and then reached up and ran it wetly over some imagined grime on the man's cheek, collecting the flesh of his face in a ripple at its edge, like a mammal cleaning her own defenceless young. It was a small gesture but it resonated loudly, and seemed as wrong as her name. Then she was gone to a quiet exit, to a few sly, unheard comments.

– What a loony. Probably queer in the head, probably into other girls, right boys?

– Yeah, or sick fetishes. All that crazy stuff about little girls! I never heard anything like it!

It was apparent to them that Grace was deranged in her mind, and in her style, like everything else they had been led to expect was deranged one way or another in this sprawling, rabid mass of pavilions and fairground rides. So they let her go, unsettled by her and yet able to reconcile somewhere within themselves that unsettlement was just her function while they visited Coney, just as Cy's function was to tattoo and hurt them and scare them a little with his dour gruff and his loud ink, just as the fire-swallowers and the contortionists and freaks would shortly create some kind of disturbance in the gut if they paid their dime's entrance into the amusement parks.

There were broken rules about broken rules at Coney. Everybody claiming residency or employment there lived by them and almost nobody understood them. Visitors acted out, as they never would at home. The Island's business folk delved into the most absurd, most stigmatic, most contemporary corners of their brains and sold their wares. That was the saying, that anything goes. The human fracas, the folly, the malediction, coming from deregulation and eternal carnival was as natural as the hysterical behaviour of small children when provided with a corpse in velvet pageboy attire and a Ouija board. Cy had learned that you didn't refer to the strange constitution of the place, because by nature it warped in the mind, slipped will-o-the-wisp from the hands of definition and litigation and could quite possibly send you raving mad as you chased after it. Better to just merry-go-round at Coney, up and down, to the creepy tinkling music of the mechanical hammer-driven pianos and the operatic wail of sirens and the grunting percussion of bumper cars. Better to just ride the anarchy like one of his tattoos of bare-breasted women riding fork-tongued serpents in the foam of a green sea. So he listened to the group berating Grace and he neglected to defend her, as his procedural, gentlemanly, elsewhere-located self might have.

He would not have a chance to open and look at Grace's paper until after ten that night, when he finally boarded up the booth, the last customers sloped away and he went to Varga to wind down. He put it into his shirt pocket suspecting that there would be something either vaguely unacceptable or of direst meaning on the page, something which might throw a spanner in the works of their relationship, or prune his burgeoning affections. And he would need a strong drink in his hand when his suspicions were confirmed or confounded. Until then he would try not to think about it. He'd simply do his job. He'd be the crowd's fearsome huckleberry.

~

War was a peculiar thing. Cy seemed to remember that from a long time ago when he was a stilt-legged boy, a fact gleaned from conversations along the promenade of Morecambe and the shenanigans of its residents. It brought out the best and the worst and the downright incomprehensible in people. It made them slough off the dead skin of reason and deepen the roots of nationality. They became creatures of habit, more so than ever before – he remembered the queues for tea at the kiosks of his hometown and the fund-raising dances and the well-attended meetings of every organization, which went on long after peace-day, long after they were essential strictures. For there was relief in repetition and routine. War sent people out looking for principles and decency and even fragments of God to be woven up in chain-mail and used as armour against all the bestial suffering and immoral wickedness inflicted by other human beings, those accused of creating a covenant with evil. But it also gave them an excuse to behave very badly themselves under the big black umbrella of a far worse phenomenon. He remembered that Morecambe's courts had seemed fuller than ever during the Great War, of pick-pockets and bigamists and even bank robbers. He remembered that his mother had said some folk simply rang louder when the breath of war was blown through them. What would Reeda have made of this conflict now? With so much human fodder. Something so premeditated and sinister at the core of it, and seeming set to go on and on. He wondered how his countrymen and women were faring, the radio and newspaper reports were distressing to say the least. He wondered if he should write letters to Jonty and Morris, send friendly word. The talk in Brooklyn was angry and pessimistic, paranoid and ultimately impotent, there were tales of horror filtering through the Hasidic communities, and there were desperate attempts to contact foreign relatives, applications sent to official quarters to allow immigration. Shaken heads, candles lit in windows and synagogues.

If nothing else this war had created a boom within the tattooing industry. Not only were military motifs selling incredibly well, but the American government's obscenity ruling meant that indecent markings would prevent entry into the navy or other forces, and so old work was being redone. Like the nude bathers and sexy dames of the film industry reformed under the rigid Hollywood codes, rude tattoos were now history, the era of naughty fun was over. Boys were being rejected daily for the promiscuously clefted, high-nippled lovelies on their bodies, and they were flocking to him for repair. The penalty for illicit liaisons was not irreversible. An applicant could get designs altered, that was the concession, they did after all want people to sign up, there was after all a war of unmitigated proportions going on, predicted to worsen very shortly. Now he was dressing all the naked women he once had drawn. Bare-breasts were slipping heavily behind snug new dresses. Pendulous buttocks were shimmying under frills and lace. The sassy maids were, with his help, pulling on some black shaded stockings to go with their heeled shoes and nurses' uniforms. The boys were sheepish and sad to see their sweethearts going.

246

– Bye, Bessie, bye-bye, Marie. See you next time, honey. Thanks for a good time.

Cy tried to preserve elements of sexy candour to the girls, a jut of hip, a beckoning finger, lowered lashes, but he could not help feeling like some kind of puritan, a despotic father. No, it felt like the morning after, each girl was getting dressed and the trysting was over. So many lovers, and all of them leaving . . .

~

It was an eye. In the centre of Grace's page there was an eye, immaculately open, static, unblinking. It looked almost hiero-glyphic, black-rimmed, black-lashed, there was a lot of black ink to it in fact, and it was scrolled in a helix at the corners. He might have known there would be no birds or butterflies or delicate posies for her. Nor portraits of the presidents on her thighs or religious symbols, which four decades earlier the carnival women had first stunned the public with. The bar at Varga was crowded that night. He sat at the counter, and moved the empty glasses on the bar away from the piece of paper that was laid out in front of him like an after-school study, simplifying the clutter and chaos around the page.

– Scotch tonight?

– Thanks.

Valerie attended to him with her usual perfunctory duty and he returned to the image in front of him. The iris was green, green, the most mysterious of pigments, and it con-tained a substantial amount of non-detail, which gave the image an amulet appearance at its centre. There were no divi-sions like the true human eye contained or faint irregular spokes, quantitative information, flecks, inflections, broken sections, and percentages. Only a pure green sphere like a jewel or an old curse. It was unremitting, unforgiving. His head hurt just looking at the thing.

Riley's voice joined him at the bar, swaggering into its most natural arena, telling him they were all witches, the women of the world. With their ability to manage pain, their smell of fresh and salt waters. And she was no different, his little Grace, his bold little poppit. No different at all. Some hereditary mange or vindictive spore or kinked strand of blood they shared made them wild, made them want to buck and nip and scratch. That's why they would roll you over and climb on top when you were so far gone in lust you couldn't defend yourself and they would look down with open eyes like they were taking something from you, like they were about to commit slaughter. His swarthy ghost here now, wanting to start a bitter conversation as ever with Cy that would make him seem clever and be validated just from provoking argument, from flicking an already twitchy nerve to make it jump. Cy was damned if he'd comply with him tonight, the old bugger.

– Go away, Eliot Riley. Go on, sling your hook.

– What's that, hon?

Mary was watching him while her sister poured his drink from a dusty bottle into a tumbler. He shook his head and held up an apologetic hand. The whisky arrived in its glass over ice. He could not recall when exactly he had taken solely to hard liquor. But there were times that it seemed an appropriate drink, the only possible retort to the place in which he worked and his profession. He thought back to his first ever beverage, under the stewardship of Riley in the Dog and Partridge. Ale for junior. It seemed like such a long time ago. Varga was busy, bodies kept moving past him, knocking him gently from side to side. The door of the bar was open but there was no kind movement of air. It felt humid tonight, as if the atmosphere was preparing for one of the tremendous early-summer thunderstorms that New York often received, with purple spears of lightning and loud booming and crashing above as if some deity were spring-cleaning. His shirt was sticking to his lower back, he had been sweating with concentration all day. He sensed something on the way, a troublesome front, and he thought of the fishermen of

Morecambe who could predict the weather patterns, who could taste the foreshadow of rain coming in off the Atlantic and who could say to land-lubbers that it was only an hour behind them in the great bay. Until an unforeseen storm rose up like the spastic finger of Poseidon and they simply disappeared, that is.

Cy leaned back on his stool and peered into the gaming room. It was too full and too smoky to see if Grace was playing yet tonight. Grubby, crumpled money was being passed between hands. He rubbed his face, took a long drink and felt the liquid burn his gums and throat. Valerie poured more whisky into his glass and set the bottle on the counter next to him, tapped it with a red fingernail. He must have had that look to him, the expression of a swimmer far out at sea in need of a life-ring or an exhausted miner groping for a canister of oil in the obsidian blackness as his lamp flickers out, for Valerie was not one for any kind of compromised distress, hers was not a half-way house. He returned his attention to the page. Yes, he could easily copy this design. It was not difficult. He could tell Grace he would tattoo her. And of course he would be happy to work on her, to have her company in his booth, get to know her and her body a little better. But at the heart of the matter, he did not understand Grace's eye. Why on earth did she want it? What was the point of one image repeated? Why not mix it up a bit? Partly it was too simple, ridiculously simple, and he knew he must be missing the point of it all. Or she was doing it merely for her act in the circus perhaps, but it seemed a far length to go to. Again he had the sense that he must concentrate hard, double-clutch the gears in his brain because of her. He lit a cigarette, parked it in the corner of his mouth and set about finishing off a generous glass of whisky. An eye, over and over. How many times would she want it done? How much would he charge? He had wished to impress her with feathery detail and delicate shading, to give her body flight. He liked the idea of women and winged creations. Like angels or harpies, these designs always looked suitable on them, their bodies housed the compositions so well, along breastbones, on shoulders, along their backs which had perhaps once already contained the stub and stem of wings, depending on how you might regard them. He had wanted to show off his skills, have her select some of his own designs, and he had wanted to have some kind of personal artistic partnership with her, like Arturas and Claudia.

He leaned back out from the bar and looked into the gaming room again. The bodies within were shifting like pieces of sand in an egg-timer and finally they emptied to one side. And there was Grace, sitting across from someone Cy could not see, the first opponent of the evening. She was wearing the same kick-pleated skirt and blouse as the night he had first met her. But her hair was down, it reached to the edge of her back's curve and a little beyond, so that an inch or two of it hung above the depression and curled in the air. They had not begun playing the match, she always wore her hair back when she played, he knew this irrelevancy to be true of her, if not much else. She looked beautiful from this far away, in profile, her strong features amended by smoky light. Before Cy realized that he was staring at her indulgently she met his gaze. He put up his hand in a small diplomatic wave. Grace nodded her head. She did not smile fondly at him as she had earlier in the day, and he thought perhaps she had not recognized him. Then, refuting this assumption and still looking his way, she held up her hands in a flamboyant European gesture, the palms tipped up, and she shrugged, as if saying she did not know the answer to some question that had been recently posed, or she was asking for his comment. He understood. He smiled so that she would know her idea was good, plausible, logistical. So she would come to see him tomorrow. And maybe, just maybe, it would be their beginning.

∽

By three in the afternoon the next day it was apparent that she was not going to show up at the booth. He had waited all morning with growing anticipation and nervousness for her arrival, missing his lunch break because he did not want to risk leaving the vicinity in case she took it upon herself to choose that exact moment to come. Nor did he dash across to the hotdog vendor for quick, convenient sustenance, conscious as he was that the flavour of onion and spicy meat on his tongue might carry and impose itself upon her. Between customers he would stand and try to spy the tall black head of the horse moving down the alleyway as Grace led him. She had said she would be working at three. And now it was past that. The day had trickled away and with it the chance of seeing her privately. Disappointment sat in him like wet coal in a grate, resilient and cold, and it would do nothing but extinguish any flame of optimism he tried to pass over it – that she might have had an emergency, that she might have forgotten a pre-existing appointment, she might not have changed her mind about the work but instead some kind of prosaic if nefarious conspiracy had ensnared her, kept her from him. And at any moment she might appear in her purple circus costume with plimsoll slippers on her arched feet and apologies in her so-dark, sloe-dark eyes. No. No. She simply wasn't coming.

∽

At around about the same post-meridian hour as of the previous night, and with a dangerously empty belly, Cyril Parks was occupying the very same stool in Varga Oyster Bar that his backside had collaborated with twenty four hours earlier, drinking the rest of his bottle of whisky. On this occasion he had removed the vessel from Valerie's hand as she first began to pour and set a wad of notes on the counter top. He would not have minded the presence of a friend or two that night, somebody to pass conversation with, Turo, Henry, one of the alley vendors perhaps, just so that he would not be left alone with the voice of Eliot Riley in his head and the urge to drink it quiet. There were one or two familiar faces in the bar, no one he particularly cared to invite to join him for company's sake. He may as well settle in with the rough stuff for another harangued and haunted evening, hastening the point at which the phantom presence of his former employer was annulled to the best of his drinking abilities. Grace's piece of paper was still in his pocket, he had carried it with him since she set it next to his equipment as if it were some precious treaty. He couldn't help feeling that there was a riddle to it he was compelled or obliged to solve. And perhaps the solving of it would bear her to him, in reward, ridiculously enchanted though that notion seemed.

What was she thinking with this damnable green and black eye? How would Riley have strutted into her psyche and found that out? What personality-picking remark would he have selected to open her up? And how would she have responded? He could suddenly see the two of them in his mind clearly, Grace and Riley, squaring up against each other, eyes straining open and wearing expressions like fighting cocks about to strut and peck and sever the ligaments in each other's necks. It was a horrible image. Thankfully, he could console himself that while he found occasional similarities between them in temperament – the blowhard singularity, the egoism, the jingo – he was sure each would have tolerated the other not one jot. No, Riley couldn't have cracked her if ever he'd have cared to set about it. Not even the great correspondent to human messages as Riley had entitled himself, with his provocative commentary and his manipulative conversations with people that led them to disrobe all their secrets, not even he could have unscrambled her code. And what did Eliot Riley know of women anyway, with his crude ballads mocking their names and his references to their tusses and their sagging tits, trawling his deep-sea nets through the murkier levels of their equanimity and dredging up primordial rage and banshee curses the like of which they had never before issued nor knew they could, and their tempers and their tears? And what of his curious relationship with Reeda Parks, which proved enduringly affectionate but was never converted into proper courtship, instead it was left eternally void? Who did he think he was to have once asked if he'd have to apprentice Cy in the ways of women as well as the trade?

– Fuck you, Eliot.

– You might want to eat something tonight, honey. The shrimp is real good, fresh in today. Shall I have a plate made up for you? C'mon, why don't you eat something?

Cy shook his head to Mary's offer, took the picture out of his pocket and opened it.

– What you got there, hon?

– Oh, just some work. It's a funny thing.

As kindly as her sister was regarding him, Valerie seemed equally cankerous and careless. And he wondered again if a deal had been struck at birth that they would split their personalities where their bodies were not.

– How long you been here?

– About seven years.

– That so. Well. It isn't right to talk to nobody like you do. You should stop being so broody and so self-involved. Don't you know it distracts people? Don't you know they won't care to have you around, the ones that want you now. Why, you must be about as dumb as dirt.

Cy smiled at Valerie, unoffended, and turned his attention away. He'd a mind that the eye spoke subtly of rejection, looking at it now he felt that quality. It was cold and it unsettled him, and he was not easily unsettled by the work he did. Thinking back over all the strange images he had tattooed on all the odd folk, he could not say this was the most unusual by any means. Not when compared to broadswords slicing open Asian heads and cartoon characters with cocks the size of lampposts and fish and chip packets on a shaved venal mound. But the eye was in a league of its own. It had meaning upon meaning, there were currents writhing under currents where that symbol was concerned, like the sea. He had the distinct impression that Grace possessed a fast-flowing undertow also, a restlessness behind her own dark eyes. His mother had had that feature too, as if she were always busy behind her face. Like she had movement in her which was kept from him behind those two grey, clandestine portals, a river within herself. He thought of his mother's working eyes, her eyes after she'd walked the promenade with her stubborn, politicking friends, her young son at her side, and her brass plate empty all those years. He thought of her quirks and her strengths, her scruples and her ignominy, that thing about her which had prompted Mrs Kirkstall of the Grand Hotel in Morecambe to grasp her firmly by the wrist and ask, Reeda, whatever's in you?

He poured more whisky into his glass. His head hurt from concentration, and the drink now decanting his brain cells. He knew he should eat a decent meal, or go home, sleep, wake up the next day without that feeling of parchment and pickle in his body. But he had hold of an idea now, an idea about his mother and Grace. An idea about the eye. And he did not want to let it slip away, he wanted to muster up the answer, and in any case turning his attention to it had made Riley's marring monologues seem temporarily distant, replaced.

The page on which the eye was printed was old and parchment-like, and it had a serrated edge, a give-away. It had been torn from a book, quite mercilessly. The tear was rough, perhaps the crime had been done quickly, in the presence of those that could punish or disapprove. Cy folded the paper closed. Yes, there was a bit of witchery to that after all, to that theft. The destruction of sacred material was vaguely occult, certainly abhorrent, wasn't that what he and the boys at school had been taught? And they had been birched hard over an open, suspended palm when any kind of destruction of written script occurred, it was one of Colin Willacy's pet peeves. His grammar-school standards of comportment were right there now, prancing alongside him like a collarless dog at heel, tame and ludicrous amid the riffraff and rabble of Coney Island. But had Grace not had her reasons for the crime? Had it not been justified?

He imagined her ripping the page from a leather bound book in an old library full of antiquated material written in another language, while guns cack-cack-cacked outside and townsfolk ran about helter-skelter and pell-mell, and fell in the street. Fires swept through buildings. Children were hoisted into the arms of those that they should not be lifted by and carried away from their childhood, and religious men had their throats cut as they prayed. And it was the brutal, old world that had made her do it, the world that was now once again exploding, perhaps reminding her of what, in another life, she had been forced to see. All those stories her eyes had told him when they met! What had she seen, and brought to America like an invisible souvenir of the past? It must be similar to the anguished tales throughout this refugee city. Brooklyn itself was full of recovery and reckoning, was it not? Old and new, the stories of immigrant Poles and Russians and Czechs were told in sorrowful ritual and stitched into the patchwork quilt of the place. Was that the purpose of the eye, a declaration of all that she had seen?

Grace was probably playing chess in the back room right now, he could go in there and pull her up from her seat, shake her and demand that she explain herself, and why she hadn't come to him that day when she said she would. Or he could kiss her and wait. He stood up, swerved hard to the right and abruptly sat again. He had accomplished what he set out to do. He was drunk. And it was late. The bar was winding down, the last greasy plates of seafood being collected. The picture of the all-seeing, witness eye on the bar counter in front of him was blurry now, shifting like lotus on the surface of water. Two-thirds of a bottle of O-be-joyful and his idea about Grace was almost good enough. Almost a good enough fiction to convince him and make him right about the image, so that by the soft-hearted direction of Providence she would come to him, if he concentrated hard on his invention of her violent, war-torn past. He put his sore head in his hands and closed his eyes and the drastic visions and the tender parable crumbled like a vase under the caterpillar track of a tank on a road through a deserted village, an artefact fallen from a cart and left behind after the exodus of residents, their internment in ghettos and camps, only to be ground to dust.

~

They were at the water's edge. A swarf of broken shells littered the shoreline, the beach was all sediment, strewn with them. High tide had the boats shifting against their moorings and echoing the lapping melody of the waves inside their hulls. He felt that his body was clean and blank and unwritten. Grace had on a dress made of pieces of old thrift ribbon and mélange clothing. Her hair was unbound. From her came a quiet, elegiac song he had never heard before, with lyrics he could not understand. Then she spoke.

– I think Claudia is a little upset with me.

– Why do you say that?

– She thinks I should have gone to Turo. I've known him longer. She thinks it is an insult to his reputation.

– I can see how she might believe that.

She turned to him. There was a smear of blood in the corner of her mouth. A small purple bruise along her cheek made up of many tiny blue and red dots.

– You can see nothing. You don't know what to choose.

– You remind me of someone, Grace.

– I know, that guy you always talk to when you're drunk.

– No. Not him. Some women my mother used to know.

A trickle of blood ran from her mouth. She must have felt it for she wiped at it with the collar of her dress. As she pulled the garment up to her face the first button of it came undone. Looking down at her he could see the swell of one of her breasts revealed, the skin brightening where her chest bone pushed up against it. He felt unafraid.

– And she liked them, these women?

– Yes, very much. They were good friends.

He was certain she would not prevent him as he reached for her and she did not. Her mouth did not taste like blood, the tongue moving against his lips was warm. But her body felt cold, too cold for the temperature of the dream. After they had kissed, her face was bruised worse, severely so, black and sunken and concussed on the side like rotting fruit, and one iris was leaking ink into the white part of her eye. A gash had formed along her jaw and there was a wet red bubble in her nostril. He slipped his hand into her open dress, ran a thumb down across her nipple, he felt his blood move, swelling fuller in his veins, and felt himself beginning to harden. She sighed, and brought her own hand up to his and held it, moved with it on the outside of her dress as he touched her, guiding it. He could hear the keel music and the ruptured tambour of shingle washing up against the shore, like the sound of keys on a metal ring or a trowel scraping loose mortar off a wall.

∾

When Cy woke his face was on the sticky, fishy counter, and the room was empty except for two drunks in the corner arguing unskilfully with the sisters about payment. Through the retreating haze of alcohol he could see the glass in his hand was empty. The whisky bottle was gone. He thought he could hear the sea but he was not sure if it was just the sonic residue of his dream.

– Is she here?

– Is who here, honey?

– Reeda. No. Is, I mean, is Grace still here?

The twins approached him at the bar. Mary reached over and squeezed his leg.

– Just you left now, hon. Come upstairs for the night, if you like. It's a long walk home.

She had her hand an inch from his flaring crotch. The tip of her forefinger was agitating gently, as if smudging charcoal on a drawing. Valerie seemed to be at the other end of the room, gathering empty glasses, though she was only ever at her sister's hip. So that was how it was done between them, he thought. Just by consideration, just by remuneration. Or in the slick, erroneous moments of distraction when the other was engaged.

– Thank you. But I should go. I'm useless after that amount of scotch. A complete rum-dum, if you know what I'm getting at.

– Oh. OK. Wait then while I find you some cold cuts to take. I'm betting you live off nothing but graveyard stew.

The twins moved into the kitchens together. On the bar next to Cy was a stack of old chessboards and some loose rolling pieces. The gaming was over for the night as was every other use for the bar. He rubbed his face, which felt numb, and blinked hard to restore his vision. Slowly he took the folded piece of parchment from his shirt pocket again and opened it. Even as he looked at the eye it looked back, so that he couldn't really see it and have it be assessed – not in the way that seen things are taken and consumed by the viewer. That was the source of trouble with the image. The eye out-manoeuvred his gaze, it failed to be inanimate and resisted being used or judged as an object. It was like the swans of Morecambe that could pull out of quicksand the moment they sensed the draw. Truly, he did not know who was pri-marily looking at whom, Cyril Parks or the eye, because his gaze was mirrored, deflected, equalled. It was as if the image was playing a game with him.

A second later he found he was on his feet and walking fast back towards Sheepshead Bay, without having collected his picnic or saying goodbye to the sisters. Then flagging down a late-travelling car as it passed him heading in the right direction.

～

Grace did not appear angry to be roused so late. There was little surprise on her face when she saw Cy there, tall in the corridor and bending towards her doorway, as if she was well acquainted with such nocturnal intrusions. He had not needed to bang on the door long for her to come and open it, which meant that he had not the time to reconsider his actions or contemplate the possibility that she may have company in her bed.

– Are we on fire?

– What's it called when you finish a game the winner? Checkmate? But what about when nobody can win? That happens also, yes? How about when it's a draw?

Grace yawned, ran her thumb under the strap of her nightgown which had slipped down off her shoulder.

– Perpetual check.

– Look. It's not up to me of course, and I would never talk anyone into something permanent that they were not convinced of, but you see, I think that you should do it. I think you should have the tattoos. Even if it's not by me. Even if you go elsewhere. I think it would be . . . spectacular.

She laughed, raised her eyebrows, and watched him for a moment, with the same look of quizzical contemplation that she had worn when they parted the night they had first met. Then she stepped closer and whispered to him as if divulging an obvious if previously unmentioned secret.

– Well of course it's going to be you, Electric Michelangelo. Of course you.

From inside the apartment he could hear the radio or gramophone playing, the soft twine of classical music, the urgency of violin strings. He had no idea what that meant, whether she slept well or suffered from insomnia. He had no idea what time it was but he knew that they existed now like actors inside the shared hours of their building's theatre. And he knew, with her standing there against silk or satin, a person of collected ideas and injuries against the orchestra, even unknown to him as she still was, that she would never again be a body confined to the frail dimension of nitrate shadows and chalk and dreams.

There were instances when Cy's needle unwittingly delved down into a soul and struck upon meaning, then confidential matter came up, unstemmable as arterial blood or gushing oil, and customers confessed the reason behind the art. He caught their stories in a bucket in the shop or booth and mixed it with ink and used the serum to paint translations of the very stories the tellers were haemorrhaging on to them. He could interrogate people without a single word, just via the incisor in his hand, drawing their lives out of them as he drew symbols on to them. The tales were revelatory and awful and enlightening. These were not house walls he was painting, after all, they were empathetic people, made of flesh and bone and experience and tragedy and joy. They had the hearts of his mother's understanding, tossed-together, torn-asunder. They were broken and healing and abused, careless and worshipping of each other. To tattoo was to understand that people in all their confusing mystery wanted only to claim their bodies as their own site, on which to build a beacon, or raise a rafter, or nail up a manifesto, warning, celebrating, telling of themselves. It was to understand that in order for a body to be reborn and re-yoked, first it needed to be destroyed and freed. It was emancipation and it was slavery, the ashes and the phoenix. It was beauty and destruction, it was that old trick. That was the contract.

One day he might go mad with the knowledge of too much brutality, the violations, the ripping up of hearts and minds and bodies. All the terrible information his needle bit into, all the secrets it lanced. All the memories of people who had come to him and bled their history, which he recorded like a photograph album or a diary of pictures on their bodies. The roped dead-man's hand holding the scales of justice that he put on the precipice of one man's back, whose mother had been raped and killed by her own brothers, who had his revenge righteously against each one in turn, and now he wore his hangman's history. The red and black garden that he had sown on one woman's torso, with green thorns around it to keep intruders out; she had been cut by a criminal from her soft parts to her beautiful lower lip, up along the length of her like a fish, like an almost-gutted fish, and her nipples cut away like scrap – she wanted flowers there now because her spirit would grow back and it would keep on growing. One day he might go mad from the twists and turns in the maze of the soul, the variety of human misdemeanour, and his strange role – recoverer and repairer of body, commanding forgiveness of the past as it became a sign on skin, as if in atonement.

Some customers were simply talkers. They spoke to him with fast care, as if pulling eggs out of boiling water on the spoon of a hand. Some had to babble themselves through the procedure, because the voice was one of the best antidotes known to pain and instinctively it overwhelmed their mouths. Mostly people did not adopt silence, could not manage a place of mind where the body was incidental or erased. Most struggled. Most could not trance. Most did not hear that original tat-tat-tat-to sound of the old way, under the seamless industrial click-clack of machinery, under the flic-flac dance of coils and drive shafts hammering away. So they could not follow the drum and beat track to rapture, hypnosis, the absence of pain from the cutting sensation, the suspension of the brain in nectar.

The talkers talked of anything and nothing. They were desperate for the anaesthetic of their voice and they provided a variety of colourful and obscure information. There was even science or poetry on occasion. One young man had formulated a meteorological theory about the weather below Coney Island's boardwalk. It affected women sexually, he said. There was a climate change when you went under. The sand went from open-beach broil to cool, private moisture, like being inside the mouth of a whale or the chill of a forest. Men took their sweethearts there to kiss and fondle and that was his intention. His girl had agreed to go with him, a sweet

261

gal, but harder than a bank safe to break into her clothing. It was a realm of striped shadows, arboreal, sap-fresh, all the laughter and the ride sounds were muffled like they were under a canopy of trees. He kissed and pulled her dress down off her. They felt like insects, he said, slowing in the wood shade, not driven into frenzy by the heat. In the cool Atlantic spit of the place he had lifted her skirt and found the corner of her menstruation belt, and thinking that a refusal in itself he had been surprised shortly afterwards to find himself pushed inside her, stinging a little on his tip. And as they made love they could hear the footsteps of the people on the boardwalk up above, like it was another world. The tattoo was of his new son's name. By the time the story of his conception was finished so was the last letter.

This was the prittle-prattle of ordinary and eccentric human adventure, the tittle-tattle of the milky lallygagging herd. But always there was the obscenity, the debris of hatred, the fetid curd. More common than compulsive banter and irrational explanation were the bitter revelations, of sin, imposed or sanctioned. Customers revisited old injuries of the mind and body in his booth and he could sense them wanting to slip past that pain with a decoy, or intimidate it with newer pain of his equipment's manufacture. There were the beatings, the cheatings, the welts from the buckles of belts on the hide of sanity, the ploughing of fists through faces, the avalanche of cocks against orifices, the rapes, the killings, the loss of loved ones from a blade, a gun, poison, lunatic voices in the head. There were the gangrenous scars of the undead. What was he if not a conduit for the brutalized stories and the mending characters of a new country? His needle found out their suffering like a surgeon's scalpel. People were pricked and spilled their lives like pus. And one day he might go mad from it all. It was a price of the profession Riley had said to him, drunk as disaster on the prom that night, and creating a fuss. He was a fucking midwife, boy, that was his job. Sharp tools were entrusted to his hands, but the demands of the trade required further skill. For unless brought to him howling and bloody and immediately from the canals of their mothers at birth, there was absolutely no such thing as a blank human canvas.

〜

Because she was not a good match with the way he recalled her in their meetings or imagined her to be, Cy found it was possible to put his hands on Grace's body professionally and it was not unbearable to have her sit in the booth and remove her clothing. She was in large part a stranger. For the past few weeks he had been courting a figment of his imagination with her vague composition. When he remembered her it was softly, flatteringly. In reality she was harder, with the serrated edges of a lumberman's saw. It was a complicated thing to have to bring her actual flesh and personality and the unreal flash design he had drawn of her into some kind of correlation. It was similar to battling with drunken split-vision as the lines of what is doubly seen roll apart, distort, roll in and pass each other again. But this reconstitution perhaps distracted him initially from all the things he thought he would be driven crazy with arousal over – the hollow channel down the middle of her upper stomach where flesh dropped off from the sternum, the shadow-line dividing the muscles along her thigh, the bone that rose to the surface here and there in a pleasing skeletal geography, hipbones, nipples, the inviting crease of buttocks. Scenarios he had imagined to death, usually in the morning with his hand shovelling away at his cock – dampness along her back as he reached round her, dampness between her legs as he pushed into her, a kiss that worked her bottom lip with his tongue – were eclipsed by what was in reality quite different and surprising and actual. There were her textures, the thin, fruit-skin dappling on the back of her upper thighs, the blossom soft area where chest and breastbone panelling became something fuller, innumerable tiny pores, the sunken dimple in both her shoulders which were strong and taut from years of holding balances on equine platforms in the circus. There were the things she said, which skirted conformity and politely ordained conversation, choosing grave and often taboo ground instead. He began to realize that there was a hopelessness to any wistful portrayals he might make of her, for he only had to dismantle them in her presence again when her mannerisms, her harsh language, her confrontational proclivities, her spitting casually in the street like a heavy smoker, the tough nodes of her behaviour, and her corporeal immediacy refuted his designs. But damn it if he didn't begin to fancy her new incarnation also. The livelier, lived-in version.

He always arranged the boards of the doorway when she visited so that there would be privacy – he generally did this for work on breasts or thighs – and he put up a sign with the time that he would be available for un-appointed work again. He placed boards and a sheet atop of the stools to construct a makeshift bench for her to lie on. Maximus, if he was accompanying her, was content to be tied up outside. There were times when Grace would talk to him through the boards, in one or other of her languages, and Cy felt that she may be flirting with the horse or that she preferred communicating with the animal rather than with him. She had meant what she said, she wanted a full body design. She was uncompromising and courageous that way, true circus stock. They arranged that he would work up to her very edges, up to her hands and neck and to the soles of her feet, to the point at which her clothing would seal off the images, but beneath the line of her underwear, as if she were wearing a complete bodysuit. Only her face, neck, and hands would be left unmarked. The eyes would vary in size, depending upon the landscape where they would be hosted. Larger on her navel, smaller on her arms. Her new skin would cost her twenty-five dollars. It was a fair price. She paid him up front, all at once, and he took the money from her with surprise, for it was no mean sum, and he would have worked out a method of layaway payment with her. She observed his expression as he folded the notes and joked with him.

– What? You thought it would be a new two dollars every week with the corner missing?

He chuckled at her insinuation. Such bills were considered lucky or seedy in this country, depending upon which circles a person moved in. They had a dubious pedigree – two dollars was the standard bordello rate in the northern states and a torn corner indicated that the prostitute in question had provided a service of lascivious excellence. He locked away the cash. Then he turned his attention to the best commission of his life.

– Ready?

– Ready. OK. On y va.

He began with her legs. He had drawn a stencil from her picture but by the fifth or sixth tattoo on her calf he felt confident he could perfect it without any preliminary tracing. His motion was better controlled if he was not a slave to a line of migration. At the back of his mind he suspected he might encounter scars on her, it seemed likely that an acrobat and an immigrant might have them, but she did not. There were moles like miniature door-handles and creases in her limbs from the repetitive hinging of joints. A sorrel birthmark stained her left hip. Past the line of her clothing the skin paled, like the bleached grass under a lifted rock – she seemed not as concerned with maintaining overall porcelain skin as many women were. With medical discretion he moved back pieces of clothing off only the area under scrutiny. When he needed to pull her underwear up over her more he asked her to do it and he turned his back until she had finished unsnapping closures. When it came to the work on her buttocks and lower abdomen, he ensured his gaze was absent as she undressed, as she lay down and stood up from the bench. She was not tall, but lying down she reached almost the full length of the booth. Its confines kept them enticingly close, always within arm's reach. And her body moved him, it did, the scent of her was genuinely existent, elemental, occasionally fused with the overtones of a musk-based perfume, but otherwise natural, and she was intoxicating.

It would have been easy to examine her more closely while he worked, the black hairs at the side of her slip, her soft dark seam, revealed when she pushed the thin material to one side. It would have been easy to brush his hand along an area of tenderness, accidentally or with deliberation, to see if her breathing changed, or if her eyes went under the first glaze of arousal. But he held back. With more difficulty than he ever had before, and with more of a sense than ever that to fail would be contemptible, he remained professional. So it was that her body slowly became known to him, as readily as if they had been lovers, though it was expressionless, voyeuristic discovery. And he fought to keep control of that aspect, swallowing his inclinations, forcing back the longings, denying his end of it. There were erogenous areas that were so alluring and so tightly sewn together with their visual stimulation, the simply seen desire to touch or run his tongue along, that it took appalling discipline to unpick the hem and separate the two, and he wondered if he were not undoing instinct itself. Love was truly one of the oldest feelings in the world, he thought, one of the original emotions, such was its magnitude, so convincingly did it exercise its power.

– How are you managing? Need a break?

– Nope. You need a break?

– Just a quick cigarette. Helps me concentrate.

Her coat on the stool smelled faintly of the horse and sometimes outside the booth Cy could hear Maximus clopping a hoof on the alley paving as he turned to face the frothy breeze off the sea, grinding his teeth or whinnying or shaking his mane, and they might have been sharpening stone together or skinning rabbits in a peasant shack on the wild Mesolithic moor of another age, not situated at the last riotous edge of a vast modern city.

～

Grace was not immune to pain. It pierced her eyes and deepened the horizontal lines in her brow. For the first few minutes of every session her hand would agitate against the closest surface or the fingers would seize into fists, becoming knaggy and rigid. Her muscles quivered, protested. Her breath was now and then drawn quickly and blown out with difficulty, if in the barbed tension she had forgotten to breathe or his equipment had hit a sensitive, easily offended area of flesh, a spur of bone. It gave him imprecise satisfaction to know that she was human after all, that while she had the will and wiles to make any argument mature, demanding all-out warfare or surrender, while she spoke a dozen languages and was hard boiled with mystery, she could also be hurt. But she quickly pushed past the discomfort, making herself relax as she had herself instructed the unfortunate soldier to, letting her body absorb and dilute the pain of incursion into its skin. She endured long, long sessions. And he worked slowly, meticulously on her.

– You're doing very well. Must have had your Bovril.

– My what?

– Never mind, it's just an expression. It's what they forced us to take as children telling us we wouldn't get rickets and polio. That and cod liver oil. I just meant you are taking it well. Never mind.

– Sometimes it's like burning. Today just nails. I prefer the nails.

This was a strange period of work for Cy. Soft. Honest. Intimate. He put away all the barking and braggery of the trade, the slapdash rhetoric, the rude commentary. It was not necessary in any case to sideshow her; she was in it for the duration. They conversed about many things, cultural, political, the new psychology of warfare, subjects which ordinarily found no relevance at his place of work. Or they remained quiet, contented to be so. Grace liked to call him by his moniker, as if she thought it was appropriate or humorous or simply more valid than his true name, and it was how she always addressed Cy. The irony was that during the hours spent with her in the booth he never felt quite so much himself as he worked.

∼

– Look at these things on your wall. Do you think these symbols you have will always remain appropriate, Electric Michelangelo?

Grace was on her back looking up at the flash designs. They were midway through a session. Only an occasional bluster of wind made its way into the booth, lifting the corners of the papers delicately, so the walls seemed to be covered with bright, twitching-winged butterflies.

– Oh, I don't know, I suppose so. Some are hundreds of years old, and everybody understands them. I've been here several years, and I've been doing this for a lot longer than that, and they've not gone out of fashion yet. I hope you aren't trying to put me out of business, petal.

– Petal! So funny! No, but look, I'll give an example. Lots of people do not believe in God. He's a joke, a big hole. Almost gone. They have money now, in their lives – no need for a heaven lined with gold any more. That was just to get the poor to believe.

– People will always believe in God. They need to, especially lately. We're all weeny in the grand scheme and unsatisfied, money or not. Besides, have you seen how many new temples are going up in Brooklyn?

– OK, yes, yes, when you are getting persecuted and killed for your faith abroad you have to make it mean something, otherwise why did you die? But what about these little girls? So silly – not like any girl I know. Who goes round with the boots of a pirate and tits out like balloons? Huh? Shouldn't they be different? Since they have discovered that we have brains and we can vote now and work and we don't have to marry you stinking brutes to buy a house.

Cy smiled. Quickly, he had come to realize that there was no matter, no issue, no problem which she considered unnavigable by human intellect. She was the least agnostic person he had ever met.

– Men will always like the girls. It's just a basic fantasy, a bit of fun. It's just one way of talking, that's all.

– Oh is it? Well, what will be our fantasy? A big prick waving in the open air? Strong muscles? Shit. Are we really so simple? Things change, you know, signs change. Look at the swastika. It's very old. Look what it's become, goddamn it, turned on its side, they are using it to torment us. These terrible armies that have it now, who will want it any more when the Reich is done with it?

He sat back from her, shrugged, and put down his equipment. He wiped his brow on the back of his wrist. Sweat had gathered along the lines of his palms and he wiped them on his trouser leg. He was conscious from time to time that she might be on the verge of some kind of personal disclosure. Of the things he had come to know about her there was little in the way of confidences. He knew facts, she was a trained funambulist and she set up a flatrope between two trees in the park to practise, she suffered from asthma, her drink was Pernod. But nothing personal had been offered.

– No. I understand that.

– Do you? You know what they are saying now? That in these places where they are keeping the Jews they tattoo a number on to them. Tattoo them. Like branding cattle. Like stamping eggs. You cannot know how awful this is for them, for so many reasons. Some of these indignities are carefully designed, some are merely accidental. But this one, this one is both.

She said this so plainly, plain enough that it left too much room to hide the accusation. He balked. She could be, with little if any effort at all, a menace to his sobriety.

– Where on earth did you hear such a horrible thing? A spy? An informer? Who?

Her eyes swept across him, dismissive and scant. Either she did not consider it an important enough question to address or she was not going to reveal her source.

– We are just so complicated now. I just wonder why we want such simple things. A picture stops working at some point. Now you can wire money from bank to bank – not just put it in a box under the bed. It doesn't exist, not really, it's like a dream of money, an idea of money. Look at these abstract artists that break everything up and tell us tradition is not worth keeping. You've seen Braque?

– Yes.

– And?

Her bare belly was stretched across the chair like tight hemp on an easel. She had that look in her dark eyes that she always got when the conversation turned weightier, became more profound. An insulted look. The beginning of ire, a smoulder that would, if blown upon for any length of time, turn from an ember into blazing fury. Cy was not keen to have her become fervent under the needle, she moved around too much, gestured too violently in that condition, making it impossible to work so he took care not to provoke her when his hand was engaged. Then again, in these moments of respite, when he was smoking or preparing a new part of her skin, she did become rather compelling and fetching as she ranted. He shrugged again, he seemed to do that frequently in her company.

– Well. I for one do not understand this new abstract art. I don't understand Picasso. And I don't understand Braque. It's too messy. Where does the picture begin and end and what does it mean? Maybe people like simplicity because everything else is so troublesome and vexing. Symbols are powerful. They convey a lot without words.

– No, no. It's good to have such complication. I like it – sometimes I have to get up and walk around the chessboard to see all the angles at once, otherwise perhaps I'm missing a move.

– OK, steady on now, Sally-Ann. We've some eyes to finish up here before nightfall.

He picked the equipment back up, flipping the cord out of the way, and Grace perused the booth walls again.

– But you know, you see that one there . . . look now . . .

Cy followed her pointing finger to a red heart, levitating among many others.

– . . . that will probably never go out of fashion, as you say. We remain truly crazy, don't we?

She reached behind her and unhooked her brassiere, brought the garment forward off her body, over her arms, and placed it on the floor. Cy leaned forward, spread the fingers of his right hand out along her breastplate, rubbed the area with alcohol solution and petroleum jelly, and then moved the needle to her upper body so that it was sitting directly above her own version of the red organ.

∽

– Shall I make this eye smaller to your shoulder?

– No. I don't think so, just until it would come to the hem of a dress. Not past the collar though. No point in paying to see the Lady of Many Eyes if you can see her tattoos on the street when she walks, is there? The people will only stare when they have paid bucks to stare and they are stared back at.

– It's just that it may give it more beauty to be left alone on a surface, away from others – the eyes are quite close together and crowded this way.

Grace smiled patiently. She looked up at him, he was working near her collarbone. She had on a tweed skirt that was dampening with perspiration. Her upper body was naked, her breasts suspended by the air. There was a large scabby, healing tattoo exactly centre on the flesh of her stomach, already observing the world through its conjunctive, crusted eye. It looked like something deformed from one of the freak shows. Several more tattoos on her breasts and arms were still too new to have scabbed and one or two were temporarily hidden under gauze. Her arm was raised on the counter and held back, flattening the plane of skin he was currently working on. In another situation she might have been offering herself to him erotically, arching her back and eager to feel the pressure of his mouth on her breast. She had recently shaved under her arm, there was just a small, dark growth there. She continued to smile at him. Cy rolled his eyes humorously and answered his own question.

– Yes, yes. I know. More eyes the better. Yadda yadda yadda.

– Oh, dobrze, so he speaks other languages now. Welcome to Brooklyn.

He laughed.

– Hardly. Is that what you'll call yourself, then? On the circus card, I mean. The Lady of Many Eyes?

– Perhaps. Yeah, why not?

– Sorry, I have to pull a little bit here, harder doing it freehand. I'm not . . . making a pass, actually.

– All right. I'm not making a pass at you either.

He was again conscious of touching her. He was conscious of the difficulty in not touching her, having to rest the side of his palm along the flesh of her breast to steady his work, otherwise the equipment was too upended and it was like leading a hopeless metal dance partner around a soft, snagging ballroom floor. He was conscious of her nipples, that they hardened and became erect if touched even slightly, and he wished they would not, but at the same time he was glad they did.

– I will make good money, better than the circus. They will pay to see me looking back at them. It will be a good joke. It will be funny, like being the invisible woman.

– I didn't ask.

– Otherwise my body already belongs to them. I don't care if it is not thought of as beauty. I don't need it to be. They can think what they like, but what they cannot do is use me with their damn eyes. Not ever again. Don't pretend you don't understand this. Not knocking on my door in the middle of the night with your chess questions for me, all red in the face like a sunburn.

– No. Yes. I mean I think I do appreciate the idea. I've said so.

272

He paused, bit down on his lip a little. He sensed the evaporation of her blithe mood but continued anyway.

– I just don't know why. I don't really know much about you, you're . . . no cakewalk. What's your story, Grace?

She was known by many in the district. And she was talked about with both affection and scorn. Since meeting her he had heard whispers and elaborate slanders about her, as Claudia hinted that he would in the gaming room of Varga the night their association was made known to him. He had heard that she had saved a life only to destroy it herself later, that she was a rich Arab's mistress, she was the sister of Oskar Manheimer, notorious banker and loan shark, that she had been trained by some elite intelligence force in a foreign country, that she was a Nazi espionne, that she collected the gilded jewellery of famous murderesses, and even that she lay with her own horse for pleasure. And while he did not pay much heed to the scandalous wake that followed her, he may have inadvertently assimilated some of it. He was once certain he had seen her in the East Village, in a third-storey window above a café, threatening a man with a blade, pulling on his hair. But she had been on his mind that day, and he might have seen her anywhere, in any guise, under the contours of any dark-haired woman. He wanted to say to her now that he didn't care what people thought of her when she rode Maximus bareback down through the borough on the dirt roads, when she cursed and argued and sat with her legs apart as she played chess in Varga, when she drank clear anise alcohol that turned milky green as she added water, like an old apothecary. And if people thought her attitude wasn't becoming of a lady, Cy didn't care to vouch for that presumption. Reeda Parks had smoked her dead husband's pipe in public when she fancied to. Women she did not know had growled at his mother for sticking her principled neck out for them. She had blistered the political sensibilities of many about Morecambe town with her coal-stoked courage, her divergences, the proverbial brass balls of her. And through it all he was not sure his mother failed to qualify for the title of lady. He wanted to tell Grace those things but thought she would laugh or become angry at the insinuation that she was abrasive, or a goon. She was staring off into space, a small vein in her throat palpitating. He tried to keep his tone light, while he dug deeper into the sealed layers of her.

– They will still look at you. Is it that you want them not to look at you lecherously and won't you still have to take your clothes off, mostly, for these doo-dads to show, and doesn't that defeat the purpose? I mean, if you don't want to be looked at like . . . a woman of . . . of certain reputation. If it's about exposing your body and being judged, then I don't see why you'd do it.

Two marble black eyes on Grace's face suddenly gleamed at him, livid, impersonal, and even the tattooed eyes on her body seemed to swivel in his direction like possessed cadaver parts in order to apprehend and intimidate him.

– Nie? Nie? Och, Idiota! It will always be about body! Always for us! I don't see a time when it won't. I can't say you can't have my body, that's already decided, it's already obtained. If I had fired the first shot it would have been on a different field – in the mind. All I can do is interfere with what they think is theirs, how it is supposed to look, the rules. I can interrupt like a rude person in a conversation. I can be rude. Isn't that so? This is America, we can all be fucking rude.

– Listen, I'm sorry.

He shrank back, attempted to smooth things over. Apologies had gone a long way since his arrival in this country. They were considered largely unnecessary and dated. Even his accent implied apology, that he had manners over and above those he was currently demonstrating. It was the universal trick of the English. And people were often charmed by that here, and thought him less unsavoury, regardless of his trade and his appearance.

– Sorry, sorry, he's sorry. OK, all but Electric Michelangelo can be rude. I see it now.

274

She was not angry. Her eyes were passionate actors playing their part. Her voice had come out for effect and emphasis, performance, the way that the Greeks drinking in Varga shouted to their families down the telephone receiver, or the mayor of the city heralded his agenda through a megaphone. He was getting used to her outbursts, recognizing them as tools she employed to toil harder for her cause. And her ambushes never seemed to strip anything vital from him, rather they seemed designed purely to warn him of the presence of dangerous bandits in the territory through which he travelled. In truth he admired more than feared her passion. But there were instances, like now, with her breasts lighting up the air before her and her face in a state of flushed excitement, when he just could not take her being nude and zealous and so close by. It made him ache. He did not know how long he could go on not reaching for her.

– I'm almost done with this section. But I won't finish it today. Can you come back tomorrow?

～

And then, when he had all but perfected the repressive art of self-restraint, Grace threw another flaming tenpin into the fiery arc of urges he was juggling. She put her hands on him. As if to seduce him. As if to begin what he was having difficulty beginning. The trouble occurred one not so very unusual afternoon in the run of things when her eccentric new body was nearly finished and they were once more cooped up tight together like birds inside an aviary. He had been talking about Eliot Riley, talking shallowly, for he did not want to get maudlin or bitter, nor mawkish, telling her anecdotes about the apprenticeship that had left him heavily printed, telling her about the Nivea lotion preservation he had inherited, and Riley's unhappy relationship with alcohol. He had mentioned the events of his life that had led to his chosen tattoos and how he had written his mother's name on himself reversed in a mirror because his master would not do it. He was working on her back as he talked when she snapped her fingers in order to stop him. She stood up. Her breasts had made creases in the flat skin on her sternum as she lay on her stomach. She looked freshly pressed and laundered.

– Show them to me.

– Oh, really no, ask me another time. Buy me a soda. We'll see what we can do.

She lifted his shirt out of his breeches, through the braces, opened the buttons, as if she had every right to do it, and then placed her hands on the flanks of his stomach. She did not ask permission and he did not grant it, she simply took up his garment and addressed his skin with her cool hands, more gently than any communication he had ever known to leave her. Under her fingers was the tall black galleon leaning into a gale, its sails full, with names tangled into the rigging like Columbus's memories, and under that was the deeper dermis, and under that, a crackling electric head of nerves that gathered energy and held it, as if he were a copper coil in a fuse.

– Who is Stanley? Don't you want to tell to me?

Cy tried speaking.

– He was my father. Er, that's an old motif of a clipper, one of . . . Sailor Jackie's original designs, my father was . . . Well, he was a fisherman . . . who died at sea . . . just before I was born . . . only a day or so before in fact . . .

His voice melted away. Her fingers were redrawing the ship, too soft to be idle, too precise to be misinterpreted. He felt his chest rise and then fall heavily. She followed the line of the mainmast up along the cavity of his chest to the left side, increasing the pressure of her fingernail as she moved it so that the sensation became a scratch. Her hand rested for a moment and then she began to stroke his body again, quietly.

– Ah. Then you must be superstitious. You must think you were unfairly treated and this strange coincidence has set a pattern in your whole life that nothing can be done about. You must throw a pinch of salt over your shoulder when it spills, and crush up eggshells after you've cracked them open, always waiting for somebody to tell you a good bright thing to take away the darkness. A szerencsecsillag vezessen utudon. Yeah, I think this is what you want. At some point you'll have to forgive him, won't you, the man who taught you this art and disappointed you? He could not ever have satisfied. You're forgiving him in Varga every night already when you drink.

Her hands were like emollient even as her words seemed to pull open the corners of his old wounds. He sighed, moaned, he could not help it. The words she spoke and her touching him felt like two separate lovers working at his body. So long as he was in a position of checked propriety and ethical administration he was in no danger of abandoning restraint. But he knew he could not take her coming to him like this. It was too thrilling a concept, too powerful a stimulant. And if she kept speaking, he thought, if she used her words like a second intrigue, allied with that first contact of touch behind his fabric barriers, the battle would be lost and he may as well throw her down. All this time Cyril Parks had commended himself on his propriety and manners as she sat in her undergarments or without them, her small redcurrant nipples hardening when he coloured them into black pupils, dislocated from desire, so that their tips might have been scorched by the sun, not touched by a laden, motorized quill and a human hand.

She wasn't watching his body now. Her eyes were closed and she was done talking. The tattoos seemed dead on her, stony, inanimate as mineral lode bound tight into the rock face. Looking down, he sensed the true arrival of a different weather system settling around her, the absence of disturbance. It had come without warning or forecast, as with everything else that was immediate and unforeseen about her, the eruption of rage, the hiss of defiance, laughter, that which she could turn her mind to, the turning of games and tables and opinions. There had been no indication from her that day as she arrived that she would soon deliver a response to his unassuming romantic notions. There had been no suggestion that she wanted to give him this gift. He sighed again as her fingertips swept along the waistband of his breeches. All the languages and conveyances she knew and this dialogue of touch might have been her most natural. He wanted to put his hands in her hair, or on her breasts, there was nothing separating him from that, but he kept them gripped tight on the dresser behind him. He might have said her name, he did not know. He might have made love to her and meant it, hunting out her preferences, slaughtering them with generosity, but that he was sure afterwards she would walk away, casually. Her hands were almost too light on him now as she moved them, making him tense and lock his muscles together so as not to convulse and jerk as new nerve endings sparked under her caress. He found he was biting down hard on his lip. Blood was tricking along his pelvic bone and he had the unmistakable sensation of becoming heavier, fuller, firmer. He knew if he drew Grace in towards him now, so that their skin met, her body would feel a fraction colder than his own, and the state of her would tell him her mood was made of vapour. It would be like touching a soft white effluent, like that quiet portion of the northern lights, the last, most obscurely hidden element of the atmospheric wonder, the humble white pulse of illumination almost lost behind the seeping blood of the sky. And his hands would move right through her. Like Aurora Borealis, he knew he just had to let her be, in all her loveliness, not knowing how much of herself she would disclose, how much she would come to him, until she was gone.

Then, as always, in the opposingly hemisphered life of Cyril Parks, with beauty arrived its disagreeable, diametric partner. Grace was stepping in towards him, perhaps to take the pearl of his ear into her mouth or to find his neck, when a fist began to pound savagely on the side of the booth.

– Hey! English asshole! Got a bone to pick with you. Hey! I know you're in there, saw you go in.

Grace held very still for a moment, varnished with calm, as if having been lacquered and set midpoint in the arc of her kiss. Her shoulders were shining. The cursing and banging continued. Then she seemed to wake from the mood and the restive energy rushed back into her. She removed her hands and nodded.

– Yes. Yes. Go.

Cy's eyes were unconvinced, and loyal to hers, telling her that there was nowhere he would rather be at that moment than absolutely right here with her.

– Go on, go. It's all right.

After a moment of composure, the unpleasant redirection of his pleasant hardness with his back turned away from the woman who had encouraged it, Cy appeared from behind the piece of vibrating wood. His belly was still out, his white shirt billowing like a sail around the tattooed ship, and he was wearing an expression that informed the intruder he might have been about to discover the divine secrets of the universe before being interrupted. Outside was a man who had been holding his own vinous face in a pose of disgruntlement all afternoon. He was sauced, soused, drunk enough that he could not maintain a plumb line of balance. He pointed to his forearm.

– Not happy, buddy. Remember me? Not happy.

– I can see that. What are the chances of you coming back later this afternoon?

– Hah! It's a mess, you did a shitty job. And I want my money back.

The man looked dishevelled, wired and exhausted at once, as if he had not left the Island since his visit to the booth four days ago. Coney Island was persuasive when it wanted to be, cajoling its weaker-willed visitors into enjoying its offerings longer than stamina and finances should feasibly permit. Until they were deprived of money and reason and sleep, and then they spoiled, and everything they had done sickened them and they would try to retrace their crimes in

279

order to repair the damage. But this was one argument that Cyril Parks never ever lost. He could not afford to. He took hold of the arm in question and examined it, then pushed it away.

– No. You've picked it. You've picked the scab off it. I told you not to. I told you it would itch like crazy for a few days like a chicken pox but not to touch it. Did I not tell you that?

– I never touched it. You fucked it up in the beginning and I paid you good money too! Sign says freehand, that's why I came, thought you'd be a pro.

– No. You picked that scab off, like a little kiddie because it was itchy and you couldn't keep your fingers off it. I can see the spot where you did it. It's patchy. That doesn't happen unless it's been messed with, right? The colour's come out just as I said it would. I'll fix it for you, but you'll not get a penny back off me. Not a cent, y'hear me. That was quality work when you walked out my door. I should charge you for the time, but I won't. Count yourself lucky. Now, can you come back later? I'm very busy.

The man had not come down to the booth to be placated or back down. He had come to transfer the responsibility of his rash and ruinous vacation at the fair to another party. He lingered. He wanted his say and to feel that he had won a little victory, salvaged something of himself. At that moment, Grace stepped out through the incomplete entrance of the booth, redressed and scowling faintly. Glad to have an audience for the drama, the man let fly a string of insults.

– You're a lying English bastard. You're not touching me again, no way. You did substandard work on me and now it's fucked and it'll always be fucked. You've probably messed up this poor lady too, goddamn bastard. You Coney freak – I knew not to come down to this wackplace for a tattoo.

There were occasions when Cy had to use his full height, standing up slowly, unfurling, and widening his eyes, to become the professional tough man of the business in order to settle disputes or knock the wind out of a conflict. This would have been exactly one of those times – the complainer was certainly about to get punchy, he wanted nothing less than to fight – and a brawl would have doubtless ensued had it not been for the knife that sliced the air an inch or so past the man's nose, close enough that he felt its sharp metallic breath on his face, and it struck the boards of the booth with a dull sucking thud as the blade's tip was swallowed by wood. The weapon's blue hilt shone like ore in the summer light. A few pedestrians paused on the Walk to observe the scuffle, or to catch the act. Incredulously the rumpled man turned to look at Grace. Cy also turned to her in shock. She had her arms crossed over her chest, as if she had never so much as taken aim. But her face was transmogrified and looked suddenly old though, weathered and deeply lived in, like a caravan tinker widow's, or as if it had come up like a grim fairytale from under the façade of a younger woman. Her eyebrows were raised high on her lined forehead in questioning and challenge.

– My God! You damn Romany bitch. I oughta call the cops and have you arrested for that. This place is nuttier than a peanut factory. I oughta report that kind of behaviour . . .

Grace unfolded her arms, walked between the astonished men and collected her knife with an abbreviated tug. As she folded it away the handle and blade appeared to be disappearing into each of her palms, and then, after a quick legerdemain and sleight of wrist, it became uncertain which closed fist contained the weapon. The man did not care to find out. With a look of contemptuous alarm he walked away, two patches of bright discolouration left under the sockets of his eyes. Grace looked at Cy and shook her head.

– You are a kind man. I think if you ever truly had to sting someone, you wouldn't survive it.

She made a buzzing sound like that of a flying bee, with her tongue on the roof of her mouth, and then she stopped the noise, abruptly.

$\sim$

By midsummer of 1940 there were one hundred and nine tattoos on Grace's form, from the soles of her feet to the base of her neck, so that she looked like a most extraordinary tree of eyes. She visited the Electric Michelangelo on sixteen separate occasions for him to complete the work. And in retrospect, when Cy would try to relive his journey across her body and remember the revolution of its archaic landscape under his unyielding bevelled brush, perhaps those were the times he was making love to her after all.

~

The last tattoo went on to the lower portion of her back, in the deep well at the curve of her spine. Cy worked slowly on it, knowing that this piece was, in a way, the conclusion of their affair, the last vertebra of its own backbone after which it would be an independent anatomy, free to come and go as it pleased. Her body was wet and slippery, the humidity of the summer had arrived even on the coastal outskirts of Brooklyn. Her tattoos shone under a sheen of sweat, as if she were oiled for a show. Neither one of them had mentioned the encounter in the booth since it passed. Cy did not know how to bring it up, for his part there was no way to refer to it, her allusive hands, the foggy arousal, the one-sided duel. Thinking back on it, Cy had not known which one of them seemed angrier or more frustrated by the rude interruption, or who had displayed which kind of daft chivalry. And yet she had not touched him again since then. And he not found it in himself to break his professional codes, even as his heart battled with the memory of that initial embrace. There had been few interactions inside Varga, for she seemed always busy or moving quickly or planning furiously in front of her chessboard. There had been no late-night visitations to her apartment door. To have found her with another man would have devastated him now.

When he had finished transferring ink he bent forward and put his lips against the raw skin of the last eye. She tasted of carbon and blood and salt, she tasted of life. She was lying on her stomach on the bench with her head resting on her arms, her dark hair curling damply around her ears and neck. He doubted whether she even felt the touch of his mouth after the precise bitchery of the needle. His lips might have felt like a cotton cloth administered to catch her sore fluids. Or like the ghostly kiss of somebody from another lifetime, a gesture reaching out past the grave.

– So. You're done. And the best of luck to you, duckie.

It was hot, kettle-steamed June. The smell of the organic city had already begun to ripen, wafting through the sidewalk grilles and gutters, out to the Island. Within a week Grace would be healed and on display in Luna Park, infatuating and unnerving customers with the optical illusion of her body. Within a month she would be gone.

– History's Ink –

The acid, afterwards that's what the assailant confessed it had been, sulphuric acid, burnt through her dress and her flesh almost until it reached bone. It would have eaten through her ribcage and sternum also, had it not been for the administration of an alkali directly after the assault. The man must have timed his attack well, it was agreed later, for the offence had a quality of premeditation to it, and perhaps he had practised with cups of murky solution or buckets of soapy water on a piece of sacking, or an old fur coat from the clothes market or on a recently butchered animal carcass, observing the speed of corrosion and imagining it on human skin, timing the two stages of the plan.

Nobody truly saw what happened, but multiple accounts of that night would exist shortly after the incident, twittering speculation and tweedy, academic overviews. Varga was jumping with customers and cuckoo mad as usual. The man's name was Malcolm Sedak. He had been beaten by Grace in two tournaments that summer season, though this proved to be incidental, for he had been beaten by many other players also. He had seen her revolving on the turntable podium in the Human Picture Gallery of Luna Park with her friend Claudia, the third week of her new career. He had something against her, that much he confessed. Little else was known of the connection, the animosity. But the channels of gossip and gasconade at Coney were as slick and obstructionless as the Human Fountain's frequently rinsed pipes. Interpretations flushed through the area. There had been a political association or a grudge or an untenable situation of some kind. Amongst other things, Grace was rumoured to have under-world connections, so it was not a slender assumption to make. He had probably seen her working with her horse in the circus long before she became tattooed and had heard some of the dark fables that told of her inner workings or had been involved directly with her iniquitous dealings.

He came into Varga an hour or so into the Wednesday chess evening. Not to play. Not to spectate. It was ten o'clock at night, a still hour outside, with just the ocean's nocturnal lilt and levy sounding, but noisy and crowded in the bar as always. He moved between bodies on a leisurely heading towards the bar, unhurried, enchanted, as if moving the wrong way through a carousel of animated creatures, because his mind must have been musical and cog-like at that stage, the carnival having become his ordinary streetwalk to work. Then he climbed down from the ride at the point which he wanted to get off, by Grace at her table with the buffed-horn chess set, up by one pawn only on her opponent and playing the sly Russian game that contributed to the rumour that she slept with a black queen under her pillow at night.

The man had on a long overcoat, curious for summer, some may have thought, sinister, it was deemed afterwards. Safe inside the garment was a colourless-brownish liquid in a sealed container. It was removed congenially like a full money wallet, opened, and directed by an appendage as smooth and elegant as an orchestra conductor's. Lento acid. The contents of the slow-flung vessel seemed dense and oily at first to Grace when she looked down at her soaked mid-section. Like the buttery juice of a bowl of chowder, accidentally spilled over her. Until the dress dissolved. Then it seemed as red and thin as fire's very centre on her stomach, her breast, her upper legs, her core. She began to scream. She had the voice for it, which was another surprise. Customers who knew her said they were amazed how well she suited that level of inserenity and panic. Usually such a constitutional woman, masterly in all things including a raised voice, was their aphorism. How long did he wait, the man with the antidote? Four seconds, five? Ten? A lifetime for Grace, being consumed by the ravenous acid. Then the disintegration of her body was arrested by another sweeping gesture, this coat-kept container releasing an ammoniacal dilution over her. Lento alkali. And for a moment she was chemistry. And witnesses swore they saw her smoke, reacting, changing matter. Malcolm Sedak was four feet away, less. He could have hit a barn door twice with his eyes closed and hung upside down like a bat. He could not have missed.

It was such a strange plan. Damnation and salvation in tandem. Because he had not wanted her dead, Sedak told the doctors, the police, and the press. That would have been murder, that would have been wrong, in his mind. He had wanted her body altered, put back to how she belonged, restored to grace and femininity, restored to God's blueprint for her kind. As if the acid might have licked off the tattoos like the tongue of a mother cat, leaving behind a blank white skin to be preserved by the salve. As if she would not be scarred or seared or turned in part to soup before she set. As if any pain during the procedure might return her in penitence to God's original purity of naked cleanness, as if the desecration of her was really a baptism, an annunciation, a rising from her unleavened state. So there was an innocence of terror to the confession and explanation Sedak gave. He was the Lord's hired lunatic, the Divine One was paying the wages of his mercenary heart. He had met Grace in Varga one night. There was something unholy about her from the beginning; that guile, the heretical bile that lifted in her mouth when she spoke, the gall in the gut of her words, the retch of her dark hair, the very peccancy of her sex, that thousand-fanged stare, and she might have been his, once, but for herself, but for her cloven-kolo self in the centre of her being. It was the bark of her cunt that put him on edge. And in her absence, in the appropriate light of his room, he knew that what he had seen were demons inside her, multiplying, and he went down on his knees to face the salivating snarling teeth, loud at the entrance of her womb, and he prayed for intervention, prayed until the voice of God came, until the voice of God came in comfort like the sound of his own mind. The Lord said gather all the evidence you can. So he went to her place of work; it was all some kind of duty to God, the stalking, the watching. And there he saw her monstrous body, with its living orbs that watched him back, that struck him impotent from that moment on. When he touched himself for pleasure it burned. She was Satan's daughter. Satan's whore. She put the blackness of hell on him with her Argus eyes and he knew she was far beyond grace. He wanted the curse on him lifted and her anaphrodisiac power gone. He wanted to rid the woman of her sin and sickness even, for he did not blame her, in this matter she was securely the Devil's victim, a pawn in his deviant game.

All this came out calmly across the interrogation table. By the time of his police interview Sedak had regained consciousness and was just able to speak again through the orthopaedic wire in his jaw. But at the time of his mission he was speaking quickly, desperately, in a language not English, even though his hands drifted, drifted through the final motion of their slow parabola. His words sounded almost like a chant. One or two of the people in the bar could understand what he said, New York after all had dozens of tongues spoken in every single one of its corners, the city was encyclopaedic and there were translators everywhere. They said the madman had been using an exorcismic verse from the Apochrypha. And his enemy had been the evil eye.

Somebody found Claudia next door to Varga, eating her clams outside where the sky was navy blue and peaceful, while others held the man down and Grace screamed on. They dragged her enormous pounding body off Malcolm Sedak only when he began to lose consciousness and it was feared she'd kill him, and the wail of a siren bit through the air near by as a police van turned into the alley. Until then her shoulder muscles looked like crankshafts, mechanical and covetous of the work. Claudia stepped through the back

287

room doorway at the urging of Mary and Valerie just as the cops came in the front, as if in a choreographed comedy, though nobody laughed, leaving the man on the floor looking like matzo paste. So at first the police were confused about who exactly the casualty of the attack was: two human wrecks had liquid around them on the floor made by their own sick and seeping bodies. The emergency telephone call had been confused at best, part-lost against the racket of the establishment. Thinking the man with the slack bloody grin that ended clear up by his ear lobe on one side of his face to be the likeliest candidate they went over to him and stooped to observe the damage. Remembering the India–China chess dispute not three years hence, the detective said right then and there that he hated coming down to Varga on account of all the crazy Polack folk and the Russian reprobates and the sorry-assed circus freaks. And he wished he could leave them all to their fucked-up Coney Island carnage.

Grace was quiet by now, diagonally across the board from them, behind the gaze of the authorities. Someone had already given her a hefty, hushing dose of morphine, injecting it into the nape of her neck which she always massaged when she played at the gaming tables, some kindly wayward doctor with access to syringes and vials, or some light-fingered hospital goof or junkie, though nobody saw who administered it, or admitted seeing as much. Seemingly Coney had ambulanced and taken care of its own. Around Grace was the strong tang of acid, tart-sour like the sprinkling vinegar for the oysters and fries served on the boardwalk, making people choke instinctively. Some of her colourful skin had flooded into the air as sulphur smoke. She was a struck match. Her body had almost finished leaking when the police got round to her and it was trying to congeal its outer layer, like a newly shed serpent. She had the look of a sleeping snake too, dead-eyed from the drug. Some people were blasé, still playing chess and drinking at the bar. Varga's chess tournaments had once again become the scene of unimaginable and accommodating violence.

~

Of the six tattooed women on the Luna podium Grace had been the newest and the least demurely dressed. The gallery had put in for a nude licence for her and been refused by the city authority, though she was always willing to do it, she said. She wore only a feeble bandeau around her breasts and a pair of short silks. The others, including Claudia, whose stage name was Mrs Bismarck, were clad as if for bathing, in long suits, and each had a circus card next to her foot. Their names were Nell Nerona, who had fake body make-up rather than authentic tattoos but said she had been abducted by Indians out west and painted while held hostage inside their wigwams, Texas Bobbie, Lovely Loretta, who had been at one time a bearded lady and had worked with Barnum and Bailey, Polly the Painted Pear, and the Lady of Many Eyes. Most were moonlighting from other circus professions, and they made more money than they knew what to do with, some had even bought stocks and shares. All but the last were dressed under their costumes in a jumble of assorted images – they had bootlaces tattooed on ankles, and portraits on their legs, hearts, doves, roses and ribbons, Allied flags, apostles and stars. Grace was the only attraction to consist of a single repetitive image. She was all eyes. And since there was a mesmerizing, confusing quality to her body, all the eyes watching the show were hers. By the third week in the gallery she had made close to a hundred dollars, four times as much as the tattoos had cost her. She had been booked to appear in a show at the Grand Theatre in Greenwich Village, and had even been invited to enter a beauty contest in Philadelphia.

~

Henry arrived at the booth as Cy was putting the last board up for the night. There was an awful, clear sobriety about him, though he had drunk almost a half bottle of Grey Goose in the bar by then on his night off, and in addition his blood was shimmering with several other ephedrine or opiate chemicals. He had a beautiful, soft, southern voice, Cy remembered thinking that night, like down on a Georgia peach, and that made the ensuing story seem like one even children would be entranced to hear, frightening and monstrous elements though there were. If anyone else had told Cyril Parks of the events minutes ago he might have laid out his fists before thinking of the guiltless messenger. Like Eliot Riley would have, when anger got the better of him, disabling his reason and he'd go about duffing the air, too drunk to reach the offender. Cy might have hooked the words right off another man's face with his knuckles, having suddenly and fully inherited the bare-knuckle legacy of Riley, when he heard about Grace. But for that soft southern voice that made the story he was hearing into a happier imitation of the truth. Then, when the tale was told, Henry said he couldn't truly tell how much morphine he'd given Grace. And that he might have given her so much morphine as to accidentally kill her, if the acid hadn't killed her already. But her pain had been so bad it had made him sorry for her, sorry enough that his thumb went down twice on the plunger, once to the post-operative millimetre marker, then beyond it to that privileged realm meant for only those long acquainted with the lag. And what would Cy recommend he do with this?

Henry took a hand out of his pocket and his two fingers were still tucked through the brass loops of the syringe and his thumb was sitting on its plunger, so it looked like he was pulling out a bizarre revolver.

– It seems you ain't the only man with Miss Grace's blood on your needle, Mr Parks.

Then the two of them walked down to the end of Steeplechase Pier and took a weight from one of the crab traps stacked on the edge and they tied it round the syringe and the empty box of glass silos and tossed it all into the water.

In the aftermath, when Grace had been taken to the hospital, everyone wanted to know about the villain who had attacked her, what his name was, where he came from, what he ate for dinner. That was the talk at Coney Island. It was as if the rankness of the act was tantamount to the incident, and the crime won the day in terms of public curiosity and attention. Not many people asked about Grace, she had received only the vengeful smite of the newly infamous. And she was, in any case, a slut to trouble, was she not? Sedak was fined forty dollars to clean up the bar and he was remanded to the Brooklyn asylum. There was talk in the newspapers of getting restrictions put on the sales of chemical substances and fertilizers, tightening up the laws, until the distributors argued back in letters to the editors that such recourse would damage their private individual sales and send them under, and the debate blew away. This was America. Consumer freedom was what made the country great. And if the public could not be trusted with what they bought, that did not constitute a penalty in rights, did it?

Grace did not die. She struggled to keep her body a consistent element. Though she was not allowed visitors for fear of infection, the nurses kept Cy informed of her condition while he stayed at the hospital, which was not good, not good at all. He arrived the night of the attack and was greeted by a creeping crêpe-bandage and disinfectant smell identical to that which he had encountered in the Lancaster infirmary years ago, and he slept along the wooden chairs in the waiting room, while the floor was polished by a man with a loud machine spinning a buffer. In his dreams the noise became the sound of his electric needle as he put blue ink along the mastectomy-buckled chest of his mother.

– Are you a relative?

He was asked this simple question time and again, hourly, as if in the continual asking there might be some sudden change of status that allowed him access to Grace, because she had no one else, no blood connection, and that deeply troubled the nurses – that lack of an immediate family. The only answer he could give was a shake of his head and nonsense.

– She lives in my building. I painted her. She's my Sistine Chapel, you see.

It was all the relationship he had to make his claim with. Then, towards the end of the first night, when he grew exhausted with hypnotic dreaming on the uncomfortable wooden chairs, and he grew desperate for news of her well-being, he began to unravel and he gave out confidential material.

– I love her, I'm in love with her, you see. She lives in my building with her horse, though I never see her there, ordinarily I see her at the bar and at work, and I love her.

The faces of the nurses were dull with work and unsmiling, but not unkind. He was polite enough, this man, if unkempt and odd and throwback looking. And love went a small way towards repairing the damage they imagined caused to Grace by her missing people. They would keep him informed, they said, as best they could.

For four days he lived in the hospital reception and waiting area, his eyes red ringed, his clothes becoming sweat stained, under the watchful and ever patience-diminishing gaze of the nurses as they moved past with metal trays bearing equipment and food and medication for patients. Occasionally there was a bustle to the uniformed women, a flap and squawk of activity, as an ambulance van howled up to the double doors of the hospital and a bloody wreck was admitted. Cy noticed the differing shapes of shotgun and revolver holes in bodies as they were wheeled past him, and he thought back to a time in the Bayview when he had first been made privy to the visceral despair of the human body, its remarkable waste. After each frenzy he would lie back down and stare at the fans on the damp-stained ceiling, the nurses looming above him like gulls. The walls began to shrink in.

Just walking to the water fountain mounted on the tiled wall opposite the chairs seemed too far to travel. After two days he was disallowed use of the orderlies' washroom. The antiseptic smell began to make him paranoid, convincing him the nurses knew Grace was dead but were not telling him so, and convincing him that all the women in the wards were destined to share the tragic fate of his mother, that if he ran in among them they would all seem beautiful and meaningful in their beds just because for the time being they were still living.

Claudia and Arturas came and sat silently next to him, then left, no more able to gain access to Grace that he. One or two other people came and went quickly, acquaintances of Grace's, characters that were furtive and suspect and seemed unwilling to talk to him. He slept through the day while the tubular lights burned the back of his eyelids and he left the chairs at night to wander the grounds when the air cooled and the receptionist ushered him out, her sympathy also at last waning. The third day he took a shit in an alleyway next to the kitchens at dusk and got some on his foot, so he was aware that he smelled of it back in the waiting room and that the nurses could smell it too, but he was beyond caring by then. He remembered the occasion he'd dressed up like a boggart in the Lune marshes and how the smell of dirt had stayed on him a week after he washed it off, how humiliated he'd felt. But even fouled and derelict, he would not leave to get cleaned up, he would stay for Grace's sake. Superstition told him that desertion, even temporary, would signal her immediate death, and tiredness and hunger pumped that ominous sense around his wrecked and ransacked brain.

On the fourth evening his stomach was sore with famine and he began looking through the waste material at the back of the hospital for leftover food. He was seen by a doctor leaving for the night in his car who notified security and Cy was removed from the grounds with a stern warning. He walked several miles back to Sheepshead Bay with the soles of his feet thinning and blistering against the leather of his boots. It was a hot wet night in the streets of Brooklyn, and the humidity washed garbled phrases out of him that were slurred and pointless, the way the quicksand had loosened his tongue when he was a boy. There was a moment when he could not go on, from weariness and bitter sadness, and he sat down on a bench and held his stomach and his body cramped with sobs. An old woman walking past with her dog jabbed at him with her stick and in a hissing fit of conniption told him to go away. He kept moving, stopping only once more at an all-night store where he bought a quart of liquor. When he arrived home he drank it with determination and slept on a sheetless bed, he had not brought his washing down from the roof, not having been home since the morning of Grace's attack, and now it was being rained wet again. Within an hour Señora Ubago had pinned a note on his door stating he was late with his rent.

In the morning he bought fresh boiled bagels from the bakery and fruit from the market, though by then his stomach resented the intrusion and he had to concentrate hard to resist being sick. He ate standing outside his building, gingerly, watching the living pass by, fearing the dead under their feet. On the way back to his room he paused next to Grace's door and was suddenly horrified to think of the horse, unfed and unwatered, closed up in a tiny space. He had no idea where Maximus was, whether he had been left at the circus or not. The door was ajar very slightly and upon closer examination the wood around the lock was splintered and split. Evidently Claudia had had the same idea about the horse. Or some opportunistic felon, some nosy gumshoe, after hearing the news of her downfall, had taken the opportunity to burgle Grace while she was indisposed. He moved for the first time inside her apartment and it was like coming into the country-side. There were patches of hay in the corner and a warm barnyard smell enriched the air, the odour of livestock and rusk. Maximus had imprinted his character on her home as well as if he were a husband. Cy thought to himself again that it was simply implausible and impractical for her to have pulled off such a feat. And yet she had done it. A patchwork blanket was folded over the back of a chair, it was covered with coarse wiry horsehair and a few pieces of bridlery hung from a hat-stand, but there was no saddle to be found anywhere. The apartment was one of the smallest in the building and some nights Grace had kept the largest horse Cy had ever seen in it without the building manager's knowledge. The old Jewess must surely have known! She must have known or suspected, or for ludicrous reasons agreed to it all. Though there was Grace in his mind's eye, going to the trouble of putting sacking on the horse's hooves as she led him back inside over the incriminating marble floor, asking for his cooperation to step high and quiet with her gypsy-blood whisper in his twitching ear. There she was, rugose and beautiful at once, arguing with strangers over any cause she saw fit, and giving up her body for a belief, or a move in a political game, or for nothing at all. It seemed such a stretch, so innately impossible when she was not here to prove it, but he had long ago given up on what was possible in life. In this city of a thousand impossibilities, the whole world could dream, with methods and strategies as appalling and wondrous as a war of angels. A trip to the bright white moon or to the green ocean floor was possible in Luna Park, buildings grown from magic beans were possible, eighty storeys high and more, Coney's freaks were possible and Manhattan's thronging, semi-harmonious crowds, the fine dance of people moving on sidewalks and between motor cars, all of it was possible. And love, love for a woman made of eyes was above all else possible.

As he looked around Grace became no less of an enigma. There were no tommy guns in cases, nor reams of money stashed in satchels to condemn her. Beside the quirks of evidence of her equestrian involvement the rest of the apartment was ordinary, like a stage set in a minimalist play. There were books stacked on an old table, he flipped one open and the print was in English. In a bowl were some apple cores, bitten through and turning brown. An empty sack of oats was peeled back on the wooden floor. In the kitchen the sink was plugged, filled a quarter full of water with straw floating in it, the smell of an animal's thirst hanging just above the surface like a cloud of flies over a pond. The window was open and outside by a tree in the old courtyard was a pile of dry horse-shit, and hanging from the window ledge, a bag that could be fixed to the animal's hindquarters to catch its dirt. Nothing else but these few mean things told him of Grace, or gave him a leg-up into her life. She was as she came, self-contained and layered. She ate, slept, breathed.

He moved back towards the door and was about to leave when he noticed a strange artisan-looking object in the corner of the room on a bookcase. It was made of flat rectangular wooden slats stacked up on each other with fibres of paper in the very middle, like an old-fashioned press. There were four screws at the four corners of the contraption that bit firmly into the wood beneath them. He began to unscrew the bolts, a little at each corner in turn because the pulpy muscles of the press were keen to kilter out unevenly as it was opened. When the bolts were off he lifted out the boarding and between the cen-tre paper was a pressed flower, so flat that it might have been paper itself if its brown-pink pigment against the white page had not distinguished it. It was a thing so frail that Cy dared not remove its ironed stamen and petals, seeming no more opaque and no more transparent than one layer of human skin from any race. He replaced the top of the press as best he could, it was a tricky fit and he was aware that the original position-ing and frieze of the flower had been done with great care. Then he left and closed her door.

Upstairs he washed and shaved, put on a new pair of slacks and a clean blue shirt under his suspenders and he tied back his hair. He had looked like a vagrant for the last few days, like a wild dog rustling through rubbish and dirt with its nose. And he'd smelled like the drunks he had been hauling up from their own piss and blood and mistakes all his adult life. His mother had always said that a clean face and a pressed collar could get a ticket aboard a carriage to the city of London even if the change was wrong. Reeda Parks had never ridden a horse-drawn tram in Morecambe, let alone a train to the capital, but he thought of her philosophy tenderly as he paid for his ticket back to the hospital.

True enough his improved appearance opened the door for greater insight into Grace's condition. The doctor, a short, greying, varicose man, shook his hand and described the injuries. It seemed she was still an undecided compound, not quite solid, not quite liquid, but something in between. Though her internal organs had been unscathed by the acid – if the shock of such a strong corrosive on her flesh was great, the alkali had been downright confusing – there were equations and proportions of damage to the skin which meant that this durable but delicate organ was presently working out of sync with the rest of the anatomy. And it could influence other organs. Such was the plexus fashion in which the human body relied upon each of its critical vessels and components for survival and harmony. At that moment Cy heard the voice of his mother again, trilling at the back of his head. One without the other we are made poorer, Cyril, remember that.

Only time would tell for Grace's recovery, the doctor went on, and though he could say she should live, she was borderline damage percentage and that made things unduly complicated. Then the man cleared his throat confidently and looked at Cy as if waiting for a reply. Cy's head was effervescing with information like seltzer powder dumped into a glass of water.

– I didn't know skin was classed as an organ. I didn't know that.

– Yes, it is. You do understand, then?

– Yes.

And so it was that in a hospital in southern Brooklyn Cyril Parks learned his final lesson about the medium of his profession. It was the body's largest organ. He knew so much about skin, how it was essentially imperfect, but that was its very nature, how it told stories where the mouth did not, how it flexed, how it folded and faded, its shades and shapes, the provinces of geographic elasticity and density, how it aged, how it bled, how it housed his ink. But he did not know that it was an organ, like the liver or kidneys or the spleen. An organ, vital to life as the loving, brackish human heart.

∼

The sister of the women's ward told him to go home. They did not know how long Grace would be there, she was very sick. Each day was as unpredictable as the last as far as her injuries were concerned. She told him to get back to work at the factory. He'd been courteous to stay so long but he should concern himself with the security of his job, she said, mistaking the ink staining the rims of his fingernails for perpetual conveyor-belt grime. When his lady friend got better, if she got well enough to leave, she would come and find him no doubt. Sister's eyes were dense and shining dully like cannon shot, they said she understood he loved this poor, broken woman, but it was time to pull his life together now. She opened and closed the situation for him, and he was grateful to her for that. Sister was a tall woman that finally reminded him of his mother, thin-haired, possessed of abilities to comprehend and ignore bodily excretions beyond the capacity of her peers – she had in her hand a jar of something pale blue-grey and intestinal suspended in liquid and resting on her papers as if it were an ordinary glass of drinking water. There was a watch pinned upside-down on her uniform so she could time health as she took pulses.

Cy had known that one day he would meet someone in the image of Reeda Parks, he'd suspected all along there were others of her kind, and Reeda had been following him around in his memory for hours, weeks, years it seemed, vying for precedence with Riley. Now she stood before him, resurrected, with a page of notes about her patients and the exact quantities of their medication pencilled darkly in a column, the essential anatomical waste in her hand, and her sufferable maternal dogma. And he knew if he really wanted this woman here before him now to be the ghost of his dead mother, this indulgent and purgatorial country would oblige him and endorse that wish, making the apparition real, come to him to shore up his soul in its time of distress. So he kissed her cheek quickly because he missed Reeda, he did, and though Sister was perhaps a little intrigued by the gesture she nodded, glad as all matriarchs are that her advice had been acknowledged, and he left her to her duties.

～

He might have tattooed five hundred people that summer or he might only have tattooed five. The rest of the season was passed in a blur, with him stewing, brooding, festering, gathering all communication up in a tight knot at the back of his mind and putting the fear of God into anyone who sat in the chair for work. Nobody cared to guess at the despair behind the frown and the complete lack of verbal engagement did wonders for his reputation. Perversely he thrilled the customers with his convincing portrayal of one of the most authentic, stony bruisers in the profession, for silence is the most threatening proposition of them all, a vacuum that will hold all the fears and treachery of those it confronts and still have room for more. Rumours even went around that he had cut out his own tongue for a dare before force-feeding it to a rival. His hands cooperated, they were reliable that way, and there was more trade than ever, but the rest of him was retired. On the lathe of his rage he reduced to sawdust all the pleasantries and banter he had once laid down. He had always been inclined towards a quiet disposition, Eliot Riley had disliked it of him, and it seemed he had been forcing talk all his adult life, for one reason or another. Now he had not the will nor the encouragement to produce one single unwarranted word. His mind felt alien and hectored at Coney, the whiz-bang-boom and hurly-burly of the place harassed him, made him dizzy. There were bizarre conversations that he simply could not comprehend.

– Hey buddy. Know where I can buy a pogo stick?

– What?

– A pogo stick. Where can I get me one? Pogo-pogo, everybody wants a go!

– I don't understand. I don't understand what you are saying to me.

At night he drank his fill and it wasn't enough. He began to take a drink before work, which he had never done previously, not for pleasure or vice or venom, not even for the sake of his master who had done the very same thing to counter or further blackness of his spirit – not in Riley's name, Amen – but just for that first reassuring sting of liquor on the tip of his tongue.

And Coney Island looked sick to him. Overnight it seemed as if the fairground had morphed from a potentially ugly thing into a hideous creature, a full-blown monster, like a wyvern wriggling from a rotten egg. He looked around the place and it was skewed with disparagement, whole screens of groaning amusement arcades seemed to be lit now by an eerie, holocaustic Brooklyn light, or seemed reflected in distorting funhouse mirrors. It was all wrong. Occasionally, on afternoons that were less hectic or when he became fed up with work and with the rumpus of the parks, he slipped back into the animal pit of the Luna circus to see Grace's horse. Claudia had been paying for his stabling since the incident, she would not hear of him being sold on and she paid extra to the zoo hands to exercise him daily and treat him well. There were amazing animals behind the tents and domes, many of which seemed lessened in their tame proximity to each other, their relegation to part of a collection, as if they were only suited to independence within broad khaki expanses of native land. Tigers rolled lazily about in their cages, yawning like house cats. The pair of giraffes had thick scabs on their knees as if from endlessly practising their curtseys. None of the beasts seemed real. They were fading under their old paint and needed sparkle. Maximus always seemed very still in his stall. After Grace's complaints Cy expected him to be feisty. It would take the animal a second or two to come over to him and then he would rest his head on the gate while Cy rubbed his nose.

– Hello, boy. Got some peppermints for you, don't tell the missus. She hasn't forgotten about you. You're still her favourite boy. She'll be back for you soon. Then she'll ride you up to Canarsie and back, I promise.

The horse's eyes were inordinately sage and sorrowful. They always had been, it was the mark of the species, but now, in this place, and with all that had happened, the animal seemed more human to him than beast, and its eyes acted like a trip-wire on his softer emotions. It was difficult to leave Maximus; Cy would spend an hour just petting him and interpreting the evolutionary sadness of the creature. There was a gentle thera-py to the visits. The inner stillness of him that Cy had first seen pictured on the brick wall of the building where he lived was present at all times and acted like a salve. So often since the attack Cy had felt on edge, or angry, storing malignancy with-in himself instead of venting it outwardly. And Maximus calmed him, helped him to relax. So that when he left the tusk-light of the circus stalls he would, for a while, feel better, until the hoary, rakish atmosphere of the exceptional present began to rub his nerves raw again. And the biggest amusement parade on earth sucked him back into its frenetic supernova, collapsing his energy and his sanity along with it.

In daytime the light of the sun seemed to be wasted over the glaring place, and when night came and the horizontal shad-ows took the legs off the piers, told them they did not exist any more, the garish floodlamps created rubbery cartilages and tissues of muscle underneath Coney that seemed to keep the entire island afloat on a large falsely illuminated lip. But it wasn't only the Island that chilled him and set him on edge. Coney was just the exotic pet of an eccentric owner. The sickness went beyond it. Everywhere it seemed there were potential madmen and acts of sensibly plotted perfidy or fundamentally corrupt faith waiting to occur, and he did not know how people could stand it, how they could live day to day with that kind of potential in their back yard. Society was suddenly filled with loose hinges and smouldering fuses and he barely felt able to leave his home. Even in the tepid streets of Sheepshead Bay he felt he wanted to look over his shoulder. At any minute there might be weapons produced or chloroform gags or speeding vehicles revving their engines in alleyways ready to throw off their emergency brakes. Because where had Malcolm Sedak come from? He was just a face in the crowd, a darn in the fabric. He was just New York. He was just America. He had stepped out of its undergrowth with his plan and his pledges to God and his diabolically limp cock in order to tear Grace down, to dissolve her. And Cyril Parks hated him, wanted to hate him, had to, he aimed everything he had at the man. He fell into it with determination. But the hating seemed not to have an end or a floor and he kept on falling, his hatred escaped the confines of a single repulsive being, spreading systematically outwards, outwards. He hated the venue of Grace's demise and got more and more tense within its walls until he fought with a complete stranger one night who had done nothing more than ask the sisters about that fateful evening in passing while smoking a cigar, and Valerie kicked him out. He hated the Island and was spiteful to his customers. He hated the stale smell of the subway and the meritless citizens who rode it and the ensigns of the country. So that more and more things were to blame.

Cy's mindset was not helped by the compulsory and continual updates of Malcolm Sedak's hospital incarceration by Henry Beausang, who worked in the institution and had access to all kinds of information. Like the crazy's unrepentant stance. Like his cock's happily restored ability to function. Like the colour of his supper plate. But Cy had to know about him, to feed his anger and his spite, to assure himself that Grace's enemy was contained, and had not dissolved through a wall only to re-form in the outside world, like an old disease, like the plague.

~

When the first September chill came in off the Atlantic and refused to budge one morning, Claudia and Arturas came to see him and told him this would be their last season at the Island. Since he had not seen them in Varga owing to his banishment it came as a mild shock. They were going to California, by way of an enormously varied land mass. The beaches along the coast were golden and ripe with bodies awaiting ornamentation, Arturas said. And perhaps Claudia might try her hand at the movies, she could act lines or silently terrorize peroxide-blonde actresses with her sheer zombie size or as Frankenstein's sutured bride.

– They better have good hotdogs in Los Angeles. It's all I can say. Will you join us, my English friend?

– No. I've been thinking of joining up. Going back over. May as well be of some use.

Arturas gave Cy a look that was set painfully between disbelief and hazardous comprehension. As if something latent between them, a tiny, precious, unifying thing, which they had both always tried to protect in the middle of a nest of unmentionable conversation, in the middle of their professional rivalry, and in the middle of a grotesque and sundering war, had now been broken. Turo took Cy's offered hand and shook it, and with his other hand he reached for the back of Cyril Parks's neck, pulling him forward until their foreheads met.

– We will have a drink then in Varga, for old time's sake?

– I can't. I'm barred.

What he wanted to do was take hold of Grace's hand and into it pass something of his own heart, but instead he held back, and he found himself watching her remove a cotton dress, a garment softer than candyfloss from a spinning machine which some friend or nurse had been thoughtful enough to get for her, to cover the fraught body. She unbuttoned it down and open through the front, making it into one long piece of material, and she slowly peeled and unwound herself out of it. Then she was naked in front of him but for her shoes. She had not put on underwear, her breasts and pubic region had been included in the savagery of the acid and were still healing. Before he could harness his horror, Cy was crying openly, an uncontrollable weeping that forbade neither his voice nor his face from expression. Grace stood before him, on the sidewalk next to his booth, with her dress in her hand and her scars open to the sky. She stood there as if she were a peep-show whore in a film about the undead. Or one of Coney Island's monsters. Litter tumbled past them with an insistent, autumnal breeze behind it, empty wrappers, paper bags and cartons once containing food. And there amid the trash she was extraordinary against the familiar background of the alley but no less ruined.

She had walked with absolute care up to Cy as he was opening the booth, like someone recently woken from a spell of being knocked unconscious, and it was further than she had walked in three months, from the station to the end of Oceanic Walk, though he did not know of her small victory. He had not seen her once during the period of rehabilitation, having recoiled from the effort of trying to get to her as hard as he had initially made it. He was removing the lock from the hinge of the booth when he turned and saw her walking towards him, at first not recognizing her, for she moved like an old lady with well-retained posture and rheumatic difficulty. Then it was her hair with its traces of red and the dark features of her face that gave her away, and his blood froze for a moment before lurching forward again.

– Grace? My God, is that you!

She was almost to him when he spoke, treading with rigid care on the pavement, so even before she revealed her body to him he knew the damage must be extreme. And without a word she stood before him and stripped away her clothing.

If her eyes said love, if they said it to him then in accompaniment with the gesture, his clamouring heart and the racket of his blood drowned the message out, so he would never know for sure. He could not fathom the bravery of that exposure, somehow stronger than the twenty men and the team of Clydesdales it took to drag that ridiculous runaway motorbus from the sands of Morecambe Bay when he was a boy, after its steering pin had snapped and it had careered through the prom wall, decapitating passengers on its tumble. Stronger than the brawniest arm in the fairground slamming the mallet down on to the Beef-o-Meter to ring its bell. Stronger than diamond or atomic propulsion or wrought iron. Her. Naked. Scarred. The boards of the booth were not even fully down yet to provide her with some privacy inside. But her expression said that the landscape was irrelevant, she might have been lost in a desert or on the presidential lawn or on the moon for all she cared.

Early passers-by slowed to see if this was some kind of radically casual, unorganized treat, a show of Coney's titillating spontaneity, shameless when it came to human dignity and the rules of physical conduct. Perhaps she was one of the ugly bodies they had been promised they would see, escaped from the big top. But Cyril Parks knew this show was for one man alone and no carnival barker would call a roll-up, roll-up. She gave him a full, wordless minute to see her, while his mouth contorted and he wiped at his eyes and tried to control himself.

Her stomach was tight and hard as wood ash, collected in lumps and ridges, so she would never be able to bend over and slip a strap through the buckle of her shoe again, she would always have to retrieve a dropped item by bringing her upright body down on bent legs, blind to whatever was underneath her. Her pubic hair was mostly gone, just a few strands remained below a bald patch, so she looked like a little girl. He could see the slit line of her against a stripped membrane. Her left breast was made smaller than the right by the acid, which had swept through fatty tissue with abandon, and the nipple there looked like a piece of misshapen rock, chipped glass. The tattooed eyes on her torso had been erased in places, in others they had washed together in bizarre, nondescript patches of concentrated dye. Green from the largest ruptured iris on her abdomen had collected above her appendix, and it seemed in comparison a beautiful emerald seam against the strip-mined earth of the rest of her. No. She was like a fresco with a jar of paint stripper knocked over her. She had run, dried and hardened. Several of the eyes on her arms, legs and back had survived, but otherwise she was as streaky as an abstract painting. She put a hand up to his face and moved his tears away with the heel of her palm. She gave him those moments before she spoke, she had probably not in any case known how to prepare him verbally for the sight. Nothing she could have said would have cleared the way.

– So. The doctors can move skin around on your body now. From here to here, they cut it off and put it back on. This is called a skin graft, they can only just do this thing. Mostly it still doesn't work. It is amazing that they can do that, I think.

Cy took a chestful of air and nodded, his diaphragm shuddering. He put his hands on his hips and tried to breathe calmly through gritted teeth, he felt as if he had been running fast for the last few minutes. But he did not look away from her. And then she reminded him of something. Her voice with its different, unlocated accent and the dark white and grey body with its patches of green – she was like a thing which he had encountered only twice as a boy from the train window as he rode to his Aunt Doris's house, and he had thought it haunting and raw even then. It was the rock pavements of the Yorkshire moors where the earth's bone surfaced in bands and petrified rivers against the swaying grass and the living ground. She was now in part dead, like the stone of the moors, while regions of her still grew, and her tone was the dirge-like song of the wind.

A man in front of them on the other side of the street whistled in their direction and crossed over to get a more intimate view of the nude woman.

– Turn around girly-girl, let's see your better side.

Grace obliged him, turning around inanimately like a gigot on a spit, and the man stopped coming and took his eyes off her. He adjusted his collar and hurried away.

Cy took the boards of the booth down quickly, his hands shaking as he stacked them, and they both stepped into the small enclosure. He offered her a seat and she shook her head.

– It takes too long. Up and down. Not worth it any more. But, I'm finding ways.

He sat down on the stool. He had to sit. He had to remember to breathe, to tell his lungs to operate. He was now in a direct line with her midriff, the region of the worst damage. There was amazing detail to the scarring. The hospital gauze had left cross-hatching on the plateaus of skin. There were peaks like miniature mountain ranges, black gullies. Those wounds! She had always said it would be about body, hadn't she, that the battleground had been chosen by others and a war would be fought there, and won or lost? Hers had been the site of an almighty uprising, on a territory mapped out and claimed by an administration that had every intention of preserving empire and dictating the law of the land to its colony. So all she could do was find a way to overwhelm the government with quick wits, a trick of the light in battle using shields and mirrors and superb body armour, blinding them for long enough to disable their forces and vanquish them. And for a time the victory flags had flown across her body.

How must that have felt for her, he wondered. Like a full brass plate and a cheer from the crowd? Like Liberty's fiery torch? And he had known what she was up against all along, hadn't he, him with his booth walls drowning under images of sex and stylized female bodies? Yes, he had known.

Grace had been outnumbered by the men of history, she had neither the political strength nor the support of her own people, but she had found a way to win her freedom, and for a time she had celebrated the identity of her body as her own sovereign state. And now the land had been razed again, it was desolate, death-soil. But her eyes, those dark, solemn, prolific eyes still glimmered and said her mind had not lost that spirit of rebellion and never would. She was gathering the last few insurgents, the hardiest survivors in their caves and forest hideaways, and they were forming a pact of defiance, they were stockpiling arms. The revolt was far from over. She'd damn herself. She'd go to the gallows bloody and brutalized but unbroken if she had to.

He knew the only pity and consolation she would accept, the only tears she would stand for, were his. He could see that in her face, the finite sympathy and tolerance for him. Her flag-maker. Her ally. The man who rewrote her body's history. The man who loved her. She gestured to herself.

– They moved skin from my leg to here above my ribs. They said it would die or continue to live, but either way it would protect the inside. It was not cosmetic, they tried a few things. I signed forms saying they could. I don't know how they did this, Electric Michelangelo. It is a miracle. I had to stay covered until it was healed enough for the air – even the air can bring infection to you – or I would have come sooner. They want me to put a liniment on that will make it hard, with some kind of metal in it, but I can't reach so well. You must stop this face now. I need your help. Here. You can do this for me.

She took a tube of cream from the pocket of her dress and held it out to him.

– I don't want to hurt you. It looks so . . . painful.

– No. I can't feel it any more, sometimes an itch, but mostly it's like this . . .

She took his hand in hers and placed their two first fingers together like the steeple of a church, while the rest inter-twined to make its roof. Then she made him slide his other fingers up and down the joined steeple. It was the dead-finger trick that the boys of his school had once done to make each other squeamish, the sensation was of a lifeless body part and now it seemed doubly awful. He took the cream from her, put a small amount into his palm and smoothed it as best he could over the rocky patches at the top of her legs. The skin was less absorbent than slate. Skin was supposed to drink in moisture and hers would not take a sip. She put her hand in his hair, stroked it while he anointed her. He felt his eyes begin to brim again and he pulled her towards him gently and began to kiss her stomach, her hips, the ruined abdomen and breasts, his mouth soft and damp on her, her body tough as granite until his tongue found the safer, softer channel of skin inside her. He felt her hand close in his hair and pull on it gently, mooring them closer together. She whispered a word to him, twice, which defied any liguistic pronunciation he had mastered, but he knew it was an affirmation of some kind. Kedvesem. Kedvesem. For a few moments he felt her body swaying exquisitely against him, like the lip of a wave breaking at his mouth. Her breathing became husked within her chest, constricted then ameliorated from the errata of her respiratory condition, and her head fell back. Her rhythm was overcome by a series of small jolts, electrical currents, as if her body had been shocked, her life being taken or given back by a connection of energy, and then she was still.

– Grace . . . I've wanted to say . . .

– No, just this. Dziekuje, Cy. Tell Claudia that she must have Maximus now. But I can't take care of him any more, you see. He will like to see all of America and if they take him to California he will like to see a different ocean. Tell her there is no other horse fit to carry her but Maximus . . . because . . .

because he is as magnificent as she is and she will be his queen . . .

Her voice broke then, suddenly, shattering apart like glass with her last words, and for a moment all the sorrow of Europe came flooding out. Cy looked up at her, expecting to glimpse a little girl or an unmade woman, the smallest in a stack of matrushka dolls. But already that pure, hatchling, embryonic thing was gone. Grace was staring at a point in space, forcing water away from her eyes to its underground channel, sealing the marrow of her spirit back up. Then she took a step away, picked up her dress off the counter and put it on, prohibitively across her shoulders, and buttoned it up the front.

– Tell her she can put molasses in his oats and it will keep him strong. For you Electric Michelangelo, I think you don't need molasses. I think your heart is very strong. But I wonder if it is strong enough for just one more favour that I will ask of you before I go?

She was saying goodbye, almost. He had always believed that knowing her would include her walking away and it was true. Soon she would be leaving and he could not ask her where she was going because he did not even know where she had come from. He wanted to tell her to stay, that he wanted her, that she had haunted him like the wind on the pavements of rock on the Yorkshire moors since they had first met. The mechanical bobsled whooshed past on its first run of the day with people laughing in its carriages and a lost hat spun down from above and rolled on the pavement as if procuring for change. And he knew if he said those things to her now his voice would be as absurd as that hat.

Coney Island would have had her back, in all her damaged, viable glory, because of the new horror of her body even, but that she would not be taken back. And Brooklyn would have cared for her intensively as its own, always. But something in her was shifting, already travelling, as if this place was now the province of an old failed world, a nameless country that had crawled its way after her from some undesignated spot

310

on another continent, wherever she started from, wherever she had first kicked out the camp fire and mounted her horse. Grace was a refugee again, perhaps she had always been so, with a refugee's identity that was defiant and pliable and eternally battling just as it was perpetually saddened and disinherited, raped and stripped of its homeland wherever it went. Her ethnicity was everything and nothing. She was beyond even America in that respect. And he did not understand how she existed at all. And yet, and yet, it did not matter. She had him still.

– Yes. Of course, I'll help you in any way I can. You know I will.

– OK. It was a good move he made, crude though effective, but it can't end here. Meet me tonight. The fountain at twelve o'clock. If you come, you will have to give up your sting, I can ask for nothing less. So think about it carefully. And if you can manage, don't drink anything, it must be done cold in our minds you see. We'll embrace now – there will not be another appropriate time.

She kissed him on both cheeks and smiled.

– Remember to look for that star, you will find it. And remember to tell Claudia about the horse. Oh, Electric Michelangelo. A szíved mindig emlékezni fog rám.

She placed the fingers of her right hand gently on his chest, against the ship, above his heart, just as she had touched him within the booth months before. Then she turned away. He watched her walk carefully down the alley, her body stiff, the cotton dress soaked through at the waist, and he was unable to call out to her. He needed her to be somehow more broken by what had happened, because she was so valuable to him, and that left him silent. He watched her go and it was ordinary. Not the profound departure of lovers on the screen separating a last time, not the muted light of evening on the set of Brooklyn, not even piano music drifting down from Varga to accompany their alba. Just human blood in his veins and the shadow of the booth getting smaller as the sun rose in the sky. The smell of new grease on the runners of the bobsled coaster, onion butter from the sausage stand, and salt in the sea air.

Only when she was gone from sight did he finally have to scream out, a lupine howl from his long upturned throat, and he slumped to the floor. His chest ached. A chronic feeling was pulling hard in him, backwards and forwards, forwards and backwards. He could taste her brine in his mouth. And all he could think about was the great sucking blowing sea at Morecambe Bay, how the tide travelled in and out, in and out, relentlessly, further than almost any other piece of shore on the British Isles, and faster than a grown man could outrun, like the maddening insolvency of love.

～

That night, Henry Beausang told the police, The Avenue psychiatric hospital was unusually quiet. Most evenings there were minor incidents, such as the singing refusal of patients to take sleeping pills or a fork stuck in the back of a wrist, burrowing for artery. A man soiling himself in some kind of incoherent protest. The inauthentic laughter of the delusive as restraints were called for. But that night the corridors of the ward were hushed, the crazies all shuffled off to bed without much assistance. And he did not like that kind of quiet. No, sir. For it meant trouble later on, usually of the fiery variety or sly eluders running through the hospital grounds with their cotton gowns flapping open at their pumping backsides. He was irritable and, he confessed, he thought he'd have himself a drink to settle the nerves. Not a large one, just enough to take the edge off. He was used to eerie spells of calm with trouble squatting on their backs, hell the state of Georgia was full of them come Klan season, so that didn't make no never mind. But something told him after this one a portion of damn hard work to put things straight would be required and he'd be as busy as a long-tailed cat in a room full of rocking chairs. Did they know what he meant by that cold quiet before the storm? One or two of the cops nodded in agreement, bewitched a little by the peachy voice. And maybe he'd had a drop more drink for good measure, said Henry, that there was his vice, you see. Anyhow, he was doing the rounds on the upper level when he thought he heard the cage elevator arriving and opening and he went to see which doctor or orderly had come up in need of him to wheel a gurney. But he was wrong, the elevator was not running, it was stuck between the first and the second floors, both lights were on and the needle was ticking its finger indecisively at two numbers. It was an old Otis service elevator with a soprano singing pulley and you could stop it with a red throw-switch in an emergency but sometimes it acted up and got a mind to stall wherever it damn well fancied. So he went on with what he was doing a few hours past midnight, which in truth was nothing much more than looking in on the strapped madmen as they rocked in their beds, thatching the ceiling with their nightmares, and tugging on his bottle from time to time. He went to the medicine station and spoke with the nurse there about nothing much, she'd vouch for that, and they took a drink together too and shared a cigarette.

About three o'clock the hospital lights in the corridors were at their most sullen and he was well warmed by the white brandy. Piracy and crime had not yet wrought havoc on the wards and he began to relax. The upper level was all clear. No patients standing like cemetery statues at the window to be put back to bed and doubled up on meds or strapped down. Looking out of the wired window himself he could tell that it was one of those huge, heavy-moving October skies that made you feel you were on the bottom of a black ocean. The cage elevator was still stuck between floors so he took the metal fire-stairs down to two. This was the unit where Malcolm Sedak was being kept, along with about fifteen other men who had run wild about the city of New York upending lives and maiming relatives – those sick, maladjusted dogs needing to be kennelled out past the normal law. The rooms in this ward had the character of cages where animals await

313

extermination, the smell of faecal minds, and he did not like being there. No, sir, he did not. Half of the patients were lobotomized, and half the rest were heavily acquainted with the electric tongs and the mouth strop. A sense of deliberation on everybody's part was always present and that gave the ward a feeling of oppression. The floor had a security gate as well as locks on the individual cell doors. There was ordinarily a guard at a post there, who would operate the lock, but he was gone now and the gate was open an inch. That could just have been the man checking into the wing if he'd heard a splay noise, or maybe not. Henry had a feeling that there was some bad ju-ju on the waft tonight, so he took another slug of brandy for luck and went on through into the ward. Expecting nothing but low fluorescent illumination in the corridors he was surprised to see a little patch of orange remarking to him around the corner of the corridor. Then there was a bitter taste to the air, as when they tar the roads. At that point he got a strong sense again of wrongful interference and he was right, for he came upon the evidence. Someone had lit a damn fire in the metal bin where they dropped the waste and laundry, there was an odour of smouldering pitch in the air and there was that smoky, black-wagging tail oil gets when it burns. It was a poor attempt to burn the asylum down, that was for sure; he had known far better in his time. The fire was contained and in no danger of spreading, even while smoke lay up on the ceiling and made him sneeze.

He took a quick look about, escaped patients had a way of taking blunt instruments with inhuman force to the back of the heads of orderlies when their attention was turned. But there was no one else in the corridor. Then he heard a shuffling muffling sound coming from the storeroom. He opened the door and inside was the missing guard, gagged and trussed up like a rag dolly stolen by some little thing's mean older brother. Now, Henry had no particular enjoyment of this fellow, that was the truth, he confessed. The fact of the matter was the man had got Henry cautioned for drinking on the premises not a month earlier, so he thought on it a while and decided he was best left bound a moment until he extinguished the fire and investigated the situation further, least that would be his story if asked at a later date, which he was now being. Henry winked at the policemen then, comfortable within his own yarn, knowing the tale of his imperfection and incompetence was winning them all over. He did, however, slip down the man's gag to find out who had gotten to him. Two of them, one big, one smaller, faces covered like bandits, he was told. They had taken the keys to the cells, so surely it was a bust out, said the man, he should secure the main gate.

Quickly Henry checked the doors of the rooms, but all were tight, there appeared to be bodies in every one of them. He took a fire blanket and threw it over the metal bin. Curiously, there was a metal fire iron sitting up against the side of the cylinder that he had not noticed for the leaping flames before. It was only later that night this object took on any significance, turning the stomachs of the cops as they bagged it up for evidence. The other orderlies were called, doctors were summoned, and the usual protocol for lockdown began. They opened up the doors on level two one by one to check the patients and see who, if anyone, had been liberated and replaced with a phoney made of rolled-up bedding. In the ninth cell was Malcolm Sedak, there was a strong smell of smoke in his quarters, and, yessir, in a way an exchange of bodies had been made. He had not been belted in to sleep since his arrival at the hospital, it was not compulsory procedure, and he had never struggled against the nurses to truly warrant it. In fact the man had been one of the calmer crooks in the hospital. He'd maintained an air of accomplishment, dignity and satisfaction, which had truly offended Henry, particularly as his crime was brutal and against a lady, he had heard. But when they pulled the sheets back off him they found the buckles and straps were tight across him. Dear Lord, sweet Jesus, but it was not the same man that had been put to bed a little after sundown. There was a stained pillowcase over his head – not tied so Henry did not think there had been an attempt at suffocation, just slack on him like a redneck hunting hood. His nightgown had been slit off with a knife or scissors around his body and it was lying on the floor next to the bed. Had they known of the extent of his facial injuries they might not have brought the pillowcase off him quite so quickly as they did for he began to moan hellishly as it took patches of wet yellow skin away with it. He had been burned severely around the cheeks. Worse still, when the cover was fully removed from his head, they saw that the man's eyes had been put out by some kind of branding device, and he was blind.

Having finished his tale with drama and emphasis, Henry pulled out his almost empty bottle and took a swill and he held it out to the nearest policeman. Oh and the cell keys, incidentally, he said, were hanging tidily back up on a hook by the gate, as if someone had only been fixing to borrow them all along. Nobody had even thought to look for them where they belonged.

Charles Henry Beausang the Third spent four hours lying to the police about possible suspects and mapping his whereabouts in the hospital all evening for them. The elevator's switch had been thrown between floors and the hatch opened and the cops had a hard time believing that this had not been brought to the attention of anyone earlier. One or two other points did not add up. Nobody had been roused by the smoke in the corridor. And, given the time the fire began, and when the injuries were perpetrated, there should have been more smoke. None of the doors on the lower level had been forced and the night watchman, well acquainted with the sauce as he was too, had seen nobody entering or leaving by the reception door. Yeah it was fishy, said the inspector, fishy, fishy, fishy. Then again if the hospital was run by drunks and half-wits, what could you expect. There followed some severe lectures about the inappropriate imbibing of alcohol on duty and the fact that this establishment housed some of the region's rankest criminals, put there by the hard work of the city's police department. All this Henry took with credible humility and shame, the bloodless blush of a professional flim-flam man. He did not know how long it would take the police to find Malcolm Sedak's records in order to piece together the puzzle of who might have been involved with the crime. The man himself was incomprehensible when he spoke. He babbled like a child with night-terrors and kept trying to touch his missing eyes behind the bandages.

What Henry Beausang omitted to tell the authorities was that he had left the back door of the hospital specifically unlocked, he had presented the watchman with a bottle of rum, and he had loitered up on the third floor an hour longer than necessary. Nor did he mention that he had left open a window on the second floor so that the smoke might billow out evasively, just as he had been instructed to do.

By the time the police detectives had reached the booth on Oceanic Walk, The Electric Michelangelo had dismantled his place of work for the winter. By the time they reached Den Jones's barbershop, via the eventual cooperation of some remarkably tight-lipped and unhelpful Coney informers, several dead-ends, one or two obvious decoys, Cyril Parks was no longer anywhere to be found in the country. Nor was Sedak's original victim around to throw light upon a very dark matter. In fact there was no record of this woman in existence at all other than her recent medical file. The city was becoming ever more a place where ghosts and demons could live their half-lives unknown and uncharted by the authorities, it seemed. The investigation was perhaps more abbreviated than it needed to be, but nobody felt truly torn up for the victim. This was after all a vague quid pro quo affair, and the file was permanently closed, or at least relegated to a spot at the back of a very full cabinet, by January of 1941. Yes, Den Jones finally confirmed, there had been an Englishman tattooing in the back room for a couple of years – but he had gone up to Montreal or Toronto as far as he knew. Something about the Canadian Air Force and doing his duty in these troubled times. To the best of Den's knowledge he had never so much as stepped out with a girl to the movies or the music hall, let alone revenged a lady made of tattooed eyes.

～

Much later, with white in his hair and two world wars behind him, Cy would dream of America, and it would visit him as a series of faces. There were the faces of Brooklyn, that could break his heart with their history, their handsome melancholy, the wet-lit eyes that were, in cold weather, very prone to tears. He dreamt of Henry's face, made prematurely old by violence, stupid with alcohol, but gorgeous from adventure as he bid Cy farewell by the station that crisp, culpable morning in the fall of 1940. Other friends put in appearances, Den, Claudia and Arturas, the sisters, in capacities that were helpful to him when his dreams were troubling. Grace was an infrequent vision. She came and went within pockets of darkness, wrathful and beautiful, dampness on her face as she bore his needle, weeping with empty rage as she lifted down the fire iron with heated sibilance on to her opponent in the terrible game she had played. Her eyes, once swirling so full of precarious, suggestive information, always appeared closed under the heavy brow. At times he woke up assured that, during the night, he had solved the eternal puzzle of who she really was, what had created her, but whatever nocturnal handiwork his brain had done, by morning it was always misplaced or deconstructed, picked apart by devious elves. He was left with just a stray idea – a sense that she was medieval after all, as he had imagined her on that first night by the fountain with her horse, but in straightforward cruelty and justice not courtly love. Or he became convinced that his imagination at that time, oft-inebriated as it was, had run riot, and she had never

318

really had him hold a rag in the mouth of a man who was only his secondary enemy while she murdered his vision. He wished to see more of her but wishing only made her harder to invoke, resistant to his dreams, and perhaps that was his own return form of anopia, an eye for an eye, losing sight for lost sight. Sedak's childish visage came and went in nightmares – accompanied by scenes of the fighting he had endured on behalf of one or other of the countries he had in his life been affiliated with, Cy had never been sure which – and it was the face of a restrained child about to be punished for a crime he suddenly understood, a juvenile soul taught by some unsuitable influence or example that he could express his tainted religion, his prejudicial extremes, that his hatred should be credited with self-tolerance in the land of the free. The blind, ruined face of his and Grace's conspiracy came to Cy most spectacularly and horribly the night after he had stood in Lancaster court dock for non-payment of rates and had noticed an old branding iron hung above the judicial bench. He dreamt he was being dragged into the dark sockets of Sedak's missing eyes. And he woke in a fit of sickness, and ran to the bathroom to vomit. There were the ordinary faces of the century in his dreams, by their thousand under wide-ribboned hats or tulip bonnets on the boardwalk, and there were those extraordinary faces – bearded, pigmy shrunken, half-human half-amphibian or reptile scaled. And sometimes, because the dreaming mind is truly a creature of sign and symbol, it was the emblematic face of Coney Island itself that came to him, looming above like a full oval moon, that dapper, lunatic caricature with a commodious grin and slick, centre-parted hair, mocking and mimicking the crowds from the double gateway of Steeplechase. This image had staying power, and when he looked into the mirror to shave come daylight it would seem that the face was trying to be his reflection, all he had to do was bring his smile into alignment.

≈

Number eleven Pedder Street was dark and damp as he pushed open the door. It had the consecrated forlornness of a crypt, the sense of a threshold violated by his presence. The electricity had been cut for well over a decade when Cyril Parks finally collected the key from the solicitor's office, so he flicked on his Zippo for illumination and burned away the cobwebs hanging from the doorway. He moved inside the downstairs rooms and put his duffle bag down on the floor, rubbed his aching leg. He had presumed the town would be streaming with nostalgia when he returned, the way a stone that is lifted out of water rushes with the memory of where it has been kept. But the streets from the train station to his destination had seemed no more vested than they ever had been when he was a resident. In the solstice twilight of the winter of 1946 he had come back to his hometown. As he walked the familiar roads he saw new places of business had opened, shops and hotels, though many of the older venues were still running and had made it through the war. But everything seemed smaller, sturdier than he recalled, and commonly organized after the anomie of his travels. The houses and churches and grander buildings of Morecambe Bay had always had a flat perspective with simple shadows at this time of day in December, he remembered, when the sun beat an early path over the barrowing Irish Sea, as if in an illustration from a nursery book. His returning eye was kinder than he expected, and it conveyed, with its visual wares, a sense of comfort. It was like stepping back into a place of sympathy, an old comfortable shoe, rather than revisiting a realm saturated with once-were spirits and cumbersome, erstwhile lives.

What he did remember vividly as he walked from the engine sheds past the Bayview and the old fairground to a familiar door on a small winding street, was that first premeditated journey to Eliot Riley's quarters, when the night had been pronounced and dense brown and his will had had a life of its own. He remembered his boyish heart, knocking like an open window in a gale at the thought of encountering what lay beyond the complacency of the present. That walk had been fast and eager, with his long, youthful stride carrying him well, though trepidation had made it pass with super-awareness, slowness, the town reverberating and chiming with exhaustive materials. Now he moved with greater difficulty, and a heavy limp to his right leg gifted to him by the war, but it seemed to take no time at all to navigate the old place, and reach his destination, as if Morecambe had shrunk in the wash even though the town had bled through its borders since he had been away. And he wondered how his life had fitted into this snug place while seeming so grand and unruly for the characters and the incidents of it.

The walls of the Pedder Street parlour were bare and cracking. There were a couple of flash pictures still mounted on the walls that he had not bothered to collect up before he departed, or he had chosen to leave them behind, he could not recall. On a dusty rail there hung the musty velvet curtain with its theatrical tasselled bottom behind which the master had apprenticed his lad, and there was another private section where the apprentice had followed the lead of his dubious mentor. Cy could almost smell the pickled fish and stouty breath in the air, and hear the bawdy, chastising words about craftsmanship, and the hobnailed opinions on every other thing, coming from the ghost of Riley. But they came from a place far back in Cy's mind that made them mannered and coloured like art and there was no emotional frottage or suffering to the recollection now, it was just life, just the pan-bright tones of what had been. There was an absence of keen junk about the place that most quickly abandoned dwellings have strewn about, so the house forgave him his hasty, barely put-together exit. There had never been many articles present anyway. Just the chairs for the customers in the waiting area where they once viewed the plethora of images and the wooden stools next to which were railings fixed on the wall. A fine sheen of lime dust covered the furniture. It could have been a small amateur stage vacated by players a long time ago at the bidding of a bankrupt production manager.

He went upstairs with his flaring lighter beginning to singe his thumb. He waited for a moment in the blackness for the casing to cool before bringing back the flame. There were the bedrooms and the small kitchen, the old bath that had been filled with cold water and a drunken man on many occasions. On the chimney mantel the bird skulls were lined up, though a couple of them had collapsed in fragments under a shroud of dust. He wandered through the shadowy rooms, watching the light pass over Riley's old books, the statue of the Virgin Mary, tenacious as ever at the edge of the shelf, and what was left in the wooden crates that had once held his meagre possessions – some old clothing, stiff and mothy in heaps, a sketch book, a set of watercolours and a brush, a gunpowder tea tin in which there were his father's cufflinks and a photograph or two taken inside the Bayview during happier times. After a while he remembered the Jewish meno-rah that had sat preposterously in the window downstairs, that had wound up in Riley's possession through he knew not what ridiculous turn, and he went to find it. There were a few grubby, waxy stubs left in the tiers which he set the flame to and this provided enough light for him to wash his face with his last ration of serviceman's soap in the bath-room sink, after first letting the water run clear of sediment and rust.

〜

The sea in the bay was out and almost beyond sight, which was a disappointment the next morning as he approached the promenade, he had wanted to get close enough to it to feel the spray, but it meant that there was plenty of driftwood and kindling on the beach for him to collect for the fireplace. The previous night had been cold, with one military blanket only and his coat as protection against the frosty, stony air. It seemed he had not come so far really in two decades, he thought to himself, picking up debris on the shoreline for the Pedder Street parlour. The Lake Distict fells were a misty smear along the horizon. He had remembered them as mountains which were taller, fuller, the way landscape in paintings becomes exaggerated. In the shallow basin of the empty bay were a number of slimy, weed-covered anti-landing-craft obstructions that spoiled the view across the counties giving the vista a modern, interfered-with look. Post-war relics dotted the town behind him also, pill boxes near the piers and the ugly shelters built on the Sunshine Slopes. But other than this the town seemed unscathed by the conflict itself – he'd bought a copy of the *Visitor* that morning and it seemed like the same old paper that ever it was, with the same contentious, conservative opinions, the same gamely gossip and extravagant advertisements. Morecambe still had its pluck and it still professed to having soft air.

As he strolled along the bare flats there was the pungent smell of long, deep silt, like the creational clay of the world, and he thought about all the folk of Morecambe Bay he had known. He thought of his mother. Later, he would go and lay flowers on Reeda's grave and clear away the moss and dirt from the carved lettering of her headstone. He knew the visit would bring him a gentle peace and in a way he was looking forward to it, though the graveyard overlooking the sea was a forlorn place. He would tell his mother about America, and that she would have been glad she wasn't around for the next war for it had trumped the last in terms of horror. Before he knew it he had walked as far as the Trawlers' Cooperative building and since he was of a mind to do the respectful rounds he decided to pay his regards to the photograph of his father, leaning, as he inevitably still would be, on the stern of the *Sylvia Rose*. But the door of the construction was locked and bolted and the handle would do no more than rattle under its chain.

– What do you need, pal? We're shut up for the holidays until the social on New Year's Eve.

Cy turned to see a middle-aged man with dark red hair and a long mackintosh coat approaching him. He was about to say it didn't matter, that it was just a courtesy visit, but the man suddenly stopped in his tracks and peered hard. Then he executed a small clog on the pavement and put his hands in the air.

– Cyril Parks, as I live and bloody breathe! Is that you, you great string bean? Course it is, I'd know that great long lank of Lancashire lad anywhere.

– Morris? Morris Gibbs.

The two shook warmly and clumsily, cradling each other's elbows with their free hands. Their eyes locked for a spell, disarmed and intrigued at once. It was as if neither had reconciled his own age until that point in his life, until confronted with a face from his youth that was now older, aged privately and separately. Morris shook his head, bemused.

– Well, what you been up to, Parksie? Must be, what, going on fifteen years now.

– Oh. This, that and the other. You know.

– I do indeed. Indeed I do. Still practising on pig heads?

– No, I've moved on to their arses now.

Morris laughed loudly and slapped him on the back.

– Well good for you. Fancy a jar? Come on, we'll have a bit of a yarn and catch up. Not busy, are you?

– Not exactly busy. No. But, well look, I don't drink any more, Morris. Not for several years now. I'll have some tea if they've got it.

– Right you are. Tea it is. Look in need of a good cuppa, you do. Heard you'd buggered off to Yanksville.

Cy abandoned his foraged firewood and they sat in the smoky warmth of the Horse and Farrier for an hour, talking of old times, which suited Cy as the recent chapters of his life were still too fresh with reddish paint to handle yet. Morris had been fishing since he left, he was one of the last to still work the Skears in the old way, with a pony and rake, for which he was proud if poor, and he still had his brother's granddaddy eel in the jar, kept in the garden shed though because his wife would not allow it in the house. And none bigger had yet been found. Cy was glad of the company, the reminiscences, and glad to see his old friend. He inquired after their childhood third. Morris sighed.

– Jonty died in the war, Cyril. Early on, poor bastard, in the Battle for France, 'forty it will have been. Bad year that, bad year. Left behind a wife and three little kiddies – well, I think you met Irene before you left, didn't you? She took in a number of vaccies, mind you; she's a good sort.

Cy nodded. Both of them stared into their drinks for a time. Difficult conversations and deliveries of news such as this were not unknown to either of them. They had become no easier with the passing years nor in their growing proliferation. There was still the compulsory awkward pause, the bitter sadness, the struggle to go on.

– Well, I'll be honest, I miss the daft bugger. Were you . . . er . . .? No, never mind, I can see that you were. Still, you're back now. How long are you staying? And where?

– Not sure. A while, I think, I've no plans. I'm staying at Pedder Street – above Riley's old place.

– Bloody hell, that's rather grim. That place has been boarded up for donkey's years. Some little devils broke in and took it over not long after you'd gone, so the Council fastened up the windows and changed the lock. Well, listen, you'll come round ours for your Christmas dinner. I'll not hear otherwise. Neither will the wife, and she's fierce when she's on the sherry come yuletide, so you best say yes. It's good to have you back, Parksie.

~

Nobody truly knew when the decline began to occur. With hindsight, it would be easier for locals to blame certain aspects – the simultaneous decline of old industries, the closing of mills and foundries in the north that furnished the seaside resort with its weekly business, package holidays available cheaply on the continent, affordable airfares, or an outside world that just suddenly sped up and left Morecambe to its old-fashioned ways. Even Cyril Parks with his testy Coney Island radar, his American-honed sense of a fading amusement industry, could not quite predict or interpret or become attuned to the evolving ebb of life out of his hometown. At first he was too occupied with work to dwell on being back and living in the haunted house of his unhappiest years. The town was busier than ever in season and he could barely cope with the summer trade. He arrived home almost penniless but with a house in his name. He fixed up the neon sign and remounted it above the doorway. He bought ink from Lancaster, and fashioned some equipment. Then the crowds began to arrive and only one or two, the hardier, older holiday-makers in Sunday suits who had been coming there for their seaside break since they were short-trousered and their fathers were besuited, only they could remember a time when Eleven Pedder Street was run by the best and most notorious tattoo artist in the northern counties. Riley had otherwise faded into folklore, his wrangling personality and his drinking taking precedent over his art in the opinion of the community, and there was no need for Cyril Parks to be forgiven for treading on his grave. The money began to roll in. After a while Cy hung paintings on the walls upstairs and bought new curtains for the windows. He let the local children string up Guy Fawkes effigies early in November from the flagpole below the bedroom window. Within a couple of years he had installed a new central heating system, because he'd be jiggered if he'd keep fetching firewood, so the waiting area was no longer quite as Baltic in temperature as it once had been. His roots began to creep back down, finding and following the path they had made when he was young. He was, after all, sand-born and sand-bred. He was, after all, Morecambrian.

When the decade rolled past the half century, they were still coming via bursting trains from Manchester and Scotland,

Oldham and Leeds, and they still wanted their arms and backs decorated. He kept thinking that maybe he wouldn't stay, maybe he'd sell up and move somewhere new, start afresh. He had only come back like a homing pigeon, because some magnetic grain in his head had drawn him there after the war ran him out of good reasons to see the world. And he'd stayed by reasoning that while there was a dependable income he may as well benefit. Rationing was over, the larder spies retreated, and rich traditional dishes once more were set on the tables of hotels and guest houses next to swan-folded napkins – again speculation abounded about who was sending potted shrimp to another King George and the Duke of Windsor and Cy was reminded of the way his mother's consumptives relished her treats and secretly assumed that it was she. Music flooded across the Atlantic from America, and in the local dancehalls the fashions of the day took their measure from the pinball-punching, Coca-Cola swilling, rocking and rolling USA. In that decade vacation venues stuffed visitors into every nook and cranny. The recommenced illuminations drew spectators in by their thousand, celebrities came to flip the switch and electrify peacocks and garlands that ran the length of the prom, and Cy turned out to watch the festivities too and celebrated. And it felt easily remembered, and it was easy to be home.

When things fell away they fell away fast, in the blink of an eye Cy thought, and before long establishments were closing, theatres were taking final curtain calls and arcades were dismantling their tuppenny attractions before the wrecking balls began. The northern workers just stopped coming. Motorists did not pull off the A6 at Carnforth but kept on going north to the pretty towns and mountains below the rain clouds. The Prom station closed. Smug jokes were made in other British pavilions about the once comedic-authority, now pathetic and brash-becoming town of Morecambe. By then Cy wasn't leaving. Whether it was loyalty to the townsfolk or the dwindling if faithful crowds, or old age creeping in, wanderlust waning, or whether it was just the never-and-always-changing view across the bay that he so loved, he didn't care to contemplate. You could go to new places but the heart still pumped the same blood about the veins, and influenced the behaviour of the same brain. Over the years he felt a gradual settlement such as he hadn't known before. He was accompanied less and less by the ghosts of Riley and Reeda, of the war and America.

When, in the last column on the last page of a national paper in 1965, he read that New York's Steeplechase was closing down, the last of the big Coney Parks to survive the war, he felt a twinge of regret and a tug at his sentimental sleeve but he wasn't sorry not to have been there until the end. No, Morecambe Bay it would be, come high or low economic tides. For better or worse. And where would he have gone anyway, in search of that stripy carnival nostalgia, that simplicity of entertainment? The older seasidey ways he was used to were dying out. The lettered rock and the melting cones no longer brought sticky, sugary pleasure, the waves were too cold and bound with seaweed, the repetitive jokes and merry songs of the collective nation failed to rouse and remedy the modern weary spirit of the population. People did not want to make do with a shared washroom and tinned fruit when they could have private facilities abroad, the Mediterranean was warm and appealingly blue, the food was exotic and the children could split off from the parents so that each could have made-to-measure fun in the sun. Even the blind fiddler at the old harbour, who was now a hundred if a day, could have seen that the changes were unstoppable and the damage irreparable. And regardless of all that, besides the folding tatty umbrella of an industry that had always sheltered his trade, wherever he was in the world, fairground fed or not, those who came to him would remain the same. Tattooing was unto itself its very own art form, old as the hills and stranger than time. Whether in rich, far-flung resorts or condemned cottages, glamorous prestige or ragged poverty, human hearts and souls were variable and would always require painting.

~

Nina Shearer waltzed through the front door of Eleven Pedder Street in leather and torn trousers, with purple glitter on her cheekbones and Egyptian kohl around her eyes, on Cy's sixty-fifth birthday, just as he was thinking about retiring. He was vaguely expecting her, at least he was in the habit of expecting unusual and meaningful events on significant calendar days. She herself was in the habit of tutting and sighing before almost every comment she uttered, as if perpetually annoyed or put upon by what she was about to say. Her hair was raked up at the sides above her ears by two painful-looking plastic combs and it was very difficult to tell how many colours of dye were present in it, or how many perms it had endured.

– D'ya do piercing here?
– No, love, I don't.
– Why bloody not?
– I'm a tattooist. Not a sodding hairdresser.
– Well, I'll just do it myself again then.
– Fine.
– Fine.

She stood with her hands on her hips looking boldly at the walls of the shop. Nothing about her surroundings appeared to intimidate her, the tattoo parlour may as well have been a florist's. Not many people had that variety of astringency, thought Cy, that natural counter-balance, the wherewithal or presence to dampen fire or dry up floods. Only a handful of people he had ever met had the ability, reacting with their environment to take away an extreme quality of it, like pepper with salt or sugar with bitterness. He had a feeling his list might be about to go up by one. There were several piercings in the cartilage of her ears, through which heavy rings and several studs had been inserted. Her right eyebrow was swollen in a pink lump at the corner where a new jewel wound had recently been made. She couldn't have been much beyond the age of eighteen and her make-up served only to make her seem younger, overdone as it was. Her eyes might have been a marshy green but as with all colours when set against the borders of black they seemed brighter, much brighter. She was pacing about in the shop, snapping her chewing-gum against her teeth and putting on a show. There was a restlessness to her, forthrightness, an echo of some of his favourite people, and Cy found the corner of his mouth pulling up in a smile.

– Can I help you, pet? Going to get something done, are you? Or just browsing?

– Nice present for me mam on Mother's Day that'd be, eh? Why don't you cut your hair, it's too thin to be worn long. Your scalp comes through. You look like an old hippie.

– And you, young lady, look like trouble with a capital T. Go on, piss off.

She looked at him, looked him over with her scornful, cheeky, eyes. Everything about her manner informed him that she would go in her own good time and not a moment before, there was no point in making his case. She looked back at the walls again, her arm bracelets rattling and tinkling as she reached up to touch the flash cards. Cy waited for her to finish her dramatic production. But either she was a thorough little madam or something had caught her attention, for she moved closer in to scrutinize the pictures.

– How much?

– How much for what?

– Any of these.

– Depends on the size and the time it takes. Or if you want it done freehand. That's extra. Look in the corner, it should say.

She stopped chewing and put her hands in the pockets of her leather coat. The burrs and brassiness seemed to be rubbing out of her. Her head dropped to one side. And there under the costumery and the kinks and claws stood a serious girl in admiration of what she saw, like a buff in an art gallery. Cy let her be a while and put the kettle on in the back room. When he came back out she was sitting on his work stool with one of his designs in his hand – it was the word 'Mother' with flowers woven through the lettering. There was a strange watery look in her eyes, as if she might be about to shed tears but also as if gladdened by inspiration. She began talking to him with the immediate confidentiality and the lack of inhibition of a thoughtful, expressive youth whose ideas are too large to contain, too important to go unsaid.

– She's had a rough time lately, eh. Dad's in the nick again since he got made redundant and the pub's not doing well 'cause everybody buggers off to Spain come summer these days. Who'd want to come to Morecambe anyway and sit in a deck chair in the pissing rain for their holiday or ride on a stinking donkey on the prom? Full of old cronies that just want to play bingo, not exactly a riveting venue, is it? I want to go to art college in Manchester but I'll end up having to help out in the pub until I'm bloody sixty and past it, no doubt, 'cause she says I've got to help out. Oh, it's not her fault. He's the one that kept nicking from the till so he could lose it all at the dogs. Fucking selfish prick. She'd skin me alive if I got this done but she'd like it really – she'd sit and cry for a bit but she'd be touched deep down, the silly cow. I've only got three pounds, mind, and it says five on the corner.

– Well, all right, I approve, love. I approve. But don't call your mother a cow. Tell you what, get yourself over to the corner shop and get us a bottle of silver top for some tea and we'll talk about a price when you get back.

He wasn't sure that she would ever set foot in the property again. But ten minutes later, just as the teapot was beginning to stew, she waltzed back in with the milk and a packet of custard creams.

∼

331

Gaynor Shearer might have had nice big nipples and svelte buttocks in the days of the first Bathing Beauties, but her granddaughter Nina was a royal pain in the backside when she wanted to be, and quite frequently when she wasn't even trying. She was of a new breed, loud, inquisitive to the point of interrogation, she had a filthy mouth, an unapologetic manner, and under it all Cy liked her very much. After four or five more visits, a couple of which were in the capacity of customer, the rest of which saw her turning up on rainy mornings, blagging tea, with bottles of milk pilfered from doorsteps in between the Horse and Farrier and Pedder Street, he offered to apprentice her. For the proposal he got a smile with her bottom jaw stuck far out and a loud kiss on the cheek.

She had a genuine interest in the profession and it became apparent that her aspirations for art college were not built without the foundation of talent. She drew many new designs for the walls, abstracts, which were in vogue, and emblems she considered attractive to both sexes. She said that people did not know themselves anymore, not as they once had, and they did not know how to define their lives. Abstracts were old, mysterious, inexplicable, and that made sense, folk were drawn to them for that very reason. It was as close to sage philosophy as she got. Cy gave her the old art books that had once belonged to Eliot Riley, their condition was appalling but there was no sense in them going to waste, and she told him flippantly that Michelangelo was too old-fashioned for her liking, though his sketches were obviously not too bad. She preferred something with a bit of oomph. Van Gogh. Edvard Munch. Egon Schiele, the randy bugger. Matisse. At that Cy smiled and thought fleetingly about telling her his fantastic tale involving the great artist's temporary reincarnation, and that there had been plenty of oomph in that bizarre existence. But he didn't, and before long she was rabbiting on about how the north of England needed a good art gallery, something to rival the Tate, and one of those dilapidated crusty old lords should donate an empty castle, lying around like an old wellington boot as it would be, for those very purposes.

There was a quality of susceptible stray animal to her as well as a smartness of mouth and a propensity for backchat. She tuned the radio to howling punk rock that gave Cy a headache and laughed at his records and cassettes of jazz and swing, saying he was an old relic who should be put in a museum. She nagged him constantly to cut his long hair and take out his ear-ring, reminding him so completely of Den Jones that he expected to walk outside during one of her lectures into the Brooklyn light and see the turrets of Coney Island puncturing the horizon in the distance and hear that faraway, once-upon-a-time hum of amusement park paradise and hell. She told unwelcome stories of getting with boys exactly to her liking in the grottos of the bay and the roller disco that made Cy blush and falsify coughing fits so he could leave the room. Sex was, in her book, a topic entirely open for discussion. Mostly she asked an endless drill of questions whose punches were seldom pulled and whose shameless promotions were never hidden. Why did he do this? Why did he do that? Why should she have to learn about motors and coils and welding and silly little gippy oily shitty parts when the stuff could be ordered out of a catalogue? What was so special about blue bloody ink and just what had he had to do with it all anyway? How did he get his gammy leg? Where were his medals? Did he believe in boggarts? Didn't he think this boy really liked her because he'd given her a kiss down-you-know-where, or that lad was a dick-head because he thought women shouldn't drive forklifts at the sausage factory? Shouldn't tampons be available on the NHS and didn't he think that if *men* had to have the curse of Eve every month they would be? Didn't America seem like a marvellous country on the telly or at the pictures where everybody's problems got sorted out and they were all happy? Why wasn't he married? Was he queer? Why, and this question really intrigued her, did he always talk about love like there was an empty chair next to him at whatever table he sat?

Occasionally Cy lost his rag, and yelled at her to shut up. But the raised voice fitted so perfectly and so sinisterly within the walls of the parlour, like a fist in a glove, or a pickaxe in a splintered trunk, that it shook him at his core and his outbursts never lasted more than a few moments. She required few apologies to resume her conversation. And though by the end of the day he often felt exhausted and irritated by her unrepentant, iridescent, volatile company, or like he was sloshing full and heavy with her mental bilge and sinking slowly, the shop was always a little too quiet after she had gone.

~

– Can I start piercing folk?

– No you bloody can't. Not in my shop. It's gimmickry. It's for people who don't understand the craft.

Nina tutted loudly and tossed out the remaining inch of leafy tea from her cup into the sink. Cy was reading a book in his room, with his leg up on a stool, waiting for a customer to appear. This was an argument they had had before.

– It's not fair. You wouldn't even have to do any of the work. I could be in charge of it.

– Oh, it's always lip from you, isn't it? Never a moment's peace. Does it say Nina Shearer's tattoo parlour on that sign up there? Does it?

– Fascist.

Cy smiled and looked up from his book at her.

– Speaking of, have you been to the polling station yet today, missy? Have you voted?

– No. They're all a bunch of great fat farts, why should I bother?

– Listen. I don't care if you never put a single tick in a single box, but you get yourself down that polling station right now. You've got your voting card?

– Yes. But why the bloody hell should I go if I'm not ticking any boxes? You've gone soft in the head.

– Well, go and write 'you're all a bunch of great fat farts'

334

across it and hand it in! At least they'll know you've been there and had your say.

Nina was giving him a look of bemused pity, as if commiserating with his insanity, his obviously retarded condition. Or as if he had suddenly grown another head. And damn it if Cy didn't want to kick her up the backside and give her a hug both at once.

– All I'm saying, pet, is that you shouldn't take these things for granted. That's all. Now off you go.

~

With almost no effort at all on nature's part and before Cy knew it, it was September again. That time of year when powerful news was broken to unsuspecting Lancashire lads and the clash of seasons brought unrest in the nether regions of the human spirit. A time when the women Cy had loved most dearly in his life had taken a step back into themselves in preparation for solitary struggles and departure. But he was as far away on the calendar from the anniversary of Eliot Riley's demise as he could be and that was a favourable place to be. Cyril Parks was not unhappy. The days had that blue hue to them, with the rush of water along their sides, and they were refreshing. A storm in the night had tossed up timber and treasure in his dreams and he had seen his old booth spinning on the alleyway, oversized chess pieces were dancing with each other in Varga, Reeda was smoking an opium pipe made from a shell at the Bayview's kitchen table with Riley, Jonty was kissing nurses in the war. And he had seen Grace, on horseback, riding fast across the open sands of the bay, standing up in her stirrups as if she might leap from the horse as she rode on into the ocean. His blood had been exhilarated when he woke, fiery, like electricity. And he felt young again. That morning he had walked along the path by the ravine, feeling the wind kiting his coat, pushing back against him, pushing him upright and straightening the bend in his long spine. His leg had not hurt so very much when

usually it provided nothing but a deep dull ache in the steel-shanked bone. The air had been saturated with that unmistakable salty tonic that only coastal regions have, and he drew deep lungfuls down into him, laughing because it was unnecessary, because he didn't have tuberculosis. He thought of Grace on the walk, the dark borders of her against which the lighter colours and aspects shone. He thought of her dark hair with its red undertraces, her hands gently pushing against the tattooed ship on his stomach as if she was launching what it carried, a heart pierced by a tall mast, and the way she always called him by his moniker, as if identity was only a matter of choice. He thought of her eyes, both real and tattooed, and he knew that she had never truly left him, not in the way old loves are eventually reconciled or abandoned. Somewhere in the world she was still living perhaps, still raging, and though he wouldn't like the job of painting it, the world was getting smaller by the day, the corners around which she might walk were getting closer. She was subjective and brief and random in his life, but she was still strong in him, and interlocking, like crystal in stone, like roots in the earth. And his heart was densely occupied and his soul was lying fallow. It was why he had never married, it was why whenever his apprentice told him some unkown lady had called for him in the shop, his stomach always dropped and lurched. And it was why he had never taken away that empty chair of Nina's remarking, even while courting others, even while getting near to that honest place where he should think about the possibilities of dying.

When he returned home he looked through some of his stored possessions, usually it made him feel old to do so, but not today. There was a dime entry ticket to Luna Park, some old British money, photographs, a sentimental beer mat from the pub where he and Morris Gibbs had taken tea together after he first arrived back in the town, and then he had come across his oldest mermaid. She was brown around the edges and the ink was fading so that her fins appeared orange-tipped, not red, and the green of her tail was dappled. He could remember making her with his set of school paints, keeping her flat in a book through all the years that Riley would not allow her up, and he could remember the skin of the men, and some women, on to which she had finally been transferred by his needle. He had said over and over that she was unique but he did not really know if she was so very different from the others.

In the afternoon he opened the shop, though business was very slack off season, and it was dark as deliverance in the parlour. Nina arrived wearing a parka with fake-fur trim on the hood. Overnight her hair had gone from peroxide blonde to a burnt crab-cake brown. He could never keep up with her. She was carrying a bunch of candles.

– Leccy's gone off. There's a pylon down from the wind by Moffat Ravine.

– I know, I saw it this morning.

– So, there's no power for any of the equipment. What now?

She kicked the door closed behind her and the bell jangled emphatically. Cy took the candles from her and began to insert them into the branches of the menorah which was still adorning the windowsill above the metal tools and cartridges on the counter. Then he bent down and took out a box from his bottom cupboard containing a bamboo shaft and a hammer and he began to roll up his trouser leg.

– Well, I'll tell you one thing for certain. They won't be asking us to switch the lights on this year, will they Nina, my dove?

– Acknowledgements –

Thanks to the professionals. To Kevin Preston at Advanced Tattoo Clinic in Morecambe for his generous and colourful insights into the craft of tattooing. To Scott Harrison at Fat Cat Tattoos in Astoria for his steady hand and humour. And to Jonathan Shaw at Fun City Tattoo for first terrifying me in the East Village years ago. Yours is a beautiful and terrible art.

Thanks to the Brits and Europeans. To Roger K. Bingham for his fascinating and illuminating book *Lost Resort?*. To Adam Ferguson for his extensive bad language, his entrepreneurial heart, and for the borrowed days. To Ashleigh Martin for breaking her plastic spade and bucket on Morecambe's shore, and remaining happy all the while. To James Stamper for some bits and bobs which he'll deny. To Mat Fahrenholz for his translations, his constructions and his profoundly inspirational art work. To György Abelovszky for his translations and that last-minute lucky star. To Fiona Renkin for her translations and for just being a rock from the local quarry. And to Elizabeth and Anthony Hall for their continued support, their assistance with research, and for not screaming blue murder over their daughter's tattoo.

Thanks to the Americans. To Jesse Berger for sharing his Coney Island anecdotes and boardwalk memories. To Joshua Berger for his amazingly efficient parking skills, his ability to locate obscure warehouse museums and his creative tinkering. To Lawrence Wakin for the accent, the slang, and for being the human *Encyclopedia Brooklynia*. To Dick and Marie Wood for their transatlantic recollections and the spirit of gin-hidden speakeasy America. To Jane Kotapish, without whose grace I would be the poorer, without whose eyes I would never have seen New York tipping just so against the light. And to EMR, endlessly, for the brighter side.

Thanks again to Lee Brackstone for his help milling the grain. And thanks to Trevor Horwood for the final spit and polish.

The Electric Michelangelo is a work of fiction. Characters, events and organizations are either products of the author's imagination or, if real, not necessarily portrayed with historical accuracy.

Insights,
Interviews
& More...

"Above All Else, Hope"
An Interview with Sarah Hall

WHILE SARAH HALL'S *first novel,*
Haweswater, *dealt with the devastation of
a rural English village, her second novel,*
The Electric Michelangelo, *turns to the
rarely broached topic (in literature at
least) of tattooing. Both novels have
received huge critical acclaim:*
Haweswater *won the Commonwealth
Writers' Prize for Best First Book, while*
The Electric Michelangelo *was one of the
six short-listed titles for this year's Man
Booker Prize. Thirty years old and born
and raised in Cumbria, Hall has been
described as "one of the most significant
and exciting of our younger novelists" by
Britain's* Guardian. *Here, she speaks about*
The Electric Michelangelo's *complexities,
challenges, and rewards.*

❝ The subject of
tattooing certainly
appealed for its
literary freshness
and unbroken
ground. ❞

*You've chosen to place people from the fringes
of society at the center of your novel. Was it a
deliberate move? And why do you think that,
of all so-called fringe pursuits, tattooing in
particular is so poorly represented in literature?*

I never really thought of the characters as
fringe figures—they always felt quite ordinary
during the writing, or at least not outside of
the realm of normality, while hopefully
still having colorful interesting traits and
operating as they do within strange industries.
For example, I think Reeda has maternal
qualities which are familiar and sympathetic,

and Riley exhibits some pretty typical abusive behavior. And in this way the reader is invited to acknowledge and recognize regular human aspects in the principal players. Having said that, the subject of tattooing certainly appealed for its literary freshness and unbroken ground (tattoos seem to exclusively crop up as erotica or crime scene clues in fiction), as well as its inherently fascinating folkish history, and its curiosities. In practice and in literature, it has possibly been seen as a prohibitive distasteful thing. There doesn't seem to have been a great examination of it as a legitimate art before—it's only recently that it has begun to be taken seriously as such. I think it's still a misunderstood and complicated art form too, difficult to qualify and quantify, for all its rudimentary, overtly symbolic aspects, and its gentrification and popularization of late. So it remains a vexing subject to grapple with in literature, as well as in life.

There are a number of strong female characters in the book, but for the most part the book centers around Cy. How difficult or easy was it to write a book with a male protagonist?

It was always the natural and comfortable voice. The lines came out that way, as the character developed. I think I briefly considered a female protagonist, thinking that preconceptions about professional male roles have to be consciously broken at some point if perceptions are ever to be changed, but that wasn't primarily what this book's agenda was about. Historically there were a few female tattoo artists about in the 1930s, odd-bods in the trade, so there was the authentic option for a female voice. In essence Cy is a conduit of life and ▶

Meet the *Author*

SARAH HALL was born in Cumbria, England, in 1974. She received her master's of letters degree in creative writing from St. Andrews University, Scotland, and has a bachelor's of arts from Aberystwyth University, Wales. Her first novel, *Haweswater,* won the Commonwealth Writers' Prize for Best First Book and is forthcoming in Harper Perennial in 2006. She lives and works in the United States and the United Kingdom, traveling between the two throughout the last few years.

"Above All Else, Hope" *(continued)*

experience and the commemoration of both things through art. Gender might not matter in that regard. Also I think I possibly see less gender separation in human and character cognition than some other people do.

A lot has been made about the violence in the novel, but in reality both of the main dramatic actions occupy little space in the book. Why did you give them such little time? I was also struck by how little we learn about Sedak, as if his motives could be taken at face value. How important is he to the story?

I always find mystery villains to be the most frightening. The ones you don't see too much of, or know too much about, they seem the most sinister. In *The Electric Michelangelo*, Sedak operates as some kind of foil to Grace's political feminist stance (we're not supposed to admit to literary devices as writers, but we do use them), and he is an advocate for the female form being classically defined. He's supposed to represent a threat to personal and bodily freedom, especially those freedoms pertaining to women, and he is a Christian version of a religious fanatic— the novel's setting at this point in the plot is America, and that's no accident, in fact I think it's relevant. I don't consider the book to be overly violent. And violence when it occurs is also perpetrated by women—for example Grace's revenge. Sedak is important for what he represents, the enemy of Grace's ideology and liberty, and he's also the challenge through which she exits scarred but unbroken.

> ❝ I think I possibly see less gender separation in human and character cognition than some other people do. ❞

In the review of The Electric Michelangelo *in* The Guardian, *it was described as "above all, an analysis of pain." How accurate is that?*

It's a very fair point, but I wouldn't agree with the "above all." In examining the good and the bad aspects of life, and how these ultimately influence identity, the latter has to be measured and described, but hopefully the book's not just hung up on that darker end of things. There's a lot of love in there too, and light. And it's as much a novel about healing as it is about pain and wounds. The nature of a scar—damage and recovery. This is seen most obviously in Cy—he has quite a few forks in paths along the way. He inherits the benevolent influence of Reeda to the malevolent influence of Riley (though neither character is purely one-dimensional by any means), and he ultimately chooses his restoration and founding, breaking the cycle of drinking and pessimism he could have wound up in, but retaining his difficult occupation. When he becomes master to his own young apprentice at the novel's conclusion he does so with compassion and balance.

> ❝ It's as much a novel about healing as it is about pain and wounds. ❞

There's a very touching scene, when Cy watches the execution of Lula, the circus elephant, that's followed by, "[T]hey had molested entertainment, consumed it and driven up their tolerance for being entertained, they wanted bigger, they wanted better, more muck, more magic, and they were not getting it." Is that more than just a comment on the Coney Island of the novel? Is it significant that Cy returns to Morecambe Bay at the end? ▶

"Above All Else, Hope" *(continued)*

Yes, the elephant is more than just a motif for Coney's demise. And I think the idea of wrongness was a little bigger than just the ugliness of an entertainment industry or consumerism—America of course is not the only country guilty of such things, then or now, so the abandonment of that country by Cy is not somehow asserting British superiority by any means. I was wondering how we follow on from Gatsby really— the "borne ceaselessly back into the past" comment at the close of the book—though I have far less literary dexterity than Fitzgerald. But it's about the idea that the past is influential and not disposable or replaceable. So Cyril Parks, with a big symbolic tattooed ship on his chest, goes home, and addresses his past and makes peace with his life for doing so. And again, this is also the inherent affirmation and protocol of tattooing—your marks record your life and permanently stay with you.

> **This is also the inherent affirmation and protocol of tattooing— your marks record your life and permanently stay with you.**

Would you describe yourself, or indeed The Electric Michelangelo, *as feminist?*

Yes. No. More yes than no. I'm not even sure what falls within and without that arena anymore. I'd describe the book as peculiar unto me and all I'm interested in, which includes a lot of women's issues, especially the body, as well as a whole host of other stuff. I'd hope to appeal to both reading genders equally.

You leave a lot of questions unanswered in The Electric Michelangelo, *which has upset some critics. Did you ever think about different endings? Developing further the ultimate story of Grace?*

That's probably the least of their concerns, isn't it? There may have been criticism if all had alternately ended well with a happy couple under a sunset. Probably most writers entertain ideas about different endings during the process, and then settle on one. *The Electric Michelangelo* finishes how it finishes, and I didn't see another way for it—it ends with hope, above all else, hope. For my part, as a reader, I enjoy fiction that allows me room for personal interpretation and mystery and insolvency—somehow it seems more honest to life, so that's how I try and write too. I don't care so much for neatly tied up literature. Unless it's a bloody good poem. ∾

> " I enjoy fiction that allows me room for personal interpretation and mystery and insolvency— somehow it seems more honest to life, so that's how I try and write too. "

Reprinted by permission from Andrew Lawless, November 2004. For more information visit http://www.threemonkeysonline.com.

Sarah Hall on **Researching the Colorful World of Tattoo Art**

AS A SMALL CHILD I was taken on annual summer seaside vacations by my parents and with my brother, and over the years I really developed a fondness for that old fashioned style of holiday and for the nostalgic coastal resort towns of Britain with their ice creams and deck chairs and pavilions and "tuppeny" attractions. Later in life I developed a serious interest in folk art, particularly body orna-mentation, and in studying the history of western tattooing I found I was led back to these venues once again. I realized that tattoo artists tended to gravitate to water and to such beach towns, where they could operate under the umbrella of colorful seasonal industries.

Morecambe, where the first part of *The Electric Michelangelo* is set, lies just to the south of my home territory of Cumbria in the northwest of England. It is notoriously throw back and run down, but maintains an atmosphere of joviality, good-time culture, and seaside fun. There are also several tattoo studios in operation, so it provides an ideal setting for a novel concerned with this topic. After a move to the United States six years ago and much time spent in New York, Coney Island became another favorite seaside haunt of mine and provides the backdrop for the second half of the novel. In researching the American section of the book, I spent a lot of time out at Coney, talking to old Brooklynites (several of whom were fishing off the pier with chicken bones and hot dogs during the discussions) about their memories of the Island

> 66 I realized that tattoo artists tended to gravitate to water and to such beach towns, where they could operate under the umbrella of colorful seasonal industries. 99

in its heyday—the freak shows, boardwalk, circuses, and famous characters. For getting that personal human flavor of history, I enjoy and, in fact, prefer this style of researching and anthropology to referring to texts and the internet. It's a lovely way to work—people are eternally keen to talk about their memories and lives, and I'm keen to hear them.

Much of the novel's initial research was related to the curious and fascinating craft of tattooing itself. I was first tattooed in the East Village almost ten years ago, and I remember the enormous personality, both ferocious and comedic, of the artist in question. It was one of the strangest and most painful and panic-stricken experiences of my life, but I had a sense of something greater and more profound underlying it, and that was a real hook, a real intrigue. Why on earth would we choose to decorate ourselves in this manner?

Little has been formally documented about the art form, and I had a desperate desire to achieve authenticity in the book, so for *The Electric Michelangelo* I turned to two actual artists for assistance and education, one in Astoria, Queens, and the other in Morecambe Bay, England. Both were incredibly helpful, and provided an abundance of anecdotal and professional information, from stories about the big men with which they had apprenticed and vivid tales about customers, to methodically laying out their equipment (ink, needles, etc.) on the countertop and explaining its usage to me. Both guys were deeply generous and fascinating. One recurring theme during such collaboration and investigation was that of bipolarism, not only as a psychological aspect for the artists but also with regards to our traditional western motifs—classic hearts and daggers, ▶

66 People are eternally keen to talk about their memories and lives, and I'm keen to hear them. 99

Researching the Colorful World of Tatoo Art
(*continued*)

love and hate, and the commemoration of good and bad in life. I chose the Dylan Thomas quote at the beginning of the novel for this very reason, and, coupled with its sea reference, I felt it was the perfect summary and motif for the novel.

I became increasingly intrigued by the trade and those working in it, by its philosophy and the relationship of the human body to life and art. So I hope the novel deals with these aspects at their very root, and I hope it is an attempt to examine the integrity and mystery of an art form that is often misunderstood and disreputable, but always compelling. I even manipulated the writing style of the book itself, adopting a bold colorful language and a symbolism to compliment the subject matter. Truthfully, the book was a joy for me to write, for many reasons—for its content and style, for its declaration and poetry.

And to refresh my memory of the tattoo experience I had more work done a few years ago in Astoria. The old adage about suffering for your art may never be truer.

> “ It is an attempt to examine the integrity and mystery of an art form that is often misunderstood and disreputable, but always compelling. ”

Mike McCabe on New York City's Tattooed Past

TATTOOING *had a distinct presence in New York in the early twentieth century. Chatham Square, which is now the Chinatown district of Lower Manhattan, was an especially popular place to find a tattoo artist, then known as a "tattooer." Later, the epicenter of tattoo art became Coney Island, Brooklyn.*

In his essay "The New York City Tattoo: The Origins of a Style" Mike McCabe writes.

ANY SAILOR at the time who wandered a few blocks down South Street from the docks would have found himself in the middle of a run down, overcrowded tenement area where the population often exceeded 15,000 people per square mile.... With a war on, New York was full of ships and sailors. The fast, colorful tattoo work of the town soon became the favorite of the fleets, setting a standard for the rest of the world.

With the Depression, everything began to change. Merchant shipping started to dry up and with the U.S. Navy in the Pacific, it wasn't long before Chatham Square saw breadlines instead of lines of customers eagerly waiting for a tattoo. The beer halls and burlesque theaters that had catered to the tattooing crowd began to close up. Many tattooers packed it in and moved on. Those who stayed dropped their prices considerably. The forecast was not good.

It took the Second World War to revitalize the trade, although it never returned to its former glory. By this time most of the trade ▶

> " The fast, colorful tattoo work of the town soon became the favorite of the fleets, setting a standard for the rest of the world. "

11

New York City's Tatooed Past *(continued)*

had moved to Coney Island where a few tattooers from the Bowery had summered through the years. With the extension of the subway system, Coney Island blossomed into a playground of popular entertainment known the world over. Each summer saw millions of people escaping the steaming streets of Manhattan and Brooklyn for only a nickel subway ride.

Coney Island and then the Madison Square Garden district soon became the new centers of tattoo in New York City. A section near the boardwalk in Coney Island even earned the nickname "Tattoo Alley" where well known artists worked on servicemen and civilians alike. ᘓ

❝ Coney Island and then the Madison Square Garden district soon became the new centers of tattoo in New York City. **❞**

Reprinted by permission from Mike McCabe, 2000, and Damian McGrath, Editor, Tattoos.com. For more information visit http://www.tattoo.com/bowrey.htm.

A Brief History of
Morecambe

The Electric Michelangelo opens in Morecambe, a British seaside resort town known at the turn of the twentieth century to be a haven for those people afflicted by tuberculosis. Sarah Hall talks about this town's fascinating history:

> The women that ran the bed and breakfast joints and cheap hotels in Morecambe had the reputation of being quite ferocious, really. It was a very shoe-string affair, the poor sick workers of the industrial north couldn't afford much of a holiday and only got one week off a year from the mills, foundries and mines etc, and they all headed to Morecambe for a cheap cheerful break—hence the flim-flam about Morecambe's air being restorative for lung diseases that was put about by locals. . . . Cruel in a way, but it gave people hope. This is one of the reasons I like the town so much—it really catered to society's poorer factions, showed them a good time, and offered what rewards it could for their toil. They all shared bathrooms and ate potted shrimp and went to shows in pavilions and bathed in the cold Irish sea. Even under the worst circumstances people tried to do their best—which is of course a very old fashioned British attitude.

As Morecambe's official website notes, "The seas have taken their toll over the years on various projects undertaken at Morecambe, but it still remains one of the United Kingdom's most popular holiday resorts, enjoyed by different people from throughout the world."

∿

66 This is one of the reasons I like the town so much—it really catered to society's poorer factions, showed them a good time, and offered what rewards it could for their toil. 99

Reprinted by permission from Peter Beverley. For more information visit http://morecambe.co.uk/

An Excerpt from
Haweswater

SARAH HALL'S DEBUT *novel , Haweswater, was published in the United Kingdom by Faber and Faber Ltd. in Spring 2002. Critically acclaimed upon its release, it went on to win the Commonwealth Writers' Prize for Best First Book. In 2006, Harper Perennial will proudly give this powerful novel its first American publication. Below, an excerpt from the book.*

LET THEM BE ASSURED that none of this was within his control, this they must understand before all else. He was simply a messenger, he said, come to tell them of their future. By the second sentence the locals had him pegged as a salesman, not the first to make it down into the valley and not a very good one, however well dressed. There was a silent pause, immaculately executed by the man. He might have been about to wheel out a marvel of the modern world from behind him. He smiled widely then, at the crowd of working men, and frowning women, as if to encourage confidence in him. Then his expression changed and was replaced by concentration, he began speaking softly, shallowly, and at the same time his accent heightened and became mannered. It was a voice for addressing others regarding serious matters, a well-oiled public-speaking voice. As he spoke, he moved his words out and away from himself, and it was as if he was speaking of another place, another land, as if this was in accordance with some eventual reckoning that reaches all quiet and secluded areas in time. The modern world was just

> 66 Let them be assured that none of this was within his control, this they must understand before all else. He was simply a messenger, he said, come to tell them of their future. 99

behind the man. What he was selling was the end of their valley.

It began as a simple proposal. Manchester City Waterworks had been hunting in the Lakeland and the borders for a site suitable for special development. This valley had been considered among others. For the past fifteen years geologists and engineers had surveyed the area, boring holes in the rocks of the valley and testing the water. Their results, when they reported back to MCW, had been favourable. The valley had been excavated by glaciers, which melted away to leave the small lake in the basin. The rocks along the sides and floor of the valley consisted of compacted slates and grits, layers of volcanic ash and lava which became hardened by subterranean heat and pressure and could not be eroded by the passing of water, as aspect vital to the scheme. In the words of the geologists and the surveyors, it was an old, firm valley, the site was admirably suited for development of the kind that the Waterworks was considering. In fact, this valley, with its own natural shape, created as the earth's muscles cramped and pulled with ferocious sloth millennia earlier, was perfect. Six miles down, at the bottom of the dale, where the fells curved towards the ground and flattened inwards, hard volcanic rock came to the surface, and it would be possible to lay down a flat arm of cement and brick. An arm belonging to a colossal stone god, capable of holding back a full valley of water. It would be a dam unlike those built anywhere else in the country. A wonderful piece of architecture and engineering, megalithic, inspired. Yes, the site was perfect, but for one thing.

On the damp boards of the valley floor was a little village. The smallest of places. ⌒

> " An arm belonging to a colossal stone god, capable of holding back a full valley of water. It would be a dam unlike those built anywhere else in the country. "

The Web Detective

Go online for further background, history, and information:

http://www.themanbookerprize.com
for more information on the Man Booker Prize

http://www.threemonkeysonline.com
a monthly online publication dedicated to current affairs and culture, written by teams based in Ireland, Italy, and Spain

http://www.tattoos.com/bowrey.htm
the premiere host of reputable artists, studios, promoters and publishers in the bodyart industry from around the world

http://www.morecambe.co.uk/
for more information on the town of Morecambe

Don't miss the next book by your favorite author. Sign up now for AuthorTracker by visiting www.AuthorTracker.com.